ABOUT THE AUTHOR

MIKE BENNETT was born in Catfc
leaving school his career highligl
warden in a safari park, video
dustman. He has just graduated from Brighton University.
One Among the Sleepless is his first novel.

one among the sleepless

One among the sleepless

mike bennett

SEED

One Among the Sleepless
By Mike Bennett

Published in the United Kingdom in 2002 by
Seed Publishing
PO Box 26
Hove
BN3 1WU

www.seedpublishing.com

ISBN 0954146301

Cover Design by Surface Impression
www.surfaceimpression.com
Printed in the United Kingdom

The author would like to thank Hayley Ann, Kerry Boettcher, Peter Pavement, Pauline McGrath, Luc Woods and Amy Flowers for their help and advice in the creation of this novel.

For Pauline.

Prologue

PETER OPENED HIS EYES and knew that once again, he was in hell. Though his was not a hell in the traditional sense, where cackling demons thrust fiery tridents at his backside for all eternity. His was a hell of bass after midnight. His demons had amps and speakers and lived not in a fiery pit, but in the house over the back. He raised his head from the pillow and stared into the darkness of his room, concentrating on the muted musical thud in the air about him. He grimaced as he recognised it. "Get Down Tonight", by KC and The Sunshine Band.

'Ohhh, you fucking bastards.' He beat his fist against the mattress. His adrenal gland dropped a rush of hate and anger into his system, propelling him from under the duvet and clear across the room. He pulled the curtain aside and glared out into the night. A single light burned in the dark from the ground floor window of the house directly behind his building.

'Oh, here we go. It's party time again.'

He stepped back and to one side, positioning himself behind his mounted telescope. He placed his eye to the eyepiece and inched it gently to the right, twisting the focus minutely at the same time. The contemptuous expression on his face became sharper, taking on clearer lines of loathing as the image in the eyepiece sharpened in its turn. The telescope, focused on the illuminated window, revealed a young man in his underwear. He was grinding slowly to the beat of the music, his hands caressing some invisible partner in a dance that was more about penetration than footwork.

'Oh, you tosser,' he murmured through gritted teeth. 'What kind of a fucking wanker are you, eh?'

Peter gently pivoted the telescope to follow the young man as he grooved across the room, writhing his way to a point in front of the sofa. Here, two other similarly attired young men sat and applauded their dancing friend.

'Wankers,' Peter lifted his eye from the lens. 'What a bunch of fucking wankers.' He shook his head in disgust then once again lowered his eye to the telescope and focused upon the dancing man. 'Look at him. Just look at him.' The leader of the pack. The strutting cock. Look at him, as good as masturbating in front of those cretins. And them: look at them whooping and cheering; the way they laugh and make those absurd finger-flicking displays. Shitheads. Oh, oh look. Here he goes, over to the stereo. Is he...? Turning it...? Wait for it... ah!

The dull thud of the bass got louder. The fucking bastard. Just listen to that. You can feel it, even from here. Oh, oh here we go. All of them up and dancing around the lounge. All as good as bare arsed, the curtains wide open. No one cares! Is that... ah yes. A spliff! A spliff, man! Ooooh, pass it 'round, man. Pass it 'round. Pathetic. Not a thought for other people. Fuck the neighbours – we're having a laugh! Christ it makes me so... so fucking angry!

Peter lifted his head from the telescope and straightened up. 'I can't take this fucking shit any longer. I just can't fucking stand it.' He closed his eyes and took a couple of deep breaths to try to calm himself. Visions of violence, fantasies of savage retribution swarmed in his head against the dull pounding of the distant drums. In his mind, axes fell into hi-fi systems, blazing speakers exploded and men in pants ran screaming into the night. He swayed gently from side to side as the images that danced through his mind began to distill into coherent ideas. An uncertain smile fluttered at the edges of his mouth as one scheme blurred into another. Then suddenly, he froze. He opened his eyes.

'Oh yes,' he whispered.

He looked again to where his stoned and happy tormentors danced, and he began to laugh. He raised his hands in front of him, bringing them together and extending his index fingers to make a pistol. He slowly brought his weapon to bear on the small square of light in the darkness, hesitating as he got his aim just right.

'Bang.' His fingers kicked back in a slow-motion recoil. He fired again, and then again. When the last imaginary bullet was fired, Peter raised the barrel of his gun to his lips and blew away a phantom coil of smoke in a gesture of finality. He smiled. Even though his intended victims carried on, quite oblivious to their execution, Peter knew. Smiling in the darkness, he knew their days were numbered.

PART ONE

Chapter 1

'WHAT IN THE NAME OF CHRIST is she doing up there?' Wayne snatched up the TV remote control, and pressed the "mute" button. He dropped it down beside him, just beyond the reach of his fiancée Ellen, and glared at the ceiling.

'I don't know, Wayne,' said Ellen, wearily. 'Just turn the sound up and ignore her.'

'She's like an elephant on a pogostick. Crashing about the place… Look!' Wayne pointed at the paper lampshade that hung in the centre of the ceiling. 'Look! The fuckin' lampshade's wobbling.'

'Wayne, turn the sound up,' Ellen reached over him for the remote control. 'I'm losing the plot.'

Wayne grabbed the remote and held it away from her at arm's length. 'You're losing the plot? She's lost the fuckin' plot, upstairs, eh? How to Behave in a Civilised Building. Chapter one: "Be Fuckin' Quiet".'

Ellen got up from the sofa with an air of palpable annoyance, and walked to the TV.

'Don't turn it up, El. Listen… it's not normal.'

'You're not normal,' Ellen turned the volume up manually, and the earthy cockney banter of certain Eastenders once again filled the lounge.

'Listen,' one Eastender said to another. 'We need to talk.'

As Ellen sat down again, the ceiling made a sound like rolling thunder.

'Right!' Wayne grabbed the remote and switched off the TV. He stood up balefully.

'Wayne!'

Wayne ignored his fiancée's boiling tone and held the remote out to her in a successful attempt at arresting her attention. 'I'm going up there and seeing about this fuckin' racket once and for all.'

Ellen took the remote and switched the TV back on. 'Don't be daft. She's probably screwing some big bloke up there. He'll chuck you down the stairs for interrupting him.'

'We'll see won't we,' Wayne strode purposefully across the room to the door.

'Wayne?' Ellen realised this wasn't just bluster; he was really going upstairs. 'Wayne, leave it. Really love, it's none of our business.'

Wayne ignored her and left the room. From the hallway, Ellen heard the front door open, then Wayne's voice, distant now as he replied from the hall. 'It is my business: it's my fuckin' paper lampshade what's swinging around like a horse's bell-end.'

He added something else, but Ellen didn't catch it due to a cockney grievance on television. She bit her lower lip and quickly muted the TV. Suddenly, the normally engrossing antics of the Eastenders had become pale by comparison to the thudding of Wayne's feet as they ascended the carpeted stairs outside their front door. Ellen held her breath, and listened.

Lucy swished the schoolmaster's cane through the air for effect, and surveyed the tremulous fat rump that awaited her on the other side of the room. Its dough-whiteness was scored with innumerable red lines that blurred across the centre into an island of screaming soreness. She addressed the owner of this uncomfortable seat with the kind of contempt that he both expected and paid for.

'Well, you snivelling little wretch? Have you learned your lesson yet, or do you need further instruction?'

The wretch spoke. 'I don't... feel chastened enough, Mistress. I, I think another six should put me right.'

'Very well then,' Lucy slashed the air with the cane, adding a little seasoning to her promise. 'You shall have your six, and by God, if I see your fat arse in my rooms again before the end of term, I'll make sure you never sit down again this side of Christmas. Do you understand me?'

The wretch, from his kneeling position, wailed in the affirmative.

'Good.' Lucy drew back the cane and ran at him. At the sound of her approach, the wretch braced himself. He closed his eyes on the tears that were welled there, squeezing them out to mingle with the sweat that beaded over the surface of his fat, empurpled face.

The cane whooshed through the air as Lucy closed upon him. She struck the tensed and waiting buttocks with all the force she could muster, staggering a few steps past him with the momentum of her charge. The wretch hissed through gritted teeth, a suppressed cry of pain almost escaping.

'Silence!' Lucy snapped. 'You know that blubbing will only make things worse for you.'

At this point there was a knock at the door.

'Shit,' said Lucy. The wretch looked at her. 'Stay there, Donald. I won't be a minute.' She left Donald hanging onto the end of the sofa and went into her bedroom. A moment later she emerged in her dressing gown. She opened the front door. There was a man outside. He seemed both vaguely familiar, and absurdly huffy.

'Yes?' said Lucy.

'Look,' the man blurted. 'I know we haven't met before, and these aren't the best circumstances for a how-do-you-do, but I live downstairs. And frankly, I'm going round the twist with all the banging about that you're making up here.'

'Oh.' Lucy now recognised him from chance passings in the front hallway. 'I'm sorry. I was just... doing my aerobics.'

Wayne, who had been steeled for combat, relaxed slightly with what seemed to be her sincere apology. 'That's OK.' His eyes momentarily explored her dressing gown. 'It's just that it's... extremely distracting.'

Lucy smiled. 'I am sorry, I get a bit carried away with them. I'll definitely try and be a lot quieter in future.'

Wayne smiled awkwardly and nodded. 'OK then. Like I said, it's not a perfect how-do-you-do but,' he proffered his hand. 'My name's Wayne.'

Lucy shook it briefly. 'I'm Lucy.'

'Hello, Lucy,' Wayne suddenly felt absurd. 'Well, I'll be off then. See you around.'

'Yeah,' Lucy nodded. 'See you around.'

Wayne, still smiling awkwardly, turned and padded down the carpeted stairway.

Lucy closed the door. She dropped her smile and her dressing gown simultaneously and went back into the front room. Donald, still prone and hanging onto the end of the sofa, looked up.

'Who was it?'

'Some wanker who lives downstairs,' said Lucy. 'He doesn't like all the noise I make when I run over to whack your miserable arse.'

'What does this mean?'

'It means either I stop wearing the heels and start wearing gym shoes, or I stop getting the extra force into my stroke by running across the room and just whack you on the spot.' She looked at him questioningly, 'It's your choice, Donald. You're the customer.'

Donald let his eyes run the length of her, starting with the black patent leather high heels, running up the stockings and suspenders, the lacy panties and brassiere, and then back down to the high heels.

'Keep the shoes.'

'You're sure?'

He nodded, then looked down shamefully at the arm of the sofa.

'Okay.' Lucy crossed the room with slow, deliberate steps and picked up the cane. 'Now where were we? I seem to recall a certain naughty little blighter being up for five of the best. But, hang on.' She paused and looked curiously at Donald. 'Who ever heard of five of the best? Surely six, don't you think?' She prodded Donald's flabby flank with the tip of the cane.

He nodded, silently, penitently, lowering his face and raising his bottom for the punishment he so richly deserved.

It had been a busy day for Peter. It hadn't been that much more hectic than any other working day, it was just that lack of sleep had made everything seem that much more burdensome. He felt as though there was a weight constantly pressing down on him, as though gravity was conspiring with his body clock in a joint effort to press him down somewhere – anywhere – and make him go to sleep. Often throughout the day he had fought back: on the bus, at his desk, even in the queue at the petrol station, waiting to pay for the contents of the wine bottle he now clutched in his nervously sweating hand.

Now of course, he was wide awake. Fear, adrenalin, maybe just good old fashioned hate; all were keeping him wired and alert as he walked, as naturally as possible, along the darkened streets. Some of the bottle's contents spilled from its open neck, running down the glass and making Peter's already moist hand slippery. He cursed under his breath and switched the bottle from one hand to the other, wiping his wet palm across his chest. Beneath the fabric of his coat, he felt the firm tubular presence of the length of hose concealed in the inside pocket. He smiled.

It was close to midnight. As he walked, Peter occasionally looked around to ensure he was unobserved. It was possible that there still might be the odd drunk stumbling home late from the pub, or maybe a dog walker. But there wasn't. He was entirely alone. He noticed a slight trembling in his breathing as he came upon the house he was looking for. Whether it was fear or excitement, he wasn't sure; but he was sure of the house. Often he had stood outside it, contemplating pounding on its door and demanding silence of the bastards within. Always he had gone home, frustrated and impotent; afraid of being laughed at, threatened or even hurt. But not tonight. Tonight he was taking action. He listened to the muted thud of the music that emanated from behind the front door of the house. A nervous smile rippled across his features. He looked furtively about. Still there was no one else around. No one to witness him as he quickly opened the garden gate and took a few quick strides up the path to the front door. He dropped down to one knee and, holding his breath, gently prized open the letterbox. Inside, he saw a darkened hallway. At the far right end of the hall he could see a closed door with a thin strip of light shining beneath. Peter licked his lips. He knew it had to be the room he could see from his window. Their playroom. The bastards. They were probably off their tits on drink and drugs right now. Maybe they were screwing some girls who were equally out of their stupid heads. God knows he had seen such things through his telescope in the past. Peter grimaced in disgust at the image, pushing it from his mind and ignoring the tingling in his loins it caused.

'Bastards,' he whispered. He slipped his hand into the folds of his coat and pulled out the short length of rubber hose. He quickly attached one end to the neck of the bottle. Then, with trembling fingers, he slipped the other end of the hose through the letterbox. Slowly, he eased the bottle up so the liquid within began to gurgle out into the pipe. He could just hear the splashing of the liquid as it landed inside. He could see it in his mind as it soaked into the carpet or doormat, splashing the woodwork on the other side of the door.

When the bottle was empty, he quickly withdrew the hose from the letterbox. With hands shaking harder than ever, he detached it from the neck of the bottle and shook the excess drops from the pipe. He shoved it awkwardly back into his coat's inside pocket. The coat would stink like hell, but he didn't care. It was old, out of style. Hell, he chuckled, he could burn it. Wiping his hands on his coat, he reached into one of the pockets. He withdrew a crumpled note with a drawing pin already pushed through the top of it. He opened it and pinned it to the door just above the letterbox. Then, with a final glance about, he got to his feet and walked briskly back down the short path and into the street.

Once the pavement was again beneath his feet, he chanced a quick look back down to the other end of the street. A little laugh escaped him. He shook his head. Unbelievable. Unbelievable that the street wasn't thronging with raging neighbours, all of them fighting to batter down the bastards' front door and lynch them by the flex of their hi-fi. He gave a short, derisory snort. Fear, that's what it was. These people, these good but meek people: they fear them. Just as I did, before tonight. But not now, he thought. Not anymore. I've struck a blow here tonight; a blow for peace and quiet; a blow for common decency.

'Oh yes,' Peter suppressed a laugh, enjoying the way that the adrenalin created by his fear now coursed through him like the champagne of triumph. He clapped his hands together gleefully. The noise was loud in the silent street and he hurriedly straightened his arms to his sides, distancing himself from any appearance of outward jubilation. He glanced back behind him to check that he hadn't drawn attention to himself. No one was observing him: no pedestrian, no car, no twitching curtain. He made a fist and, somewhat self-consciously, punched the air before him in triumph. Then, with a small, awkward bow to the rows of darkened houses, he turned the corner, and was gone.

'Now, what I really want to happen, scientifically, is the development of robot women.' Gaz grinned, happy to see his opinion was shared by his friends, or at least the male ones. Jimmy and Glen nodded at his wisdom. Of the two girls, only Kay seemed amused. Gaz drew on the joint and passed it to the other girl, Sally. By far the better looking of the two. 'Spliff?'

She shook her head and smiled politely.

Gaz shrugged and offered it to Glen.

'Nice one.' Glen took a hefty toke and sat back in his armchair.

As Gaz resumed his ramblings about robot women, Sally shifted her position on the sofa and glanced beside her at Kay. She sank inwardly as she saw Kay laughing. Coming here had been Kay's idea. Sally had felt uncomfortable with these guys from the minute they met, but Kay adored them. Especially, Kay had confided in the toilets earlier, the apparent leader of the pack, Gaz.

'He's gorgeous,' Kay had gushed as they waited in line for a cubicle to be vacated. 'He looks like Ricky Martin, don't you think?'

Sally mentally aligned images of the two men in question. She shook her head. 'No, I don't see that.'

'Maybe a young George Michael?'

Sally raised her eyebrows. 'Is that a good thing?'

Kay sighed. 'Oh, don't be such a drag, Sal. That Glen seems to like you. In fact, you could probably have your choice between him and the little one, whatsisname?'

'Jimmy,' said Sally, without enthusiasm.

'Yeah, Jimmy. He's nice.'

'Then you have him.'

Then Kay turned to her. 'Oh, I get it. You're just jealous because Gaz likes me and not you.'

'Oh, don't be stupid, Kay. No offence, but I think he's a wanker.'

'Excuse me? He may be a lot of things, but with those looks he is not a wanker.'

'Oh, I'd say he probably spends a lot of his time wanking... Over his own image in the mirror.'

'Oh, that is gross, Sally. Utterly gross,' Kay turned away toward the toilet cubicle, from inside which there came the sound of a flush. 'Look, they've asked us back to their place after the pub and I'm going. If you want to fuck off home, that's up to you, but I want to enjoy myself tonight.' The cubicle opened and a girl stepped out and moved past them.

Kay turned to Sally. 'And who knows.' She smiled smugly before stepping into the toilet cubicle. 'Maybe I'll be enjoying myself for longer than that. Perhaps a lot longer.' She pulled the door in behind her, closing it on both Sally and the conversation.

Sally had considered arguing further, but what was the point? Kay had made up her mind. She had elected to come along with her because it would have been bad form not to. She liked Kay, most of the time, even if they did have wildly different taste in men. In fact, now that she thought of it, they had wildly different tastes in just about all things. However, she didn't want to lose Kay's friendship, at least not over a trio of cocksure dickheads like these. Plus, she felt uncomfortable leaving Kay alone with them. If nothing else, she could provide Kay with a good excuse to leave if she needed one later. And as the talk turned to robot women, she began to hope Kay might. But no, bizarrely, the opposite seemed to be the case. She sighed as she realised Gaz was still rambling on about his utopia.

'Yeah, what'd really suit me would be an island of these robot chicks, all programmed to keep me happy.'

'Yeeahhh, man,' said Jimmy.

'Yeeahhh, alright,' added Glen.

The two nodded their stoned appreciation. Glen passed the joint back to Sally. She smiled and held up a hand. 'No, thank you.'

'Urh?' Glen's face contorted.

Sally raised her voice to be heard above the Jamiroquai track that pumped from the expensive stereo equipment. 'I said, no thanks.'

'Why not?'

'I don't smoke.'

'Don't tell me you never smoked dope before,' Gaz said, patronisingly.

'Oh, I've smoked dope before. Which is how I know I don't like it.'

'You must've been doing it wrong.' Gaz glanced at his friends knowingly. Then as an idea occurred to him, he turned back to her. 'Have you ever used a bong?'

Sally rolled her eyes ceilingward. 'Yes.'

'Properly?'

'Is there a wrong way to inhale smoke?'

Gaz's eyes widened and he turned to Jimmy and Glen, 'Is there? Lads? Is there?'

Jimmy and Glen laughed and nodded. 'Is there?'

Sally, becoming bored with the conversation, interjected, 'There seems to be some uncertainty on the matter.'

'Fuck, no,' said Gaz. 'Course there's a wrong way. You've obviously been doing it wrong.'

'Obviously.' Sally looked at her watch.

'That's it, man.' Jimmy pointed at Gaz. 'She needs the bong.'

'Get the bong,' said Glen.

They all began to chant as Gaz crawled across the carpet to a sideboard that clung to the shadowy edges of the room. 'Bong. Bong. Bong. Bong.'

Sally turned her face to Kay's ear and said in a voice inaudible to the others, 'It's like King Kong. Primitive tribe chanting the name of their god?'

Kay frowned, 'Eh?'

'Maybe there's a giant ape in the sideboard.' Sally smiled. 'Like in the film? King Kong?'

Kay said nothing.

'The natives worshipped the ape? The big ape?'

Kay, whose eyes betrayed the depths of her stoned condition, smiled uncertainly.

'Never mind,' Sally surrendered. 'Forget it.'

A moment or two passed before Kay brightened and slapped Sally gently on the arm. She laughed. 'I geddit. King Kong. Ape.'

Sally smiled. 'Yeah. Ape.'

'Nice one,' said Kay.

Sally looked at her watch.

Gaz returned to the table with the bong.

Sally looked at it with mild curiosity. She'd seen one before, and this one wasn't particularly awe-inspiring. A seven or eight inch plastic tube that swelled into a spherical bowl at the base. Connected to this bowl was a small spout with a tiny metal cup for burning a lump of dope in. Big deal.

The bong chant died out as Gaz, the high priest, began to speak.

'This is the bong.'

Sally smiled wanly. 'So I gather.'

'This little beauty will change the way you experience dope forever.'

'I'm not actually interested in the experience of smoking dope forever. Thanks all the same.'

'Oh, come on,' said Jimmy. 'Don't be scared.'

Sally managed a smile in spite of sudden homicidal urges. 'I'm not scared. I just don't want to.'

Kay rubbed Sally's arm. 'Come on Sal, don't be a drag. There's plenty of time to be an old maid later on in life.'

Sally gave Kay a disapproving glance, but it was wasted on her. Kay's sensitivity had obviously been dulled by the dope. She stared at Sally querulously and nudged her arm. Sally shook her head and looked away.

Gaz was leaving the room with the bong. 'I'll just put some water in it. Don't go away.'

Sally considered doing just that; making her excuses and going away, a dignified retreat. Or was it? A voice inside nagged her. She realised she didn't want Kay scoring any points with these tossers at her expense. Oh, Kay the live wire; the interesting one. Maybe it was just vanity, but the prospect of being seen as an old maid when she was only in her late twenties niggled her.

'Go on Sal,' Jimmy pleaded. 'Just one hit.'

Despite knowing that to do so would be to play into their hands, Sally found herself nodding. 'Okay then, just a few puffs, then I have to get going.'

This was met with a rowdy chorus of approval.

Imperceptible to the others, Kay squeezed her arm and sent her a furtive look of thanks. Sally met her eyes with a hardness that caused Kay to look away to Gaz, who was returning from the kitchen. Sally saw the bong now contained water. Gaz sat down cross-legged by the coffee table. He picked up his lighter and the lump of hash that lay on the table. He flicked a flame into life and began stroking it against the resinous lump, heating it.

'Come on, baby,' Gaz coaxed. He put down the lighter and broke a small piece off the lump of hash and placed it in the firebowl of the bong. He then held it aloft.

'All hail the bong,' he said in reverent tones.

The boys began their bong chant again.

Kay joined in.

Sally wished she were an old maid.

She watched as Gaz touched the flame of his lighter to the firebowl, lighting the lump of dope. He placed his finger over a small hole near the neck of the tube and sucked on the open top. Sally watched as smoke bubbled through the water and filled the tube. Gaz looked up at her and winked. He let his finger off the little hole and sucked the smoke into his lungs. When he had a lungful, he took his mouth away from the bong and placed his hand over the opening to keep the smoke in, where it swirled like a trapped ghost. Grinning, he passed it to Sally.

Sally had dabbled in this kind of thing in her first year at university. She'd not long been on campus, and the group of people she had fallen in with immediately, weren't greatly dissimilar to the present company. Their social ties soon became unravelled as they all found more kindred spirits to hang out with. Though while she'd been part of that particular gang, she'd dallied with one of these things on more than one occasion. She knew it was important to breathe in easily and not to cough. More than anything, she was determined not to cough and splutter – it would be like sweet music to the ears of these dickheads.

She took the bong, slipping her hand over the top as Gaz removed his. Her eyes were fixed upon Gaz's as she raised it to her mouth, letting her hand move away as she sipped easily at the ghost in the pipe. So far so good. Then, pressing her lips to the rim and placing a finger over the tiny hole, she drew gently upon the bong. The water in the bowl bubbled and she felt fresh smoke enter her throat. She suddenly felt the urge to cough, and so stopped inhaling, slipping her hand over the top of the pipe and holding the smoke she'd already inhaled. The room swam slightly as she felt the initial physical hit from the cannabis bloom through her body. She felt it rush to her feet, swirl around on itself, then rush back up to bloom again.

Gaz exhaled the smoke he'd been holding in his lungs in a long stream. 'Nice one. How's it feel?'

Sally exhaled the smoke in a blue stream before her, nodding as she did so. 'Fine.' She offered the pipe from side to side, to both Jimmy and Kay in turn.

'Whoa, there cowboy,' Gaz intervened. He motioned to Sally. 'Have another blast.'

'Really.' Sally shook her head. 'I'm fine, thanks.'

'Aw, go on. One's nothing. You need at least two puffs to get anywhere.'

The chanting began around her again. 'Bong. Bong. Bong. Bong.' Sally shook her head slightly and once again raised the bong to her lips. First she removed her finger from the hole and sipped the remaining smoke in the pipe, then, exhaling it through her nose, she drew again, this time deeper. She looked at the lump of dope in the burning bowl glow like an ember as she did so. When she had a lungful, she slipped her hand over the top and passed it to Jimmy.

'Alriiiight,' Gaz clapped appreciatively. The others, including Kay, joined in the applause. Sally exhaled, feeling both ethereal and contemptuous in equal measure.

'Nice one.' Jimmy smiled as he took the pipe.

Sally felt there was more than approval in his tone; there was surprise. They'd thought she was a naïve fool who'd cough and puke. Someone for them to feel superior to. Well, she'd spannered that for them. Now she could exit with their respect. However little that mattered to her, she knew it mattered to Kay. And Kay could fuck off. Sally felt as high as a kite, but she wasn't going to allow them the satisfaction of knowing that, if she could help it. She got slowly to her feet. 'Well, thank you for that, but I have to be going now.' The room swam slightly, but she wasn't fazed.

'Eh?' Glen looked bewildered.

'You can't go,' said Gaz. 'The fun's only just beginning.'

'Not for me. I have to work tomorrow.'

'But tomorrow's Saturday.' Jimmy sounded wounded.

'I work in a shop,' Sally explained. 'Saturday's the busiest day of the week.'

'Oh, stay a bit longer, Sal,' Kay slurred. 'For me.'

Sally glanced down at Kay, sending in the briefest of looks, a message that was decidedly sub zero. Not one the others would recognise, but one that she hoped might penetrate the fog that enshrouded Kay's brain. Whether it did or not, she couldn't know. Nor could she be bothered to find out. 'Sorry. Got to go.' She turned, walked to the door and exited into the hallway. As she went she called over her shoulder, 'Goodnight.'

Gaz got to his feet, so did Glen, followed by Jimmy. Kay watched from the sofa as they stumbled around the coffee table and into the hall.

Gaz called after Sally as he entered the hallway, 'Sally, wait!' To his surprise, she did. She stopped at the front door and looked down. Alriiight, his mind sang. But she didn't seem interested in him. His inner jubilation sagged.

'What's this?'

The others crowded the doorway behind Gaz and he felt himself pushed forward. 'What's what?'

'On your carpet.' Sally shifted her weight and felt the moisture in the fabric beneath her feet. 'It smells like… petrol.' She opened the front door and stepped outside. Her feet left dark, liquid footprints on the concrete path.

'Petrol?' Gaz frowned uncertainly as he approached the door.

'What's going on?' asked Glen.

'Take this, man,' said Jimmy, offering Glen the bong. Which he accepted and hastily drew upon.

Gaz reached for the hall light switch and flicked it on. He looked down at his feet. Liquid oozed beneath his trainers. 'What the fuck is this?'

Glen exhaled smoke. 'What the fuck is what, man?'

Then Sally noticed the note pinned to the door. 'What's this?'

'What's what?' said Gaz, suddenly wishing he weren't so stoned.

Sally read aloud: "Turn the music down, you bastards. This is just a warning."

'What's this shit on the carpet?' Glen bent forward at the waist. As he did so, the small glowing coal of hash tumbled from the firebowl of the bong and hit the sodden carpet.

Gaz's mind, which had been struggling to put all this weird shit together, still hadn't figured it out as the hall burst into flames.

Chapter 2

DUSTY SURVEYED THE HIGH STREET through his vintage Ray Ban Balorama sunglasses. Despite being a little scratched here and there, they still reduced the glare of the morning sunshine to a comfortable level. Over the last few years, many comforts had abandoned him, but not the sunglasses. He settled back against the bus shelter, enjoying the otherwise empty bench; the other people at the bus stop seemed to prefer to stand. Dusty smiled. He wasn't waiting for a bus. He was just sitting, watching the world go by, contemplating life, and as he happened to be at a bus-stop, busses in particular.

They came in many different colours, he had noticed. A different colour for the various different routes. He watched as a green bus slid up against the kerb in front of him and opened its doors to disgorge some of its passengers onto the street. As they disembarked, there was not one among the passengers who didn't check him out. Usually a furtive glance, sometimes a longer look, either with or without an expression of disapproval. Dusty ignored them.

When the bus had taken on board its new passengers, it pulled away from the kerb and eased back into the traffic flow, leaving a stinking blue cloud of exhaust in its wake. Dusty fanned the toxic odour away from his face.

'Foul.'

A woman who now stood at the front of the loosely defined queue glanced in his direction.

Dusty looked up at her. 'Don't you think?'

The woman started slightly. She smiled politely, then looked away.

'They ought to bring back the trams.' Dusty waved in the general direction of the traffic. 'None of this congestion with trams. None of this pollution. You know?'

Other eyes in the queue now looked surreptitiously in his direction.

'This part of town,' said Dusty. 'It's like a bus trap. They get lured by the prospect of big fares and then find themselves all wedged in, trapped by their own bulk and lack of manouvrability.' He turned to the queue. Immediately all eyes shot away from him. 'Oh, it's not so bad now. But in about 15 minutes or so, when you people are gone and rush hour really starts to cook, that's when it gets ugly. Bus-ugly. Their bumpers can almost get interlocked as they struggle to free themselves from this.' Dusty waved at the street. 'This hell of their own devise.' He paused to see if anyone was going to respond. The passengers stared stoically into neutral space.

Dusty nodded sagely. 'And of course, as they toil – inching this way and that – their engines churn out that toxic stench. It belches from their tin-pipe arseholes like an endless blue fart of death. You know what I mean?'

A man who stood a few feet down the queue smiled.

'Ah, you do know what I mean.'

The man nodded.

'Horrible isn't it?'

The man nodded again.

Dusty turned back to the street and settled himself back against the shelter. 'Bring back the trams. That's what I say.'

Peter's head bumped on the window of the bus as it turned into the bottom of the High Street. As he travelled to work, the events of the night before were still running through his mind like a looped reel of film. He enjoyed again the mingled feelings of fear and excitement as he crept though the night: the petrol fumes rising through the fabric of his coat, the liquid sloshing gently in the bottle next to his heart. Christ, it was so daring, so heroic, so... crazy. He grinned to himself. I'm crazy. I'm certifiable. And why? 'Because they made me this way,' he whispered. 'They drove me to it, Your Honour.'

He sniggered, delighted, both with his actions and with his defence of them.

The bus halted. Peter shifted his attention to the people at the bus-stop. Then he noticed something out of the ordinary. Sitting on the shelter bench, just beyond the usual array of passenger types, sat a tramp. But there was something unusual about him, and it took Peter a second to realise what it was. Amidst the fuzzy mist of long hair that blended seamlessly with a beard of equal fuzziness, was a band of blackness that Peter recognised as a pair of sunglasses. Odd, he thought. It was quite a fashion statement, considering the rest of his attire. A dirty-looking baseball cap was pulled down onto the wild nest of hair, and a long, shabby raincoat covered most of his relatively big frame. Peter's scrutiny of the tramp's eyewear ended abruptly as the tramp suddenly turned to look at him. Peter blinked, startled, then quickly looked away, just as the bus moved off again on its next twenty yard lurch.

He scratched his head, refocusing his attention on the here and now. Ahead of him in the aisle, a small, fat woman bundled up in a large coat was approaching the vacant seat beside him. He shifted his position to make more room for her, and she sat down. The woman turned to him and offered him a small smile of thanks. He returned it, then both of them turned away to gaze vacantly ahead into the middle distance.

Dusty had caught the young man's eye. He had looked at him for only a moment, but in that moment, he had known: this was The One. He got to his feet and moved quickly to where the last of the queue was about to be swallowed into the interior of the bus. He climbed aboard. The driver's eyes widened for a few seconds when he saw his new passenger. 'Yes, please?'

'Where does this bus go?'

'Universities.'

'Of course,' Dusty realised. 'A green bus. Take me there.' He reached into his trouser pocket for change.

The driver pushed buttons on his ticket machine and a ticket popped out. He looked blankly ahead.

Dusty frowned. 'How much is that?'

'Pound.'

'That's very reasonable.' Dusty handed him a pound coin.

'Thanks, I'll tell them you approve.' The driver let out the handbrake.

Dusty took the ticket and looked down the length of the bus. At once, the hundred or so eyeballs that had been fiercely trained upon him suddenly shifted onto neutral territory. Some went for the windows, some for the ads along the rim of the roof, the rest opted for the floor.

He looked at The One. He seemed unaware. Dwelling on deeper things, no doubt, thought Dusty. As the bus lurched out into traffic, Dusty weaved his way down the aisle, grabbing onto support handles as he went to prevent himself from stumbling. He saw a vacant seat opposite The One and made for it. Unfortunately, a woman sat between them, but this wasn't too much of an inconvenience. As he sat down, he took pleasure in noting that The One had seen him, a quick sideways glance, but it was enough. Contact had been made.

Wayne opened the front door to number thirteen Charrington Street with a bump from his shoulder. The door swung inwards and banged against the wall. He struggled in with his shopping, the four carrier bags swung awkwardly, their handles were stretched and cut painfully into his hands. He kicked the door closed and walked to his front door. Ellen was out; he'd have to fish for his keys. He planted the bags at his feet, relieved to be unburdened, albeit for only a few moments, and groped in his jeans pocket for his keys. Just as his fingers managed to distinguish keys from small change, scraps of paper and various other dregs, he heard a door upstairs close firmly. He turned and looked up the stairs to the first floor landing just as Lucy stepped into view.

Wayne smiled. 'Hi there.'

'Oh.' Lucy smiled vaguely. 'Hello.'

'Listen, I, er, I'm sorry about the other night, I...'

'No,' she interrupted, coming down the last few steps and standing alongside him. 'It's me who should be apologising. And I do.' Her courteous smile took on a more genuine warmth. 'It won't happen again.'

'That's...' Wayne's mind groped blindly for a witty remark, gave up, went with the dull but polite. 'That's very good of you, it's, er, Lucy isn't it?'

'It is. And you're Wayne?'

'I am.' He gave a little laugh. 'At your service.'

'Oh, I'll remember that when I need a light bulb changing.'

'Do.' Wayne leaned casually against his door. 'Light bulbs are my speciality.'

Lucy forced a polite laugh and stepped in the direction of the front door. 'Well, I imagine I'll see you again.'

'Yes. I'm sure you will. I look forward to it.'

Lucy glanced back at him as she opened the front door. She smiled briefly, then stepped outside and closed the door.

As soon as the door was between them, the smile dropped from Wayne's face. He grit his teeth and cursed. 'Bugger!' He opened the door to his flat and picked up his carrier bags. He stepped into the flat and let the door swing closed behind him. As he walked to the kitchen he mimicked himself aloud. 'I look forward to it.' He shook his head. 'Good move, shit head.'

He put the bags on the kitchen work surface. What did she mean about that light bulb thing? Was that flirting? Was she asking me up to her place to change a light-bulb or, he smiled lasciviously, to change a light-bulb?

As he unpacked and stored away the various groceries, he continued to ruminate over their meeting. Does she have a boyfriend? A husband? There's never any mail in the box for a man at that address. At least I haven't seen any.

He recalled her smile and how it had gone from the impersonal to the personal in the course of their chat. I wonder if there's anything happening there? If maybe she does fancy me? He remembered the sight of her the other night: the make-up, the high heels, and the dressing gown. What did she have on under that dressing gown? He felt a tingling in his loins.

Shit! What am I doing thinking like this? I'm an engaged man. Am I insane? He stopped unpacking and looked long and hard at a can of peas. Maybe I am. Maybe I'd like nothing more than to go upstairs and roll around with her on her living room rug, bumping and banging and making a massively un-neighbourly racket right over Ellen's head as she's trying to watch TV. The thought had a perverse appeal to him. He closed his eyes and let it take shape in his mind. He mentally opened the dressing gown she had been wearing the other night and beneath he discovered a lacy black bra and panties, stockings and suspenders, and a little tattoo on the swell of her left breast. It depicted a heart with a scroll unfurled across it. The scroll held a single word: "Wayne".

He drew in a breath through pursed lips, and his hand went to his crotch where he felt a straining against the inside of his fly. Opening his eyes, he put the can of peas aside. Suddenly the shopping lost all meaning; the slow thawing of the frozen foods, the imperceptible warming of the fresh, cold milk. Everything was irrelevant that stood between him and the bathroom. He ran to it as if to a reunion with a long lost lover. He locked the door behind him. Then, with wild abandon, he began to grapple furiously with the various buckles, buttons and zips that stood so annoyingly between him and himself.

*

Peter silently thanked the Lord for the woman who had seated herself next to him on the bus. If she hadn't, he felt sure the tramp would've sat next to him. He had noticed, from the moment the tramp got on board, that he seemed to be looking at him. Of course, there was no way to be certain, what with those impenetrable black sunglasses he wore. But the tramp's face seemed to be turned in Peter's direction every time that Peter dared to look at him. Peter now chanced a quick sideways glance. Shit, he thought, he's looking at me. He is looking at me. Oh, Jesus, he thought with horror, what if he fancies me? What if he's going to try to rape me? Mercifully, his rational mind stepped in, and with strictest teacher tones snapped, don't be absurd! Tramps don't rape office clerks on buses – or anywhere else for that matter. There has to be some rational explanation for this. He tried to imagine one and couldn't. He took another sideways glance beyond the woman. A spotty youth was standing there in the aisle looking at him expectantly.

'I said,' the youth sneered. 'Have you got a fag?'

'Me?' Peter muttered, confused. Obviously he had been too distracted to notice the youth's question the first time he asked.

'Yeah, you.' The youth was about fourteen or fifteen. He wore his hair in that greasy, fringe-combed-forward look that the nation's young men seemed to so relish these days.

'No.'

The youth scowled. He seemed about to turn his scavenging attention elsewhere when Peter added. 'And anyway, you're not allowed to smoke on buses.'

The youth turned back. 'You what?'

'I said you're not allowed to smoke on buses. There are notices at the front that say it quite clearly.'

'I don't give a shit. We'll smoke wherever I fuckin' like. Won't we?' He spoke in the direction of the back of the bus. Peter turned to look and saw three more greasy-fringed herberts slumped in all directions along the back seat. Their replies, sneering and directed at Peter, consisted mainly of, "Yeah", and "Wanker".

'So what're you going to do about it?' said the youth in the aisle.

The other passengers remained staring intently forward. The driver drove on, indifferent. Peter felt his heartbeat quicken. He looked away.

'Oi!' the youth persisted. 'I'm talking to you, arsehole.'

Peter felt his face flush red. He suddenly felt incredibly hot. His mind raced with reactions, but none of them seemed appropriate. He sensed movement behind him; the others were getting up from the back seat and coming to join their friend. Oh God, he thought. Oh God.

'I think you ought to sit down and be quiet,' said a deep voice beyond the youth.

Peter turned to see that the tramp had gotten to his feet. He stood behind the youth and was considerably taller than him.

'Who's gonna make me?' said the youth, but his voice had lost its cockiness. He was trying to save face.

'I will,' the tramp's tone was matter-of-fact.

The youth looked to his friends. They had resumed their seats and now looked anywhere other than at their comrade in the aisle. He was alone in this. The youth turned and, saying nothing, walked coolly to the back of the bus.

Peter turned to the tramp. The tramp was looking at him. Peter nodded. 'Thank you.'

'You're welcome.'

At the next stop, the youths sauntered arrogantly off of the bus. As it resumed its journey they shouted obscenities and made assorted rude gestures towards both Peter and the tramp. Peter looked away. The tramp paid no attention.

No wonder they shut up, Peter thought, looking at the tramp. He looks crazy in those sunglasses. A real loony.

They approached his stop. Peter reached up and rang the bell. He got to his feet. He was about to turn to the tramp to say goodbye, when he noticed the tramp was also preparing to disembark. The smile froze on Peter's face. The tramp merely looked at him. The bus came to a halt. Peter turned and made his way to the front. He muttered his thanks to the driver and got off. He didn't look back. He heard the hiss of the bus door closing and the sound of the bus moving off on its journey. Still he didn't look back. The seeming composure of his stroll disguised the wild panic that gripped him. His heart pounded and his legs trembled. He longed to run as fast as he could down the few short streets to his office, but he couldn't. He had to be cool, had to remain calm. But at the same time, he had to know. He had to look behind him. He forced himself to walk to the edge of the pavement to make an unnecessary crossing of the road. It gave him a good, natural-looking reason to look right and left. He stepped up to the kerb, and with as much nonchalance as he could muster, he looked left, back the way he had come.

The tramp was so close that Peter's nose registered him before his eyes came around. A sharp smell, like ammonia. He loomed over Peter like a tree.

'Hi,' said the tramp.

Peter made a small sound in his throat, but it was lost in the sound of passing traffic as he turned and ran off down the street.

Chapter 3

'HOW ARE YOU?' Sally didn't sit down as Kay had done. She didn't plan on staying long.

'Oh, you know,' Gaz sat fully upright in his bed. 'Mustn't grumble.'

'You are brave,' said Kay. 'I brought you some grapes.'

Gaz took the proffered bag. 'Thanks.' He popped a grape into his mouth. 'Want one?' He offered the open bag back to his visitors.

'Ohhh,' Kay purred. 'Thank you.' She took a grape.

Gaz turned the bag to Sally and raised his eyebrows.

Sally shook her head. 'No thanks. I'm on my lunch break, I can't stay long.'

'Doesn't take long to eat a grape,' said Gaz.

Sally smiled. 'Really. Hospitals take away my appetite.'

'Me too.' Gaz smiled and ate another grape.

'Yeeeah, man,' said Glen from the bed opposite.

Sally looked over. 'How are you Glen?'

'Alright, yeah, I'm alright.'

'I'm afraid we only brought the one bag of grapes,' said Sally. 'You'll have to share them.'

'I brought the grapes,' Kay whispered to Sally.

Sally looked back to Glen. 'I mean Kay brought the one bag of grapes. I didn't buy any.'

'Hey,' said Gaz. 'You came to visit, that's the main thing.'

Sally smiled politely.

'How badly burned are you?' Kay asked Gaz.

'Oh, not badly. Thanks to you guys.'

Sally looked up from her watch. 'We didn't do anything.'

'You phoned the ambulance.'

'And we put them out when they were on fire,' Kay added.

'They weren't on fire,' said Sally.

'Yes we were,' said Glen.

'Not much.'

'Our shoes were on fire.' Gaz spat a pip into his hand and tapped it onto the bedside table.

'And my jeans caught too.' Glen nodded.

'So did mine. A bit.'

'Alright. So you were on fire, my apologies.'

Gaz shrugged. 'That's alright. It's nothing serious.'

I know, thought Sally.

'They've only kept us in for observation,' said Gaz.

'You're just being brave.' Kay touched Gaz's thigh reassuringly. 'They wouldn't keep you in if it wasn't anything serious.'

'Yeeaah, man,' Glen agreed. 'We're both brave and serious.'

Sally rolled her eyes. 'When are you out then?'

Gaz popped another grape into his mouth. 'This afternoon.'

Kay leaned closer to Gaz's bed. 'Really?'

'Well I'm glad I didn't contribute to the grape fund,' said Sally. 'Do you think you'll manage to eat them all before you go?'

Gaz smirked. 'Oh, yeah,' and threw a grape over to Glen who, caught unawares, failed to catch it. They all watched as the grape bounced from Glen's bed and rolled across the floor to settle beneath the bed of his neighbour. Glen looked up, sad.

Sally took a grape and walked over to Glen's bed. She handed him the tiny fruit. Glen took it, smiling. Behind her, Gaz winked suggestively at Glen. When Sally turned to go back to Kay's side, Glen returned the wink.

Kay, who saw the exchange, swelled visibly with pleasure. To her, this was a clear indicator that the couplings had been decided. Glen was interested in Sally, that meant that Gaz was interested in her.

Sally took her bag from beside her seat. 'Listen, I have to go.'

'Oh, Sal,' Kay whined. 'Not yet?'

'I'm afraid so. I'm delighted to see that you two are in such good condition.' Sally stepped out into the aisle. 'And things being what they are,' she looked at Kay. 'I imagine I'll see you around.'

Gaz winked. 'I hope so.'

'Yeeaahhh,' said Glen. 'And soon.'

Sally smiled thinly and left.

Gaz turned to Kay. 'Weird bird, your mate.'

'Yeah, she is,' Kay agreed. 'I dunno why I hang around with her half the time.'

'Why do you?'

'I dunno.' Kay shrugged. 'I met her on a temp-job years ago.' Kay helped herself to a grape. 'We stayed in touch afterwards. Go out for drinks now and then, y'know?'

Gaz nodded. 'Nice girl.'

'Yeeaahh,' said Glen, lasciviously.

'Oh, yeah,' said Kay. 'She's brilliant.'

Gaz frowned. 'Bit weird though.'

Kay nodded. 'She is, yeah.'

'Can I have another grape, man?'

Gaz threw another grape over. It bounced from Glen's ineffectual catch and they all watched as it fell to the ground, rolling to its final resting place somewhere beneath Glen's bed.

Glen looked up and smiled. 'Nice one.'

When Ellen came in, she could hear Gary Numan's "I Die, You Die" coming from the front room. She paid it no attention. She knew that this meant Wayne would be dancing in that funny 80's-type way of his in front of the mirror. Wayne took the whole thing very seriously, and she knew from experience that it was best to just leave him to it. She went into the kitchen and saw the spoils of Wayne's trip to the supermarket in their half-unpacked sprawl about the kitchen. She sighed. From the front room, she heard Numan fading and seized the opportunity to intervene before Wayne got another one of his precious 45s onto the turntable.

She caught him slipping "We Are Glass" from its plastic-protected sleeve. 'Hi sweetie,' she said.

Wayne turned, surprised. 'Oh, hi. I didn't hear you come in.'

'I'm not surprised, you dancing fool, you. You'll have the neighbours complaining.'

'Oh, come off it. It's midday.'

'I wasn't talking about the volume. I was thinking more of the content.'

Wayne stiffened visibly. 'Leave it Ellen. I don't want to hear it. We've had it from the music press for years, we don't need your scorn as well. You just don't understand him.'

Ellen sat down and picked up the *Radio Times*. 'Oh, I understand him. He sings his little songs, he flies about in his little plane. Sometimes he features his little plane in the videos that go with his little songs.'

Wayne turned away. He put "We Are Glass" back into its sleeve and picked up "I Die, You Die" again. 'This,' he waved the single at her, 'this is about you. You and people like you.'

'Oh?'

'Critics, cynics, people saying nasty things. Jealousy, that's all it was, all it is, all it ever will be.'

'I see.'

'He was – is, a man before his time.'

'Uh-huh.' Ellen flicked through the pages of the magazine.

Wayne stood looking at her, waiting.

She continued to leaf through the TV listings.

'Well?' Wayne folded his arms.

Ellen looked up. She knew the expression on his face from numerous other conversations just like this one. He was hurt. Indignant too, but hurt mainly.

Ellen sighed. 'I'm sorry, Wayne. And I'm sorry to Gary as well.'

Wayne relaxed a bit. 'He's a persecuted genius, El. And we, the fans, we've always taken our small quantity of persecution too. Persecution for loyalty.'

'I know, love.' Ellen was reading about *Coronation Street*. 'And he'll always have his fans, won't he?'

Wayne straightened proudly. 'He certainly will.'

'And his little plane.'

'Yeah.' Wayne turned back to the stereo. 'That too. Now, what do you prefer: "We Are Glass" or "Cars"?'

Ellen, who preferred silence, looked up from her magazine. 'Do we have to listen to music right now? I feel a little headachy.'

Wayne looked put out, but yielded. 'Oh, OK. But later on maybe?'

'Sure, later's fine.'

'Brilliant.' Wayne came over and sat down beside her. 'Good morning?'

'OK. You?'

'Oh, yeah, not bad. I got the shopping.'

'Did you get fruit?'

'Shit.' Wayne slapped his forehead. 'I forgot.'

Ellen looked up from the magazine and sighed. 'You always forget the fruit. It's a good thing I can rely on it, otherwise we'd have too much now.'

'You mean you got fruit?'

'I got fruit.'

'Did you get yellow bananas?'

Ellen raised an eyebrow. 'As opposed to?'

'Speckledy brown ones.'

She collapsed the magazine in her lap. 'Wayne, they're properly ripe when they're speckledy brown. When they're yellow, they're only just ripe.'

'Yeah, well I don't like speckledy brown ones, they look wrong.'

'What do you mean, they look wrong?'

'When you see a picture of a banana, it's not all speckledy brown is it? It's yellow. That's because they're supposed to be yellow. Do you see?'

'What does this have to do with the taste? They taste better when the skin is speckledy brown.'

'That's a matter of opinion.'

'Well if you care so much, how come you always forget to buy your precious yellow bananas?'

'I've got more important things on my mind when I'm shopping, El,' said Wayne, frantically trying to think of something important to have on his mind when shopping.

'Like?'

Flummoxed, Wayne shrugged. 'Stuff.'

'Oh, of course.' Ellen nodded. 'Stuff. Whatever you do, don't forget to get stuff when you go shopping, Wayne.' She hoisted the *Radio Times* and resumed reading with an air of closure.

Wayne stood up. For a moment he just hovered, wondering what to do. He opted for leaving the room indignantly. A few moments later, he reappeared in the doorway holding a banana. A yellow banana. 'This banana's yellow.'

'I know.'

'They're all yellow.'

'I know.'

'I thought you got speckledy brown ones.'

'Did I say I got speckledy brown ones?' She looked up at him. 'Why would I do that when I know you only eat the just ripe variety?'

Wayne smiled. He came over and sat down next to her on the sofa. He snuggled up against her to the extent that she had to give up on the TV listings altogether and toss the magazine aside.

'Wayne!'

He peeled back the skin of the banana and offered her the protuberant flesh. 'Want some 'nana?'

'Get that thing away from me,' said Ellen, feebly resisting his attempts to feed her.

'Oh come on.' He pushed the banana to her lips. 'Take a bite.'

Ellen opened her mouth to protest and he slipped the banana in. She made a noise and tried to turn her head but he moved with her, she couldn't escape. She bit down and took a mouthful of the fruit.

'Mmmm,' said Wayne. 'Yummy 'nana?'

Ellen sniggered. She nodded and said through a mouthful of banana. 'Yummy 'nana.'

'Good thing you remembered to get fruit, El,' Wayne kissed her cheek. 'Fruit is sexy food.'

Ellen pushed at him. 'Oh get off, Wayne. I've got a headache coming on.'

Wayne, still horny, despite his earlier masturbatory diversion, persisted. 'Sex is the best cure for a headache.'

'Is it fuck.' Ellen struggled to her feet.

'Oh, come on, El,' Wayne pleaded. 'My love banana is speckledy brown – all properly ripe and good to eat.'

'You eat it, then,' Ellen said as she left the room.

Wayne called after her. 'I would if I could. Don't think I haven't tried.'

'Oh, I'm sure you have,' she called back from the bedroom. 'I'm going to take a nap; try to shift this headache before it takes hold.'

'Okay,' Wayne called back. He smiled. He looked at the bulge in his trousers and wondered at the limits of his spinal elasticity. He leaned forward, bringing his head near to his lap. It was possible. Maybe if I tie my belt around my neck and knees, like they do in Ellen's yoga video? He got up and headed in the direction of the bathroom, undoing his belt as he went.

Peter sat at his desk. He studied the second hand on his watch as it slowly ticked around the dial. He was mentally counting down the seconds to one o'clock, lunchtime. When the hour finally struck, he looked up over his monitor at Mick Nixon.

'Lunch, Mick?'

Mick glanced up, then across at the clock on the wall. 'Is it that time already? Shit. Time flies.'

'When you're having fun,' Peter finished, sarcastically.

'Having a bad day?' Mick asked, taking his jacket from the back of his chair.

'You could say that.'

They walked across the carpeted office. Around them, ranks of co-workers clattered away on keyboards, gazing numbly into the shimmering depths of their monitors.

'I've had a bit of a weird morning,' said Peter.

'Oh?' Mick smiled. 'I didn't think weirdness was able to cross into the sterile world of Richardson and West.'

'It isn't. And it didn't. This shit happened on the outside, on the way in.'

They stepped into the lift and Mick selected the ground floor button. 'Fill me in, dude.'

Peter closed the story half an hour later as they sat finishing their Big Macs.

'Phew.' Mick wiped his fingers on his serviette. 'Hyper-weird. What happened when you got into work?'

Peter shrugged. 'I dunno. I looked behind me through the glass doors as I came in, and I could see him standing down there on the other side of the street. He hadn't moved. That was the last I saw of him.'

Mick sucked milk shake dregs noisily through his straw. 'A saviour in rags.'

'Yeah, but why me? And why follow me afterwards?'

'Maybe he was hoping you'd give him a few quid for helping you out, now that you were away from the crowd on the bus. Did you give him anything?'

'No.' Peter's eyes widened with dawning realisation. 'No, I didn't think to. Do you think that was it?'

'Makes sense doesn't it?' Mick shrugged. 'Guy's homeless, needy; does a guy a favour…?'

'Shit. It just didn't occur to me.'

'Well, there you are. You need to adopt a more charitable disposition, then these things would occur to you naturally.'

Peter nodded. 'You're right. I am an uncharitable bastard.'

'I know. Talking of which, how are your uncharitable feelings towards the boys in the house over the back of yours?'

Peter shifted uncomfortably in his plastic chair. He'd forgotten all about his late night visit to the house around the back. 'Oh,' he said nonchalantly. 'Business as usual. Jamiroquai last night. Must've stopped about one or two.'

'Fuck, Pete. Why don't you call the police?'

'I have.' Peter popped his last French fry into his mouth. 'They say there's nothing they can do. It's a domestic situation.'

'That's bullshit. They just can't be arsed. What you need is a big mate, dressed up as a copper, to go around and give them a warning.'

'And when they take his badge number and phone the real police? Do you want to do it?'

'Well,' said Mick doubtfully. 'I'm not very big.'

'It wouldn't work.'

'Okay.' Mick leaned forward. 'Forget the police outfit, just get the big mate to go around there and threaten them with violence.'

Peter smiled. 'They do some martial arts shit.'

'How do you know?'

'I...' Peter floundered for a second. He wasn't about to disclose how he'd seen the lads high-kicking around in their lounge through the lens of a telescope. 'I've seen them, in the street,' he lied. 'Kicking and stuff.'

'Really?' Mick frowned distastefully. 'Wankers.'

'Yeah.' Peter shook his head. 'Tell me about it.'

'I dunno what you can do then.'

'Killing them would be nice.' Peter pushed his finger through the polystyrene burger box.

'So have them killed.'

'Oh?'

'Doesn't cost much these days,' said Mick with a worldly air. 'Just go up to King's Cross, get talking to a few desperate characters. Tell 'em what you want doing and that you'll pay a hundred quid.' Mick tapped a hand on the table and waved it at Peter dismissively. 'Boffo! They're dead.'

Peter smiled. 'Yeah, right.'

'I'm serious, Pete. There's people'll do anything for a bit of the old folding.' Mick rubbed his fingers and thumb in a cash-happy gesture. 'Know what I mean?'

Peter said nothing. He was staring fixedly out of the window.

'Pete?' Mick tapped the table. Peter didn't move, he didn't even blink. Mick followed the other's gaze. Outside the restaurant, beyond the plate glass windows decorated with colourful ribbons and images of the world's favourite burger-munching clown, a man with a long, frizzy beard and jet black sunglasses stood looking in at them.

'Whoa, dude.' Mick shifted back. 'Is that him?'

Peter nodded silently.

'Maybe he wants a cheeseburger.'

Peter gathered his jacket and got up.

'Pete?' Mick looked from Peter to the tramp and back. 'He's just a tramp, mate.'

'I don't like being watched when I'm eating.'

Mick got up. 'But we've finished eating. C'mon, it's too soon to go back.'

'I'm behind in my work,' Peter said impatiently. 'Are you coming?' He started towards the exit.

Mick followed. 'Wait up, Pete, for fuck's sake.' A woman who sat with two children shot Mick a disapproving look. He ignored her. 'Pete?'

Peter pushed open the door and left the restaurant. Mick watched as he plunged into the crawling traffic and wove his way rapidly to the other side of the street. Stepping out of the doors after him, Mick watched as Peter walked quickly away in the direction of their office. Mick shook his head in mild exasperation and turned to where the tramp still stood looking into the window of the McDonald's. He seemed to have no interest in Peter whatsoever. Probably just hungry, thought Mick. He wandered along, waiting for a break in the traffic before crossing. When he got to the other side of the street he saw Peter up ahead, waiting outside the office building. As Mick approached, he noticed how Peter stared back in the direction of the McDonald's. There was a look of genuine fear on Peter's face.

'What was all that about?' Mick asked, as he joined Peter outside the building.

'I didn't want to walk past him.'

'He wasn't even looking at you, Pete. He was looking into McDonald's all the time. Seeing how the other half live, y'know?'

'He wasn't.' Peter continued to stare back at the restaurant. 'He was looking at me.'

Mick gave a light, dismissive laugh. 'You are par-a-noid, man. I mean really, this noise thing has caused you to lose so much sleep that you can't figure stuff out any more.'

They entered the building that housed the offices of Richardson and West. 'I can figure stuff out just fine,' Peter said as they walked up to the elevators. 'That tramp is watching me.'

Mick smiled as a thought occurred to him. 'Maybe he's in love with you.'

Peter looked at him, unamused. 'Don't be stupid.'

They stood among a small crowd awaiting the elevator. The lift arrived and everybody stepped inside.

'Seriously,' Mick persisted. 'You'd be quite a catch, in tramp terms.'

Peter ignored him. He hoped everyone else would too.

Mick settled next to him and stared neutrally ahead. He cleared his throat. 'You're just afraid you might enjoy the feel of his beard tickling your neck.'

Despite himself, Peter smiled. 'Shut up, Mick.'

Mick touched him lightly on the arm. 'I just want you to know, you have my blessing. I'm over it already.'

Peter glanced at the other passengers, all of whom were pointedly ignoring them. Then he looked at Mick. 'Thanks, honey.'

Mick smiled and gave him a gentle punch on the arm as the doors rolled silently closed.

Ron Chigley stared at the front of his house and wondered whether it was worth the hassle any more. In the three years since he and his wife Margaret had bought this place and let it out to tenants, they'd had nothing but headaches and trauma. Not the kind of thing they need an abundance of at their time in life.

'At my time in life, this is the last thing I need an abundance of,' said Ron.

Jack Woolfe looked at him. 'No, Ron.' His burned-out, roll-up cigarette bobbed on his lower lip as he spoke.

'I just don't understand it.' Ron looked at the scorched door in bewilderment. 'How can a bloody balls-up like this happen in a respectable neighbourhood like this one?'

'I dunno, Ron. Blimmin' kids innit.'

'Bloody right it is.'

Ron and Margaret bought the place just as prices began to rise towards the end of the 1990s. Before the last tenants moved in, he had an estate agent in for a free evaluation and was delighted to learn that he'd doubled his money on the place.

'You know, I've doubled my money on this place in the last three years?' said Ron.

'Don't surprise me.'

'I don't know why the hell I don't just sell it on and have done with it.'

His brother-in-law, Martin, had the idea of letting. He'd made a packet buying and letting property out in the Eighties. Martin had put in more partition walls than there were real ones in just about every place he'd owned. He'd turned two-bedroomed houses into six-bedroomed houses, and four-bedroomed houses into hospitals. At least that's what he could have sold them on as.

'Could've sold them on as hospitals,' Ron announced. 'Made a fortune he did, our Martin.'

Jack lit his cigarette, took a puff, then let it to go out again.

'He called himself a property investor,' Ron scoffed. 'His tenants called him a slumlord. You know what I mean?'

Jack nodded.

'I didn't want to be like Martin, Jack. Sure, I wanted to make a sound investment, a nest egg for our retirement, but not at the cost of causing people to live like pigs. You know what I mean?'

Jack nodded.

Ron looked at his watch. 'Where is that flippin' blighter?'

'Probably in the pub.'

'Do you think?'

'Dunno. That's where I'd be if I didn't have nothin' else to do.'

'But he does have something else to do. He has to meet me here at two. All of 'em do.' Ron held up his watch so Jack could see it. 'It's fifteen minutes past, Jack. There havin' a laugh at me aren't they?'

Jack nodded. 'Laughin' at you in the pub.'

'Do you think?'

Jack nodded.

'Sods.' Ron shook his head. 'Give 'em a nice place to live; all the facilities; all mod cons, and what do they do? What do they do?'

'Laugh at you in the pub.'

'No, Jack. They set fire to your flippin' house, then they laugh at you in the pub. That's what they do.' Ron was breathing heavily. He was working himself up into a temper. His chubby cheeks glowed like the plastic coals on an electric fire. He began pacing up and down the garden path. Jack looked impassively at the front door.

Somewhere beyond the neighbouring hedges, a car door slammed, then another, then another. Voices could be heard. Cheerful, boisterous.

Ron looked at Jack.

Jack looked at the front door.

'Mr Chigley.' Gaz appeared from behind the hedges and opened the garden gate.

Ron fixed Gaz with a stern look, which he then turned upon Glen, Jimmy and some young tart as they ignored the gate and stepped over the two foot high, ornate plastic chain fence that separated his property from the street. They ambled in casually over the lawn. Ron noted that at least they didn't tread on the neglected, but nevertheless provided, flowerbeds.

'Sorry we're late, we've only just been discharged from hospital.'

Hospital? Thought Ron. Of course, hospital. What was I thinking of? Pub! Idiot Jack and his idiot pub talk. 'Of course, hospital. A terrible business,' his boiled facial expression cooled to a warm, benign one. 'How are you all?'

'We're all fine,' said Gaz.

'I'm relieved to hear it,' said Ron. 'Thank heaven for small mercies, eh?'

'And big ones.' Glen grinned.

'Yes.' Ron nodded uncertainly. 'And big ones. After all, not being burned to death in a house fire is quite a big one, isn't it?'

They all agreed it was. Even Jack.

'Anyway, shall we take a look at the damage?' Ron indicated Jack. 'I've brought Jack along to assess the repairs situation. You've met Jack haven't you?'

'No.' Gaz waved casually. 'Alright Jack?'

The others did likewise. Jack nodded once for all. He lit his cigarette and took a puff. Then let it go out again.

'Yeah.' Gaz walked up the path and past Ron towards the front door. 'It's mainly just the carpet and some scorching around the door and the walls. Nothing too serious.' He took out his keys and opened the front door. 'We contained the fire very quickly; had it out in no time.'

Ron looked into his hallway. The smell of things burned then doused with water hit him like a fist. That and the other smell. 'Petrol?'

'Er, yeah. Petrol. See, the whole thing started yesterday afternoon.' Gaz began to spin out the well rehearsed lie that they had concocted in hospital over the last few hours. 'Glen here's been planning a drive over to Bournemouth in the next few days, and he decided he'd have to get a spare gallon of petrol for the car. In case of emergencies.'

Ron nodded.

Gaz continued. 'So he says to me, "can I borrow some money off you to get some petrol?". I say, "sure", and give him a tenner. He goes off to the petrol station down the road with the tenner and one of those plastic petrol containers you carry in the car for just such an emergency.'

Ron, frowning slightly, nodded.

'Anyway, he fills it up and comes home. Now, being a conscientious type, he stops off at the bank machine on the way home to pick up a tenner to pay me back with. Then he comes back, and the first thing he does is comes in and gives me back the tenner. Didn't you, Glen?'

Glen nodded. 'Oh yeah, gotta get the priorities right. Always pay my debts off straight away.'

Ron rubbed his chin thoughtfully.

'So he comes into the house with this petrol can and gives me back the tenner. "Cheers," I say. And off he goes to put the can in the back of his car. Only, like a tit, he trips over the doormat on the way out and spills petrol all around the doorway. See, he didn't screw the top on the can properly, did you Glen?'

'No.' Glen rolled his eyes. 'Like a tit.'

'Naturally we did our best to clean it up. But petrol's a deeply penetrating thing, as I'm sure you're aware, Mr Chigley.'

'Very penetrating,' Ron agreed.

'So there it is. In the carpet. We all agreed to get the carpet cleaners in as soon as possible. After all, we don't want to bother you with such matters, do we? I mean, it was our fault, and it's our problem. Right?'

Ron, impressed by the assessment, nodded.

'Anyway. That was the plan. Unfortunately, it all went a bit pear-shaped later in the evening.'

'What happened?'

At this point, Kay came forward nervously. 'I'm afraid I had a bit of an accident, sir.'

Ron looked at her. 'Oh? Miss...?'

'Oliver. Kay Oliver. I'm a friend of the lads.'

'I see. So, what was the nature of this accident?'

'Well,' Kay began. 'I'm a smoker, you see, and I came around last night to see if the lads would like to come out for a drink.'

Ron nodded.

'And when I came to the door, I was, I was smoking a cigarette?' The end of her sentence rose questioningly in the antipodean fashion.

Ron shifted uncomfortably at the thought of a smoker in his house.

'Well, Gaz comes to answer the front door and, as soon as he sees the fag in my hand, he says, "put that out, Kay, you know this a no-smoking household."'

'I do tell people, Mr Chigley, but Kay here hadn't been around before. She didn't know the rules.'

'I see. Quite right, too. But anyway...?' Ron nodded to Kay to continue.

'So I drop the cigarette on the ground, to tread it out with my foot, and the stupid thing bounces on the concrete, through the front door and lands on the mat indoors.'

'Woosh!' Gaz mimed the conflagration.

'Jesus.' Ron looked shocked. 'And you were standing in it?'

'I was.' Gaz nodded. 'And then Glen comes charging out to help me, and manages to catch fire himself.'

'Well, it's a deeply penetrating thing,' said Glen. 'Must've gotten all over the soles of me shoes.'

'Goodness.' Ron shook his head. 'What happened next?'

'Well,' said Gaz. 'We ran out onto the front garden and managed to kick our shoes off before they burned us to death.'

'What about your other clothes?'

'Well they weren't soaked in petrol in any way. So although they caught slightly, they were easy to put out by just beating at them with our hands.'

'Are your hands burned?' Ron asked.

'No, not so's you'd notice.' Gaz shrugged. 'But the pain's still there, mind you.'

'What about the fire? How'd you put that out?'

'Well, fortunately Jimmy was inside, and naturally, by now he's aware that the house is on fire, so he runs to the kitchen and grabs a couple of saucepans, fills 'em with water and comes out to douse the flames.'

'I did.' Jimmy nodded.

'How many pans did it take to contain it?'

'Only the two.'

'And another one to make sure,' added Gaz, unhappy with the dramatic image painted by the truth.

'I see.' Ron raised his eyebrows. 'Sounds to me like you were bloody lucky.'

'Oh, we were.' Gaz nodded. The others agreed.

Ron sighed. 'Well, I think we can safely say that this terrible accident doesn't affect our relationship. Jack here'll sort out any repairs that need to be made, and I'll get onto my insurance people in the morning.'

Gaz smiled. 'Thanks Mr Chigley. You're very understanding. Not like some landlords.'

'Not like our Martin,' said Ron, inscrutable to all but Jack, who nodded. 'He'd've charged you all for the damages then sued you for personal trauma or something. Then he'd spend the money on a whole new load of partition walls. Eh, Jack?'

Jack nodded.

Gaz, confused, nodded anyway.

Ron rubbed his hands together. 'Anyway. I'll be off now. While I'm here, do you lads have the rent cheques?'

Gaz turned to the others. They looked back blankly. 'Er, I think they're around somewhere, Mr Chigley. I know we wrote them out yesterday, but, in all the excitement, I've forgotten where I put them.'

'Oh, well, I suppose that's understandable. I'll leave you chaps alone to get yourselves sorted out, and then get back to you in a few days time.'

'That's good of you, Mr Chigley.'

'Not like some landlords,' mumbled Jack.

'No,' Ron agreed. 'Not like our Martin.'

Jimmy and Glen inched slowly back into the shadows of the hall. Seeing them, Kay slunk away as well. Slowly, the three of them backed away into the house, watching Ron Chigley talk to the ground about Martin. Gaz turned and looked at them, a smile fixed awkwardly on his lips. Jimmy waved and the three of them stepped quickly out of sight and into the front room. Gaz turned back, his idiot smile firmly in place. Still addressing the ground for some reason, Ron Chigley rambled on about partitioned rooms and vast amounts of money. Gaz turned his smiling face to the handyman Jack. Jack lit the cigarette that dangled permanently from between his lips, took one puff, and then seemed to forget it again.

With a long internal sigh, Gaz, secure in the knowledge that the police wouldn't be coming around to investigate their happy home, resigned himself to the fact that they wouldn't be going down the pub just yet. But when they did, he reflected, they'd raise a glass to good old Mr Chigley.

Then they'd spend the rest of the afternoon laughing their hairy arses off at the gullible old fart.

'Can I help you?'

Peter Reynolds was startled by the voice. He turned and saw a small, smartly dressed woman in her forties standing next to him, her hands clasped in front of her chest. He recognised her as one of the reception staff. 'No. Thank you. I'm, I'm just waiting for someone.'

'Oh,' the receptionist indicated the chairs against a far wall. 'Would you like to have a seat?'

'No. No thank you. I prefer to stand.'

The receptionist smiled. 'I'm sorry sir, you're rather in the way just where you are. Would you at least mind standing a little to one side?'

Peter considered this. Where he stood now he had an excellent view of the street. He'd had an excellent view of the street for ten minutes now. As far as he was aware, he wasn't causing an obstruction. 'Must I?'

The receptionist smiled. This strange young man had been staring out of the front door now for what seemed like half an hour. People were having to walk around him just to get in and out of the building. Everyone had been giving him strange looks, not least of all the reception staff. 'If you wouldn't mind,' she said with the utmost politeness.

Bitch, thought Peter. 'Actually, I think I may have got my times mixed up.' He smoothed his hair back with both hands and sighed casually. 'I'll just be on my way.'

'Very good.' She watched as Peter stepped up to the doors and with curious slowness, eased them open. It was like he thought they were wired to explode if handled too harshly. He turned and smiled at her. She smiled back. He looked out into the street; first left, then right, then left again. He turned again and, smiling, gave her a little wave. She waved back. Peter swallowed dryly, stepped out into the street and was gone.

The receptionist dropped her smile and returned to her desk. When she got there her colleague, Jenny, who had watched the whole thing, asked excitedly, 'Well?'

'Nutter.'

'Really? What did he say?'

'Reckoned he was waiting for someone,' said the receptionist as she sat down.

'Do you believe him?'

'I never know what to believe with these people.'

Jenny tapped her chin with a pencil. 'I must say, I've noticed him before. Not in a sexy way mind you – he wouldn't be my type. But there's something different about him. Do you know what I mean?'

'I know what you mean,' the receptionist nodded. 'He's a nutter.'

He is The One.

Dusty watched from the first floor window of the public library opposite Peter's office building. He watched as Peter emerged, cautious and tense.

He knows, thought Dusty. He knows that I know, and he fears exposure. But still, I have to know more about him. I have to know everything about him.

He got up from his armchair, tossing the newspaper he had been hiding behind back onto the periodicals table. He walked quickly across the library, and down the stairs into the entrance lobby. The librarians looked at each other as he passed. Dusty read their silent transmissions. He was able to understand the secret codes of librarians, having spent many hours watching them on cold or wet afternoons.

Librarians have a hidden language of minute facial expressions that the ordinary public neither sees nor understands. He had seen them mock people to their faces as they asked whether or not a certain book was in. He had watched as librarians communicated complex and elaborate sexual fantasies about men or women in the library to one another while the man or woman in question went about their literary perusals, unaware that they were being psychically undressed and violated in front of everyone else in the library.

Oh yes, librarians – they held no secrets from him. Right now, they were communicating their mutual gratitude that he was leaving. They sensed he could understand them, and this made them uncomfortable. At the doorway, Dusty turned and looked at the librarian who stood at the returns desk. The librarian calmly met Dusty's gaze and raised an enquiring eyebrow.

'Don't even think it,' said Dusty.

The librarian was unperturbed. He regarded Dusty with an air of cool curiosity.

'Oh, you're good.' Dusty stepped into the revolving door.

The librarian looked across at a colleague.

Dusty, having gone around once, stepped out of the revolving door and back into the library. 'Dream on, librarian. Your friend knows it, and so should you.' He stepped back into the revolving doors and stepped out into the street.

'Beasts,' he muttered as he trotted down the steps and off in the direction that Peter Reynolds had taken a moment earlier. 'The things they'd do if they could.' Then, at a volume he knew the librarians would be able to hear, he shouted, 'Perverts all!'

Peter was beginning to feel relaxed. There was no sign of the tramp. Maybe he'd gone back to wherever he came from. Maybe he'd found someone else to spook.

'Who gives a shit,' he said, 'as long as he isn't following me around.'

Up ahead he could see that the queue at the bus stop was tiny. The bus had probably just recently gone. Shit, he'd have to wait a bit. It was that tramp's fault, making him hang around for so long in the foyer. He wandered up and joined the back of the queue.

As he stared absently at the backs of the people in front of him, his mind wandered back to what Mick had been saying earlier about killing the wankers over the back. Of course, soliciting some strange King's Cross vagabonds to murder them was out of the question, but somewhere in the muddy depths of Mick's stupid advice there lurked a curious pearl of wisdom. Mentally, Peter groped for it. The King's Cross desperadoes? The big mate? The visit? The threat? The ideas bobbed about in his mind for a while before eventually fusing into a notion; an unlikely one, but no harm in playing it out in his mind.

Peter saw himself approaching the big tramp in the sunglasses and…? And what? He painted in a McDonald's and saw himself buying the guy a cheeseburger. This works. I buy him a cheeseburger and then? Then I ask him how he'd like to earn fifty quid. Is that too much? Is that enough? Irrelevant, since it isn't going to happen. Anyway, he saw the bum accepting the deal; they shake hands. He sees himself wipe his hand on his trousers underneath the table. Then it's dark; the tramp goes to the wankers' house and gives them the warning to turn it down, or else. Then what? They attack him with that kung fu thing they do. Can the tramp handle it? Yes, he's pretty hard. Maybe before he was a tramp he was in the army. Maybe in the Falklands or something. He beats them up. Then he smashes their stereo… over their heads. Excellent.

He smiled to himself, mentally replaying the bit where the stereo smashes over their various heads. Stereo and speakers. Brilliant. He looked up. The bus was approaching. He reached into his coat pocket and fumbled around for his return ticket. He couldn't find it.

'Shit,' he cursed under his breath.

'Lost something?'

The voice came from behind him. Peter turned, and felt a cold, low voltage electric shock run through his entire body. He couldn't speak. Instead, he gaped like a fish at his own frightened expression reflected in the smooth, obsidian blackness of the tramp's sunglasses.

Chapter 4

MICK BENT DOWN and began to move the small wheels of the number coded lock that secured the rear wheel of his bicycle to its frame. The underground car park was manned throughout the working day by an attendant, but the lock provided him with an extra sense of security.

The numbers clicked into place and the lock came apart in his hands. Mick wrapped the chain around the bike frame beneath the saddle. Of course, if someone were determined to steal the bike, then no chain, or any number of chains, would make much difference. But then, unlike so many mountain bikes, if someone were to steal Mick's bike, they'd have a job concealing it beneath anything so transparent as a new coat of paint. No one else in this town, or anywhere else he'd seen for miles around, rode a Raleigh Chopper.

The Harley Davidson of the bicycle world, the Chopper was Mick's single greatest joy in life. Throughout his childhood, he'd pestered his parents to buy him one, but they were pragmatic people. They saw no practical advantages to the strange, hulking contraption that for some curious reason was so adored by theirs and indeed most of the nation's sons in the 1970s. They felt the racer they'd invested in for young Michael was a splendid machine, and saw no point in buying him another bike. Mick shook his head. How could they have understood the allure of the Chopper? How could they have known that to the young Mick, it was the embodiment of sex, power and freedom.

How he had sullenly sat perched upon his fine, skeletal racer, watching while Chopper owning boys like Malcolm Barnes seduced girls with the prospect of 'backies' on those big, padded seats. He recalled now the plastic, beak-like saddle of his racer; how it felt like the head of an axe between his arse cheeks. No girl would ever want to ride with him on a racer – it wasn't designed for two. For one thing, it would be unmanoeuvrable with two people on it, and for another, just supposing you did get some chick onto it – then where do you sit? You don't – your arse just goes up and down in her face as you pedal, and she's got nothing to hold onto – except your hips, and she's not going to do that, not at the tender age of twelve.

How he'd envied boys like Malcolm Barnes, riding around the streets with his black leather gloved hands. One hand on the handle bars, the other dangling casually at his side. His expression said it all: 'Check me out – I can steer one-handed.' And he did, he used to steer that Chopper leisurely past pubescent young girls who were drawn, moth-like to the colourful iron horse between his legs. They took it in turns to sit on the saddle; their feet dangling either side and their hands on or around his waist as Malcolm took them up and down the street. And then Vicky Rhodes, the hottest girl in the second year, had started going out with Malcolm – not for his looks, but for his Chopper.

Oh, the cruelty. Oh the agonies of burgeoning sexual frustration. He recalled Malcolm, jumping over ramps constructed of planks with one end propped up on a couple of bricks. How he used to fly for whole inches through the air before the weight of the Chopper brought him back down onto the tarmac. But the distance travelled was irrelevant. It was the spectacle. 'Put another brick under it,' cried Malcolm. 'Prop it up even higher.' How the girls gasped. This was Catford's very own Evel Kenievel; a daredevil for whom brick quantity was merely an adrenaline barometer.

How Mick had waited, had scrimped and saved the money from his paper round until, at the age of fourteen, he had enough money to buy… a decent cheap stereo. For the times had changed, and now music mattered far more than bicycles. At seventeen, the young worker, he bought a moped. But that had ended in a minor road accident and Mick went back to biking it. He'd ridden racers most of his adult life since then, shunning cars (despite their potential allure to susceptible young women) in favour of the tried and trusted bicycle. It wasn't until his thirtieth year that, entirely by chance, he discovered his own Raleigh Chopper.

He'd been thumbing through old seven inch singles in a second hand store when he noticed a big red reflector, glowing like the eye of Hal in *2001 – A Space Odyssey*, in the shadows at the back of the shop. The singles were suddenly forgotten beneath his fingers as he realised what he was looking at. He moved slowly towards it, the classical shape revealing itself to him with every step he took. It was a mauve one, the word "Chopper" written in orange along the crossbar. He reached out and touched the black plastic grips on the handlebars and felt the past wash over him. He'd had innumerable goes on Malcolm's Chopper, and he knew the touch achingly well. His eyes drank in the details of the bike with the slow appreciation of one who has loved from afar, finally beholding the naked and yielding contours of the adored. The gear stick replete with red grip, the big, chunky tyres with their thin red trim, the kick stand, and of course, the big soft seat with its backrest and curious metal extension that protruded skyward with no discernible purpose.

He looked for a price tag and found it dangling from the suspension springs beneath the seat: fifty quid. Bargain. He hurried to the shopkeeper and placed a £20 deposit down before rushing off to the nearest cash machine and drawing out the rest of the money. That afternoon, he rode home with one hand on the handlebars, the other dangling casually at his side. 'Check me out', he thought, smiling like an idiot, 'I can steer one-handed too.'

'Check us out,' Mick whispered now in the gloom of the car park. He ran his hand affectionately over the saddle, giving it a little pat before kicking up the stand. He mounted the bike and pushed off, heading towards the glow of daylight at the entrance. He pedalled lazily past Charlie, exchanging a wave before riding out into the afternoon sun. He reached down and shifted up into second gear before he turned the Chopper out into traffic. He had long grown accustomed to the staring of passers-by. Some sniggered, but most, he knew, looked with envy and admiration at his magnificent bicycle. As he had done in childhood, they now pined for the opportunity to cruise the streets on two of the grooviest wheels ever made.

As he rode, Mick considered his lunchtime chat with Peter. Old Pete had seemed really freaked out about this tramp business. Like the tramp actually gives a shit about him. That he might even mean him harm. As if! What kind of tramp gives a toss about Mr Totally Average Reynolds? For that matter, he speculated, what kind of anybody?

Peter was about the least magnetic guy Mick knew. To most people, Peter was just a sad boy; a neurotic best kept at arm's length. Yet he enjoyed Peter's various eccentric episodes. He found the wild rants about the late night exploits of his neighbours particularly enjoyable. Mick shook his head as he recalled Peter's account of the three guys dancing around their flat in the nude. No wonder Pete was going crazy. This tramp development just had to be a new symptom of that craziness.

Mick turned out onto the main road. As he moved into the centre of the traffic flow, he saw Peter at the bus stop. He was about to call out to him when he noticed that Peter looked almost absurdly frightened. Then Mick saw what Peter was looking at. The tramp stood behind him, the one from McDonald's, the one that Pete thought was after him. At that moment a double-decker bus pulled into the bus stop, obscuring Mick's view. He looked about, weighing the chances of getting to the kerb, but he was too boxed-in by cars. He had little choice but to move on with the flow of the traffic. As the bus moved away from the kerb, Mick looked back to where a moment before Peter and the tramp had been. The bus stop stood empty.

Mick watched as the bus moved off down the road. Behind him a car hooted and he realised he'd braked to a halt. Mick looked again at the receding bus; he couldn't manoeuvre through this mess of traffic and pursue it, even if he could catch up with it. Reluctantly, he turned the handlebars of the Chopper to the right and pedalled slowly towards home.

Peter looked around at the empty seats. Where wouldn't this guy want to sit, he wondered, before realising the folly of the thought. He sits in trash all day long – what does he care? As Peter looked at the seats he heard the tramp addressing the driver.

'Palmeira Square.'

That's my stop, thought Peter with fear and outrage. He must've heard me tell the driver where I was going.

Peter quickly sat in one of the seats nearest the front of the bus. He looked down at the floor ahead of him, knowing the next pair of feet to pass down the aisle would be those of the tramp. There they were; old boots, battered and scuffed. The laces in one boot replaced by string that looked like it too would soon need to be replaced. Peter watched as the boots walked up the aisle, stopped, and turned. Peter felt the seat sink beneath the weight of the tramp as he sat down beside him. He realised he'd stopped breathing and forced himself to inhale. Immediately he wished he hadn't; the guy smelled acrid, like ammonia. Peter turned and looked at the object of his terror.

The tramp smiled at him. 'Mind if I sit here?'

Peter looked around the bus, empty seats abounded. 'There's lots of empty seats. Wouldn't you rather sit alone?'

'No. I like company.'

'Well, I'm sorry,' Peter stood up stiffly, 'but I don't.' He stepped out into the aisle and walked to the back of the bus. His heart hammered in his chest as he turned around and faced the length of the bus before sitting down. At the front, the tramp was looking back at him over his shoulder. Peter looked away. He didn't see the tramp get up and walk towards him, but in the moments before he sat down beside him again, he smelled him.

'Isn't this the troublesome end of the bus?' asked the tramp casually.

'I…' Peter stammered, horrified to find himself again in the tramp's company, 'I thought I told you I wanted to sit alone.'

'And I thought I told you that I like company. It was awfully rude of you to just get up and walk off like that, especially after I helped you out this morning.'

Peter found himself unsure of what to say. His mind struggled to deal with the etiquette surrounding social gaffes with members of the vagrant classes. 'I… I'm sorry. It's just that I've had a difficult day.'

'Anything I can help with?'

'Sorry?' Peter frowned with deepening consternation. This was getting more and more like a bus journey into the Twilight Zone.

'Anything I can help with? I haven't always lived this way, you know. I used to be things.' He turned to face Peter and his eyebrows raised over the rims of the sunglasses. 'Other things.'

'Like what?'

'All sorts. I'm very versatile.'

'Who are you?'

The tramp proffered his hand. 'Dusty. Dusty Gibbons.'

Peter looked at the hand and, not wanting to be chided again over his manners, shook it briefly, with the barest pressure. 'Peter Reynolds.' There was something odd about the tramp's name. Something he couldn't quite put his finger on. 'Dusty Gibbons?'

'That's me.'

Then it dawned on Peter. 'That sounds kind of familiar.'

Dusty turned again to Peter. With a slight smile, he revolved his right hand in a slow circle that came to an end in a kind of two fingered salute pointing off to his left. Peter recognised it from ZZ Top videos he'd seen on TV in the eighties.

Peter smiled, he couldn't help himself. 'Yeah, right.'

Dusty's eyebrows again bobbed over the rims of his sunglasses.

'You expect me to believe you're someone from ZZ Top?'

'Believe what you like.'

'Sharp dressed man?'

'You know it.'

'So what's your excuse?' Peter gave a quick, ironic glance up and down Dusty's attire.

Dusty turned to face the front. 'Clothes maketh not the man.'

'I don't recall that one being a hit.'

Dusty said nothing.

'I mean, you do look a bit like someone out of ZZ Top.'

'People have commented upon that.'

'But they're from Texas, aren't they?'

Dusty shrugged.

'You sound like you're from… I dunno, here.'

'Here, there and everywhere.' Dusty smiled. 'I've been other things.'

'So you said.' Peter nodded. He continued to consider Dusty's appearance. 'You're also too big.'

'Thanks. I try to keep in shape.'

'I see.'

Dusty turned to him. 'Enough of me. Let's talk about you.'

Peter shifted in his seat. 'Me?'

'Yes. You were telling me about your day.'

'Oh. My day. Yeah, it, er, it was a bad one.'

Dusty nodded sagely.

Then, almost without knowing he was saying it, Peter said, 'Actually, it's not so much work that's difficult, but my home life. I have some problems at home.' Damn, he thought. Why did I say that? Damn Mick and his stupid ideas.

'Oh? Anything I can help with?'

'Huh?' Peter groped for a response. 'I, ah, I don't think so.'

'I'm very versatile.'

'Yes.' Peter smiled awkwardly. 'Yes, you did mention that.'

They rode in silence for a moment, both rocking with the gentle rolling motion of the bus. Dusty watching Peter, waiting for a response. Peter frowning, inwardly absorbed as his mind improvised and projected a patchy film of his cocksure neighbours engaged in a pitched kung-fu battle with this intimidating stranger. The film ended with the tramp, broken and bleeding, raising a shaky finger to point up at Peter's bedroom window and saying with his last, dying breath, 'It was him, he made me do it.' The three blokes look up and smack their fists into their open palms in a united gesture of revenge. Who put petrol through the letterbox? Why, the same guy who sent this hit-tramp, that's who.

Peter turned to Dusty and flinched at the close proximity of the other's bearded features. Wincing afresh at the odour. 'No, actually. Thank you for asking, but it's a personal matter.'

'Wife?' Dusty asked bluntly.

Peter shook his head, 'No.'

'Girlfriend?'

Peter laughed a little. 'No, it's not a woman.'

'A boyfriend?'

Peter turned, shocked. 'No!' he blurted. 'Jesus, do I look like that?'

A few other people on the bus turned at his resounding denial. Peter blushed and looked away from Dusty and out of the window.

'What does a gay man look like?' said Dusty. 'In my experience they look much the same as anybody else. I'm sorry if I offended you.'

Peter said nothing. He watched the traffic through the window.

'Rent?' said Dusty. 'Mortgage payments?'

'Listen. I don't want to talk about it. In fact I don't want to talk to you at all. If you must sit next to me then there's not a lot I can do about that – it's a free country. But I don't have to talk to you, so if you'll excuse me, I'll just sit here and mind my own business.'

Dusty looked at him for a few moments, then turned to sit facing forwards again. They travelled the rest of their journey like this: unmoving, unspeaking. As they neared his stop, Peter again felt anxiety rising within him. He had felt quite strong earlier; he'd managed to overcome his fear of the tramp with the stupid ZZ Top fantasy. He'd even managed to get angry with him. But now they were entering a new juncture, a new moment where the tramp might somehow take the upper hand. The bus approached the stop. Peter got up.

'Excuse me,' he said to Dusty, carefully averting his eyes from the sunglasses. He reached out and rang the bell. Dusty moved aside, allowing Peter to pass, as the driver pulled the bus into the stop.

As Peter made his way down the aisle, he prayed silently that Dusty would stay on the bus, even though he knew the tramp had only paid to travel this far, and was surely behind him even now. He stepped off the bus and didn't look behind him. Instead, he looked up at the back of the bus as it moved away. To his utter astonishment, Dusty was still aboard. The tramp had been waiting for him to look up, and as the bus moved off down the street, he gave Peter his ZZ Top salute. Peter looked away, relief and disgust overwhelming him as he crossed the street.

As soon as the bus left Peter behind, Dusty got to his feet and rang the bell. He moved quickly to the front of the bus and stood by the driver. 'Must've been dozing. Missed my stop.'

The driver glanced at Dusty in his mirror. 'Next one's just up ahead.'

'Phew.'

The driver turned and looked directly at him.

Dusty smiled. 'Don't want to have to walk too far to get home.'

'You live around here?' asked the driver as he pulled into the stop and opened the doors.

'No.' Dusty stepped off the bus and began walking back towards the corner where, just a moment before, he'd seen Peter Reynolds disappear.

Peter hurried homeward, glancing over his shoulder every now and again to make sure the tramp hadn't decided to jump off the bus and run after him. He groped in his trouser pocket for his keys as he neared the converted town house, the top flat of which was his. He stepped up to the front door with his key poised and ready. Quickly, he opened the door, slipped inside, and then closed it firmly behind him. The familiar sights and smells of the hallway were as a balm to his anxieties. He looked ahead at the carpeted stairs as they ascended into the upper regions of the house and felt a sense of safety wash through him. Sighing, he slumped against the wall with relief. He stood there a moment, his head lolling gently. Then, quite suddenly, the sheer absurdity of his situation overwhelmed him. He shook his head and said aloud, 'Fucking hell.' He laughed, and looked up at the stairs, 'What a fucking day I've had.' He stayed like that for a few moments, the laughter subsiding gradually as he shifted his weight back onto his feet and began the slow trudge up to the top flat, and a cup of tea that most definitely had his name written all over it.

Dusty shadowed Peter at a distance. He followed his progress through the windows of parked cars and in the reflections of opposite houses. He watched as Peter looked over his shoulder, nervous, like a rabbit. It wasn't unusual behaviour, even for The One. I am strange to him, thought Dusty. I smell unfamiliar, perhaps unpleasant. In a world populated by false and scented people, how mysterious am I? 'Very mysterious,' he muttered aloud. 'Very mysterious indeed.'

He watched as Peter withdrew his keys and stepped up to the front door of one of the big houses. Dusty fixed the house in his memory as Peter opened the door and disappeared into the shadowy hallway within. The door closed. Dusty straightened up from behind the car that concealed him. He walked across the street and down to Peter's house. It was number 13.

'Unlucky for some,' Dusty whispered. He walked up to the door and placed his ear against the cool painted surface. Inside he heard a voice laughing quietly. Dusty smiled. It was The One. Perhaps he wasn't so angry after all. Perhaps he was playing a game with Dusty. After all, he thrives in a world of falsehoods. He is no doubt a master of illusion. Dusty turned and looked at the building's intercom system. Beside them were listed only the flat numbers, not the names of the occupants. Dusty listened again at the door. Silence. He knelt down and peered in through the letterbox. The hall was empty. He waited. A door closed distantly somewhere inside the building. He could clearly see the door of the ground floor flat. 'So,' he said. 'You obviously don't live there, then.'

He lowered the letterbox flap and got to his feet. He cleared his throat, then pressed the doorbell for flat one. A few moments later a tiny metallic voice came through the speaker.

'Hello?'

'Hi,' said Dusty. 'Is this the dark-haired guy who just got off the bus?'

'No,' the voice sounded guarded. 'What do you want?'

'Oh, I'm sorry. It's just I saw this guy get off the bus and he dropped his wallet. I tried to catch up with him, but he came in here before I could.'

'Oh. Well you might try flat three,' the voice suggested. 'Bloke called Reynolds.'

'Thanks. Sorry to bother you.'

'No problem.' There was a crackle as the line went dead.

Dusty stepped back and craned his neck to look up to the top floor of the house. 'Flat three. Mr Reynolds.' He smiled, then turned and walked slowly back up the street.

As soon as he finished speaking on the intercom Wayne went straight to the window. He peered through the net curtains at the tramp that stood on the doorstep. 'Who the fuck are you?'

He heard the bathroom door open and hurried into the hall. 'El, quick, come and see.' He gestured frantically for her to follow him.

'What is it, Wayne?' She thought with his manic flapping that something must be wrong somewhere and she followed him with a rising sense of apprehension. When she entered the front room he was standing craning his neck at the window. What could it be? A fire up the road? A police siege? 'What is it Wayne?'

'He's gone,' Wayne sounded deflated. 'Shit, you should've seen this guy.'

'What guy? What are you talking about?'

Wayne turned from the window. 'There was this guy on the intercom looking for the bloke up in flat three. He said he'd found his wallet.

'So?'

'So he was like, unwashed. A tramp.'

'So?'

'So it's a bit unlikely isn't it? A tramp returning a wallet?'

'Tramps can be honest people too, Wayne. Just because you're not. Don't measure them by your standards.'

'What do you mean, I'm not?'

'Well if you found a wallet, would you return it?'

Wayne thought a moment. 'Depends.'

'See?'

'Yeah, well this honest tramp didn't seem to go in and hand the wallet over. He just said he was going to, then cleared off.'

Ellen shrugged, 'Maybe Mr Flat Three's out?'

'He said he'd just seen him go inside.'

'Well maybe he's having a dump!' Ellen sat down on the sofa. 'I don't know. It's none of our business.'

'But that's not all,' Wayne went on.

Ellen looked at him wearily. 'What?'

'He was wearing sunglasses.'

Ellen shook her head and fell back in her seat.

'Have you ever seen a tramp wearing sunglasses?'

'What? Do I look as if I go around trampspotting?'

'You know what I mean.'

'No, Wayne, I don't. So what if he was wearing sunglasses? It's sunny!'

Wayne shook his head. 'You don't understand, El. It's weird. The wallet thing; the sunglasses.' He hesitated, as though something had occurred to him. 'You know, he looked kind of familiar?'

'Oh?'

'Yeah, like TV familiar.'

Ellen smiled. 'Maybe it was Danny Baker doing a soap powder ad. He looks like a tramp.'

'No.' Wayne was deep in thought. Then he brightened. 'I know! ZZ Top.'

Ellen furrowed her brow. 'ZZ Top?'

'Yeah. Like one of the beardy guys from ZZ Top.'

'I see. You think ZZ Top are calling for Flat Three?'

'No.' Wayne smirked sarcastically. 'I said he looked like one of them. Not that he was one of them. Jesus, what would ZZ Top want with old personality boy up there?'

'Maybe he has good legs.' Ellen took her pack of cigarettes off of the table and shook one out.

'Eh?'

'They like legs, don't they? Like that song of theirs?' She shrugged absently. 'Maybe Flat Three has a gorgeous pair of pins.'

Wayne nodded. 'Yeah, right. Look, I just think it's weird, that's all. Tramps calling for Flat Three? It's weird.'

Ellen lit her cigarette and sighed smoke in Wayne's direction. 'Okay, it's weird.'

'So what do you think we should do about it?'

'Get over it and move on with our lives?'

'No,' said Wayne, exasperated. 'I'm serious.'

'Oh come on, Wayne. What can you do? Someone in dark glasses calls for Flat Three and you have a mental hernia. Forget it. It's none of our business.'

'I can't forget it, Ellen. What if he's somehow attracting homeless people? That's a risk to all of us, isn't it?'

'Attracting homeless people? Do you know how nutty that sounds?'

Wayne shrugged.

'So what are you going to do about it?'

'I could go up and see him,' suggested Wayne. 'Talk about it. See if he's lost his wallet.'

'Okay then, off you go.'

Wayne didn't move.

'Well?'

'I said I could do it, not that I would.'

Ellen smiled. 'Okay, then.'

'But I'll keep an eye out for old Flat Three.' Wayne illustrated his intent by twitching the net curtain and peeping outside.

'Oh, I know you will.'

Wayne continued to peer out, as though he was expecting a horde of vagabonds to come hurtling down the street and lay siege to the building at any minute. Ellen reached for the *Radio Times* and began flicking through to find out what delights awaited them on TV that night. Maybe Delia was making a pie or something fascinating like that. She noted with interest that *Hollyoaks* was just about to begin. She picked up the remote control from where it lay on the arm of Wayne's end of the sofa.

Wayne turned at the sound of the TV coming on. 'What are you doing?'

'Watching *Hollyoaks*.'

'Is it on now?'

'I sincerely hope so.'

Wayne came over and sat down next to her at his end of the sofa. 'Where's the remote?'

Ellen handed Wayne the remote control and he set it carefully back upon the arm of the sofa. He smiled at her, then turned to the TV.

Ellen watched him from the corner of her eye as he settled into a silent stillness, slipping almost immediately into a trance-like state. She smiled. Baby and his dummy, she thought, gone bye-byes.

Chapter 5

LEANNE WALKED FROM ROOM TO ROOM in the big, empty house. She couldn't believe that it was finally hers. At last all the bother with estate agents and solicitors was over and she was finally the owner of Meredith House. Hers by birthright, now, despite the machinations of Rick Galsworthy, hers by law. She suddenly felt tears of joy welling in her eyes and she stopped to dab at them with her hanky. Once her vision was clear, she saw ahead of her the open door of the master bedroom. Had she left it that way? She had no recollection of doing so. Had the estate agent been here then? Yes, that must be it. She walked down the corridor past the huge windows that let the sunshine flood in and into the bedroom. Once in, she stopped in horror.

'Hello Leanne,' said Rick. 'Fancy seeing you here.' He sat on the bed, a sheath of papers he'd been leafing through lay on his lap. He tossed them aside.

'What are you doing here?' Leanne asked. She tried to keep the tremor of fear she felt in her heart from reaching her voice.

'I might ask you the same question,' said Rick. 'Since this is my house that you're so plainly trespassing in.'

Leanne gasped in astonishment. 'Your house? What do you mean?'

Rick held up the sheaf of papers. 'It's all in here, Leanne. My house.'

'But, but,' Leanne stammered, 'that's impossible. I closed the deal on this place myself just yesterday. This is my house. My home.'

'You mean with Harper and Lewis?' Rick laughed dismissively. 'I own Harper and Lewis, Leanne. No sooner had your signature dried on the contract than they faxed it to me for my signature; the final signature.'

She looked at him with disbelief. 'You mean, you're...'

Rick nodded. 'I'm the owner; the seller. This has been my place all along.'

'That can't be!' cried Leanne. 'You can't! Not you!'

'Oh I can, Leanne,' said Rick, getting to his feet. 'I can, and do. I put this place on the market just so you'd come running for it. I had Harper and Lewis put everybody else off from the start. And let me tell you I turned down some very lucrative proposals on the way as well. And do you know why?'

Leanne shook her head.

'Just so as I could get you in the position where you are now. All keyed up and believing that Meredith House was finally yours. That your grandfather's estate had once again passed back into Meredith hands after the old fool gambled it away all those years ago.' Rick smiled cruelly. 'You never did know the name of the man he lost it to, did you Leanne? You never knew that the old card shark on the other side of the table was Damian Galsworthy – my grandfather.'

Leanne felt hot tears welling her in eyes, they spilled over her long black lashes and down her face. 'But why?' she asked. 'Why do this to me?'

Rick walked around the bed and came towards her. 'Because I hate you, Leanne. Ever since you spurned my advances, dismissed me as unworthy of you, I've vowed to hurt you like you've hurt me. And if the only way to pierce your heart is to use this house as a dagger, then I will. I have. I've plunged this dagger into your breast and now I'm twisting it.'

He ran his finger down his cheek, mimicking the tracks of her tears. 'Those tears that run down your cheeks,' he said, 'they remind me of mine on that night that you told me that you could never love an Aries. Oh, how I cried. How I wept. And now, how I relish your weeping. Your pain.'

'You,' Leanne sobbed, 'you bastard.'

Rick threw his head back and laughed. Then, he fixed her with his burning blue eyes and said, 'The only way you'll ever get your hands on this property, Leanne, is if you marry me.'

She gasped.

Rick suddenly threw open his blazer and grasped the waistband of his trousers.

Leanne looked aghast as he began to unfasten his braces. 'What,' she cried, 'what are you doing?'

'Oh, come now, Leanne,' he said. 'Let's not play games. We're both adults aren't we?' His braces sprang loose and his strong, sun-tanned hands quickly opened the clasp of his trousers. Before Leanne could protest, the trousers fell to his ankles. He smiled as he noticed her eyes, drawn inexorably to his underpants.

Leanne could see his aroused manhood like a coiled python behind the hugging white fabric. But there was something wrong, something... frightening.

'I want you, Leanne,' he said. 'I want you, and I mean to have you.' He grasped the elastic waistband of his jockeys and yanked them down to his knees.

Leanne's hand went to her mouth to stifle the scream that she felt rushing through her as

The door buzzer rang again. Lucy looked up from the home computer and cursed. She got up, removing her glasses and walked with irritation to the intercom.

She picked up the receiver. 'Yes?'

A tinny voice replied diffidently. 'Hello? It's Arthur.'

'Arthur?'

'Yes, eight o' clock? Arthur?'

She looked at her watch. Shit. It was eight already. She'd become so engrossed in her fiction that she'd forgotten all about her reality. Arthur, rubber boy. Eight o' clock, Tuesdays. Shit!

'Er, Arthur? I'm not feeling very well tonight. I've got a migraine. Would you mind terribly if we called it off tonight?'

'Well, I've come quite a long way you know.'

'Yes, but I'm not going to be able to... put you through adequate discomfort, if I'm in discomfort myself, am I?'

'But my wife will wonder what I'm doing back so early,' said Arthur querulously. 'I'm supposed to be at the ornithology club 'til at least nine-thirty.'

'Well then go to the ornithology club 'til at least nine-thirty.'

'I can't. There isn't one.'

'Arthur...'

'I really think I should come up, you know. I...'

'Arthur!' Lucy snapped. 'I said no. Now go home. Go to the pub or go and have a wank in your car, but don't bother me tonight. Do you understand?'

There was a moment of silence, the receiver hissing quietly against her ear like a seashell, then, a considerably smaller voice replied, 'Yes, Mistress.'

Lucy smiled. Sometimes the power she had over these poor men's souls amazed even her. 'Now off you go. I'm sorry, but I'm not well tonight. Okay?'

'Yes, Mistress. I hope you're feeling better soon.'

'I'm sure I will be.'

Arthur coyly enquired, 'Same time next week then?'

'Yes, Arthur. Same time next week. I'll make it up to you.'

Arthur's voice took on a note of hope, 'Will you?'

'Oh, yes. I'll make you cry real tears, big boy.'

'Oh, thank you, Mistress, thank you.'

'Yes, yes. Goodnight Arthur.'

'Goodnight Mistress.'

She hung up the receiver and walked back to the computer. Shouldn't do that, she thought. Should've just got on with it. She sat down behind the monitor and read over what she'd been writing. She tried to place herself back there in front of Rick's uncoiled python, but it was no good. The muse had fled. She saved the document and switched off the PC. A moment later, she emerged from the kitchen with a glass of vodka and a packet of crisps. She flopped down on the sofa and began flicking through the channels. She soon found, and settled with, a Kurt Russell movie.

Half watching, she considered the horror in Rick's pants. Would Mills and Boon go for this? Was she taking things in the wrong direction? The ice clinked pleasingly as she sipped the vodka. Fuck 'em, she thought. I can't change Rick any more than I can change the past.

'He's written in stone, baby,' she told Kurt Russell.

Kurt ignored her and shot a terrorist.

She took another sip of her drink and smiled. Poor old Arthur. She wondered which of her options, if any, he'd taken.

'The wank.' She envisaged him in the passenger seat of his little car, thrashing anxiously away at his lap. His facial expression one of mingled fear and desire. The fear of being discovered in the act, and the desire, well, probably much the same.

'Masturbate.' Gaz concluded.

'Yeeah. Nice one,' said Glen.

Jimmy frowned, confused. 'Yourself?'

'Yeah.' Gaz drew on the joint. 'It's the third night.'

'I don't get it. Why do you masturbate yourself when you've gone to all the bother of getting this bird into the bedroom with you?'

'It's all part of the ritual. You're simmering, see?'

Jimmy shook his head. 'No.'

They sat around in the lounge of their house. Two lava lamps threw warm orange and red shadows around the room. A thin blanket of smoke hovered in the air like a heavenly plateau. *The Best of Marvin Gaye* CD advanced to, "Let's Get it On."

Glen sniggered, stoned. 'It's like Gaz said, man. It's the third night of the ritual.'

'Oh? You explain it then, Glen.'

'You take the bird out and… you really get on with her.'

Jimmy nodded. 'Yeah.'

'Then, you take her home. But – ' he pointed at Jimmy. 'No kissing.' He looked at Gaz.

Gaz nodded.

Encouraged, Glen continued. 'Next night, by the end of the date, you're both really hot, and you kiss.' He paused for Jimmy to signal his understanding.

'Yeah…?'

'So this goes onto the third night.' Glen checked with Gaz.

Gaz nodded.

'On the third night, the pair of you are dying to fuck. Kissing just isn't doing it anymore, right?'

Jimmy smiled. 'Right.'

'So you go in, and up to the bedroom. Then, once you've had a good old snog, you go to separate corners of the bedroom – making sure you got a clear view of each other – then you undress. Slowly.' As he spoke, Glen couldn't help stroking his sides seductively.

Gaz grinned. 'Yeeah, baby.' He passed the joint to Glen.

'Nice one.'

'And then you have a wank?' Jimmy's face was a knot of incredulity.

'Yeah.'

'What's the fuckin' point of that?'

'No touchin' yet, man,' said Gaz. 'You're in too much of a hurry. You gotta savour the tension.'

Jimmy laughed and shook his head. 'That's mental, man. You can have a wank any time. Why'd you want one now when you've got this bird all fired up?'

'She's having one as well, Jim,' Glen explained.

'Eh?'

'She's not allowed to touch you either,' said Gaz. 'Only herself. You're not the only one who's sexually inflamed. She's over in her corner of the room, masturbating over the sight of you, masturbating over the sight of her.'

Enlightenment dawned on Jimmy's face. 'Ahhhh, I get it. Yeah… nice one.'

Glen and Gaz nodded at him, both smiling inanely. 'Yeaah,' they said together.

'So what happens on the fourth night?'

'The fourth night,' said Gaz. 'The fourth night, you get back to the bedroom. Go to your corners to undress and start stroking yourself a bit, but then –' he pointed at Jimmy, who took the joint from Glen, 'then you both go to the bed, and…'

His audience stared, transfixed.

'You masturbate each other.'

'That's it?' said Jimmy.

'That's it for tonight, baby.'

'Why not go all the way?'

'You still don't get it, Jim. It's all about suspense. About drawing it out 'til it's driving you both crazy.'

'It's driving me crazy now, and I'm not even there.'

'So it's working. Feel free to wank now if it'll relieve the tension.'

Glen and Jimmy laughed. Jimmy said, 'No, no I'm alright, man.'

'You're sure?' Gaz raised an eyebrow. 'Nothing wrong with sexual expression. Not in this house, right?'

'Yeah,' Glen nodded his earnest agreement.

'No, I'm alright, really.' Jimmy drew on the joint. 'So when do you get to fuck?'

'Not the next night,' said Gaz. 'That's oral night.'

'Night six?' said Glen.

'Night six.' Gaz beamed. 'You've driven each other mad with chained lust long enough. Now you consummate the relationship.' He sprang to his feet and grasped invisible haunches just in front of his groin and began bucking his hips wildly. 'You fuck her like a mad bitch in heat. Fuck her all night long. Fuck her 'til she's all fucked out.'

Jimmy and Glen made sounds of enthusiastic endorsement. Jimmy laughed. 'Then what?'

Gaz flopped down in his chair. 'Who cares? Chuck her.'

'That's a bit of a waste, innit?'

'Is it? The moment's gone, man. Why drag it on into all the bullshit that follows.'

'What bullshit?'

'All that, "Do you love me," shit. All that passionless, automatic pilot sex that comes after the first few weeks of wild fucking's over. All that engagement and marriage and kids and car and mortgage and fucking living death shit, man. You know what I mean?'

'Yeahhh,' said Glen.

Jimmy said nothing.

Gaz looked at Jimmy. 'You know what I mean?'

'Well, it doesn't have to be like that. I mean, if you actually do love each other.'

Gaz sat up. 'You're kidding?'

Jimmy passed the joint to Gaz. 'No.'

Gaz took a draw on the joint. It had gone out. He picked up the lighter from the litter of Rizla papers and torn cigarettes on the coffee table and re-lit the stubby remains. He drew hot smoke into his lungs, paused, then exhaled. 'You're deluding yourself, man.'

'Am I?'

''Course you fuckin' are. Love don't make no difference. Passion fades. Love dies.'

'Not always. Look at Paul McCartney and Linda.'

Gaz burst out laughing. 'What about Paul Mc-fuckin'-Cartney and Linda?'

Glen, unsure, laughed anyway.

'They loved each other right up until she died,' said Jimmy.

'Don't be so naïve.'

'I don't think I'm being naïve just because I don't agree with you on this one, man.'

Gaz noticed that Jimmy wasn't smiling anymore. He changed tack. 'Alright, man. Fair enough. Each to his own. I'm just speaking from experience.'

Jimmy nodded and seemed to relax again.

'You ever been in love then, Jim?' Gaz enquired casually.

'Not yet.'

Gaz took a couple of sipping tokes at the joint as the small twist of card that was the roach began to smoulder. He stubbed it out. 'Be careful, mate. All women are bad.'

'Yeah, right.'

'Fuckin are, mate. I fell in love once.' He shook his head. 'Mad fuckin' sex, man. I was just a kid, about eighteen. We fucked like crazed rabbits, we did. And I loved her.'

Glen and Jimmy looked at him. Gaz sat up and began sticking Rizlas together, preparing to roll a fresh joint.

'What happened?' asked Glen.

Gaz shrugged. 'She dumped me. Just finished it one day like it was nothin'.'

'Shit, man,' said Jimmy. 'I'm sorry.'

'Don't be. She was older than me. She was about twenty-one. I thought I was quids-in there, I can tell you. But she knew better.'

Glen frowned. 'Eh?'

Gaz sparked the lighter. He held the lump of cannabis resin to the tip of the flame. 'She was older. For me, it was still wild after the first two weeks. For her, it was already getting to be a drag. I didn't understand. I thought we had something special. I told her so. I told her that I loved her.'

They were silent for a few moments, then Jimmy spoke. 'What did she say?'

'She said I was very sweet, and that she was sorry, but it wasn't love, it was just sexual infatuation. She said I'd understand one day.'

Glen shook his head. 'Fuckin' bitch, man.'

Gaz rolled the joint to its conclusion and placed it between his lips with satisfaction. 'No, mate. She was right. At the time, I wanted to top meself. But I got over it.'

'What did you do?' asked Jimmy.

Gaz sparked the lighter and touched the twisted end of the joint to the flame. He drew the heat into it, inhaling the smoke and gritting his teeth in a grin. 'I fucked someone else.'

Glen brightened. 'Yeaah, man.'

'She knew then what I know now. It's only hot when it's fresh.'

Jimmy laughed, stoned.

'Fuck 'em and leave 'em,' said Glen.

'All women are bad.' Gaz got to his feet and staggered over to the CD player. He pressed the eject and the Marvin Gaye CD popped out. Gaz fumbled it out of the tray and dropped it onto the pile at the side of the machine.

Glen smiled dopily. 'What're you puttin' on, Gaz?'

'The Cramps.'

'Who?' asked Jimmy.

'The Cramps.' Glen shrugged slightly.

Gaz found and inserted a CD. He stabbed at the track select button rapidly, then pushed the volume control upwards. Then he spun in his socks to meet the stoned and confused expressions of his friends with a manic look in his eyes. Suddenly the room began to thud to the steady beat of a bass drum. Gaz began to groove on the carpet. 'Allllriiiight, lads'.

Jimmy and Glen stared, numb-faced and grinning like idiots as Gaz strutted around in front of the CD player. 'All women are bad,' Gaz sang along with the chorus, shaking his torso and gesturing pointedly at Jimmy.

Jimmy looked at Glen and grinned. 'Alright, man. All women are bad.'

'Yeeeeeah, baby. C'mon, let's boogie!'

They got to their feet and joined Gaz, the three of them shuffling around, bumping into the furniture and playing air guitar for all they were worth.

Peter's eyes opened and he stared into the darkness. A moment ago he had been leaping playfully in a summer pasture with an unknown dog bounding cheerfully at his side. Now he was awake. Ripped from his dream by distant drums. Realisation hit him in seconds. Adrenalin flooded his entire system in the time it took to draw a breath. He went from the numb bliss of sleep to a volcanic fury in the blinking of an eye. He thrashed beneath his duvet, kicking it aside and leaping to his feet.

'Fuckers!'

He ran to the window. Pulling the curtains aside, he grappled with the end of the telescope and brought it to his eye. After a moment of fumbling, all was revealed. He saw the French windows; curtains wide open as always, giving him a clear view of the proceedings.

They were dancing. Doing the twist and all manner of idiot gyrations. One of them was headbanging. Jesus, what a bunch of wankers. Peter focused on the leader. He was strutting around in some Jaggeresque fantasy like he was the singer. Now he was flexing his muscles, he obviously worked out. Peter could imagine him at the gymnasium, pumping iron and admiring his sweaty pecs in a long mirror.

'Probably turning himself on,' he muttered. 'Probably goes for a wank after getting himself all hard from gawking at his own reflection.'

He lifted his head from the eyepiece and listened. The beat of the music was almost palpable in the room. Peter closed his eyes and felt it pulsing in the air about him.

'Am I the only one? Doesn't anybody else hear this? Is everybody deaf?'

He knew he was a light sleeper, but you'd have to be dead to sleep through this. What about the people next door to them? Didn't they give a shit? He waited, hoping to hear shouts from all around demanding they shut up. He waited to see a band of wild-eyed neighbours, pyjama-clad and raving as they stormed into the bastards' home with blazing torches and axe handles. Nothing happened. The bastards partied on.

Peter went to his wardrobe and took out the old metal ammunition box from the bottom. He opened it and the smell of petrol hit him in a wave. He took out the plastic petrol can and shook it. It was, as he knew it would be, empty. But holding it, smelling it, empowered him. He had done something. 'But not enough. Clearly not enough.'

Was it time to follow up on his previous visit? Pay another call, but this time, follow through. The burning rag through the letterbox? Really do it? Should he? Should he?

He saw himself running from the blazing door. Running into someone – a passer-by walking his dog. He saw the look on the man's face as he looked from him to the blazing door and back. He felt the man make the connection and heard the man screaming, 'Arson! Arson!' Then neighbours burst from their doorways all around with blazing torches and axe handles, they point at him and scream the wild, indecipherable cries of the enraged mob.

'I can't do it. Not like that.' He dropped the can back into the box and shut it before sliding it back into the wardrobe. Suddenly, silence fell. Just as abruptly as it had started, the music cut out. Peter went to his telescope. He expected them to be squabbling over their next musical choice; their next neighbourly onslaught. Instead, he watched as they turned off their stupid lamps and made their way out of the lounge.

Was this it, then? Was the torment over for the night? Peter saw lights go on upstairs and soon after, go out again. It was their pattern of shut down. He straightened and sighed with relief. It was over. He reached for the curtains and pulled them closed before climbing back into bed. For a few moments he lay staring at the ceiling, adrenalin still coursing pointlessly through him. Then he closed his eyes. He knew it would take a long time for sleep to come, so he consoled his emasculated pride with fantasies of violence. Of raging conflagrations without the interference of dog-walking do-gooders. Of guns, knives and crude clubs with nails hammered through the ends. When sleep finally claimed him, he was smiling softly, the screams of his three victims like a lullaby in his head.

Chapter 6

DUSTY AWOKE beneath a canopy of shrubs in the cemetery gardens. The collapsed cardboard boxes that he'd slept upon were damp with the morning dew, and he was cold. He decided to rise early. He crawled out from under the shrubs and emptied his bladder against the cemetery wall. The stream of yellow liquid steamed in the chill morning air. Dusty inched his penis this way and that, enjoying the pattern the urine made as it splashed against the brickwork. When he was finished, he zipped himself up and wondered how best to proceed in his attempts to win over the jittery apprehension of The One.

He emerged from the trees and shrubs and walked out into the cemetery. He noticed the Council gardeners were here to cut the grass. He reasoned that it must be a Friday. They came every other Friday, first thing in the morning. Therefore it must be about 7.30 am. He sat on a gravestone and watched the men as they unloaded mowers and strimmers from their van. Their cheery banter carried over the stillness of the cemetery. One of them lit a cigarette. A few moments later, the small engines spluttered into life and the men began to mow and cut. As the distant sound reached him, Dusty had an idea. He smiled. He turned and headed for the hole in the railings on the far side of the cemetery which served him as a personal entrance and exit.

Ten minutes later, he was walking slowly around one of the housing estates on the edge of town. As he walked around the rim of a recreation ground, he soon saw exactly what he was looking for. A number of cars were parked erratically on the edge of the grass. People without parking spaces last night had just dumped their cars where they figured no one would care. He eyed them with the shrewd eye of a buyer. Not guided so much by his own tastes, but rather, he tried to shop with the eye of The One. He settled on a red hatchback. He walked up to it, looked around, then tried the handle. It was locked. He walked around to the passenger side. It too was locked. He frowned, thinking. After a few moments' contemplation, he glanced casually about. Way over on the other side of the recreation ground, a woman was walking her dog. That was it. He looked around on the ground. Sure enough, there was a half-brick. Dusty had noticed that half-bricks were a common feature of recreation grounds on housing estates. Why this should be, he had no idea, but it was a curiosity he was grateful for as he bent down and picked it up.

'Why?' he asked the half-brick. Without waiting for an answer, he smashed in the passenger window and unlocked the door. In a second he was inside. He moved over to the driver's side and bent down out of sight. He reached beneath the steering column and tugged down on the ignition wiring. He separated the red wire from the others, then he took his penknife from inside his raincoat and cut them all. Then he ducked down to better see what he was doing as he disentangled the other wires from one another, before striking them, one after the other against the red one. After a couple of misses, the engine fired and Dusty sat up like he belonged there, which in his mind, he now did. This was his car now, and he had to go and offer a friend a lift to work. He gripped the wheel and tried to turn it. It was locked. He sighed. He gripped it firmly on one side and yanked down with all his strength, which was considerable. The wheel lock broke. Dusty smiled.

He drew the seatbelt over his shoulder and snapped it into place, then turned on the radio. Idiots babbled and laughed through static. He looked about for some tapes and saw none. He sniffed, then opened the glove compartment. Several tapes fell into view, and he flipped them one after the other through his fingers, trying to glean the artists responsible for them through the chaos of cover art. He didn't recognise any of the names, and was just about to give up when he saw something that caused him to chuckle. He opened the box and slipped the tape into the player. Then, as music filled the hatchback, he reversed out and drove away, singing heartily as he did so.

Peter awoke to the irritating sound of someone making cat noises. For a moment he wondered what was going on, then he heard Sarah Kennedy reading a letter someone had sent to her concerning a cat. Cue another meow. He reached out from beneath the duvet and shut off the clock radio. Radio Two, his preferred station, had its weaknesses. Sarah Kennedy, in his opinion, was the biggest.

'Oh, you mental bitch.'

As he lay looking at the ceiling, the memory of the previous night seeped back into him. The momentary relief afforded by silencing Sarah Kennedy was lost as fresh misery and hatred swelled in his heart. 'Shit.' He sighed, shaking his head. It had felt like hours had passed before sleep had returned following his rude awakening last night. He kept tossing and turning, revolving between the sheets like a pig on a spit. His mind kept playing out scenarios. These ranged from violent revenge fantasies to realistic attempts at a diplomatic solution. He imagined himself going around to their place and explaining his predicament in a calm and rational manner. Then his mind played through all possible outcomes. Unfortunately, the one where the bastards were thoroughly reasonable, said sorry and never did it again was almost as absurdly unrealistic as the one where he beat them all in a kung fu showdown. It was also infinitely less satisfying.

He had thought again about Mick's idea of hiring some desperate down-and-out to murder them. The face of the tramp, Dusty Gibbons, had popped up in his mind like toast. He had promptly pushed it back down again.

The last time he looked at the clock, before he managed to doze off, it had been 3:27. He reasoned he probably fell asleep around four. Five hours' sleep. Enough for Thatcher, he thought, but not enough for me. He felt like shit. His eyes felt like someone had emptied the contents of a cat litter tray into them.

'Bastards.' He struggled upright and swung his legs out from beneath the covers. 'Evil, degenerate bastards.'

As he stood upright, he noticed that he had an erection. It protruded from his boxer shorts with a firm yet dozy will of its own. He tried to replace it within his shorts, but it resisted confinement, awkwardly pointing this way and that, making walking uncomfortable. He released it again. For a moment he contemplated masturbating in order to get rid of it, but decided against it. The best thing to do was ignore it. He padded off in the direction of the bathroom, his erection nodding dozily in front of him as he went.

After a shower and a shave he felt more awake, but his anger was unabated. He made himself a cup of tea and poured out a bowl of cornflakes, then sat down on his small sofa. He picked up the remote and clicked on the television. *The Big Breakfast* came on.

'Shit,' he grumbled. He flicked through the options; they were worse. He returned to *The Big Breakfast*. He ate his breakfast scowling at the television. 'Oh we're so fucking crazy,' he sneered through a mouthful of cereal. 'Cheerful bastards.'

He watched the programme for about a minute, then switched off the T,. preferring to eat in silence. When he was finished, he placed his breakfast things in the sink before going back to the bedroom to get dressed.

Standing in front of the mirror on the inside of his wardrobe door, he continued to play mental movies of diabolical retribution. The ones he liked best involved fire. Burning bodies running around a blazing hi-fi and similar scenarios. 'If only,' he said to his reflection as it fixed his tie into a tidy knot. He took brief stock of his finished appearance, shrugged, and left the flat.

Downstairs at the front door, he checked through the pile of letters on the mat. Nothing for him. He dropped the pile back onto the mat, opened the door and stepped outside.

He looked up, squinting at the clear, sunny sky above. For a moment, he considered phoning in sick and jumping on a train to some seaside town somewhere. A day at the beach, he thought. He smiled and shook his head, then turned to walk toward the top of the street, and the bus stop.

He walked with his head down, watching the pavement pass beneath his shoes, looking at the cracks; the old gum stains; the occasional piece of dog shit. He barely heard the music at first. As it grew louder, his mind picked up on the tune and began following it unconsciously. Then it triggered. He turned suddenly to where the music now played steadily beside him in the road. The tramp sat behind the wheel of a red hatchback smiling at him. The passenger window was down and ZZ Top's, "Gimmie All Your Lovin", pulsed out and into the street.

'Morning.' Dusty smiled. 'Need a lift?'

Peter almost laughed out loud; so unexpected and absurd were both the image and the offer. He shook his head, unable to prevent himself from smiling. 'No thanks.'

Dusty turned down the music. 'Come on. I'm going your way.'

Peter stopped. 'Oh? And what way might that be?'

The car stopped. 'I know where you work. I can give you a lift.'

Peter suddenly felt something shift within him. In that moment, the simmering pot of anger, paranoia and frustration in his soul suddenly boiled over. He pointed at Dusty and shouted, 'That's just the point! How do you know where I work? Why do you know where I work?'

Dusty shrugged. 'I followed you.'

Peter's mouth fell open. 'You... You admit it then? Just like that?'

'Sure.'

'That's illegal, you know? That's called stalking.'

'So?'

Peter shook his head in exasperation. 'What do you mean, "so?" Doesn't it bother you that I might not actually like being stalked?'

'Yes.'

This caught Peter off-guard. 'What?'

'Yes, it bothers me that you mightn't like it.'

'So why do you do it?'

Dusty looked ahead through the windscreen for a moment. 'I think you need me.' He turned back to face Peter again. 'I think I can help you.'

Peter stared at the tramp. How could he possibly know what had been going on between himself and the blokes over the back? How could he even guess? Peter suddenly felt uncomfortable. 'I,' he said, falteringly. 'I don't know what you're talking about.' Then, turning, he continued uncertainly up the road.

For a moment, the car idled in the road, then it slowly moved forwards, coming alongside Peter again. 'You hesitated there a moment.'

'So?' Peter walked on, his eyes fixed forward. 'There's no law against hesitating. Unlike stalking. If I were you I'd get lost before I call the police.'

'You'd have me arrested?'

'Yes.' Peter stopped and turned to Dusty. 'Why wouldn't I?'

'Because I'm here to help you. Having me arrested would be... rude.'

'Rude!' Peter shook his head. 'You admit to stalking me, and you call me rude?'

Dusty looked down at the passenger seat. 'Look, I'm sorry. I, I just wanted to make contact.'

'Well you've done that alright.'

Dusty nodded. He looked up at Peter. 'I can help you.'

'What -? What are you talking about?' Peter was flabbergasted. 'Are you – ' he shook his head and looked at the ground. 'You don't live around here, do you?'

'Not exactly.'

'So you're not a neighbour of mine?'

'Not strictly speaking, no.'

'You know nothing of, of noise problems around here?'

Dusty scratched the side of his nose. 'I know that noise is a problem everywhere these days.'

'Yeah, but I'm talking about right here. This street. This street and the next one?'

Dusty paused a moment. Then he said, 'People can be very inconsiderate.'

'I fucking know that, mate. I'm asking you if you know about them.' Peter gestured in the approximate direction of Gaz's house.

'Them?'

'Yes, them. Those fucking bastards over the back there?'

Dusty nodded slowly. 'Oh, I see. They're your problem, are they?'

Peter looked down. Again he shook his head. This was insane. He was discussing his "problem" with a tramp.

'I can help you with that problem.'

Peter looked up at him. 'How? Just how... can you help me?'

'However you want me to.'

Peter looked into the inscrutable depths of the tramp's sunglasses. Who was this guy? What was going on here? Can he be some kind of contract man? A vagrant who goes around looking for people who look desperate enough to... To what? asked a reasonable voice in his head. To kill someone? Don't be absurd.

Dusty sat motionless. He regarded Peter patiently, silently.

He has no connections to me or to them, Peter thought. He has no reasons. No motives. It made a horrible sense, insane as it was. He was being propositioned by a contract tramp. A hit bum. Peter shifted his gaze to the red hatchback. 'Where'd you get the car?'

'It's mine.'

'That's not what I asked.'

'You like it?'

Peter shrugged. 'It's just – It's just you don't look like the car owning type.'

Dusty smiled. 'Looks can be deceiving.'

Peter nodded. He looked up the street, then back at Dusty. 'You say you can help me with my problem?'

'Yes I can.'

'How?' Peter asked, 'I mean... how?'

'We can discuss that on the way to your work.'

Peter looked thoughtfully up the street.

'I reckon you've missed that bus by now.'

Peter looked back at Dusty. The tramp's eyebrows rose quizzically over his sunglasses.

Peter shifted his weight from one foot to the other. He nodded at the car. 'Do you sleep in that thing?'

'No.'

Peter looked at his watch. He'd missed the bus alright. What am I thinking of doing here? He asked himself. Am I going to do this? Am I going to suggest some kind of action to this guy? He looked again at the tramp sitting coolly behind the wheel. Moreover, he wondered, am I actually going to get into that stink-mobile?

He looked again at his watch. 'Oh fuck it,' he muttered. He stepped off the pavement towards the car. 'I don't believe I'm doing this.'

Dusty leaned over and opened the passenger door. 'I'll have you there in no time.'

Making a conscious effort not to breathe through his nose, Peter got into the hatchback's passenger seat. 'Sure,' he said, without enthusiasm. 'Thanks a lot.'

Chapter 7

PETER SAT DOWN. As he did so, he felt something digging into his behind. He shifted and brushed the seat beneath him. His fingers touched something hard and sharp. He drew it out and inspected it as the tramp drove up to the junction with the main road.

'What's this?' Peter held up a crystal of broken safety glass.

Dusty glanced over. 'Glass.'

'I know it's glass. What I mean is, how did it get here?'

'I tried to clean it up,' Dusty replied. 'But you know how it is. There's always a few pieces that seem to slip through the net.'

Peter looked at the glass between his fingers, then at Dusty. 'Did you steal this car?'

Dusty's eyes were on the traffic ahead. 'All property is theft.'

Peter gave a short, derisory laugh. 'That's what all thieves say.'

Dusty said nothing.

'You did, didn't you?'

'This car's mine.'

Peter nodded. 'Fine.'

Dusty smiled. 'It gets me around.'

'Yeah.'

They rode in silence for a short while. Peter was hoping the tramp would make some kind of opening gambit concerning the "problem", but after about a minute, it became apparent that he was content just to drive. 'So,' Peter began. 'So what kind of help can you offer me?'

Dusty's gaze remained on the road ahead. 'What kind of help do you need?'

Peter shrugged. 'I dunno. What do you charge?'

Dusty turned and looked at Peter. 'Charge?'

'Yeah. I mean, what payment do you require?'

Dusty turned back to the road ahead. 'No payment.'

Peter shifted to a more upright position. 'No payment?'

'No payment.'

'Well...' Peter scratched his head. 'What do you live on? I mean, doing things for people and so on. You must get some kind of payment?'

'People?'

'You help people out, right?'

'You should put your seatbelt on,' said Dusty.

Peter didn't like the idea of being strapped in with this guy. 'I don't wear them.'

'You should always wear your seat belt. Clunk-click, every trip.'

'What?'

'Never mind.'

They drove on in silence a few moments, then Peter said, 'Look, do you mind pulling off somewhere? A side road or somewhere where we can discuss… things?'

Dusty shrugged. 'If that's what you want.'

'I'd be more comfortable if we weren't moving.'

'You could be late.'

'I'll take that chance.'

'As you will.' Dusty indicated to turn off the main road and a few turnings later they were parked beneath a tree on a quiet residential street. Dusty reached under the steering column and silenced the engine.

'No key?' Peter enquired.

'No key.' Dusty turned in his seat to face Peter.

Peter held up his hands. 'No problem. It is your car after all.'

'After all.'

Peter shifted and looked out of the window. He cleared his throat. 'Er. I guess I ought to explain my situation.'

Dusty smiled.

'OK. Well, there's this house over the back of mine, you see? And there's, there's these blokes who live there, see –'

'Yes, I see.'

Peter hesitated. 'Yes. OK, well, there's these blokes and they, well, they're extremely noisy. Like I said earlier?'

Dusty nodded.

'So anyway, they've been driving me crazy. I mean, fucking crazy, yeah?'

Dusty nodded again.

Peter became more animated as he spoke. 'It's like every night, or almost every night, boom – boom – boom.' He looked at Dusty. 'That's bass, see? Boom – boom – boom, every night. It wakes me up and keeps me from sleeping. I don't know what to do.'

'Have you spoken to the police?'

'The police.' Peter waved his hands dismissively. 'What good are they? They just say it's a domestic matter and that they can't do anything. They're fucking useless.'

'What about these blokes? Have you ever confronted them over this?'

Again Peter waved the idea away. 'You're kidding. These guys aren't going to listen to me.' He shook his head. 'They're animals. Hedonistic animals. I've seen them at night. They're like a bunch of raving Caligulas. You wouldn't believe what they get up to.'

'Hmmm.' Dusty stroked his beard thoughtfully.

'No,' Peter continued. 'If I went down there they'd probably just slam the door in my face and turn it up even louder.'

'You think so?'

'Yeah, I think so. They're debauched.'

Dusty nodded. 'Have you done anything at all?'

Peter considered a moment; could he trust this guy? Shit, I'm sitting in a stolen car for God's sake. What's he going to do, drive me to the authorities? 'Yeah. I did something.'

Dusty waited.

'I went 'round there one night with a can of petrol and poured it through their letterbox. Then I stuck a warning note to the door and legged it.'

'Ingenious.'

'Do you think so?'

Dusty nodded. 'But not successful?'

Peter slumped in his seat. 'No. They were quiet for maybe a night, then it kicked off again.'

'Hmmm.'

'I can't cope any more. I need to take some kind of action, but I don't know what to do.'

'You want the problem solved?'

Peter looked at him steadily. 'I do.'

'I can solve this problem for you.'

'You can?'

Dusty nodded.

'What will you do?'

'Whatever needs to be done.'

'You don't mean, like, murder or stuff?'

Dusty shrugged. 'Whatever needs to be done.'

'I don't think that will be necessary, though. Do you?'

'Not if you don't.'

'Eh?'

'Not if you don't.'

'Right,' Peter said, uncertainly. 'I call the shots?'

Dusty nodded.

'Like maybe, do the petrol thing, but this time, actually light it?'

'If that's what you want.'

'Well, I don't know,' Peter raised his hands helplessly. 'I don't know what I want. I mean, I don't know what's going to work, do I?'

'You don't?' Dusty's tone registered mild surprise.

'No.' Peter shook his head. 'You're the expert here, not me.'

'I am?'

'Yeah. You help people like me, right? You solve problems?'

Dusty said nothing.

Peter suddenly felt as though the tramp was scrutinising him. 'Hello?'

'You are The One?'

Peter frowned. 'What?'

'The One. You are The One?'

'What are you talking about?'

'Are you The One?'

Peter looked at the tramp with deepening puzzlement. What the fuck was this? He scratched his head and waved his hand absently. 'I don't know, what do you think?'

'What I think doesn't matter,' said Dusty. 'Are you the One?'

Peter laughed nervously. 'I have no idea what the fuck you're talking about.'

Dusty pushed himself back in his seat and sighed. He lowered his head slightly.

'Are you okay?'

Dusty looked up at him. 'No,' he said quietly. 'No, I'm not okay.'

Peter shifted in his seat. 'Was it something that I said?'

Dusty nodded. 'I'm afraid so.'

Peter shook his head. 'Well I –' he began, but his voice was suddenly cut off as Dusty reached out and grabbed the back of his head. Peter didn't even have time to gasp as he was pulled violently off balance. He felt a crushing pressure on his face as Dusty's other hand suddenly clamped hard over his nose and mouth, cutting off his breath. Peter's eyes bulged with shock and terror as he felt himself being pushed down in his seat, his legs buckling beneath him as the tramp's weight bore down upon him. He pulled at Dusty's arms but they were incredibly powerful. His head felt like it was fixed in a vice. He tried to scream but he couldn't breathe, the air trapped in his lungs was beginning to burn as he felt his nose suddenly break beneath the pressure. Blood flowed beneath the tramp's fingers, finding its way into Peter's mouth and turning his panic to hysteria. He thrashed desperately within the impossible confines of the passenger seat. His chest heaved, cramping his abdominal muscles and causing spasms of pain to radiate through him like fire. Peter fought back, but already he was weakening, his fingers scrabbled frantically for purchase at Dusty's clothes and hair. He reached out for the tramp's eyes. He managed to claw away the sunglasses before the tramp raised his face beyond reach.

Small clusters of light started to flash at the edge of Peter's vision. The agony in his chest began to abate, and Peter found himself lost in the tramp's newly revealed eyes. There was an expression of sadness there, of pity, possibly even pain. Peter ceased to struggle. He gripped Dusty's shoulders with what little strength he had remaining, his fingers white and trembling as he watched a tear spill from the tramp's eyes and run slowly down the length of his nose. Peter watched from a numb, ethereal place as the tear was joined by another. It fell, slow and dreamlike. A last point of brightness spinning after him as he fell away from this world and into darkness.

It was shortly after midnight when Dusty inserted Peter's front door key into the lock of number thirteen Charrington Street. He opened the door and stepped into the darkened hallway. Then, closing the door softly behind him, he turned on the hall light and walked quietly up the stairs. When he got to the top flat he inserted Peter's key into the lock. It didn't fit. Suddenly the hall light switched itself off. Dusty froze in the darkness. He listened to the silence around him for a few moments before he remembered that places like this have timer switches on their hall lights. 'Fool,' he whispered to himself. He quickly groped along the wall until he located the light switch. He found it and turned it back on. Then he returned to Peter's door, fumbled with the small ring of keys until he found another Yale, then inserted it into the lock. The door opened. He stepped inside and switched on the light.

So this was the home of the man he had mistaken for The One. Dusty shut the door behind him and looked around. He stood in a large, simply furnished room. A small kitchenette occupied one corner. It had a cooker, a fridge and various cupboards and work surfaces. The rest of the room served as a lounge. A television stood against one wall facing a coffee table and a small, two-seater sofa. There was a poster on the wall for a film called *Pulp Fiction*. Dusty looked at the woman on the poster, she lay on a bed with a big gun. She struck Dusty as being a little too sure of herself. But then again, he reasoned, she does have a big gun. 'That helps.'

In the corner opposite the kitchenette stood a table littered with shallow trays, bottles and photographs. Above the table, extending from one wall to the other, was an indoor clothes-line. From this hung a number of black and white photographs.

'A photographer?'

He then turned to look at two doors set in the wall opposite the front door. He crossed the room and went into the one on the left. He turned on the light. A bathroom. Next he entered the other room, again switching on the light. It was a bedroom, but it was more than that. His eyebrows rose momentarily above the rims of his sunglasses.

'A shrine.'

All over one wall of the room were pinned a hundred or so black and white photographs. They varied in size, the largest blown up to A4 size. They were all of the same group of men, and one man in particular. Dusty raised his sunglasses to examine the subjects of the pictures more closely. They were an ordinary looking bunch; unoriginal, slaves to the modern style of dress and appearance. 'And thought, I'll wager.'

Dusty noticed the most photographed subject was a handsome young man of about twenty four.

'Pretty boy.' He touched a glossy image of the man's face.

The other subjects were of similar appearance, but not as good-looking. 'Clones.' He noticed that in some of the photographs, the subjects were naked. None of the pictures were posed. In each of them, the subjects seemed unaware that they were being photographed.

'Big Brother.'

He moved to the mounted telescope that stood like a weapon aimed beyond the window. Next to it, on a tripod, stood an expensive-looking camera. For the first time, Dusty noticed the muted sound of music. It's beat was gentle against his senses. He quite liked it. He went to see what the telescope had been focused upon, looking out of the rear window into the night. The darkened rear elevations of the houses on the next street dominated the view. Lights shone sporadically across their surfaces. Dusty noticed that the house that backed directly onto the garden of Reynolds' building was where both the telescope and the camera were pointed. He bent his knees and placed his eye against the telescope's eyepiece. At first, he wasn't sure what he was looking at: a room, dimly lit with warm colours. Then he saw a man walking around in the nude. He recognised him as one of the men from the photographs. Then he recognised another; he too was naked.

'Interesting. What game is this, I wonder?' Then he saw the most-photographed man. He was naked and smoking a big cigarette. He sat down and passed the cigarette to one of the others. Then a girl entered. Dusty wasn't surprised to see she also was undressed. She sat on the lap of the most-photographed man. They kissed for a moment, then one of the other men came over to them. He began stroking the hair of the girl and she turned around and smiled at him. Dusty noticed the man had an erection at the same time as the girl did. She took the man's penis into her mouth and the most-photographed man began to applaud.

Dusty straightened up. So these were Peter Reynolds's Caligulas. He smiled and drew the curtains. Then, slowly, he began to get undressed. Once naked, he went into the bathroom to run himself a bath. As the hot water began to fill the tub, he looked at his hands. They were still dirty with the dried earth of Peter's grave. The right one still had black, dried blood around the fingernails. He shook his head as he thought of Peter. A simple mistake. He couldn't blame himself. Peter had the look of The One. He hadn't been him, but Dusty now felt strongly that Peter had known him; had been linked to him somehow and was therefore sent as a sign. Dusty had followed that sign. Just as previous signs had led to Peter, so Peter had led him here. He returned to the bedroom, to the shrine, where one face more than any other grinned mischievously from the walls.

'Thank you, Peter Reynolds.' Dusty ran a finger over one of the glossy black and white pictures of the most-photographed man: Gaz. 'Thank you for leading me to The One.'

Dusty felt great pity for Peter. He hadn't chosen to be a sign. Who would? He consoled himself with the knowledge that Peter had now found peace. His body, unburdened of keys, credit cards and money, now lay in a shallow grave dug at the bottom of a ditch by the railway line. Trees obscured his funeral from the passing trains, there were no mourners other than himself. It was a desolate and rather unsightly spot, but that at least guaranteed rest. Peter wouldn't be disturbed there.

A short while later, Dusty reclined in a hot, fragrant bath. Beneath the dense layer of bubbles that topped the water, he could feel the grime of recent times ebbing gently away. He looked at his hands. Both the dirt and the blood were already gone. He sighed and slid down until the water covered his head. He stayed submerged for a moment, then rose, water pouring thickly from his hair and beard. Then he lay back and closed his eyes.

An hour later, clean and fresh smelling for the first time in months, Dusty wandered about the flat in Peter's towelling dressing gown. It was far too small for him, but he liked the feel of it against his skin. He was looking for a pair of scissors. He found some among Peter's photographic clutter in the lounge. He took the scissors into the bathroom and wiped condensation from the bathroom mirror. His reflection smiled back at him from the glass.

'So long, handsome.' He gathered together a handful of beard and eased the scissors into the damp woolly mass. A moment later, small clumps of hair began tumbling into the sink. By the time he had finished, the sink was full.

PART TWO

Chapter 8

SHE WAS ALL HE HAD IMAGINED SHE WOULD BE. Her hair, dark with a suggestion of red in certain light, fell just past her shoulders framing her face with those long, loose curls. Wayne sat on her sofa as she had bidden him. He wore only his boxer shorts. Lucy stood before him in her dressing gown. Although tied at the waist it was slightly open at the chest. Wayne couldn't see her breasts, but the way the towelling hung; the subtlties of light and shadow, suggested them vividly. Lucy looked at his lap and smiled.

Wayne looked down and saw his penis jutting up from the fly in his boxers. He grinned. 'My love antenna.'

'Picking up any signals?'

Wayne nodded. His hands went to the elastic waistband of the shorts but Lucy stopped him with a curt, 'Uh-uh'. He looked up, she was slowly shaking her head from side to side. 'That's my job. All in good time.'

Wayne removed his hands obediently and sat still.

'You said you had something for me?'

Wayne nodded.

'I like presents.'

Wayne grinned.

'Well?'

'Well?' Wayne echoed stupidly.

'When can I have my present?'

'Oh.' Wayne reached for the carrier bag at his side and drew out a large and sublimely yellow banana.

'Sexy 'nana,' Lucy purred.

He offered it to her and giggled. 'Sexy 'nana.'

As she accepted it, Lucy's fingers slid down its length and brushed Wayne's fingertips. He barely noticed, his attention was fixed in the shadowy recesses of her gown. She straightened up and the gown closed. Wayne gave a small whimper of regret. She looked at him, saw the direction of his gaze and smiled. 'Wayne? Were you trying to look inside my gown?'

Wayne looked chastened, he shook his head. 'No.'

'Oh, I think you were, weren't you? Be honest.'

Wayne looked down at his love antenna and nodded ashamedly.

Lucy's fingers went to the casual tie in the towelling belt and pulled it slowly loose. 'Well, since you've brought me a present.' The gown fell open. Wayne looked up and his breath stopped in his chest. His gaze flowed up her, from the high heel shoes, over the black-stockinged ankles and lower calves and into the shadowy realm of the now open dressing gown. His eyes crawled up her long legs to the point where the stockings ended; they were unfixed, held up, he imagined, by sheer enthusiasm. Above them there was only the smooth whiteness of her bare flesh. Wayne's eyes tried to penetrate the shadows at the top of her legs, but he couldn't, she stood in such a way as to make that impossible. He noticed she wore no panties; a fact she couldn't conceal, and, he expected, didn't want to.

'Mmm.' Lucy moistened her lips. 'I'm feeling rather peckish.'

Wayne tried to look up, but couldn't. His eyes ran over her stomach and up to her chest where her breasts were cruelly concealed by the twin lapels of her gown. Unconsciously, he bit his lower lip; she wore no bra. His heart ached.

'Sexy 'nana,' Lucy whispered.

Wayne looked up. Lucy was peeling the banana with infinite slowness, revealing its pale flesh to him in smooth, regular strips. She peeled the skin all the way to the very base. When it was bare, she took the flesh of the banana in her fingers and gently pulled the skin free, letting it drop forgotten to the floor.

'Careful,' said Wayne.

'Hmm?'

'That skin, there.' He nodded in the direction of the banana skin. 'Watch you don't step on it. Might have a nasty accident.'

She smiled. 'Oh, thank you, Wayne. I, I suppose I'd better kneel down... for safety's sake.'

Wayne said nothing. He just watched as she took a few steps closer and slowly sank to her knees before him. She held the bare banana in both hands before her face like a woodwind instrument. As he looked down over his belly, he saw the banana over the tip of his trembling love antenna. It rose like a fruity extension of himself.

Lucy smiled. 'Mmmmm, I'm feeling ever so hungry, now.'

Wayne managed to make a small noise in his throat as she parted her darkly rouged lips and moved her head forwards to take the tip of the banana in her mouth. She closed her eyes as her lips touched the flesh. Wayne suddenly realised he had stopped breathing; he gasped.

'Mmmm,' Lucy purred, as she slowly fed the banana into her mouth. Wayne watched wide-eyed, his boiling sexual desire now merging with a dawning astonishment. The banana was slowly, seamlessly being sucked into Lucy's mouth. She wasn't chewing, she wasn't hesitating to mush it with her tongue, she was just swallowing it whole. It was like watching a snake eating an elongated bird's egg. Lucy opened her eyes to see Wayne's reaction, she smiled, her lips pursing around the slowly disappearing banana. Wayne didn't notice, he couldn't take his eyes off the last few inches of the banana. It was nearly gone, Wayne whimpered as the little black nub at the end twitched slightly and then disappeared into the impossible depths of Lucy's mouth.

'Fucking hell.'

Lucy smiled. She licked her lips lasciviously. For a moment, Wayne was able to see inside her mouth. There was no trace of the fruit. It had vanished; she'd swallowed it whole.

'I-' Wayne began, but his words were cut off as Lucy placed her hands upon his knees and ran them slowly up the length of his thighs. She gripped the bottoms of his shorts and pulled. Dumbly, Wayne raised his hips and felt the garment begin to slide slowly down his thighs. His erection was pulled down momentarily but then sprung up again once it was freed from the fabric. Lucy pulled the shorts down to his ankles and then forgot them. She leaned forward, her dressing gown fell open and Wayne gasped as her breasts brushed against his knees. Wayne had hoped her hands might dawdle awhile in the vicinity of his lap, but they pressed down upon his hips as she gently pivoted herself up towards him, her breasts slowly swept around his erection and over the rise of his stomach, finally coming to rest against his own small, hairy breasts. She brought one knee up onto the couch and then another, straddling him but keeping clear of his lap. Wayne ran his hands inside of her dressing gown, he encircled her body and tried to pull her to him but she resisted, her hands now either side of his head and holding it tightly. Wayne moaned as Lucy lifted her face to look him in the eyes, she smiled, then she opened her mouth. Wayne tried to move his head forward to kiss her, but she held him fast.

Then he saw it. Rising in the back of her throat, Wayne saw the black tip of the banana. He blinked in disbelief as the fruit rose slowly and wetly back into her mouth.

'Fuck m-' he began, but before he could finish she pulled his face to hers and closed her mouth over his. Her tongue swept around his for a moment before withdrawing. Wayne's tongue pursued Lucy's back into her mouth but was suddenly halted by banana. His eyes widened as he felt it begin to slide into his mouth. It was slimy and soft, he tried to pull away but she held him too tightly. Then he felt her legs moving. His mind reeled as, simultaneously, the banana filled his mouth and Lucy dropped a hand to guide his desperate and aching cock inside her. She moaned as she moved onto him and began moving her hips in a slow rhythm. Wayne's hands flailed within the folds of her dressing gown. He tried to withdraw them so he might ease her back, but they were lost in the voluminous, gathering depths of the gown. The banana was now entering his throat, he tried to choke, but couldn't. He tried to cough or cry out, but all sound was pushed back inside him as the banana began to slide into his oesophagus.

Lucy gripped his head, again with both hands, as she began to increase the rhythm of her hips. Wayne could feel the touch of her breasts as they brushed against his own. Despite the certainty that he was about to die of banana asphyxiation, Wayne still struggled in vain to free his hands so that he might touch those fabulous breasts before he expired. A wave of dizziness rolled over his senses, the banana seemed to go on forever; it flowed from her into him, moving and pulsing like a live thing in his gullet. Behind his delirium, he felt his orgasm beginning to build. Lucy seemed to recognise this as she fucked him still harder. He felt her tongue against his again; the banana had left her. The fruit seemed to fill his entire neck. He tried to swallow it, he tried to gag, he prayed she'd flip him over and execute the Hiemlich manoeuvre. Instead, she pulled her face away and gasped his name as her body arched in orgasm. Wayne's head swam, his whole sensory system seemed to explode in slow motion as his own orgasm engulfed him. The huge banana in his throat seemed to disintegrate and he gasped lungfulls of air. Music filled his head, everything swam about him, his hands still flailed helplessly in the folds of Lucy's dressing gown... Music, euphoria, air! But then suddenly, Lucy was gone.

'Wayne?' said a disembodied voice. 'Wayne?' a hand was shaking him. He blinked, he tried to move but his arms were knotted in the tangled folds of Lucy's dressing gown.

'What? What is it?' said Wayne.

'You've come all over yourself.'

Wayne looked about. A woman lay propped up in bed beside him, her features in shadows cast by the bedside lamp behind her. Wayne squinted.

'Wayne?' It was Ellen's voice. He saw her clearly now, his eyes adjusting to the light. Confusion was rapidly dispersed by embarrassment. He lay on his back, his arms entangled between the duvet and its coverlet. He'd managed to pull the whole thing into a bundle on top of himself. He pushed the mass of bedding aside and looked down over his body. Semen lay in cooling pools over the swell of his stomach. He looked at the duvet: more semen; he'd come over that too. He let his head flop against the pillow.

'Shit,' he groaned.

'I woke up. You were thrashing about there with the duvet, sounded like you were having a choking fit. I thought you'd swallowed your tongue.

'I wish I had.'

'Scared the life out of me for a moment. I tried to wake you up, then...' She indicated his belly. 'That happened.'

'Oh,' said Wayne, dully.

'So what was it all about?'

'What?'

'Your dream. I presume you were dreaming?'

'Oh, I dunno.'

'Was I in it?'

'Yeah,' Wayne lied. 'Of course you were.'

'Was it exciting?'

'Yeah,' he said without enthusiasm.

'What happened?'

'Eh?'

'What happened?'

'I can't remember?'

'You can't remember? The spunk's not cold on your stomach yet and you can't remember?'

'I was choking,' Wayne muttered. 'I remember I was choking.'

'Choking?' Ellen frowned. 'What? On an orange probably. Was there a Tory MP in there anywhere?'

'Yeah,' said Wayne. 'You were the Tory. You were choking me with a pair of braces and whacking my arse with an umbrella.'

'Really?'

Wayne sighed. 'I don't remember.'

'I bet it was some other woman, wasn't it. That's why you can't remember.'

'It was not, it -' Wayne broke off and looked around. 'What the fuck is that?'

'What?'

'That music?'

Wayne was suddenly conscious of the room's uninvited entertainment. A steady beat emanating from an unknown source.

Ellen looked in the direction of the window. 'Over the back.'

'What's going on over the back?'

'I dunno. Started about five minutes ago.'

Wayne pushed the duvet aside and swung his legs out of bed. He grimaced as he realised he'd put his hand in a cold clot of semen. He wiped his hand on his bottom as he crossed to the back window. 'What time of night is this for a fucking party? It's the middle of the week for fuck's sake. What time is it, El?'

Ellen looked at the LED on the digital clock radio. 'One-thirty-one.'

Wayne was peering out through the curtains into the darkness outside. He could see light shining beyond the fence at the back of the garden. 'There's something going on alright.'

Ellen sighed. 'Forget it, Wayne. Come back to bed.'

'And do what? Sleep? Through this? You must be joking. You'd have to be dead to sleep through this.'

'I can sleep through it.'

Wayne raised an eyebrow.

'Just lie down and close your eyes, Wayne. You'll probably drop off in a little while.'

'I'll probably go insane in a little while.' Wayne turned and came back to the bed.

'That's it.' Ellen patted his pillow. 'Just forget-' She stopped as Wayne picked up the corner of the duvet and wiped off the semen from his stomach.

'What are you doing?'

'I'm going out there.'

'Like that?'

'Yes, I'm going to go out and investigate in the nude. The nude detective.'

'There's no need to take that tone.'

'Why do you think I'm wiping the spunk off me if I'm not going to put something on?'

Ellen shrugged. 'I hadn't noticed any unusual behaviour in your wiping spunk onto the bedsheets.'

'Very funny.' Wayne pulled on his boxers.

'You're going outside?'

'Uh-huh.' Wayne nodded, stepping into his slippers.

'Why don't you just shut the window? That should shut out a lot of the noise.'

'Why don't they just shut their window? They're the ones with the music on.'

Ellen lay down and rolled her eyes. 'Please be careful, Wayne. Don't start any trouble.'

Wayne gave a dismissive laugh. 'I didn't start this, Ellen. They did.'

'You know what I mean.'

Wayne strode to the bedroom door. 'Don't worry.' He stepped out into the hall. 'I know what I'm doing.'

Ellen listened as he retreated down towards the kitchen. 'Sure you do,' she murmured to herself. Then, with a sigh, she began untangling the bedclothes. She spread them out around her, careful to ensure that Wayne's half of the bed got all of the seed he was so fond of scattering around.

Wayne unlocked the back door and stepped out into the warm night. It was late May, and this was the first time this year they'd opened the bedroom window. Some people liked to have their bedroom window open all year round in the belief that it was healthy; but not Wayne. In his opinion, having a cold head for eight hours wasn't healthy, it was stupid. Their window was only open when the weather was warm enough to ensure a cold head wasn't a likely consequence, and tonight was such a night. Their window was double-glazed and relatively soundproof. Wayne reasoned that it was this that had so far protected their slumber from this bad neighbourliness. He'd heard distant music before at night, but it was as though it were a mile away and presented no obstacle to his sleeping. Now, with everyone opening their windows to the night air, the situation was different. He walked across the lawn to the fence at the back.

It was only a small garden, approximately thirty feet long. The lawn was an unmowed mess. Dandelions, bindweed and nettles abounded, many concealed within the long grass. A nettle found his ankle and he cursed under his breath. He felt moisture seeping into his slippers and cursed again. Undaunted, he strode on, guided by a small beacon of light in the darkness; a miniature pole star that shone through a knothole half way up the rear fence. The fence was about six and a half feet high. When he reached it he squatted down and placed his eye to the hole.

Their garden was as wild and unkempt as his. Bindweed grew over a couple of plastic chairs that lay overturned amid the long grass. On their small patio, Wayne noticed a rusted metal barbecue on wheels. Beyond the patio, a large French window stood wide open. The curtains were not drawn, and Wayne had no difficulty seeing inside. He could see two cocky looking young men on a sofa. They were talking to someone he couldn't see. He could hear the music clearer than ever now. It was some dance track. Wayne knew nothing about dance music, other than the fact that it sucked. This particular track, he reflected, sucked particularly hard. He watched them with swelling disdain. It wasn't so much their music, but their complete lack of concern for anybody else that bothered him. These blokes evidently thought nothing of throwing open their window in the middle of the night and inflicting their hideous taste in music upon their neighbours. What did that tell you about them?

'Selfish bastards. They're selfish, arrogant tossers.'

He straightened up and wondered what course of action to pursue. He considered pulling himself up the fence and calling over for them to turn it down, but dismissed the idea. Even if they could hear him, which he doubted, anyone so arrogant as to do this in the first place would no doubt just give him the finger and turn it up louder. No, he needed to think of something else. The police? No, they don't give a shit about things like this. He needed to come up with something himself. Something clever, something cunning, something uniquely Wayne. He returned to the knothole and looked again into the garden beyond. What was there that he could turn to his advantage? What could he see? Grass, patio furniture, barbecue, big window, wankers. That was all. He straightened up, deep in thought. He began walking slowly back through the grass. This time he managed to avoid getting stung by nettles. Nettles? Were they the answer? He considered a moment. No.

Then he became aware of a vague and unpleasant smell. He sniffed and recognised it as cat spray. Some fucking neighbour's mangy pet chuffing its foetid musk about. Wayne stopped and considered the smell for a moment. Was this the answer, he wondered: Cat spray? Get the cat to spray outside their window and they'd have to shut it, wouldn't they? He looked about for a cat, then his reasoning interjected. What would he do with it if he found it? Squeeze it till the spray came out? Milk it for stink? He was just about to dismiss the idea when the solution came to him. He stopped, and a smile of devious delight slowly spread across his face.

*

Ellen was just drifting off into sleep when she heard a rummaging in the corner of the room. She propped herself up on the pillow and looked in the direction of the noise. Wayne was sifting through the junk in the bottom of his wardrobe.

'Wayne? What are you doing?'

'Looking for something.'

'Looking for what?'

Wayne threw something back into the mess. 'I can't find it.'

'What?' said Ellen, irritably. 'What are you looking for?'

Wayne stood up and faced her. 'My water rifle thing.'

'That toy you got last summer for your nephew and decided to keep for yourself?'

'Yeah.'

'Have you looked under the bed?'

Wayne brightened. 'No.' He dropped from her view and she heard him begin foraging around beneath her. Suddenly the rummaging stopped. 'A-ha!'

Ellen heard his struggling retreat, then he re-emerged holding a plastic water rifle with the words "Super Drencher" emblazoned along the side. 'What do you want with that at this time of night?'

'I'm going to ensure we get some sleep tonight.'

'I was just about to get some sleep when you came crashing in here and woke me up.'

'Don't be daft, El,' said Wayne inspecting the Super Drencher. 'You can't sleep through that racket.'

'I can't sleep through your insanity.' Ellen fell wearily back into her pillow.

'I won't be long.' Wayne said as he trotted out of the room.

Ellen sighed and rolled onto her front. She closed her eyes and began counting sheep. She didn't expect it to send her to sleep, but it was preferable to thinking about what Wayne was getting up to.

Wayne went into the bathroom and switched on the light. He took the Super Drencher and unscrewed the cap of its water cylinder. Then he reached in through the fly of his shorts and drew out his penis. He turned and arranged himself so his penis and the Super Drencher were well over the bathtub, then he inserted his penis into the Super Drencher's water cylinder and released his bladder. He'd had a few cans of beer that evening, and there was plenty of ammunition for the rifle.

The water cylinder was made of a semi-opaque plastic, and he could watch as his urine steadily filled it. Wayne smiled as the smell of warm urine arose from the rifle. When it was full, he put his penis back into his shorts and re-capped the rifle. A few moments later he stepped back out into the garden. He strode through the underbrush to the fence, stinging himself again as he did so. He hunkered down and peered through the knothole.

The two blokes remained as they had been earlier, only now, Wayne noticed, one of them was smoking an unusual looking cigarette. Wayne watched the guy take a long draw on it and then pass it on to his neighbour on the sofa. Ahh, thought Wayne. A joint. A matter for the police perhaps?

'Perhaps. Maybe in the future. But not tonight.' He raised the rifle so the end of the barrel was pointing through the knothole in the direction of the French window. The hole was large enough for him to aim the gun with reasonable accuracy. He targeted the area just to the right of the window, and pulled the trigger. A high-powered stream of hot piss burst from the end of the rifle and streaked across the garden onto the target area. Wayne watched gleefully as the wall and patio area began to darken and glitter in the moonlight. He didn't want it to start splattering wetly on the same spot; unlikely as it was, they might hear it, so he fanned the stream about a little. When he was satisfied with his result, Wayne ceased firing. He took a last look through the hole and smiled. Delighted with himself, he then made his way back through the lawn towards the flat. In the bathroom, he quickly rinsed out the Super Drencher under the bath taps and then left it outside on the patio. Then he kicked off his slippers and crept back into bed beside Ellen. She murmured sleepily as he settled himself down but didn't awaken. Wayne smiled in the dark. She really could sleep through this shit if she wanted to. He was impressed. He was also remarkably pleased with himself, because he knew that thanks to him, she wouldn't have to do so for much longer. He lay in the dark, and waited for the music to stop.

Chapter 9

'OH, FUCKING, BESTIAL MAN. BESTIAL.' Gaz reached down and picked up the bottle of Red from the floor at the side of his chair. He noticed it was light, he swilled it; it was empty. 'Shit, I'm out. Anyone else?'

Jimmy raised his bottle and shook his head. 'I'm alright, man.'

Glen leaned forward to the coffee table and lifted his lightly. He looked up and nodded, 'I'm getting pretty low, Gaz.'

Gaz nodded and went to the kitchen.

'I need a piss,' said Glen.

'Cool.' Jimmy drew on the joint.

Glen got up. 'See ya in a sec.'

Jimmy released the smoke, 'Yeah, baby.' The blue stream of smoke broke and changed direction with the movement of his mouth as he spoke. Jimmy enjoyed that. As Glen left the room, Jimmy drew on the joint again. He started blowing smoke rings to amuse himself.

Glen returned shaking his head. 'Gazza's in the bog, inn'e.'

'Go outside.' Jimmy drew on the joint and handed it to Glen.

'Good idea.' Glen took the joint and stepped out through the French windows.

Jimmy blew smoke rings.

Outside, Glen laughed. 'Shit, man.'

Jimmy tilted his head in the direction of the window. He raised his voice to be heard over the music. 'What?'

Glen came back into view. He was smiling, but his tone was mildly critical. 'That's a bit close to the house innit, Jim?'

Jimmy smiled, not understanding. 'What?'

'That piss, man. You coulda' gone a bit further away, like.'

Jimmy's brow creased slightly. 'What piss?'

Glen pointed just right of the window. 'That piss, man.'

Gaz came into the room with two bottles of Red. 'What piss, man?'

'That piss.'

Both Gaz and Jimmy came over to the window to see what Glen was pointing at. A large area of dark wetness stood out from the rest of the wall. At its base was a puddle. 'Who done that?' said Gaz.

Glen looked at Jimmy. Gaz followed Glen's gaze. Jimmy looked up from the piss to the eyes of the others. He started slightly. 'Whoa, don't look at me, guys. I didn't do it.'

'Aw, come on, man,' said Glen.

'Seriously. When have you seen me go out there tonight?'

Gaz and Glen looked at each other, unsure.

'See? I haven't, have I?'

'What about when I was going to go earlier?' Glen suggested.

'You were gone like, thirty seconds, man. It'd take me more than thirty seconds to get off the couch, get out here and let go of this lot, then get back onto the couch all calm and collected by the time you get back, wouldn't it?'

Glen thought about it a moment, then nodded. 'Who did it then?'

They all looked down at the urine. 'Fuck knows, man,' said Gaz. 'That's a genuinely weird one.'

'Like, no-one could've come into the garden from outside and done it without us seein' them, could they?' said Glen.

Jimmy shook his head. 'No way, man. Not even the Invisible Man.'

'Well he might,' said Gaz. 'After all, he's invisible, inn'e?'

'Yeah. But we'd've heard him pissing, wouldn't we.'

Glen shrugged. 'Maybe. Then again, maybe he'd've pissed stealthily.'

'A stealth pisser?' said Gaz.

Glen nodded sagely. 'Like some night prowler, who, instead of stealing valuables or watching you have sex through your window; he pisses outside your house.'

'You reckon?' Jimmy frowned.

'I dunno. There's a lot of weirdos out there.'

Gaz laughed. 'I don't think there's anyone out there quite that fuckin' weird, man.'

'Except maybe you, Glen.' Jimmy added.

'What? Why me?'

'You thought of it.'

'You said it was a stealth pisser, man. Not me. It was your idea.'

'No way, man,' said Gaz. 'This is all your creation. You're a closet stealth pisser.'

Glen smiled dopily. 'Am I fuck.'

Gaz laughed and slapped Glen on the shoulder. 'Come in weirdo, and shut the window. We don't want the smell of stealth piss in the house, do we.'

Glen followed the others inside and drew the French window closed. Gaz and Jimmy slumped back into their seating positions.

'Still,' Gaz opened a bottle of Red. 'It's a weird one.'

'It is a weird one,' Jimmy agreed.

'It's a real weird one – weird one – weird one – weird one.' Glen sang in the style of Iggy Pop's, "Real Wild Child".

Gaz laughed. 'Oh, yeah. I'm a real weird one an' I like-a weird fun -'

Jimmy took up the singing, 'In a crazy fucking world I'm pissing on houses.'

They all sang together, 'I'm a weird one, Ohh baby I'm a weird one.' After this they broke into various versions of the lyrics before coming together for a rousing chorus. This dissolved into a discord of badly sung guitar solos.

'Why are we listening to this shit?' Jimmy pointed an acusing finger at the CD player. 'Turn it off and put some Iggy Pop on.'

'Have we got any Iggy Pop?' Glen asked.

'We have to have some somewhere. I know I had that one.'

'Me too.' Gaz got to his feet and went to the CD selection. All their CDs had been pooled into a communal collective that lay in permanent disarray around the CD player. A moment later, Gaz pulled out the desired disc. 'Yeeeah!'

Wayne was drifting into sleep. The music had been significantly dampened when they had closed their window. Although he had still been able to hear it, his sense of personal victory was more than enough to soothe him into restful sleep. He had been trying to return to his wet dream. Vivid visions of Lucy were hard to conjure at first, but he finally arrived at a working version. At first he had to direct her movements, but now she was moving with a life of her own. She began dancing to a vague and muted version of Iggy Pop's, "Real Wild Child". His brother Colin appeared and started playing the guitar. They were all on a steam train, smoke and steam billowed past the windows. There were lots of people on board, but they didn't seem to mind Lucy dancing in the nude. They were all playing cards. He turned and saw she was gone just as the train went into a tunnel.

*

Mick sat at his desk and looked at the empty space where Peter Reynolds should be. It was the second day that he hadn't turned up for work. He hadn't phoned in sick, and when they phoned him, there was no reply. Mick returned his attention to the data that glowed at him from the screen of his PC, but his mind refused to focus on it. It kept on replaying scenes from the last day he had seen Peter. His anxiety about that tramp, and then later, seeing him riding off on the bus with the very object of his angst. And now Peter, a man not known for his absenteeism, was absent. It was vexing. Mick ran his hand thoughtfully over his chin and began rolling his lower lip between his fingers.

'That's a nice face.'

Mick turned and saw Jenny Rose watching him. She sat at the next work station along from his. Mick realised he was pulling his lip down, baring his lower set of teeth and gums. 'Could you love a face like this?' It sounded more like, 'Could oo lugh a hase ike iss?'

'I don't think so.'

Mick released his lip. 'Better?'

'Hmm.' Jenny considered. 'Actually, I preferred the other version.'

'Damn. I'm grotesque.'

'Yes. But in a nice way.'

'Thanks.' Mick turned back to his PC.

'Not very busy today?'

'I keep wondering about Peter.'

'Peter Reynolds?'

'Yeah. I can't figure out why he's not here.'

Jenny shrugged. 'I presume he's ill or something.'

Mick shook his head. 'I don't know. I asked Lesley in Personnel if he'd rung in, and she said he hadn't. She called him but got no answer.'

'Maybe he's dosed-up in bed or something.'

'Maybe. But even so. It just isn't like him not to even make the effort.'

'Perhaps there's more to him than meets the eye.'

'No.' Mick smiled. 'What you see is the sum total.'

'How do you know? Do you see him socially?'

'No.'

'Have you ever been to his house?'

'No.'

'And yet you know him well enough to dismiss the idea he may have some mystique?'

Mick pouted. 'We go to lunch together and stuff. We talk a lot. I've asked him in the past if he wanted to go out for a few beers but...'

'But?'

'He always kind of puts me off.'

'Maybe he doesn't like you.'

88

'Oh, thanks a lot, Jen,' Mick sounded wounded.

'I don't mean you're not likeable. I'm just saying maybe you don't know him as well as you think you do.'

Mick turned back to his PC. 'It's too late. I'm mortally wounded.'

'I'm sorry, Mick. I'm sure he loves you really.' Jenny nudged the air between them. 'That's probably why he doesn't want to see you socially – he's afraid he might get drunk and make a pass at you.'

Mick turned back to her. 'You are depraved, do you know that?'

Jenny shrugged. 'It helps to pass the time.'

'But then again, maybe you're right. I fancy I've a great many secret admirers in this place, all afraid to go drinking with me for that very same reason.'

'Do you now?'

'Oh yeah. Do you fancy coming for a drink tonight at Wetherspoon's?'

'No.'

Mick raised his eyebrows and turned back to his PC. 'I rest my case.'

'Yeah. I'll just adore you from a distance.'

'You do that.'

'I will.'

'OK.'

At lunchtime, Mick went to Marks and Spencer's and bought a packet of ham and tomato sandwiches, a bag of crisps and a small carton of orange juice. When the weather was agreeable, as it was today, he liked to eat in the public gardens. He wasn't alone, there were many other office workers sitting around eating similar lunches. Most had something to read, a book or a newspaper. Mick didn't, he had a book in his drawer at work but he knew there was no point in bringing it; his mind was still preoccupied with Peter's absence. Pigeons roamed among the benches looking for crumbs or proffered titbits. Mick watched as a gang of them waddled over in his direction. They bobbed about at his feet, pecking at bits of dirt and minute trash. Idiot birds, thought Mick. He tossed them the corner of his last sandwich and they all dived for it, tearing it into pieces before waddling off in different directions to gobble down the pickings. A few seconds later they were back. Now I've done it, he thought, I've encouraged them. Friends for life. He opened his crisps and tossed them one; they pecked at it, breaking it into bits which they duly fled with.

'What if the tramp's killed him?' Mick murmured to himself. He shook his head. That was insane. Why would anybody want to murder Peter Reynolds? Especially someone who didn't even know him. Why go to the bother of stalking and killing a complete stranger? He'd heard of such things happening to beautiful women or people in the public eye, but not everyday saps like Peter. It just didn't add up.

The pigeons had finished their crisp. They agitated in expectation of the next course. Mick tossed them another.

What if Peter had run away to throw the tramp off his trail? That made more sense, and it was much more like Peter. Maybe the tramp had followed him home and knew where he lived, and so Pete had taken off somewhere, maybe gone to stay with friends or family. That made sense alright. Still, it seemed like an overreaction. He'd have to come back at some point and face the music. And it didn't answer why he hadn't called in to work. He could do that from anywhere. He wouldn't just abandon his work responsibilities – he needed his job, just like everybody else. Unless of course he had no intention of returning, either to his home, or his job. Mick tipped the crumbs from his bag of crisps into his mouth then put the empty packet into his small M&S carrier bag. He took out a cigarette and lit it. He stretched out his legs and exhaled smoke thoughtfully.

Maybe the tramp knew him from some past they both shared. Maybe this was a pattern. Peter moves on, trying to keep ahead of this guy, who maybe didn't start out as a tramp, but became one in his pursuit of Peter over the years. Peter evades him; gets away and sets up a new life in a new town. Then, eventually the tramp finds him, and then Peter has to move on again.

Mick shook his head. His mind suggested further scenarios. The tramp is Peter's idiot half-brother. Or maybe the husband of a woman Peter shagged and dumped, and then she committed suicide, and now this husband haunts Peter like a ghost. Maybe he is a ghost.

Mick laughed quietly to himself. His rational mind was trying to dismiss these possibilities as ridiculous, but his imagination persisted. If you removed the melodrama, there was something plausible in there somewhere. He wished he knew where Peter lived, then he could call on him in person. He wondered if Lesley in Personnel would give him Peter's address? It was probably against the rules, but after all, it was in everybody's best interests, wasn't it?

The pigeons had finished the crisp. They pecked at the crumbs that remained and watched him edgily. Mick rose and picked up his small carrier bag of rubbish. He dropped his cigarette butt to the floor and ground it out with his shoe.

'Sorry lads. Nothing more from me today.' He walked to a litterbin and deposited the carrier bag. He looked back to where the pigeons were pecking away at his cigarette butt. He shook his head. 'Idiot birds. Bon appetit.'

Lesley sat behind her desk. 'I can't do that Mick, you should know that.' She wiped tomato ketchup from the corner of her mouth with a napkin. 'It's against company policy.'

'I know, I know.' Mick shifted in the seat opposite. 'But surely you can see it's in all of our best interests?'

Lesley took a bite from her Big Mac then placed it delicately back in its polystyrene box. 'It is? Why is my divulging confidential personnel information to you in my best interests?'

'Because he's my mate, and I think he'd thank you if he could.'

Lesley picked up the big diet Coke from her desk and took a sip through the straw. 'Oh? Why can't he?'

'What?'

'Thank me. Do you know what's wrong with him?'

'No, not exactly. But I'm concerned about him.'

Lesley renewed her demure attack on the Big Mac. She shook her head. 'We're all concerned when a colleague is ill, Mick.'

'Yeah, so it's in our best interests that you give me his address so I can go around and check up on him. Make sure he's OK.'

Lesley chewed meditatively. She sipped her coke. 'Is he a good friend of yours then?'

Mick shrugged. 'We go to lunch together. We take breaks together.'

Lesley bit down on the Big Mac and grimaced. She drew away from the burger with a gherkin slice protruding from her teeth. 'Ugh.' She quickly removed the pickle from her mouth and dropped it into the polystyrene box. 'Yeuch. Should've got that out at the beginning. That's your fault for distracting me.'

Mick smiled slightly, unsure if she was serious. 'Sorry about that.'

'You should be.' She reached into her McDonald's carryout bag and removed a box of fries.

'Why do you eat McDonald's if you don't like the gherkin?'

'Lots of people don't like the gherkin. Do you?'

'Not really. But then I generally prefer Burger King.'

Lesley nodded and gathered a number of fries together. 'Me too,' she said, before pushing the fries into her mouth.

'Why do you get McDonald's then?'

'They're nearer.'

'Only about two minutes nearer.'

Lesley chewed a moment before again wiping her lips with the napkin. 'Two minutes is a long time in a lunch hour.'

Mick pointed at her. 'Ahhh, but the queues in McDonald's are longer. It evens things out.'

'Yeah, well I prefer McDonald's.'

Mick raised his eyebrows. 'I see.'

'So, you reckon I should give you Peter Reynolds's address?'

'I do.'

'Let me try his phone again.' She picked up the telephone on her desk and turned to her PC. She'd brought up Peter's file when Mick first came in. Now she read his home phone number and dialled. She sat back and looked at Mick. 'You're worried about him you say?'

Mick shrugged. 'Like you said, we're all concerned.'

Lesley nodded, casually looking him up and down before letting her eyes come to rest on his.

Mick shifted a little in his seat. He averted his eyes to a chart on the wall.

'No answer.' Lesley put the receiver back into its cradle. 'That's kind of worrying, don't you think?'

She sat forward again and picked up her Coke. She sucked at the straw, watching him thoughtfully. The dregs of the drink noisily entered the straw. She sucked at the bottom of the cup for a few seconds before putting it back onto her desk. 'It's a little uncommon, I have to admit.'

'So what do you say?'

Lesley sighed through her nose. She looked at him searchingly. 'I've noticed you two together at lunch and stuff. You do seem fairly pally.'

Mick nodded. 'We are.'

Lesley reached down into her bag and came up with a packet of cigarettes. 'You smoke?'

He nodded. 'But I'm trying to quit.'

'Who isn't? Want to step outside?'

Mick looked at his watch. 'I can't I'm afraid. I have to get back; my lunch is over in about two minutes.'

Lesley got up and came around the desk. 'I'll speak to Ray. I'll tell him you two are friends and that I think it's okay. He should be fine with that.'

Mick smiled. 'Thanks a lot, Lesley. I think you're doing the right thing here. I've a feeling that old Pete may be in a bind. We may be saving his life with this visit.'

'Mmm. How exciting.'

'Well, you know. He might've slipped on a bar of soap or something and be lying in a comatose mess on the bathroom floor.'

Lesley opened the office door for him. 'Let's hope not.'

'Yeah. Well, now we can find out, eh?'

Lesley nodded. She looked at him a moment then said, 'I'll let you know later what Ray says.'

'I appreciate that.'

She smiled slightly then turned and walked down towards the elevators. Mick took a deep breath then turned in the direction of his desk. As he walked he contemplated the idea that Lesley might fancy him. She wasn't his type: forties, dyed blonde hair, kind of heavy. But at the same time, it was sort of complimentary, being eyed up appreciatively by a female boss. Or was it? Maybe not. Maybe it was fraught with peril, like in that movie, *Disclosure*. Mick imagined Lesley in dominant psycho-bitch mode. He grimaced and sat down next to Jenny.

'Damn it,' he said with mock disgust. 'I'm just a piece of meat to you women, aren't I?'

She turned and looked at him. 'That's right.'

Mick nodded. 'Oh, I know. Don't think I don't know, because I do.'

'You're like,' she considered a moment, 'Spam.'

Mick dropped the act, wounded. 'Spam?'

'Yes. Spam Boy.'

Mick turned to his PC. 'Thanks a lot, mate.' He shook his head. 'Spam. I'm flattered.'

'Spam Boy's adventures in Office Land.'

'Yeah, okay. That's enough.'

'At least fifty-five per cent meat. "We use the whole of the pig".'

'Thank you.' Mick tried to concentrate on his work.

'Including lips, hooves and arseholes.'

'Enough. Please. I yield.'

'You sure?'

'I'm sure.'

Jenny sat back. 'So why are you "meat", then?'

Mick leaned toward her and whispered. 'Lesley eyed me up.'

Jenny turned back to her PC. 'Big deal. She eyes everyone up.'

'What? Every bloke?'

'No. Everyone.'

'She doesn't?' Mick was incredulous.

'She does.'

'What, even you?'

Jenny turned to him. 'Yes. Even me.'

'You're kidding.'

'Ask anyone.'

'I will.'

'Do.'

'I will.'

'Okay then.'

He considered a moment. 'Lips and arseholes?'

Jenny nodded. 'Read the ingredients.'

'I will.'

'Do.'

'Don't worry, I will.'

'It'll be like looking in a mirror.'

'Thanks.'

'Don't mention it.'

The man formerly known as Dusty lay in the bed of the late Peter Reynolds with a cup of tea, a pencil and a pad of paper. He was naked, his big form spread out, luxuriating in the sense of comfort that was still a novelty to him, even after three days. He sucked thoughtfully at the end of the pencil and gazed intently at the pad. Occasionally he wrote a name on the paper:

christian names, surnames, names of famous people, both living and dead, names of places and things. Many were crossed out, some had arrows connecting them to other names on the list.

He reached out and picked up the old copy of TV Quick that lay on the bedside table. He opened it and began to scour its pages in search of inspiration. Every now and then he made a sound of approval and jotted new entries onto his list. When he came up with one he particularly liked, he spoke it aloud, as if trying it on for size. Frasier, Tony Banks, Liam Neeson. He mixed and matched: Liam Banks? Tony Frasier? All these he subsequently struck from the list. Choosing a name was a serious business. The last one had been easy; he liked ZZ Top. The beard and sunglasses gave him the Top look, so he mixed up the surnames of the two bearded members of the band. That simple solution wasn't going to work this time. He ran his hand over his shaven scalp. 'Mr Kojak?' Uh-uh, he shook his head. No-one would ever take him seriously with a name like that.

Suddenly the telephone rang in the front room. He listened intently for a moment, considering possible courses of action, then decided it was best left to ring. The caller would soon tire of the neglect. He had constructed a number of possible answering dialogues, from Peter himself speaking with an illness that altered the sound of his voice, to Peter's landlord, horrified at the sudden departure of his tenant – along with the rent he owed. The one he most favoured was simply that of a new tenant. But that could all wait. For the time being, those who phoned could simply wonder at the whereabouts of the old occupier, before learning the identity of the new one.

Chapter 10

SALLY SAT BEHIND THE COUNTER of Stephenson's Books and watched the world go by outside. It was a sunny day, though rather cool. However, this didn't stop everyone who was able to from putting on as little as possible in the way of clothing. She'd noticed on innumerable occasions how English people, as soon as the sun so much as poked its head around the corner of a cloud after mid-April, immediately donned T-shirts, shorts, summer frocks and the obligatory pair of sunglasses. Perhaps it was a determination to throw off the winter wardrobe that dominated their appearances for so much of the year. Perhaps it was a desperate need to bare white flesh in public in the unlikely hope that it would tan to a more desirable red by tea time. Or maybe it was just the sheer dogged determination to experience at least one attribute of summer; that being partial public nudity. Whatever it was, they were at it today. Despite the chilly wind people were out and about sporting sunglasses and short sleeved tops, shorts and light cotton skirts. She smiled wistfully and thanked heaven she'd had the sense to wear woolly tights and a cardigan. Unlike the scantily clad hordes outside, she laboured under no delusions of summer. It was late spring, and a long way from the bikini season.

'Have you done the delivery, Sally?'

She turned. Leonard Stephenson had emerged from the stockroom and was looking at her with an air of expectancy. She nodded, 'Yes, Leonard. All done.'

Leonard looked about the shop. 'Much of interest?'

'Not really. Nothing new.'

'Damnation. I was hoping that new Martin Amis book would arrive today. I'll bet they've got it down at Waterstones.'

'Probably. Probably discounted as well.'

Leonard scowled. 'Swineherd. Perhaps I should pop down and take a look.'

'Could do.'

Leonard drummed his nicotine-yellow fingers on the counter and considered. 'I think I may, you know. I could pop into the bakers and get a couple of buns while I'm at it.' He looked at her. 'Do you fancy a bun, Sally?'

'I'd love a bun, Leonard.'

'Good.' Leonard smiled. 'What's the weather doing?'

'People seem to feel it's high summer. Personally I think it's a bit nippy out.'

Leonard peered doubtfully out of the window. 'I feel inclined towards your interpretation of things. I'll get my jacket.'

'I think that'd be wise. Anything you'd like me to do while you're out?'

Leonard looked about. 'Anything pressing you can think of?'

Sally thought a moment. 'Not really.'

'Nor I.' He stepped through the door marked "Private", next to the Classics section. He emerged a few moments later wearing a green Harris Tweed jacket and carrying an umbrella. 'I shouldn't be more than about half an hour. Perhaps you could get the kettle on ready for tea about then?'

'I'll do that.'

'Splendid.' He opened the door of the shop and the small bell tinkled above the doorway. 'See you later.'

She waved. 'Bye.'

Once Leonard was gone, Sally went back to her contemplation of the world outside the window. She found her thoughts drifting inevitably back to her social life, or the lack of it. Why don't you just join a club or something? The only way to meet new people is to get out there and physically meet them. She considered the wide range of options open in the "club joining" scheme of things: sports, health, academic and… and that was about it really. She didn't much care for sports, so that was that out. She'd tried going to yoga classes for awhile but found the cheesy odour of the whole experience somewhat off-putting. Then there was the academic option; going to a class of some kind. To study what? A language maybe? Learn Spanish and move to Spain. That would be nice. Go somewhere where the summer was a reality, not just a series of sunny photographs on the calendar from May to August. God knows nobody here would miss her. There was Leonard of course, he'd miss her. And his parents upstairs, they'd probably miss her too. But Leonard and his parents didn't exactly constitute a social life. Leonard's social horizons began and ended at the Black Pig, where they maintained a regular and exclusive clientele consisting of what Leonard termed "oddballs and misanthropes" – people Leonard considered brethren.

At least, Sally reflected, she had Kay. Kay and her stupid obsession with those fuckwitted blokes. She sighed and kicked gently at the counter, her swivel chair revolved slowly around. She wondered where her life had gone. Where had all her friends vanished to? Were they dead? Were they abducted by aliens? No. 'They're married. Married or similarly removed. Husbands, children, careers. Or all of the above.' She spun the chair gently in the opposite direction to prevent herself from getting dizzy. 'While I work here and hang around with Kay Oliver.' She smiled. 'Beautiful.'

It doesn't have to be this way. You have other friends, acquaintances; why don't you call them up?

'Like who?'

Look in your filofax address book, dummy. That's what it's there for.

She stopped her slow revolve and went to where her bag lay behind the counter. She pulled out the filofax and turned to the address book. One by one she confirmed what she already knew: by the time you get to twenty-eight, old friends were people you occasionally bumped into on the high street. The conversation consisted of you saying flattering things about the little bundle of joy they were pushing in front of them, and them telling you about the bundle's toilet habits. Just as she was about to lose interest, she came to 'L'. There she read a name she hadn't considered in a long time: Lucy Conner. Tel: 366541.

Lucy Conner. Whatever happened to Lucy? She'd never heard of a marriage; never been invited to a wedding or a christening featuring Lucy. Maybe she'd moved to London. Maybe she'd been to evening classes and learned Spanish and now sat around in a genuine summer. Then again, maybe she's available on 366541 right now.

'Maybe.' She picked up the phone and dialled the number. A moment later a voice came on the line.

'Hello?'

'Lucy?'

'Yes, who's this?'

'It's Sally. Sally Kenton?'

Lucy's voice brightened with recognition. 'Sally. God, how are you?'

Sally smiled. 'I'm fine, how are you?'

'Oh, you know. Getting by, getting on with it.'

'Married?'

'God, no! You?'

'No, Mr Right eludes me.'

'Me too, thank Christ. So what are you doing with yourself? How come you're phoning?'

'I work in a bookshop. I was just calling to catch up with you.'

'Big time, eh? Foyles? Manager?'

'Uh-uh. Stephenson's. Assistant.'

'Lovely. What about the other thing?' Lucy's voice took on an ominous tone. 'Kids?'

Sally smiled. 'No. You?'

'No. And no regrets there either. I have other plans.'

'Like what?'

'Oh, various. But none of them involve the patter of tiny feet or the warming of the pipe and slippers.'

Sally laughed. 'Listen, do you fancy going out for a drink sometime?'

'Hmmmm,' Lucy pondered aloud. 'What about Thursday?'

Thursday's fine with me. When and where?'

'I dunno, what do you prefer, bar or pub?'

'Pub.'

'Me too. Do you know the Moon and Stars?'

Sally picked up a pencil and jotted the details on a scrap of paper. 'Yeah.'

'Half eight?'

'Half eight it is.'

'Fabulous. It's a date.'

'Okay.' Sally underlined the time and sat upright. 'I'll look forward to it. You can tell me about these various plans of yours.'

'I will. Maybe I'll give you a few ideas.'

'Oh I could use a few.'

'Okay, see you Thursday, Sally. Thanks for ringing.'

'My pleasure. See you Thursday. Bye.'

'Bye.'

Sally hung up the phone. She smiled. Good old Lucy Conner. She wondered what Lucy was doing for a living; she had forgotten to ask her. Never mind, there'd be plenty of time for that on Thursday. She looked at her watch and realised that Leonard would be here in a minute eagerly clutching his buns and demanding tea. She stepped into the room at the back of the counter where they kept the tea things and put the kettle on.

Lesley stopped by Mick's desk at about three o'clock that afternoon. 'Mick?'

Mick had been absorbed in his screen and didn't notice her. He looked around and blinked. 'Lesley?'

She handed him a folded piece of white paper. 'I spoke to Ray, and, under the circumstances, he's agreed to allow an exception. Needless to say, this is confidential information.'

Mick took the slip and opened it. Inside was written an address. He looked up at Lesley. 'Brilliant. Don't worry, I understand the confidentiality thing.'

'Good.' She looked over at Jenny who had turned to watch the exchange. 'Hi Jenny.'

Jenny smiled. 'Hi Lesley.'

'How are you?'

'Oh, you know, busy.'

Mick looked from one woman to the other. He scratched his chin and smiled at Lesley. 'Thanks again.'

'You're welcome.' Lesley winked, then she turned and walked in the direction of her office. She gave Jenny a small wave. 'Bye, Jenny.'

'See ya.' Jenny raised her hand slightly. She looked at Mick and smiled. 'Love letter?'

Mick looked secretively at the slip of paper. 'I don't know, what do you think?' He leaned closer to her and pretended to read from the note, 'Mick, please help me. I am in love with Jenny but cannot bring myself to say anything to her. Please tell her for me and end my heartache one way or the other. Signed, Lesley.'

'Gosh.' Jenny feigned surprise. 'It says that?'

'It sure does.'

'My goodness. How can I tell David that I'm leaving him for a woman?'

'Just go with your emotions, girl.'

Jenny dropped the pretence. 'So what is it?'

'Peter's address.'

'Why do you want Peter's address?'

'I'm going to call on him. Find out what's wrong.'

'I see. Bit of private investigation, eh?'

'Sort of. I have a feeling there's something queer going on.'

'Do you now? That explains your interest.'

'I mean odd, strange, uncanny.'

'Of course you do.'

'Oh, okay,' said Mick. 'If it'll brighten your day. I'm going round to Peter's with flowers and a box of Milk Tray.'

'Sounds lovely. Flowers and chocolates always work on me.'

'I'll be sure to tell Lesley.' Mick smirked.

'Oh, ho-ho-ho.'

'My but we do have fun. Don't we dear?'

'Oh, we do,' Jenny agreed. 'Never a dull moment.'

'Except those spent on the treadmill.'

'Which I really must get back to.' Jenny sighed and returned her attention to her PC.

'Me too.' Mick took a last look at Peter's address on the piece of paper, then folded it and slipped it into his pocket.

It was six thirty in the evening when Gaz, Jimmy and Glen stepped out of their front door and began the walk to Shenanigans Irish Pub. Ted Tucker, the landlord, didn't have an Irish bone in his body, but business never seemed to suffer as a result.

'Anyone have any further thoughts on the Stealth Pisser?' Gaz asked.

'I reckon it must've been an animal,' said Glen.

'Like what?' said Jimmy. 'Have to be fairly big and very silent to have come up just outside our window and piss like that.'

'A fox?' suggested Gaz.

'Yeah, man.' Glen nodded. 'That's what I was thinking. A fox or somethin'.'

'You do get foxes in towns at night. They raid bins and stuff looking for food.'

'Yeah,' said Gaz. 'I reckon that's got to be it, lads. A fox, marking his territory.'

'Nice one.'

Jimmy smiled. 'Yeah, it is pretty cool. Maybe we should put some food out for it. I heard they like bread and milk.'

'Where'd you hear that?'

'I dunno. But it sounds reasonable doesn't it? I mean, it's better than eating trash.'

'Unless you're rich and have really posh trash,' said Glen. 'Leavin' out lots of expensive leftovers like caviar and stuff.'

'I don't think foxes eat caviar, mate,' said Gaz. 'It's not exactly on the woodland menu, is it?'

'Yeah, but they'd eat it wouldn't they? They'd eat any food they found in the bin.'

'Yeah, I suppose so. Mind you, I've heard caviar tastes like shit. It's only coz it's expensive that rich people eat it.'

'I've heard that too.'

'Then it's a good thing for our fox that we're not rich, then innit?' said Jimmy.

'Yeeeah, man,' Gaz flicked his fingers. 'Our own fox. That's fuckin' cool.'

'We can put some bread and milk out tonight after work.'

'Alrighhhht. Nice one.'

They all nodded, laughing as they neared the town centre. None of them noticed the big man in the tight suit that followed them.

The man formerly known as Dusty followed the three young men at what he considered to be a safe distance. They seemed entirely unaware of him, absorbed as they were in whatever it was they were discussing.

'Deep.' Whatever it was, their discussion was probably beyond him. The One led the conversation, as he did all things in their lives.

Over the last few days and nights, he'd monitored their activity closely through the telescope. He'd made notes of the times they came and went. Their six thirty exit lead to an absence from the property of several hours. They returned variously from twelve to two a.m. Subsequently, tonight he'd positioned himself behind a parked car several doors down the street from them, waiting for the six thirty exit. And now, here they were.

The suit he wore had been selected from Peter's wardrobe. It was too small and smelled vaguely of petrol. He had intended to go to town and buy new clothes with Peter's credit cards, but so far, he hadn't bothered. Instead, he stayed at home enjoying the flat and watching the movements of The One and his disciples as they went about their daily business. Their big cigarettes, he quickly realised, were reefers, and he was interested to discover the frequency of their indulgence in the habit. He soon learned that seldom did an hour pass without one or more of them rolling up. But then, many seers used such things to see better. That, and they numbed the tedium that modern life must represent to The One. He ran his hand over his shaved head and smiled to himself. It all fitted perfectly.

Ahead, the three young men were approaching a big pub. The whole building had been painted green. The legend "Shenanigans" was painted in white and orange Celtic script above the door. He frowned at the sight. The building stuck out from the other shops and premises on the street like a gangrenous limb. He stopped and watched from across the street as the three young men entered. He thought for a few moments, then reached a big hand into the pocket of the suit trousers. It took a moment to squeeze it into the tight opening, but once it was in, he smiled at the feel of the crisp bank notes. He pulled out a ten pound note, and crossed over the road. He hesitated for a moment to look at the pub sign that hung above the door. A drunken leprechaun, his face flushed with alcohol saluted the passer-by with a pint of stout. The man formerly known as Dusty nodded thoughtfully, turned, and pushed open the door.

Glen and Jimmy were behind the bar talking to a girl. Suddenly the girl's eyes moved to the left and stayed there. Jimmy and Glen followed her gaze to a big man in a tight suit with a completely bald head. The man was looking curiously about the walls at the fixtures and fittings.

'Nutter alert,' Glen whispered to Jimmy.

'Full on. You or me?'

'You're nearest.'

Jimmy smiled. 'Thanks mate.' He went over so he stood in front of the man. 'Hello, there. What can I get you?'

The bald man was studying a poster depicting a series of Irish doors. He turned to Jimmy. 'Pardon?'

'What'll it be?'

'Oh,' the bald man brightened. 'A lemonade, please. A pint of lemonade.'

'Ice and a slice?'

'A slice?'

Jimmy laughed good naturedly. 'A slice of lemon.'

'Ah, yes. Lemon. What else would it be?'

'I could pop some lime in there too if you'd like.'

'Why not? That'd be very refreshing.'

'Sure.' Jimmy selected a glass and added a generous helping of ice. 'Why not?'

Glen and the girl watched the exchange with undisguised fascination. Glen, who was leaning on the bar with his knuckles in front of his mouth, turned to her with a crazy smile on his face. 'Very refreshing,' he whispered. The music from the jukebox ensured there was no chance of his being overheard. The girl took a sip of her drink to conceal her amusement. She glanced over at the bald man. He still stood in the middle of the floor, some three paces or so from the bar. He was looking at her and smiling coolly. She averted her eyes back to Glen.

'What?' Glen's looked over at the bald man. The bald man smiled at him. He quickly looked back to the girl and sniggered. 'Fuckin' hell, man.'

'There we are.' Jimmy set the drink down on the bar. 'Anything else?'

Still smiling, the bald man turned from Glen and the girl and raised his eyebrows at Jimmy. 'Sorry?'

'Anything else? Or just the lemonade?'

'Thank you. Just the lemonade. How much is that?'

'One pound ninety, please.'

The bald man stepped up to the bar and handed Jimmy the ten pound note. 'Expensive. Not much of a financial incentive for alcoholic abstinence.'

'I know, mate,' Jimmy spoke with a professional world-weariness as he took the money. 'But that's the pub trade nowadays.'

'Fizzy water and flavoured syrup, isn't that right?'

As he worked at the till, his back to the customer, Jimmy glanced over towards Glen and rolled his eyes. 'That's right, mate. Drinking out's an expensive pastime these days.' He closed the till and turned back to the customer to hand him his change. 'Personally, I drink at home whenever I can.'

'I know.'

'Sorry?' Jimmy frowned slightly.

The bald man blinked. 'It's the best option – financially – to drink at home. I know.'

Jimmy nodded warily. 'Yeah. Okay.' He gave the man a last, perfunctory smile before re-joining Glen and the girl.

'Very refreshing,' Glen whispered sarcastically.

'Leave it out, man. He's a bit touched. It's not his fault.'

Glen glanced over to where the bald man now sat alone at a corner table. 'Touched is right. But by what?'

'Maybe we should call the fashion police,' the girl suggested.

'Yeeeah,' Glen resumed his position at the bar in front of her.

Jimmy joined him. 'You're pretty sharp. It's so rare to find a girl as gorgeous as you with a gorgeous brain to match.'

The girl smiled. 'Yeah, sure. That's the cheesiest line in the book.'

'Yeeah, man,' Glen sniggered.

'Listen,' Jimmy leaned close to the girl. 'I wrote the book baby. And that line's in the "heartfelt compliments" section.'

'Cheese, baby,' Glen tousled Jimmy's hair. 'Pure cheese.'

'Oi! Leave it out,' Jimmy swatted Glen's hand away and quickly combed his hair with his fingers. He offered the girl his most winning smile. 'So what's your name?'

'Rachel.'

'I'm Jimmy. And this is Glen.'

The girl smiled. 'Pleased to meet you both.'

'So what's a nice girl like you doing in a place like this?' Glen asked.

'Another great line,' said Rachel. 'You two are quite a double act.'

'Actually,' Jimmy grinned. 'We're a trio. The third of our number is upstairs with the boss. But I know he'd just love to meet you.'

'I'm sure he would. But in answer to your earlier question, I'm waiting for my boyfriend.'

'Oh.' Jimmy nodded, his smile cooling a few degrees. 'He's a lucky guy.' He looked at Glen.

'Yeah,' said Glen. 'He sure is.'

'Well,' Jimmy rubbed his hands briskly. 'I'll leave you two to chat. I've got work to do.'

'Oh, er, me too.' Glen nodded. 'Glasses to wash. Stuff like that.'

Rachel smiled. 'Uh-huh. Well, it was nice meeting you.'

'Oh, the pleasure is all ours.' Jimmy bowed slightly. 'And don't worry, we aren't going far.'

'I'm not worried.'

Jimmy and Glen turned to their various tasks.

'What do you think?' Jimmy asked covertly. 'True or false?'

Glen shrugged. 'Fuck knows, man. Could be either. Could be a dyke.'

'No way, man. She's not a dyke.'

'If she is, she wouldn't stay one for long once she's gotten her laughing gear around this.' Glen took his crotch in both hands and grinned.

Jimmy laughed. 'Alriiight, man.' Then he noticed Glen's demeanour become suddenly more professional. He followed the direction of his gaze. In the corner, the bald man was watching them with undisguised interest.

Jimmy turned his attention to the glass-washing machine. 'Whoa.'

'Touched is right,' Glen muttered. 'Listen, I'll see you in a sec.' He opened the door at the rear of the bar and started up the stairs to the flat above.

Jimmy casually looked up to the bald man and smiled.

The bald man smiled back. He raised his glass, as if in a toast. Jimmy smiled and nodded. The bald man continued to toast him, his eyes smiling across the rim of the glass.

Touched? thought Jimmy. Fucking barking is more like it. He turned away, decided that right now was a great time to get to know Rachel a little better.

Chapter 11

GLEN TOOK THE CARPETED STAIRS TWO AT A TIME. At the top was another door, it was locked with a coded keypad. He quickly tapped in the pass code and opened the door. He heard the sound of voices coming from Ted's lounge. He crossed the landing and knocked gently on the closed door.

Ted's voice beckoned. 'Come in.'

Glen opened the door and stepped inside. Ted, a stout man in his late forties, was standing by the window. He was holding a mug of coffee and stood paused in his conversation with Gaz, who sat upon the arm of an armchair with his feet up on the seat cushion.

'Yes Glen?' Ted enquired.

'I was, er, wondering if one of you guys could change the Guinness over. It's sucking suds.'

'I'll do it in a minute, mate,' said Gaz.

Glen nodded. 'Cool.'

'Was there anything else?' asked Ted.

'No, not really.' Glen thought for a second. 'How's it going?'

'It's going great, Glen. Thanks for asking. But hadn't you better get back to the bar. It'll be getting busy soon, won't it?'

'Yeah, okay. See you in a minute then, Gaz.'

Gaz held up a hand in acknowledgement.

Glen withdrew and closed the door behind him.

Ted waited until he heard the landing door close before he spoke. 'So what's going on?'

'My source has dried up, Ted mate. The bloke I get it off has moved up to Manchester.'

Ted looked surprised. 'You only had one source?'

'I only ever needed one source, Ted. Terry always got top gear, there wasn't any need for anybody else's services.'

Ted took a sip of his coffee. 'But surely you must know someone. A streetwise lad like yourself?'

Gaz shrugged. 'I wish I did, mate. But times are hard. If we had more money we might get to go clubbing a bit more often and get to know a few shady characters, but as it is, we're skint. All our money's going into the Thailand fund, so clubbing is a luxury we can't afford.'

Ted chuckled. 'How much have you got saved now?'

'Enough plane fare for three of us – ish.'

'When do you reckon you'll have enough dosh to actually go?'

'At this rate, about six months.'

'You wanna start dealing yourself, Gaz. That'll get you there a lot quicker, and it'd solve our immediate problem.'

'No thanks, mate,' Gaz shook his head emphatically. 'I've seen too many dealers get nicked to want in on that caper. That's why Terry split. Coppers had him marked.'

Ted stiffened. 'You don't think they might've traced us from him?'

Gaz smiled. 'No, he was always very careful in that respect. We've got nothing to worry about.'

'Other than the fact that there's no one dealing to us anymore.'

'Leave it to me, Ted. I'll sort something out. I always do.'

Ted finished his coffee. 'Yeah, I know you do.' He laughed. 'I can't imagine you lot going for more than twenty-four hours without a joint. You'd go loopy.'

'We fuckin' would, mate.' Gaz got to his feet. 'We fuckin' would.'

'Alright, mate,' Ted sighed. 'You going to go down and sort out that Guinness?'

'Yeah. And don't worry about gear. I'll sort it real quick.'

'I'm not worried mate. At least not yet, I've got enough stash for the next few days or so.'

'Oh? We'll have to pop up and see you after work, then.'

Ted chuckled. 'Alright, mate.'

'When's the missus get back?' asked Gaz as he opened the door to leave.

'She's gone to her keep fit class. She won't be back for about another hour or so.'

'She's keeping it supple for you, Ted. She'll be hot for you when she gets in.'

Ted laughed. 'I should be so fuckin' lucky, mate.'

'Wha-hey!' Gaz thrust his hips forward unambiguously.

'Go on.' Ted waved him away.

Gaz gave a short Sid James laugh and departed.

Still smiling, Ted shook his head and went to where Gaz had been sitting. He cheerfully brushed the seat where Gaz's feet had been. He then went over to the mantelpiece and picked up a small brass box which he carried over to the dining table. He sat down, opened the box, and took out a lump of hash and some rolling papers. He held up the lump of cling film wrapped hash. 'Fuckin' hell,' he murmured. 'If those buggers come up here tonight, I'll have fuck-all left.' He unwrapped the lump and carefully snapped it into two smaller pieces. One half he left on the table, the other he re-wrapped in cling film. He took this second lump back over to the mantelpiece where he dropped it into one of Fiona's ornamental brass pots. 'For emergency use only.' He then went back to the table, sighed contentedly, and started carefully sticking Rizla papers together, exactly as Gaz had taught him.

After leaving Ted, Gaz went straight to the cellar and changed the Guinness over. When he'd done that he went back to the bar where Glen and Jimmy were busy serving the slowly gathering crowd.

He saw a waiting customer and went over to him. 'Yes, mate?' He took the order and joined Jimmy at the Lowenbrau tap. As Jimmy poured a pint, Gaz said, 'I need to have a word. See you in the gents' in a minute, yeah?'

Jimmy nodded without looking up. 'Sure thing, man.'

Gaz poured the drink and took it back to the customer. 'There you go, mate. One pint of lemonade. Anything else?'

'No thank you,' replied the bald man. He paid for his drink and went back to his table. He put the drink down and then turned and headed toward the gents' toilet.

Meanwhile, after serving another customer each, both Gaz and Jimmy found themselves free. Gaz nodded to Jimmy and they both slipped from behind the bar, leaving Glen to serve alone.

'Just having a quick conference, Glen. See you in a minute, yeah?'

Glen nodded and continued to serve.

Gaz and Jimmy entered the toilets together. Once in, they glanced about. At first glance they appeared to be alone, but then Gaz pointed to the door of one of the stalls, which was closed. He went over to the door and bent to look underneath it. He saw a pair of scuffed, old, black boots pointing towards him. They had been recently polished, but there was no mistaking their worn condition. Suddenly the owner of the boots farted. Gaz grimaced and straightened up. He directed Jimmy to the far end of the toilet, away from the occupied stall.

'Ted obviously wants more gear.'

'Doesn't everybody?' Jimmy shrugged.

'Yeah, well, exactly. We need to make a new contact. We need to put out feelers among any likely looking punters, you know what I mean?'

Jimmy nodded. 'I can think of a couple of people already. I don't know if they're coming in tonight or what, but I'll certainly keep an eye out.'

'Nice one. Listen, go and get Glen and send him in here. I need to give him the same briefing.'

Jimmy nodded. 'Sure thing, man.' He turned and left the toilets.

Left alone, Gaz went to the sinks and looked at himself in the mirror. He ran water into one of the sinks and rinsed his hands absently under the running water. A flush sounded and Gaz looked up into the mirror. The stall door opened and a big, bald-headed guy stepped out of the toilet. Gaz recognised him as the lemonade customer he'd served a few minutes ago. The suit he wore was strangely too small for him. The trouser hems rode some five inches or so up the guy's legs, allowing an unimpaired view of those boots and his equally incongruous pair of Daffy Duck socks. Obviously a single man, thought Gaz as the man came over to the sink beside him and turned on the taps. Gaz glanced casually at him in the mirror. 'Alright, mate?'

The bald man smiled. 'I'm fine, thank you. How are you?'

Gaz turned off the tap and shook the excess water from his hands. 'I'm great, thanks. Wicked.' He ran his wet hands through his hair, checking his reflection approvingly as he did so.

'Wicked,' the bald man echoed.

Gaz looked at him and smiled. 'Yeah.' He walked over to the hand dryer and put his hands beneath it. Warm air began to blow automatically. He looked up as Glen entered the toilets. Gaz met Glen's eyes and furtively shook his head. Glen looked over to the bald man at the sinks; then he saw the man's reflection smiling at him from the mirror. He looked back to Gaz, who had finished at the hand dryer. Gaz smiled, patted Glen on the shoulder and steered him back outside.

'What's up?' Glen asked as they walked through the short corridor that led back to the public bar.

'I didn't want to say anything in front of that geezer in there. It's about our supply.'

'Oh right. That guy back there looks a bit fried, eh?'

'Yeah. Nice suit, dude,' said Gaz. 'Anyway, we need to reach out and make a new connection. I want us to start chatting any likely looking punters up tonight. You know what I mean? Nothing obvious, just testing the water.'

Glen nodded. 'Gotcha.'

Behind them, the door to the gents' toilet opened and the bald man in the tight suit came out. He smiled as he passed. 'Hi there.'

Gaz and Glen smiled lamely. 'Alright, mate?'

'Wicked,' replied the bald man. He stepped through the door and disappeared into the public bar.

'See what I mean?' Glen whispered. 'Nutter.'

'Yeah,' Gaz agreed. 'Nutter.'

They hesitated a moment, giving the bald man a head start, then went through the door and into the bar. Gaz glanced in the direction of the bald man's table. Three kids sat around it. There was no sign of the big guy. The untouched glass of lemonade was the only indicator that he had ever been there at all. Gaz looked around. Maybe the guy had come back, found his seat taken, and then moved somewhere else.

'Looks like he's gone.' Glen was obviously thinking the same thing.

'Yeah,' Gaz shrugged. 'One less potential hassle at kicking out time, eh?'

'Fuckin' A.'

They went back behind the bar. Gaz spotted the bald man immediately. 'Shit. No such luck.'

Glen looked and saw the bald man. He stood at the bar, surrounded by other customers. The bald man, happy to catch Gaz's eye, raised his hand. Gaz nodded to him and came over. 'Another lemonade is it?'

'Forget my wants and desires,' said the bald man affably. 'What is it you want?'

Gaz looked at him uncertainly. 'Eh?'

'In the toilets a moment ago. I couldn't help overhearing.'

Gaz felt his internal organs suddenly chill. Outwardly he remained unfazed. He looked at the bald man and gave a wry smile. 'Oh, we were just chatting about some shit. No big deal.'

'I can help you.'

Gaz gave a short laugh. 'Oh? Help me how?'

The bald man raised his eyebrows. 'You tell me.'

Gaz scratched the side of his nose thoughtfully. Other customers were trying to catch his eye, craning their necks or cocking banknotes. 'I'll, er, talk to you later, mate. Did you want a drink?'

'I have one,' the bald man smiled. 'Thanks.' He moved back from the bar. Gaz watched as he went back to his seat and sat down at his previous table amongst the kids who now sat there. The youngsters, probably borderline underage drinkers, stopped talking and looked at their new companion.

'Excuse me, mate?'

Gaz turned and saw the foremost thirsty punter waving a ten pound note impatiently. 'Sorry, mate. What can I get you?' He took the man's order and went to pour the drinks. As he did so he looked over again at the table. The youngsters were getting up and moving away. The bald man sat with an easy expression on his face.

Gaz wondered about what the big guy had meant when he said he could help him get what he wanted. If he'd overheard them in the bog, he knew what they were after was dodgy. Could he be a copper? No way; your undercover cop tries to blend in, not stick out like the proverbial sore thumb.

He gave the customer his drinks and accepted the money. At the till he spoke to Jimmy. 'Yo Jimbo, I think I might have made that contact.'

'Really?' Jimmy said, surprised. 'Fuck me, that was quick. Who?'

'You know that big bald weirdo?'

'Tight suit? The not so secret lemonade drinker?'

Gaz nodded. 'That's the kiddie.'

'No way?'

Gaz winked. 'Later, dude.' He smiled and turned to serve the thirsty horde. 'Right then, who's next?'

*

It was about twenty minutes before Gaz could get away from the bar to join the bald man at his table. He drew out a chair opposite him and sat down.

'What happened to your young friends?' Gaz asked.

The bald man frowned. 'Young friends?'

'Those kids who were sitting here a while ago?'

'Oh. Those young friends. I think they considered their conversation a little too personal for my ears.'

'They're not the only ones. Do you make a habit of overhearing personal conversations?'

The bald man smiled. 'I try to refrain from habitual behaviour; habits can define a man.'

Gaz took a second to digest this remark. 'Hmmm. Well, my ill-defined friend. What is it you feel you can help me with?'

'What is it you need?'

Gaz looked cautiously about. No one was paying them any attention. He leaned across the table towards the bald man and whispered. 'Hash.'

The bald man, who had leaned forward to hear better, straightened up and nodded slowly. 'I can help you.'

'What can you get?'

'I'll have to make enquiries.'

'When can you get it?'

'Same answer.'

Gaz brought his hands together and touched them to his lips as if in prayer. 'OK. Whatever you can get, I'd like an ounce to start with. Can do?'

The bald man nodded. 'Can do.'

Gaz smiled. 'Nice one, man.'

'Nice one.'

'Listen,' Gaz leaned forward conspiratorially. 'No offence, but seeing as how I don't know you from Adam, I'd prefer not to pay cash up front, you know? Rather, cash on delivery. Fair enough?'

'Fair enough.'

'Beautiful.' Gaz got the feeling that things were looking up. 'What's your name mate?'

The bald man paused a moment, as if he were reluctant to reveal his identity, then he smiled. 'Adam.'

Gaz considered a moment. 'As in, I don't know you from…?'

The bald man bobbed his eyebrows.

'Fair enough… Adam. I work in here five nights a week. Me and my mates over there behind the bar. We usually come as a package, but sometimes we do different shifts. You can deal with them just as if you were dealin' with me. We're like, one, you know?'

'You're The One.'

Gaz smiled. 'You know it, baby.'

The man who now called himself Adam smiled. He extended his hand across the table. Gaz considered it for a moment, then reached out and shook it. Adam's other hand enfolded Gaz's warmly in both of his. 'I know it.'

Chapter 12

IT WAS 5:15 THE NEXT AFTERNOON when Mick Nixon rode slowly down Charrington Street. It had not long finished raining and the Chopper's tyres hissed as they rolled across the wet surface of the tarmac. Mick counted the houses as he went until he found number thirteen. A big, tall, terraced house that looked exactly like its neighbours: tall, white and Georgian. Mick noticed all the houses had entryphone systems; at some stage they'd all been converted into flats. Number thirteen was no exception. Mick pulled up outside and kicked down the bike's stand before getting off and looking up at the house. Peter lived in the top flat. Mick looked up. White net curtain fluttered at the base of the open top floor window. Someone was in, thought Mick, either that or Peter left in such a hurry that he left the window open. He walked up the short path and located the door buzzer for flat three. He pushed it. The only sound was that of the button as it depressed into the casing. A moment later there was a crackling sound, followed by a voice.

'Hello?'

'Hi, er, Pete?' Mick replied uncertainly.

For a moment there was only a distant hissing sound, then the person at the other end spoke again. 'Who do you want?'

'Peter Reynolds.'

Another pause. 'The man who was here before?'

'Er, before what?'

'Before me.'

'Do you mean he's not there anymore?'

'That's right, he moved out the other day.'

'Oh.' Mick was surprised, despite his wide-ranging scope of possible scenarios. 'When was that?'

'I don't know. All I know is what the landlord told me. Apparently this Reynolds man ran off owing rent just recently.'

'I see,' said Mick. 'Not that it's any of my business, but you got in there pretty quick.'

'Not that it's any of your business,' the voice agreed. 'Who are you?'

'I'm a colleague of Mr Reynolds. We, that is my colleagues and I, were wondering where he was. No one has seen him since last Friday.'

'I'm afraid I can't help you. But if you do find him, drop me a note of his whereabouts so I can forward it to the landlord. He's naturally anxious to speak with Mr Reynolds.'

I bet he is, thought Mick. 'Er, I'll do that. Thanks. Sorry to bother you.'

The intercom crackled a moment and then fell silent, the guy had hung up. Mick looked up again at the top window. Whoever this landlord was, he didn't hang about when it came to getting new tenants. He must've advertised on Saturday, done the deal on Sunday, and got this guy in on Monday. Mick tugged thoughtfully on his lower lip. He looked at the other door buzzers, then, before he could think of a reason why not to, he pressed the one marked "Flat Two".

A moment later a woman's voice came through the intercom. 'Hello?'

'Hello. I, er… You don't know me but I'm a friend of the guy who was living upstairs.'

'Yeah?'

'Well, I was wondering if you'd seen him at all lately. You see, he's moved out and I don't know where to find him. I was wondering if he might've perhaps given you a forwarding address for his mail?'

'No. I never really saw much of him. He kept himself to himself.'

'No clue as to where he was going?'

'Like I said, I never saw much of him. I didn't even know he'd moved out.'

'Well, yeah,' said Mick. 'Apparently he went just the other day. Some new guy's in there now.'

'Doesn't surprise me. This is an in-demand area. I'm always getting bumf through the door asking me if I want to rent or sell.'

'Oh. Well that's a good thing I guess.' Mick shrugged. 'Anyway, thanks for your time.'

'No problem. I hope you find your friend.'

'Thanks.' The intercom crackled into silence. 'Thanks a lot.' Mick hesitated a moment, then pressed the bottom buzzer. Nothing happened. He pressed it again. Still nothing. The occupier was evidently out. Mick took a few steps back and squinted up at the higher windows of the house. He wondered if anyone was looking down at him from behind that fluttering white net curtain. He shook his head and turned back to the pavement. He climbed onto his bike, kicked up the stand and pedaled slowly away.

From the top window in what had once been Peter Reynolds' flat, Adam watched the man on the child's bicycle ride away. He recognised him as Peter's lunch buddy. Obviously, he was concerned for his absent friend. Never mind. Someone will take Peter's place in the corporate scheme of things soon enough.

'Don't worry. A new lunch buddy will come.'

Adam ran his hand over his head, enjoying the rasp of the stubble against his palm. He thought back over their conversation. His prepared story had sounded perfectly plausible to him. The question was, did it sound plausible to the lunch buddy? He leaned forward and parted the net curtain slightly, watching as the cyclist grew smaller in the distance. Watching, and wondering.

Lucy watched the man on the bicycle ride away. Nice bike, she thought, if you're like, twelve. What kind of an idiot rode a Chopper these days? She turned from the window and went back to her desk. She picked up the packet of Silk Cut and lit one, then sat down again and looked at the words that filled the PC screen:

Leanne pounded her fists against his hard chest but he grabbed her wrists and held them in his iron grip. Rick pushed her back and she felt herself falling onto the bed.

'No!' she cried. 'Get off me! Get off!' She felt her words cut off as Rick fell upon her and pressed his mouth over hers. She felt his tongue pushing at her lips and she closed them tight against him. He broke off his kiss and licked her lips lasciviously. She turned her face away and screamed, 'Help! Help me!'

'Scream all you want, Leanne,' Rick sneered. 'No one can hear you, no one can help you. It's just you and me.' Laughing, Rick reached down and pulled up her skirt.

'Keep that thing away from me,' gasped Leanne as she felt Rick's hideously malformed manhood against her. 'Keep it away, you, you freak!'

Rick suddenly cried out as if he had been speared by a hot poker. 'Arrrgh! You bitch!' he cried. He fell away from her and rolled off the bed and onto the bare wood floor. 'I'm not a freak! I'm a man, just like any other man! I'm just different!'

Leanne managed to get to her feet and straighten her skirt. She stepped over Rick where he lay rolled into a foetal position, his body curled up around his shame. 'Oh, you're different, Rick,' she said. 'You're cruel and, and evil. You would have raped me a moment ago if I hadn't told you what you surely must know already.'

'No!' Rick cried. 'I love you, Leanne. I thought that you might, that you might enjoy it after a while.'

'Ha!' said Leanne. 'Just like they do in the movies? Well not me Mr Galsworthy. The mere thought of sex with you, with or without normal equipment, is one that fills me with horror and loathing.'

Rick wailed like an injured thing on the floor. He sniffled.

'Now who's crying, Rick,' said Leanne. 'Now who's enjoying whose tears, eh?'

'I...' Rick sobbed, 'I...love...you.'

There was something about the way he said it that caused Leanne to pause. She was getting ready to kick his bare bottom and march out with her head held high. But now, she saw him for what he was: a child. A child who had never known love. For Rick's father, Galston Galsworthy, was a cruel man who cared for nothing but money. So it had been for generations in their family, and no doubt Rick was supposed to keep up the family tradition. But was he? Was this sad, sobbing child with the strangely gnarly penis a monster, or just a sapling whose natural growth had been thwarted and deformed by the dark and confined cage of his evil upbringing?

'Oh, baby,' Lucy flicked her ash. 'This is meaty stuff.'

The intercom buzzed in the hallway. Lucy removed her glasses and went to check who it was. She half expected the Chopper guy again, instead she heard a more familiar voice.

'Hello. It's Gareth.'

Gareth the cleaner. She looked about the flat. It was suitably messy. 'What time do you call this?' she snapped. 'You're early.'

'No, no, Miss Lucy. I'm on time. It's six o'clock exactly.'

She looked at her watch. He was right. 'Okay. Come on up.' She went to the PC and saved her work before switching it off. Then she sighed and went into the bedroom to get Gareth's French maid outfit ready for him.

Walking down the street towards home, Wayne slowed down when he saw the stranger on his doorstep. Then he noticed the man's finger on the buzzer of flat two. Forgetting the weight of the shopping bags that he had been inwardly cursing a moment ago, Wayne managed to put on a burst of speed that got him to his front door just as Lucy buzzed the stranger in. Pushing the door open, the man turned at the sudden sound of bustling shopping bags behind him.

'Hi,' Wayne panted.

The man smiled. 'Hello.'

There followed an awkward pause, then Wayne realised the man was unsure of how to proceed. He must be wondering who the hell I am, thought Wayne. 'I live here.' I'm not weird or anything. I've got my keys in my pocket, it's just easier for me if I follow you in.'

The man nodded his understanding and gave a polite chuckle before stepping inside.

'Visiting Lucy are you?' Wayne asked.

'Er, yes. Yes I am.'

Wayne nodded. 'Friend of yours is she?'

The man smiled awkwardly. 'Yes, she is, yes.'

'Nice girl, Lucy. A good neighbour.'

'Yes. I'm sure she is. Well, er, I must be going.' The man turned to the stairs.

'Tell her Wayne said "Hi".'

The man turned and waved. 'I will.'

Wayne watched him as he turned the corner at the top of the stairs and disappeared. Just as he was about to dig out his keys, he heard the sound of Lucy's door opening followed by her voice.

'Come on, Gareth. I don't have all day you know.'

'Sorry Mistress,' Gareth's tone was simpering. The door closed on whatever came next.

Wayne stood frozen in thought. Had he really called her "mistress"? He had, hadn't he. What the hell else sounded like mistress? His brain struggled to digest this strange new development. All kinds of images danced through his mind: the dressing gown covering the stockings and high heels; the frequent day and night visits from single men; the noises – aerobics she'd said. 'Aerobics my arse,' whispered Wayne as he looked up the stairs. 'I think she's working. A working girl.' Now that he had articulated the idea, it didn't sound that bizarre. 'An honest to goodness prostitute. In my building. Just upstairs from my flat.' He smiled and opened his door. Once inside he kicked it shut and carried the shopping down into the kitchen where he put it on the worktop.

'Fuck me,' he giggled. 'There'd be nothing to stop me just popping up there with a bunch of money and saying to her, "Alright, darlin' how much for some wild, illegal loving?"' He leaned against the fridge as he envisaged her embarrassment.

'How did you find out?' she'd say.

He'd wink and say, 'Intuition, Lucy, intuition.'

Then she'd open the door up and ask him if he wanted anything to drink and he'd say no. He'd look at her and say, 'I just want the kind of love a man can't ask his wife for.' And she'd smile knowingly. She'd walk over to him and take him by the tie (he quickly imagined a tie where in reality, one was never worn) and she'd lead him to the bedroom. Then she'd say, 'I was kind of hoping you might put two and two together, Wayne. I shouldn't tell you this, but I've been wondering what it would be like… with you.'

Wayne looked at his watch. Ellen wouldn't be back for quite a while yet. He touched his crotch. His erection strained against its confinement.

'Come on, Wayne,' Lucy whispered in his mind. 'Do it to me. Do it to me now.'

Wayne looked to the hall, to the toilet.

'Do it to me here, Wayne,' she begged. 'Fuck me, I can't wait for you any longer, sugar.'

'Yes,' he murmured aloud, as behind his closed eyes he allowed himself to be led into Lucy's boudoir. In his fantasy, his hands were reaching to open Lucy's dressing gown; in reality, they were shoving his pants down to the kitchen floor.

*

Half an hour later, having cleaned up after himself, Wayne sat watching *Countdown* with a cup of tea and a Penguin biscuit. His mental struggle with the conundrum came to a sudden end when he heard the distant sound of a door closing upstairs. His hand grabbed for the remote control and muted the TV. He listened with animal alertness as footsteps began to descend in the hallway.

Well, he thought, are you going to or not? Just step out casually and ask him. 'How was she?' 'Was she... good?' Shit, he'd sound like Eric Idle in *Monty Python*: 'Does she go, eh?'

He could ask him directly like that, but it'd be a bit fucking blatant, wouldn't it. Quick, decide, his brain demanded. The footsteps were drawing near. Just go out and see if he looks flushed, or if his clothes are dishevelled or something. He sprang to his feet and ran to the door. He stopped and composed himself for a moment as the footsteps descended to the last flight of stairs. He took a breath and opened the door. What he saw came as a surprise.

'Oh. Who are you?'

'Who are you?' the bald man asked. Wayne checked out his clothes: blue roll neck sweater, blue jeans and a pair of white deck shoes. He looked like he was off to the sailing club.

'I'm,' Wayne cleared his throat. 'I'm Wayne, Wayne Dolan. I live here.'

'That's nice, Wayne Dolan. I live here too.'

'Do you?'

'Top flat, number three. My name's Adam.'

'Oh. How do you do?'

'Very well thank you.' Adam smiled and turned to go.

'What happened to the other bloke?'

Adam stopped and turned back to him. 'He moved out last week. Ran out on his rental agreement. My name was on a list with the estate agent and I was notified of the vacancy immediately.'

Wayne nodded. 'Oh, I see. Well, nice to meet you, Adam.'

Adam smiled. 'Nice to meet you Mr Dolan.'

Wayne watched as Adam left. Once he had gone, he continued to stare at the closed door. 'What is it about that flat and weirdos?' He shook his head and went back inside.

Mick had been thinking about going home. He'd been sitting here for about three quarters of an hour now, staking-out Peter Reynolds' old building in the hope of finding some kind of clue to his disappearance. But what, he reasoned with himself, was he likely to discover? Did he think Peter would emerge from inside, or perhaps return incognito? No, but just looking at the place gave him a feeling of nearness to the mystery. He felt he could better analyze the problem if he were here, in close proximity to it. He decided he'd call it a day after he'd had a last cigarette. He lit up and leaned forward onto the handlebars to watch the house. As he did so, the front door opened and a big bald man in a blue roll-neck jumper stepped out.

Mick sank down to watch the man through the windows of the car he was parked behind. The man turned and walked up the street in the opposite direction from Mick. He had to be the guy from Peter's flat, Mick reasoned, since he wasn't the girl from flat two. Neither was he one of the two guys who went inside shortly after he himself had called at the front door earlier. Mick considered following the man. He looked at his watch; it was getting on a bit. His stomach rumbled noisily. Fuck it, he thought. He'd wasted enough time for one evening, he'd check out baldy some other time. He flicked away the cigarette and kicked up the bike stand. No sooner had he done so than the stillness of the evening was suddenly broken by the sound of distant drums. Bass drums to be exact. Mick stopped. Could this be Peter's late night nemesis at work? The three nude dudes cranking it up early? Mick steered his bike in the direction of Barrow Street, the road that wound around behind Charrington. As he did so, the dull thudding in the air grew louder.

Sally looked at her watch and wondered what was happening in *Dawson's Creek*. She looked at the TV in the corner of the room and sighed inwardly, knowing that even if she could turn it on, she'd never be able to hear it.

'Alright, Sal?' Glen asked.

Sally smiled wanly but gave no reply.

'Cheer up, babe. It might never happen.'

Sally smiled. 'It has.'

Glen frowned. He turned his attention to where Gaz, Kay and Jimmy were dancing in front of the fireplace. Sally had been trying to ignore the spectacle, but the trio were becoming increasingly unavoidable. She looked at the three of them as they moved with nauseating over-sensuality to the Jamiroquai CD they always seemed to play whenever she and Kay came around. It was like the three of them were getting ready to perform some kind of ancient pagan sex rite. No, she corrected herself, it was as if they were performing some kind of ancient pagan sex rite. Gaz and Jimmy were writhing up against Kay's body in a manner that was more like foreplay than dancing. It was, to use a popular term, gross.

She had met Kay after work as planned. Then, instead of going for coffee as planned, she'd allowed Kay to convince her that coming around to see these dickheads for coffee was a good idea. Naturally she'd objected, but Kay, as ever, had begged her to come on the grounds that she needed a girlfriend along with her.

'Why?' Sally had asked. 'You've been 'round there on plenty of occasions without me recently. I thought you were past the stage of needing moral support. In fact, anything to do with "moral" is surely an encumbrance in their place?'

'What do you mean by that?' Kay demanded.

'I mean morality doesn't seem to be something they particularly encourage in their visitors. Especially the females.'

'They don't have female visitors. Except me. And you occasionally.'

'I was talking about you, and me occasionally.'

They had walked on a short distance in silence before Kay suddenly stopped and turned to face her. 'Please, Sally. Just this once. It'd mean a lot to me. They like you and, well, it's not so, so…'

'Testosteroney?'

'Yeah.' Kay smiled. 'Not so testosteroney.'

Sally looked at her watch. 'Just for a coffee, then we're out of there, right?'

'Right,' said Kay, with the enthusiasm of a young girl whose parent is on the verge of saying yes to letting Westlife come to tea.

'Okay,' said Sally.

Now she sighed as she thought back to that moment with regret and annoyance. The mug they'd served her coffee in sat empty and cold at her feet. At first they'd talked fairly normally. Then the dope had appeared. After that the flirting started, and now this – this burlesque – had begun. She looked at them. What a bunch of charmers. Gaz took the joint he was smoking and turned it around so the burning end was in his mouth and the roach extended from his lips. He steered Kay's face to his and she closed her lips over the smouldering protrusion. Sally watched as Gaz blew and Kay inhaled. Kay suddenly fell back with an expression that suggested she'd accidentally inhaled a piano.

'Yeeeah, baby,' Gaz cheered. 'Hold on to it, Kay.'

Kay waved her hand to indicate she was doing so. She rolled her eyes comically, then let the smoke go in a long blue stream. 'Oh,' she coughed. 'Oh, wow.' She let herself fall into Gaz's arms and raised her mouth to his. As they kissed, Jimmy came up behind her and began to gyrate lasciviously against her back. Sally noticed with interest that rather than pushing him away, Kay seemed to encourage his behaviour by pushing her bum out towards him. Sally suddenly felt a tap on her shoulder. Glen stood unsteadily at her side, proffering the joint with a cheeky grin.

'No thanks,' said Sally.

'Come on, Sal,' Glen pouted. 'It's our night off. We're all going partying.'

Sally looked at Kay. Had she known this? She looked back to Glen and shook her head. 'No, thanks, I have to be going soon.'

'You're not are you? It's not even seven o'clock.'

'I know,' Sally got up. Glen looked horrified. 'Don't worry,' she assured him. 'I'm just going to the toilet.'

Glen smiled. 'Nice one.'

Sally left the room. She noticed all eyes on her as she did so and was glad to be out of there. As she headed to the base of the stairs the doorbell rang. 'I'll get it,' she called back into the lounge. She stepped over the bare, blackened wood floor from which the torched carpet had now been removed. The lock on the new, unpainted front door turned smoothly as she opened it.

A youngish-looking man in a suit stood on the doorstep. 'Hi, there.' He wore his tie slightly askew, loosened as one might do ritually when leaving the office. 'Do you live here?'

'No,' said Sally.

'Oh.' He seemed disappointed. 'Who does?'

'Who are you?'

'I'm, er, investigating the disappearance of a chap from hereabouts, and wondered if you – or rather the occupants – knew anything about it?'

'Oh? A detective are you?'

'Well, no, not exactly.'

He was familiar looking, Sally thought. She knew him from somewhere. She quickly took in his full appearance: medium height and build, cheap-looking navy blue suit, short dark hair; perhaps a bit too long at the back – a mullet, in fact. Then it clicked. 'No. I didn't think too many detectives rode around on Chopper bikes.'

'Oh.' He nodded and put his hands in his pockets. 'Yeah, people do notice that.'

'You go past my shop every day.'

'Oh? Where's that?'

'Stephenson's Books.'

'Oh, yeah,' he said. 'I know the one. Never been in there, I'm afraid.'

'You and everybody else. It's a bit off the average shopper's beaten track.'

The man nodded. 'My name's Mick, by the way. Mick Nixon. I'm basically trying to find a mate of mine who seems to have legged it for some reason that, well... I don't know.'

'Oh, really?' Sally nodded, not offering her name in return. 'I'm sorry to hear that.'

'Yeah.' Mick looked awkward. 'So who does live here?'

'A bunch of idiots. I doubt they'd know anything about your friend, they don't seem too concerned with the local "neighbourhood watch" programme.'

'Oh, party types are they?'

Sally smiled. 'They'd say so. I'd call them something else.'

A voice shouted from behind her. 'Who is it Sal?'

She turned and called back. 'Jehovah's Witnesses.' She waited, but nobody replied. She turned back to Mick. 'I hope you don't mind, but you really don't want to speak to them right now. They're all rather...' She tried to think of a polite term for their condition. 'Out to lunch?'

Mick nodded his understanding. 'I see. Like that is it?'

'It is.' Sally smiled.

The music stopped and the sound of laughter filtered out to them.

'Peace at last.' No sooner had Sally finished the sentence than the music resumed and a fresh blast of bass flowed over them.

Mick held a hand to the side of his mouth and pretended to shout. 'Spoke too soon.'

Sally shrugged.

'Well, thanks for talking to me. I, er, guess I'll be off.'

'Where's your bike?'

Mick indicated with a coy gesture. 'Behind next door's hedge.'

'Good move.'

'I'll see you then.' Mick held up a hand. 'Maybe I'll pop in for a book some time.'

'You do that. We could do with the custom.'

'I will.' Mick bowed slightly as he retreated backwards down the path.

'I hope your friend turns up.'

'Yeah.' Mick nodded. 'I'm sure he will. Like a bad penny.'

Sally waved and closed the door. She leaned against it a moment, listening to the overtly hedonistic commotion from the lounge: the sound of slap bass, the whooping and "yeahs" of the doped-up early evening revellers. What the fuck am I still doing here? She walked briskly to the lounge, being careful to avoid any eye contact. She ducked to pick up her bag and quickly turned to exit. No one had said anything; hopefully no one had noticed. She opened the front door and stepped out onto the path, pulling it quietly closed behind her. In a few moments she was walking down the road, the gentle evening breeze purging her of the smell of dope smoke and the thought of what she might have seen had she looked up in the lounge before she left. She'd seen from bending over that Glen's seat was vacant; he had to be up and dancing with the others. All four of them, squirming around in a giggling, funky knot. She grimaced. It was enough to drive you to death metal.

Chapter 13

ADAM STEPPED UP TO THE CASHPOINT and inserted the card as he had seen so many people do before. His viewpoint then had been from the ground beside the machine. Not today. Today he stood at the machine with his own card. It may have had the name "P Reynolds" embossed upon it, but it was his nonetheless. Peter kept a very orderly file of his banking affairs. He hadn't recorded his PIN number, but he had made a note of his password in the event of an emergency. Adam had phoned the bank and informed them of the loss of his PIN number. The bank had then very kindly mailed "P Reynolds" a new one. Adam now tapped the numbers into the machine. The screen invited him to select a service. He selected "On-Screen Balance". The machine then informed him he had £3, 249 to play with.

'Thank you,' said Adam.

A woman behind him in the queue wondered if he was talking to her for a second before she realised he was talking to the machine.

The machine wanted to know if he required a further service. He pressed "Yes", then selected "Cash Withdrawal". The machine asked him how much he required. 'Fifty pounds.' He pressed the corresponding button.

The woman behind him unconsciously took a step back from him.

A few seconds passed before the machine disgorged the money. 'Technology.' Adam smiled as he gathered the cash. 'What will they think of next?' He took his card and slipped it into the pocket of his trousers. He turned to the woman behind him. 'Don't know how I ever got along without one.' The woman smiled awkwardly. Adam turned and walked away. The woman mouthed a word that clearly began with 'F' as she stepped up to the machine and inserted her card.

A short time later Adam stood in front of an old building. It was long since abandoned by whoever owned it. The front door and windows were boarded up and the front garden overrun with buddleia and other wild shrubs. Over the front door, a crescent shaped, tattered awning projected about six feet from the building. At the end, in rusted metal lettering was the legend, "Chicago Club". The club stood apart from a row of terraced houses. The colonising buddleia had also found their way into the spaces either side of the building. Adam gazed at its grimey facade and wondered what it once might have been.

'Exclusive, I'll bet.' He patted the front wall. 'Now look at you. All shut up, windows all boarded and broken. What does that mean?' He stepped through the open gateway. 'Are you merely the husk? The corpse from which the soul has long since departed?' That felt better than his other explanation. 'Damned,' he whispered. He walked up the cracked and dirty path that led up to the front door. 'Possessed by tormented spirits.' He reached out and ran his fingers over the peeling red paint of the doorframe. The flakes crumbled away beneath his touch. He rubbed the tiny red debris that clung to his fingers thoughtfully. 'Just the husk, eh?' He nodded. 'Just the husk.'

He stepped out from under the awning and onto a path that had been trampled through the undergrowth around one side of the building. Around the corner he stepped into a litter of old cans and bottles. The smell of human urine and damp rot mingled with the perfume of the buddleia. Adam was no stranger here; he had found his way here in the dark on many an occasion in the past. Nor was he a stranger to the building's tormented spirits. As he came upon the side window where the boarding had been smashed in, he felt a wave of nostalgia for the life he had now moved on from.

He put his head in through the window. His eyes, unaccustomed to the dark, told him nothing. 'Hello?' he called into the gloom. Somewhere inside he heard something shift. He tried again. 'Anyone at home?'

More sounds of movement. Voices whispering, muttering. Then a voice shouted from the shadows. 'Fuck off!'

Adam smiled and climbed in through the window. Inside his feet crunched on broken glass. The room smelled powerfully of damp. He could see shadowy figures in the ballroom beyond and he waved at them. 'Hi, there.'

There was no response at first, then the same voice shouted again. 'Are you deaf? Fuck off!'

Adam laughed and walked into the ballroom. 'You ghosts still scaring away the living, eh?'

The remark caused the occupants to mutter amongst themselves a moment before one of them cautiously enquired, 'Dusty?'

Adam laughed again. 'I've been known by that name alright. Is that Harry Bates?'

'Fuck me.' One of the figures laughed and stepped away from the shadows. His features became slowly more distinct as he grew nearer to the wan light that filtered in behind Adam. 'Is that you, Dusty Gibbons?'

'Is that you, Harry Bates?' Adam asked in reply, even though he knew that it was.

'Fuck me,' Harry smiled. 'So that's what you look like under all that fuckin' hair.' He turned to the shadows that still clung to the gloom. 'It's old Fuzzy, look.'

The others began to move nearer, their voices now becoming more distinct as they muttered to each other. Including Harry, there were six of them in total. Adam could recognise most of them. One of them, Gordon, laughed derisively. 'Where's all that fuckin' mop gone then, Fuzzy?'

'I took a blade to my past and sheared away my years of doubt.'

'You mean you cut your hair off?'

'I cut my hair off.'

'Then why couldn't you just fuckin' say that then, you cunt?' Gordon scowled.

Harry laughed. 'Still the same Fuzzy, hair or no hair.' He looked at Adam's new clothes. 'Where'd you get the new outfit? Overnight delivery?' Harry referred to the bags of donations that people leave outside charity shops after opening hours. A popular source of wardrobe replenishment.

'No,' Adam brushed theatrically at the arm of his jumper. 'I got these during trading hours. Oxfam's finest.'

'You mean you paid for them?' asked another man, known as Zippy due to the large number of piercings in his lips.

'Correct,' said Adam.

'With what?' asked Gordon.

'With money. Cash.'

'Where'd you get money from?'

Adam smiled. 'A great aunt died and left me her fortune.'

'Bullshit.'

'Yes,' Adam nodded. 'It's bullshit. It's my way of saying mind your own business. Okay?'

'Or you'll what, slaphead?'

Harry Bates stepped in placatingly. 'Alright, girls, stop fuckin' about. This is no time for behaving like wankers.' He prodded Gordon's shoulder. 'This is no way to greet old friends, now is it?'

Gordon snorted. 'Old friends? Bollocks.'

'I like Fuzzy,' said an older man, known only as Griggs. 'Nice to see you, Fuzzy, boy.'

'Nice to see you, Griggs.'

'So, if you're a new man, rolling in the late great aunt's fortune,' said Harry. 'What're you doing here?'

'I'm looking for Toby.'

'That cunt?' Gordon turned back to the shadows. 'He's over there, snoring away in a pool of his own piss.'

Adam looked into the gloom by the far wall of the ballroom. He saw what could've been a pile of trash, then recognised the vague shape of a man. 'Sleeping you say?'

'Like normal,' Zippy confirmed. 'Sleep. Coma. One or the other.'

Adam walked over to the sleeping man. It was Toby alright. There was no pool of piss. But the odour of urine hung about the man in a way that suggested the pool Gordon referred to may've dried up since they last gave Toby any thought. Adam shook him gently. 'Toby?'

Toby's eyes opened slowly. 'Ungh?'

'Toby, it's Fuzzy. Wake up.'

Toby managed to speak. 'Fuzzy?' He sounded doubtful. 'Fuzzy's got hair, man.'

Adam smiled. 'I cut it off. The ladies like me better this way.'

The men behind him laughed at this. Toby shifted onto an elbow and squinted. 'Fuck, Fuzzy? You bald cunt.' He laughed. 'Crazy baldhead.'

'That's me.' Adam rubbed his scalp. 'Listen, Toby. I need to buy some dope.'

'What kind of dope?'

'Hash dope.'

'I can get you that, Fuzz. How much you want?'

'An ounce.'

Gordon laughed. 'Oh? Fuckin' auntie paying for your habit now is she?'

Adam ignored him. 'Can you get that for me, Toby?'

Toby sat up and leaned against the wall. 'Yeah,' he nodded, becoming more alert now. 'I can get you that no problem. Need money though.'

'I know that. I have money. How much do you need?'

Toby thought a moment. Adam knew he was adding extortionate personal expenses. 'A hundred quid?'

Adam nodded. 'Fine. Come with me.'

'Where are you going?' Zippy asked.

'Probably going to bum each other,' said Gordon.

Adam helped Toby get shakily to his feet. 'You okay?'

Toby nodded. 'Perfect, mate.'

'Good, let's go.' Adam patted him on the shoulder. 'I'll buy you a coffee or something.' He led the way back to the room with the broken window. Toby followed. As they passed the others, Adam waved casually. 'See you fellows later.'

Harry returned the wave. 'Don't you be a stranger, now.'

Adam smiled. 'I won't.'

'And next time,' Harry called after them, 'be sure and wipe your feet.'

Gaz and Glen were walking into town.

'Shame about Sally,' said Glen.

'Fuckin' shame is right,' Gaz agreed. They had originally planned to go clubbing, but since Sally's early departure from the scheme of things, Gaz had gone off the idea. Instead, their destination was The Northern Star, a big, noisy pub favoured by students and trendy youth.

'Why do you think she just fucked off like that?'

'I don't know. Maybe she felt herself getting the horn and fled before she did something she'd regret.'

'Like suckin' your dick, man.' Glen slapped Gaz on the back.

'She wouldn't fuckin' regret that, mate. She'd celebrate the occasion 'til her dying day.'

'Oh yeah. 'Course she would.'

'Seriously though. It might've been those Jehovah's Witnesses that called – when she got the door, like?'

'You think she ran off with them? Discovered God, an' all?'

'I dunno, do I? What else could it be?'

Glen considered. 'Maybe she doesn't fancy any of us?'

Gaz laughed. 'Maaate? Be serious!'

'I am. Maybe she likes some other bloke. Some bookish geezer. She works with books after all.'

'So what? I work with beer, doesn't mean I fancy drunk birds.'

'I don't mind drunk birds,' said Glen.

'You can't afford not to, mate. It's the only kind that find you attractive.'

'Fuck off, man.' Glen jostled him, starting a play fight. 'Least I don't have to fuckin' pay 'em.'

Jimmy and Kay, who had been walking on some distance ahead stopped and looked back. 'Oi!' shouted Jimmy. 'Leave it out, you two.'

Glen and Gaz broke off their game and Gaz waved to Jimmy. 'Alright, man. You go on, we're cool.' Jimmy and Kay resumed their conversation and walked on. Gaz waited for them to get a fair distance ahead. 'Seriously though, Glen. I'm gonna fuck that stuck-up bitch like she's never been fucked before. I mean it.'

'We're not talking about Kay here, are we?'

'No we fuckin' ain't. We can fuck her anytime. It's not her that interests me. She's no challenge, know what I mean? But Sally – now there's a different story.'

'She is better lookin' than Kay.'

'She's better lookin', yeah, but it's more than that now. It's that holier-than-fuckin'-thou bit, you know? That sort of "not good enough for me" shit.'

'You think she's like that?'

Gaz laughed. 'Just a bit, man. We're too common, maybe a bit too rough, y'know?'

'You don't think she'd like a bit of rough?'

'Oh, I think she'd like it, if she got it. But she won't let herself have it, see?'

'Yeah, I know what you mean. So what are you gonna do? Buy her some flowers?'

'No, mate. I'm gonna do somethin', but I don't know what – not yet anyway. All I do know is, afterwards, she'll fuckin' love us. She'll do whatever we fuckin' want her to. In fact, she'll fuckin' beg us to abuse her.'

Glen grinned. 'All right, man. Wicked. A spot of the old three-way penetration? Maybe a little girl-on-girl action?'

'If that's what you want, man. Her and Kay, doin' it for us on the mat while we wank off slow and easy. Maybe we join in? I dunno.'

'Fuck.' Glen flicked his fingers. 'We haven't had that scene for a while. Not since we got them two fat slappers from the estate.'

Gaz grimaced. 'Oh shit, man. Don't fuckin' remind me.'

'I've still got the camcorder footage of that one, geezer. I can show it to you if ever you need some wankin' stimulation.'

'No, man, that's fuckin' bestial. Pig sex revisited. Tape over it for God's sake.'

'Tape over it with Sally and Kay, eh?'

'Fuckin' right.' Gaz focused an imaginary camcorder. 'Get a close-up of Sally when she starts crying; we're all givin' it to her with our big dicks, and she's crying. I fuckin' love that, mate.'

'Yeah, nice one, man,' Glen giggled. 'I can't wait.'

Much later that evening, Wayne woke up wondering why his radio alarm had gone off in the middle of the night. Then he realised it hadn't; the music that had awoken him wasn't coming from inside the room, it was external. He recognised the bassline that thudded rhythmically all around him: it was "I'm Free", by the Soup Dragons. He sat up. Ellen mumbled something and rolled over beside him. Wayne clambered out from beneath the duvet and fumbled into his slippers. His mind was ablaze with curses that only consideration for his sleeping fiancée kept from his lips. He went into the hall, took his fleece from the coat hooks and went into the kitchen. Then he went out into the back garden where he located the Super Drencher among the shadows.

'I can see I'm going to have to start leaving this loaded.' He looked down to the back fence. Light from the house behind rose above it. Wayne could hear voices laughing above the din from the music. 'Unbelievable. Fucking unbelievable.' He picked up the Super Drencher and ran into the house. A minute or so later, he emerged holding the now fully loaded water weapon, its pungent ammo still warm inside. Happiness is a warm gun, he thought, and grinned. He walked quickly through the long grass, managing not to get stung by nettles, and came up to the knothole in the fence. He crouched down and brought his eye up close to the small circle of light. What he saw caused him to forget all thoughts of urine and basslines. 'Oh my,' he whispered.

As before, the curtains were open and the occupants visible within. Wayne could see three people by the big candle that flickered on the coffee table. In one corner of the room he could see a lava lamp warming up. Three people were seated on the couch. A girl and the two guys he'd seen before. They were all clothed, but from the looks of things that situation was transitional. The girl was in the middle. She was kissing one guy on the mouth, while the other bloke looked like he was licking her ear. Both of the men had their hands inside the girl's clothing. She seemed to be enjoying herself alright. Wayne noticed with growing excitement that she was rubbing the crotch of the guy she was kissing. Then the other guy broke off from cleaning her ear and started to unfasten his trousers. He said something and the girl stopped snogging. She turned around just as the guy's cock sprang free.

'Hmm,' murmured Wayne. 'Not much to be proud of there mate.'

Then a third bloke came into view. He was bare chested and carried with him a large plastic picnic hamper, the kind that supposedly keeps things cool and fresh on hot summer afternoons. The third bloke set the hamper down on the table and stood between Wayne and the people on the couch.

'For fuck's sake,' said Wayne. 'Get out of the fuckin' way.'

The third bloke obliged, stepping just far enough to the right to allow Wayne a view of one of the two blokes on the couch leaning forward to open the fastenings on the box. They all seemed fairly excited by this hamper. Perhaps there was like, ice cream or something in it? Maybe they were going to start smearing it all over the bird in the middle. Wayne's breath halted as they raised the lid of the box. The guy who opened it smiled broadly, just as the third bloke, the one who was standing, turned and pulled the French window closed. Then he pulled the curtains together, one after the other.

'What? What do you think you're fucking doing? You can't do that!'

He remained there, crouched and staring for a few minutes, hoping that the curtains would miraculously open and the show would continue, but they didn't. The erection that protruded from one leg-hole of his shorts slowly began to nod downwards.

'Typical,' he whispered. 'The one night there's a point to having their bloody window open, and they go and shut it.' He stood up dejectedly. Then, as if prompted by spite, he dropped down and put the Super Drencher barrel to the knothole. He targeted the area to the right of the window and fired. 'Might as well keep it ripe.'

Chapter 14

THE SMALL BELL OVER THE SHOP DOOR TINKLED as Mick entered Stephenson's Books. There was no one behind the counter. He peered into the depths of the store, but there was no sign of anyone, customers or staff. He turned and checked the sign in the front door window; the "open" side was definately facing out into the street. He raised his eyebrows and listened for sounds of life, but except for quiet classical music, it was silent. He shrugged, obviously she wasn't here. Fate was giving him a sign. He turned to go.

'Oh, hello,' said Sally. 'How are you?'

Mick looked back into the shop to see her emerging from a flight of stairs that led down somewhere below the shop. 'Oh, I didn't see the stairs. Hi.'

Sally smiled. 'Maybe if you'd gotten further than the doormat you'd've spotted them.'

Mick felt his cheeks reddening. 'Yeah.' He noticed she was carrying a large paintbrush and saw an opportunity to change the subject. 'Been decorating?'

'No,' She came up to the counter and put the brush somewhere behind it. 'We use it to dust the tops of books. It's very effective.'

'Oh. Excellent.'

Sally smiled. 'Well, I don't know if I'd go that far. But it's better than a cloth.'

'Good. I'll try and remember that.'

'Anyway. I don't imagine you came here for a bunch of domestic tips. How can I help you?'

'Oh, I, I just thought I'd pop in, you know? Say hello. Maybe buy a book.'

'Well you've come to the right place, sir. We have a fine range of books to choose from. And we say hello whenever the occasion demands.'

'Hello,' said Mick.

'Hello.'

'Nice shop,' Mick looked around thoughtfully.

'Thanks.' She noticed his bicycle through the shop window. 'I see you rode here.'

'Oh, yeah. It's my lunch break. I thought I'd get myself something to read, you know, help to pass the time.'

'Okay, what sort of book did you have in mind?'

'I'm not sure. Something good, I guess.'

'Lets get a bit more specific. What kind of thing do you like reading?'

'Oh, I dunno. Thrillers?'

'Any particular authors?'

Mick considered. 'Er, no.'

'What other stuff have you read that you enjoyed?'

'Lately?'

'Whenever.'

'I used to read *Man from U.N.C.L.E.* books when I was a kid.'

Sally smiled. 'Read anything more recently?'

'Not really. I'm a pretty busy guy.'

'I see. Out investigating disappearances and stuff, eh?'

Mick smiled. 'In my spare time.'

'Maybe you'd enjoy a detective thriller?'

'Maybe.' He glanced at the many titles that faced out from a nearby display. 'I was sort of hoping that you could perhaps recommend something?'

'Okay,' Sally invited him to walk with her into the shop. 'Something I like, or something I think you'd like?'

'Something you like. If I get something I think I'd like I'll leave clutching a copy of *Tin Tin goes to Tokyo*.'

She laughed. 'I don't think we sell that one, but I'm sure it's very good.' They were standing in front of the best sellers display. She picked one out. 'Ever read this?'

Mick took the book and examined the cover. '*Captain Corelli's Mandolin*. Can't say that I have. It's a film isn't it?'

'Yeah. They made a film of it, but the book's better.'

'Did you like it?'

'Yeah, I enjoyed it.'

'Do you think I'd like it?'

'Well, I don't know you, but...' Sally stroked her chin and gazed at his face with exaggerated concentration. 'I think... Yes, I think you'd like it.'

'Okay. I'll take it.'

'You don't want to read the back cover?'

'No.' Mick smiled. 'I'll take it on your recommendation.'

'Gosh, if only all customers were so easy to please.'

'Oh, I'm easily pleased, alright.'

Sally raised an eyebrow. 'I see.'

'I mean,' Mick stammered, 'I mean, I'm not demanding. I enjoy life without the need for... complications.'

'Hence your adventures as a free-roving private eye?' Sally stepped behind the till and scanned the bar code of the book. She craned her neck over the counter and looked down into the shop. Leonard had come up from the basement level and was pottering about in the sci-fi section. She quickly tapped in her discount and knocked 25% off the cost of the book. Mick watched the price fall on the till LED. He gave her a questioning look. She looked pointedly at Leonard then put her finger to her lips, 'Shhh.'

Mick nodded conspiratorially. 'Thanks very much.'

'You're welcome.' Sally put the book into a small carrier bag.

'Are you doing anything for lunch?'

'When?'

'Today. Now?'

Sally considered for a moment. 'No, I, er. I don't have any plans as such.'

'Can you take lunch now?'

'I don't know.' She leaned over the counter. 'Leonard, can I take my lunch now?'

Leonard looked at his watch. 'Go on then. It's twelve-forty, just in case your watch says otherwise.'

'Thanks.' She turned to Mick. 'Okay. I'll just get my bag. What's the weather like?'

'It's okay. Mild, I think about describes it.'

'Hmm, I'll bring a coat.'

She was glad she did. It was sunny, but there was a chilly wind as they sat in the public gardens, each with a packet of Marks and Spencer sandwiches.

'What did you get?' Mick asked, as Sally withdrew hers from her bag.

'Tuna and sweetcorn.'

'Mmmm.'

'You?'

'Egg and cress.'

Sally raised her eyebrows. 'I presume you won't be kissing the boss later?'

Mick's mouth was poised for a bite of the sandwich. He stopped and withdrew it. 'Really now. I don't see that someone with cat breath can honestly pass comment on someone with egg breath.'

Sally stopped munching her sandwich and turned to him. She smiled. 'Touché.'

Mick bit into his lunch. They ate in silence for a moment.

'So what's all this about this friend of yours?' said Sally.

'Peter? He's this guy I work with, or should I say, used to work with. He seems to have up and legged it somewhere without telling anyone. He didn't turn up for work on Monday and we couldn't get in touch with him. So I went around to his place yesterday to try and speak to him in person, but,' he shrugged, 'he wasn't there.'

'Wasn't at home?'

'No. I spoke to this bloke who's living in his flat, and he says Peter ran off the other day owing rent and stuff.'

'Sounds weird.'

'It does, doesn't it? Especially if you know Peter. He's about as weird as…'

Mick searched for a metaphor. 'As weird as this sandwich.'

Sally raised her eyebrows. 'Is it weird?'

'No,' said Mick. 'It's as egg and cress as they come.'

'I see. So Peter – he's as egg and cress as they come too?'

'He is, totally. But there's more. And this makes it even more mysterious.'

'Go on,' said Sally.

'Peter was freaked out about this tramp that he said was following him. He reckoned this guy was like, you know, up to no good?'

Sally nodded.

'Now I saw this bloke. Big feller, all hair and sunglasses. That was odd – how often do tramps wear sunglasses?'

'When it's sunny?'

Mick smirked. 'Anyway, I think old Pete's being silly, and I tell him so, but he won't have any of it. He's genuinely scared of this guy, y'know? So, later that day – we've just left work – I'm going home on my bike, and what do I see?'

Sally shook her head. 'I don't know.'

'Peter and the tramp together at a bus-stop.'

'You think the tramp followed him to the bus-stop?'

'I dunno. All I know is, they're both standing there, and Pete's looking pretty scared. Then the bus comes in and when it pulls out, they're both gone.'

'On the bus?'

'I presume so.'

'Hmmm,' Sally chewed thoughtfully, as if masticating the facts. 'Coincidence?'

Mick shrugged. 'I honestly don't know. It's a mystery.' He tossed a piece of bread to the growing crowd of pigeons at their feet.

Sally sat back and thought. 'And now he's disappeared?'

Mick nodded. 'Uh-huh.'

'Have you told the police?'

'What's to tell? I saw my friend at a bus-stop with a tramp. Please help?'

'Yeah, but there's suspicious circumstances involved, surely?'

'Is there? I mean, I thought he was being paranoid at the time. Who's to say I'm not just being paranoid now?'

At that moment the pigeons lost interest in them as the sudden clatter of myriad wings turned their attention to an old woman who had just walked into the gardens. She was throwing handfuls of breadcrumbs about. Pigeons from all around were flying in to join the fray.

Mick pointed. 'Check it out. Pigeon feeding frenzy.'

They watched a moment as the woman fed the bread-crazed birds. 'I wonder why she bothers?' said Sally.

'Maybe she's lonely?'

'Maybe. But pigeons?' Sally grimaced.

'Some people will do anything to be loved. Even if it's only by vermin.'

Sally eyed him curiously. 'Now, there's a charming thought.'

'Thanks.' Mick smiled. 'I like to try and keep things upbeat.'

They finished their sandwiches at about the same time as the pigeon woman ran out of bread. She stood in the middle of the shimmering pool of grey-feathered backs that clamoured at her feet.

'Thanks for asking me out for lunch,' said Sally. 'If you hadn't called I'd have probably just had a bun with Leonard.'

'The guy in the shop?'

'Yeah, my boss.'

'What's he like?'

'He's nice. I like him.'

'Are you and he...?' Mick enquired vaguely.

She laughed. 'Oh, God, no. Nothing like that. Anyway, Leonard's sexuality is kind of ambiguous.'

'Oh? What makes you say that?'

'I don't know... Leonard seems to find the whole idea of sex with anyone distasteful. But,' she shrugged. 'He just doesn't come across as in any way... straight.'

'So he doesn't find you attractive?'

Sally looked at him. 'Er, no, he doesn't, but that's not why I think he may be gay.'

'I see.'

'Stop it, Mick, you're implying I'm narrow-minded and shallow.'

'Am I?'

'Aren't you?'

'No,' said Mick. 'They're the last things I think you are.'

'What do you mean?'

Mick looked back to the pigeon lady. 'I dunno.'

Sally thought about pushing the issue but decided against it. She joined Mick in contemplation of the pigeon lady. A few moments passed. 'Plenty of people think I'm attractive. I don't need to go chasing after a camp old bookshop owner.'

'I can't say I'm surprised.'

'By what?'

'The fact that plenty of people find you attractive.' Mick kept his eyes on the pigeon lady and her adoring flock. 'You're a very attractive person.'

The remark caught Sally by surprise. Embarrassed, she replied, 'Thank you. I think.'

There was a pause. Then Mick turned to her and cleared his throat theatrically.

She looked at him. 'What?'

Mick beckoned her attention to himself and cleared his throat again. He looked at her expectantly.

'I don't get it.'

'I said you were a very attractive person, right? Now I don't mean that in a fresh-type way. I'm just commenting on you as a person.'

'Yeah. And?'

Mick fluttered his eyelashes.

Sally smiled. 'Oh, right. My turn is it? Okay, you're a very attractive person too.'

'Thank you. You're very attractive as well.'

'I know. You already told me.'

'I just thought I'd remind you.'

'Thanks. Listen, it's coming up on half past. Oughtn't you be getting back to work?'

Mick looked at his watch. 'Yeah, I had.' He turned to her. 'Do you want to do this again sometime? Maybe tomorrow?'

'Sure. It's been nice.'

'It has, hasn't it?'

'Yeah. It's not everyday I get to have lunch with someone as attractive as me.'

'Oh, you're too kind.'

Sally smiled. 'Yes, you know maybe I am being a little over-generous.'

'No, no. I think you're being very fair. Very fair indeed.' He got up and mounted his bike. 'How about tomorrow? Here? Same time, same place?'

'It's a date.'

'Fabulous.' Mick kicked up the bike stand. 'Well, I'll see you, then.'

'Okay. Enjoy the book.'

'I will.' Mick proudly shifted the gear stick into first. Sally held up a hand. He waved. 'Bye.'

Sally watched Mick cycle away along the winding paths. He looked slightly absurd on the bicycle. Not all the height adjustment in the world could disguise the fact that it was basically a kid's bike. Yet he evidently didn't care. 'What an odd guy.' She smiled. 'Nutter more like.'

Since the dawning of his initial conviction that Lucy was up to more than a punishing aerobic schedule, Wayne had been monitoring any activity upstairs with an interest bordering on obsession. He hadn't revealed his suspicions to Ellen. There were some things, he felt, that a fiancée didn't need to know. That they were living under a knocking shop certainly fell into that category. For this reason he kept his careful study of Lucy's world confined to such times as when Ellen was out; times like now.

Wayne sat alone on the couch, watching the ceiling and listening with the keenness of an owl on a moonless night. Twenty minutes ago a man had gone upstairs and was currently indulging in some moist, pulse-pounding transaction that left Wayne dry in the mouth with the mere imagining of it. He was trying not to imagine it, but it was hard. He licked his lips. It was the middle of the afternoon, Ellen was out at work and not due home for some time.

He waited, a cup of tea on the coffee table before him. Every now and then he'd take a sip, careful not to slurp it in case he missed a vital sound from above. Eventually, forty-five minutes after she'd buzzed the guy into the building, Wayne heard the sound of Lucy's door. There was no mistaking the sound of the door; since his last error, he'd trained himself to know every audible nuance of that particular portal.

Wayne leapt to his feet and scurried to the door of his flat. He could hear footsteps descending the stairs outside. He waited, barely breathing, with his ear pressed to the wood. He imagined the man's feet as they approached the last step, then touched the hall carpet, then... Wayne opened the door and leaned nonchalantly out into the hall. He took a second to appraise the man: middle-aged, lightweight, pencil moustache, blazer – no problem.

'Alright, sir?'

The man stopped, evidently taken aback. 'I'm sorry?'

Wayne nodded to the top of the stairs. 'Everything... satisfactory?'

The man looked upstairs, then dubiously back at Wayne.

Wayne saw the need for further prompting. 'Just making sure that things are... as they should be.'

The man replied cautiously 'Yes. Everything's... as it should be.' He scratched the side of his nose. 'You are?'

Wayne smiled. 'Oh, I'm just a caretaker of sorts. I rarely make myself known to the, er, visitors. But, you know, occasionally I like to make sure things are,' Wayne winked, 'as they should be.'

The man nodded, a smile hinting at the corners of his mouth. 'I see. Well, you needn't trouble yourself in that respect. Everything is very satisfactory. Definitely... as it should be.'

'Good. Excellent.' Wayne took the man's hand and shook it warmly. 'I'll be sure to pass the compliment along.'

The man gave a short but hearty laugh. 'Oh, there's no need for that, I never shirk on extending my gratitude, you know.'

'Of course. Well, sorry to have detained you, sir.'

'Not at all. Cheerio.'

'Good day to you, sir. Cheerio.' Wayne watched the man close the front door before withdrawing his head back into the flat. He giggled, mimicking himself, 'A caretaker of sorts indeed.' He walked swiftly into the bedroom and picked up his wallet from the dresser. He pulled out the wad of notes he'd withdrawn from the cashpoint earlier on that day and stuffed them into the pocket of his jeans. Then he took a deep breath. 'Easy boy, stay cool now. Stay very fucking cool.' It was no use. He looked up to the ceiling and began to giggle uncontrollably.

Lucy picked the ball gag up from the floor where it had fallen fifteen minutes earlier and grimaced. Bernard was a sweet man but he drooled like a dog on hot day. She walked to the kitchen dangling the gag by its straps and dumped it into the washing-up bowl along with a plate, some cutlery and about half a dozen coffee mugs. Lucy had a vast amount of mugs for a woman living alone, not because she had a vast amount of friends around for regular coffee mornings, but because she hated washing up. She put the kettle on, opened the cupboard and took out a fresh mug.

She was wearing a schoolmaster's gown and mortarboard. They belonged to Bernard, but like many of her customers, he chose to leave his equipment here. Her wardrobe was full of such outfits. She often thought she could run off and start a new life as the proprietor of a costume shop.

'As if by magic, a shopkeeper appeared.' She smiled, wondering what Mr Benn would make of her costumes. 'Oh, he'd be a regular. He's just the type.'

The kettle boiled and switched itself off. As she opened the fridge to get the milk there was a knock at the front door. She frowned. Who the hell could this be? She walked down the hall, removing the mortarboard as she did so. 'Who is it?'

'It's Wayne.'

Wayne? she thought. Who?

As if reading her thoughts, the voice on the other side of the door added, 'From downstairs.'

'Oh. Hang on.' She sighed irritably, what on earth could that prick want? She changed into her dressing gown and slipped on the safety chain on before opening the door.

Wayne stood grinning like an idiot. 'Hi.'

'What is it, Wayne? Was I too loud again? I'm sorry, but I...'

'No,' Wayne interrupted. 'No you weren't too loud, considering.'

'Considering what?'

Wayne smiled. 'Considering what you were up to.'

'What do you mean?'

Wayne looked down at his feet for a moment before bringing his eyes level with hers. 'How much?'

'What?'

'Oh, come on,' said Wayne. 'How much? I know what's going on up here.'

Lucy shook her head in disbelief and went to close the door. 'Goodbye, Wayne.' The door stopped as it encountered Wayne's foot.

'I'm serious. I've got money.'

'I'm serious too, dickhead! Now fuck off before I call the police.'

'Why would you do that, Lucy? Has prostitution suddenly become a legal profession in this country?'

'I don't know what you're talking about.'

'Don't you? Aerobics? Aerobics with a regular clientele of sorry-looking blokes?' Wayne smiled. 'I don't think so.'

Lucy's voice took on a harder, colder tone. 'What do want?'

Wayne held up his cash-swollen wallet. 'I want you.'

'I don't do that sort of thing. Nobody has me, Wayne. I punish.'

Wayne seemed momentarily nonplussed by this revelation. He nodded slowly, as if thinking it over.

'And anyway, I wouldn't have anything to do with the likes of you. My clients are gentlemen. Sad, maybe, but they're good at heart.' She shoved the door against his foot for emphasis. 'I choose my clients, Wayne. And I certainly don't choose you.'

Wayne looked hurt. 'What's wrong with me?'

'Oh, you don't find something un-gentlemanly about this whole scenario? You come up here, making propositions and thrusting money at me! It's not exactly David Niven-like is it?'

Wayne smiled. 'Okay, so what? I don't think the landlord would take kindly to the fact that you're running a brothel under his roof.'

'I own this flat, you shit. I don't have a landlord.'

'You don't own the freehold,' Wayne sang in a manner that did nothing to assuage Lucy's loathing. She looked at him balefully as the fact seeped in. Wayne grinned. 'That's right, isn't it, old Mr Anderson owns the freehold on this place. We all signed a contract when we moved in. I don't remember a clause which said, "no whoring on the premises," but I guess some things just go without saying.'

Lucy fought to contain her rage. 'Go away.'

Wayne shook his head. 'No.'

'I'm asking you, one neighbour to another, please go away. If you want sex, I can give you some numbers – nice girls, not the kind you find advertised in phone boxes, they-'

'I don't want other girls, Lucy. I want you.'

'I've told you, you can't have me. I only punish.'

'So punish me.' His smile broadened. 'You can't say I haven't earned it.'

Lucy looked at him: the shit-eating grin, the bulging wallet in his hand and the way he twitched it at her like he was offering a carrot to a donkey. Oh yes, you've earned it mister. Her mind began to flood with possibilities. She could make this bastard so sorry he'd wish he'd never been born. She looked again at the wallet; she could get paid for it too. The playing field, she decided, had radically shifted in her favour. She smiled. 'Okay, Wayne.' Her professionalism eclipsed her emotions with a seamlessness that comes only from long experience. 'You've got a deal.'

Wayne frowned, surprised. 'You're sure?'

'Don't let's get into a discussion, Wayne. I'm fickle. I'll change my mind.'

Wayne tentatively withdrew his foot. Lucy pushed the door gently towards its frame and un-slipped the chain before opening it wide. 'Welcome to my parlour, creep.'

Chapter 15

TED TUCKER SAT IN HIS OFFICE staring out of the window. He sucked meditatively on the end of a biro as he watched the pub customers out in the beer garden. Behind him, at the other desk, his wife Fiona was working on the business accounts.

'Stop that Ted,' said Fiona without looking up.

Ted froze, confused. 'Stop what?'

'Stop tapping that pen against your teeth. It's annoying me.'

Ted withdrew the pen from his mouth. Had he been tapping it against his teeth? If he had he wasn't aware of it. 'Sorry, love.'

Fiona swivelled her chair around to face Ted's back. 'You're mooning over the lads, aren't you?'

Ted swivelled his chair so that he was facing her. 'Who, me? No, no I was thinking about, er, putting a swing or something in the garden for the punters' kids.'

'Why would we want to do that, Ted? All it takes is some kid to hurt himself on it and we'd be sued out of existence. We've had this discussion before.'

Ted shrugged. 'I was only wondering.'

'If I didn't know better, I'd say you were daydreaming about running off with Gaz and the boys to Thailand for a wild life of sun, drugs and ladyboys.'

'Eh? Ladyboys?'

'Well something's woken the old man,' said Fiona, eyeing Ted's lap. 'Please tell me it isn't the thought of kids on swings.'

Ted looked down at his lap and cursed the telltale nature of not wearing underwear, something he'd been experimenting with since Gaz extolled the virtues of "letting it all hang out". He spun his chair back so he faced the window. 'I was, er, I was thinking of tonight. Maybe we could... have sex, or something.'

Fiona laughed. 'Or something? What might "something" be, Ted?'

Ted turned to face her again, no longer abashed about his lap. 'I dunno, anything. Let's have wild, crazy, experimental sex.'

She turned back to her work. 'Don't be stupid, Ted. You've been listening to too many of Gaz's stupid fantasies.'

'They're not fantasies, Fi. Those boys get up to all kinds of stuff.'

'Of course they do.'

'They do,' Ted insisted.

Fiona put down her pen and regarded him from beneath finely plucked, disbelieving eyebrows. 'Like what? Gang-bangs? Oh good heavens how extraordinary.'

'Well I've never been to a gang-bang,' said Ted. 'Have you?'

'Of course not.'

'Well they have. You might dismiss it as no big deal, but...' He let the sentence trail off.

'But what?'

'Nothing.'

'You want to go to a gang-bang, don't you? You want to get stoned on that pot you've taken to smoking and go to a gang-bang, don't you?'

'No.'

'Yes you do. You want to sleep with other women, don't you?'

'No,' Ted's voice rose emphatically. 'I just... wouldn't mind if we got a bit more, I dunno, spice in our sex life.'

'Like what? What spice do you have in mind, Ted? Cumin? Nutmeg? No? Perhaps you didn't mean spice at all. Perhaps this is just some fresh, half-arsed attempt at getting me to smoke pot with you? Is that it?

'Well it wouldn't do you any harm. It makes you more... sensual.'

'Oh, so I'm not sensual enough for you?'

'No,' Ted floundered. 'You're very sensual. I mean, really sensual. It's just... Just a bit of fun, that's all.'

'A bit of a cancer-inducing giggle, eh? A bit of a brain- damaging hoot?'

'No,' Ted whined. 'It's not brain-damaging.'

'You haven't seen yourself when you're doped-up on it.'

At that moment there was a knock on the door. Ted was grateful for the interruption. 'Come in.'

The door opened and Gaz stepped inside. 'Alright?'

Ted brightened. 'Alright, mate? How's it going? I was just telling Fiona here how dope isn't brain-damaging.'

'That's right,' said Gaz. 'Nothing of the sort. It enhances your thinking; makes you more perceptive, more creative. Why do you think so many artists use it?'

'Like who?' asked Fiona.

Gaz furrowed his brow and thought for a moment. 'Er, I dunno, I haven't thought about that for a while.' Then, suddenly struck by enlightenment, he pointed at her. 'Oasis, er, The Doors, Jimi Hendrix. Paul McCartney – he likes a bit of a puff. He's come out in public support of smokin' he has.'

'I'm still waiting to be impressed.'

'There's lots of people,' said Ted.

'Cheech and Chong!' said Gaz.

'Lots of people,' said Ted.

'Of course,' said Fiona. 'Cheech and Chong. How could I possibly have any remaining doubts.'

Gaz leaned casually against the door-frame. 'You shouldn't knock it if you haven't tried it.'

'That's what I keep telling her,' Ted muttered.

'Why don't you have a smoke with us later?'

Ted looked up expectantly. 'Have you got some, then?'

'Not yet, I'm working on it. But you have.'

'Eh?' Ted shrank back into his chair. 'Only a little bit.'

'That'll do. We only need enough to make our point.'

'I suppose so,' Ted mumbled.

'Anyway,' Gaz rubbed his hands together. 'I just popped in to say we've arrived, alright?'

'Yeah, alright, mate,' said Ted. 'I'm coming out now myself.' He got up and joined Gaz at the door. 'See you later, love.'

'Don't piss off upstairs and get brain-dead on your stupid drugs,' said Fiona. 'You're supposed to be working tonight.'

As Ted left the office, he made the noise of a long-suffering husband who feels the pressure of his wife's thumb bearing down upon him. It was intended more for Gaz's entertainment than Fiona's. She looked at him grimly.

Gaz laughed. 'Don't worry Fiona, I'll keep him under control.' He followed Ted into the pub, closing the door to the office as he left.

Fiona frowned at the door. 'That's what's worrying me.'

Ted and Gaz walked into the lounge bar. It was early evening and there were quite a few people in, mostly the office crowd having a few pints after work. Ted shook his head long-sufferingly. 'She won't listen.'

'She's afraid, Ted. Afraid of the pleasure. You're like the serpent in the garden, only instead of offering her an apple, you're offering her a spliff.'

Ted chuckled. 'No, mate. You're the serpent in the garden. And now my guts are full of your bloody apples, that's my problem.'

'Whoa now, mate. You can't tell me I've made you do anything you didn't want to do. And there's nothing to stop you from packing it all in and going back to clean living.'

'Christ, the way you talk you'd think we were involved in an opium ring. It's only a bit of dope.'

'Don't tell me, mate. I'm not the one making a fuss about it.'

'Well neither am I. It's the wife who's getting all dramatic. She thinks I want to come along to one of your gang-bangs.'

Gaz laughed. 'Gang-bang! There's a phrase you don't hear too often these days. Very seventies' Ted.'

'Well whatever you call 'em. Orgies, love-ins, you know what I mean.'

'Okay,' said Gaz. 'But is she right, mate? Do you want to come along and get down to some group love, eh?'

'No I don't,' said Ted emphatically. 'Group love? Is that what you call it?'

'Love is a many splendoured thing, Ted. It has many names, but it all boils down to one thing.'

'Right,' Ted chuckled. 'Shagging.'

They were standing at the far end of the bar, away from any customers.

Jimmy was behind the bar, he came down to join them. 'Someone say shagging?'

Gaz pointed to Ted. 'Old Fiona reckons Ted wants to come along and get frisky with us and a bunch of chicks.'

'Nice one. Go for it, Ted.'

'I do not!' said Ted. 'She's just reading stuff into the situation that isn't there.'

'I see,' said Gaz. 'You mean if I were to tell you that we were going to be shagging a couple of young and willing babes tomorrow night, you wouldn't be interested in coming along and joining us, is that right?'

'Bloody right that's right.'

'Why's that, then?' asked Jimmy. 'Afraid of comparisons?' He crooked his little finger.

'No, I'm not,' huffed Ted. 'I've got enough down here to keep any woman satisfied, I can tell you.'

'Alright then,' Gaz laid a hand on Ted's shoulder. 'What if you could bring your very satisfied wife along? She could join in too. Would that make it more palatable for you?'

'What, Fiona? At a gang-bang?'

Jimmy laughed. 'Gang-bang. Nice one Ted, not often you hear that one these days.'

Ted ignored him. 'Oh, no. I can't see that happening.'

'Have you asked her?'

Ted laughed. 'I have enough trouble getting a shag meself, I don't fancy the chances of her going to a bloody gang-' He corrected himself. 'I mean, going in for group love.'

'Group love?' Jimmy savoured the phrase. 'Sounds racy, Ted.'

'Ah, well,' said Gaz. 'You never can tell, mate. It's always the quiet ones. That's what they say, innit?'

'No, mate.' Ted shook his head and looked stoically at his hand where it supported him on the bar. 'Not my Fi. No chance.'

Gaz and Jimmy exchanged knowing looks. Gaz was just about to suggest how she might be made to reconsider, when Glen came around the bar.

'Gaz, that geezer's here.'

'Eh? What geezer?'

Glen made an indistinct, but strangely meaningful facial expression.

'Oh, right,' said Gaz, deciphering Glen's cryptic gurning. 'Cheers mate.' He turned and slapped Ted on the shoulder. 'Put it to her, Ted. Tell her she'd have a right old time. You both would.' He stepped behind the bar. 'I gotta go and see someone. I'll see you later.'

Ted shook his head. 'That boy's a fuckin' animal.'

'He sure is,' Jimmy agreed. 'We're all animals at heart, Ted. It's just that Gaz and the rest of us are in touch with the beast, while – no disrespect – you settled-down types aren't.'

137

Ted, who had been subtly avoiding any eye contact, suddenly locked eyeballs with Jimmy. 'I'm not a settled-down type. I'm totally in touch with my beast.'

'Are you though, Ted? When was the last time you surrendered to the animal within?'

Ted waved a hand. 'Oh, all the time. I'm constantly surrendering to it.'

'Well that in itself is a mistake. We mustn't let the beast rule us; we must rule the beast. This is the mistake a lot of people make. Me and Gaz and Glen, we're masters of our beasts. If you always go surrendering to the beast, Ted, you'll lose sight of the man. You'll go feral. You'll wind up howling at the moon.'

'Well. When I say I'm always surrendering to it, I mean, in a controlled way. I'm able to touch my beast, but I'm still its master.'

'That's alright, then.' Jimmy smiled. 'Listen, I gotta go, there's thirsty punters lookin' at me like I'm a right lazy bastard, know what I mean?'

'Right, mate.' Ted nodded. 'Well done.'

Jimmy went off to serve and Ted opened the door that led up to the flat. 'What the bloody hell was that boy on about?' He mumbled. 'Flamin' beasts and lost men? What a load of cobblers.'

As he let himself into the flat, he wondered if maybe Fiona might be on to something when she said that dope made you soft in the head.

The man who now called himself Adam sat at his usual table in the corner. Gaz noticed the tight suit had gone and was replaced by a white T-shirt with "Choose Life" written on it in big black letters.

Gaz pointed at the shirt as he sat down opposite him. 'Haven't seen one of those for a long time.'

Adam looked down at himself. 'What?'

'Choose Life,' said Gaz. 'Wham!'

'Wham?' Adam looked puzzled.

'Wake me up before you go-go.'

Adam shook his head, bewildered.

Gaz sang the chorus line. 'Wake me up before you go-go, der-ner-ner-ner der nee-ner-ner.' He looked at Adam expectantly.

'A song?'

'Yeah. Remember? Early eighties?'

'Dimly.' Adam nodded slowly. 'They were strange times.'

'I'll say,' said Gaz. 'Thankfully I was only a kid. I spent most of that period running around with a plastic machine gun. We were too young to care much about gender bending and shit like that.'

Adam frowned. 'Gender bending?'

Gaz waved a hand dismissively, 'Forget it. Where'd you get the shirt? You obviously weren't a Wham! fan.'

'Oxfam.'

'Nice one. Cheap?'

Adam shrugged. 'Cheap enough.'

Gaz nodded. Small talk with this guy was a limited experience. He pinched his nose and gave a curt sniff. 'Any luck, then?'

'Yeah.'

Gaz, who had been sitting with an exaggerated air of relaxation suddenly leaned forward, excited. 'What did you get?'

'What you wanted.'

'Shit!' Gaz sat back suddenly and looked away.

Adam's brow creased slightly. 'That is what you wanted isn't it? I didn't misunderstand you?'

Gaz laughed. 'Fuck, no, man. I was just, you know – surprised.'

'Surprised? Why?'

'You know,' Gaz leaned forward again. 'When you're a kid, you ask for a BMX bike – you don't necessarily expect to get one. Then when you do it's like... Fuck!'

'Then you do want it?' Adam asked cautiously.

'Fuckin' hell, yeah. Where is it? You got it on you?'

Adam nodded.

Gaz cocked his head in the direction of the toilets. 'Come into my office.' He got up. Adam followed him.

When they were in the toilets, Gaz checked the stall doors. Once he was satisfied they were alone, he turned to Adam. 'How much do I owe you?'

Adam had given this matter a lot of thought. He had thought about simply giving the dope to The One as a gift, but he felt that such a gift at this stage in their relationship would be a mistake. It wasn't the done thing, and might cause The One to back away from him. At the same time he didn't want to charge too much money. If he were to win a place among The One's disciples, he would have to be an asset. Therefore, he had decided to sell it at less than he had paid for it, but not by too much. He reasoned that Toby would've added a cut of about £25 for himself, so took that amount off, and then a bit more. 'Sixty pounds?'

Gaz seemed surprised. 'Nice one, man.'

'Is that good?'

'Yeah,' said Gaz, not hiding his appreciation. 'That's really good, baby. Can I see it?'

Adam reached into the pocket of his trousers – part of a fine beige polyester suit he'd also purchased in Oxfam – and drew out the cling-filmed lump. He handed it to Gaz.

Gaz stepped into a stall, leaving the door open so Adam could watch him. Once he'd unwrapped a section, he pinched it; it was slightly tacky, slightly malleable. He smiled and sniffed it. 'Mmmmm, fuckin' A, man.'

'You like it?'

'Do I?'

'Do you?' Adam asked, confused.

'Fuck me, yeah. This is premium gear. Sixty quid? You sure?'

Adam nodded. 'For you, sixty.'

Gaz smiled, curious. 'For me?'

'For you.'

'Why me?'

'You're The One. It seems…' Adam felt slightly embarrassed. He sought for the right word. 'It seems appropriate?'

Gaz's smile lingered uncertainly as he considered this. 'Uh-huh. Yes, I see what you mean.' Then he brightened. 'Oh, Fuck yeah. Course it's appropriate. I can't think of anyone else more deserving, can you?'

Adam smiled and shook his head. 'No, no I can't.'

'Then that's fine all 'round.' Gaz grinned, any doubts dispelled. 'If you go back into the pub, I'll nip off and get the cash. Be with you in a few moments. Okay?'

'Okay.'

They left the toilet in silence with Gaz leading the way. As they entered the bar, Gaz turned back to Adam. 'I'll be back with you in a minute. Alright, mate?'

Adam nodded. He pointed to his chair at the corner table. 'I'll be waiting.'

'Alright, mate.' Gaz stepped behind the bar and went up to Jimmy. 'Fuck me if it isn't Christmas, mate.'

'What is it, man?'

'Fuckin' dope's turned up, innit. Premium gear. And guess how much?'

Jimmy shook his head. 'Tell me.'

'Sixty-fuckin'-quid.' Gaz whispered the words with the awe they deserved.

Jimmy looked shocked. 'No?'

'Fuckin' yes, man. Fuckin' yes.'

'Why so cheap?'

'Because that geezer knows what I've known all my life, and what every chick that ever spread her legs beneath me can testify… I'm the fuckin' one, baby.'

'Eh?'

'You heard me, Jim. Numero fucking uno, eh?'

'Riiight, man. I getcha.' A customer came up to the bar and made himself known. Jimmy acknowledged him, then said to Gaz, 'Show me later, geezer.'

Gaz patted him on the shoulder and went through the door that led up to Ted's flat. He tapped in the pass code and stepped inside. The first thing he noticed was the smell. He smiled. He entered the lounge to see Ted sitting in an armchair, eyes closed, with a pair of expensive stereo headphones on his head and a smouldering joint between his fingers. Gaz recognised the tinny music emanating from the headphones, it was Pink Floyd's, "Shine On You Crazy Diamond". Ted's face was a mixture of emotions: what looked like mild constipational twinges fluttered into lip-biting moments of either agony or ecstasy.

Gaz was unsure of how best to break in upon this private rapture. Eventually, seeing the joint would soon be little more than a roach, he opted for the direct approach. He went over to the stereo and turned the volume down. Ted's eyes opened and focused on Gaz with alarm. 'Eh?'

'Ted.' Gaz waved at him. 'You remember that order I placed for you?'

Ted pulled the headphones off his head and tried to regain some semblance of composure. 'Eh? Order? Er, did,... Oh, yeah. The order. Yeah.'

'Well it's turned up, mate.'

Ted sharpened up a little. 'Oh, right. Well that's great, mate.' He extended the joint to Gaz, who accepted it gratefully. 'Where is it?'

Gaz spoke as he inhaled smoke. 'Downstairs.'

'How much is it?'

Gaz held up his hand for Ted to wait a moment, then he exhaled. 'That's the thing, mate. It's premium gear, not the usual stuff.'

'Oh?' Ted was intrigued.

Gaz nodded and held up the joint. 'Makes this stuff look like cat shit.' He took another draw on the joint and passed it back to Ted.

'Oh, right. Expensive is it?'

Gaz nodded, then released the stream of smoke. ''Fraid so.'

'How much?'

'Fifty quid.'

'Fifty quid!' Ted choked on the smoke he'd been inhaling, searing the lining of his throat. He coughed and waved his hands as his eyes filled with tears. 'Fuck a duck!' Gaz went to the sideboard and poured Ted a glass of soda water, he handed it to him and Ted gulped at it gratefully.

'Fifty quid, mate,' said Gaz. 'You don't have to buy it. I can send the geezer on his way. He'll have no problem clearing it elsewhere. He just let me have first go at it, that's all.'

Ted, whose florid features were cooling thanks to the soda, wiped his eyes. 'Hang on, mate. Hold your horses. Are you buying any of this gear?'

'Fuckin' hell, yeah. You don't get your hands on this shit too often.'

'Alright, fuck it,' Ted waved a hand. 'Get me a quarter.' Then he paused. 'No, hang on. Make it an eighth. I can't really afford to spend fifty nicker on pot. If Fiona found out she'd kill me.'

'She doesn't have to find out, does she? I mean, who's going to tell her?'

Ted shook his head. 'She doesn't need tellin' mate. She can smell the change in my bank balance. I sometimes wonder if she hasn't got something like an old sailor's leg that stiffens when a storm's coming. Only her leg stiffens when I get my credit card out.'

Gaz sat down on the sofa. 'Sounds a bit unhealthy to me, mate. If you don't mind me saying.'

'Fuckin' tell me about it.' Ted looked intently into the pattern of the carpet as if expecting it to yield up strange truths.

'Surely you work hard? What you earn and how you spend it is your own affair. It's not like you've got a bunch of kids all need feeding and clothing and stuff.' Ted continued to gaze into the carpet. Gaz pressed gently on. 'I mean, if you want to let this stuff go, that's fine. But when we'll see the likes of this shit again is anybody's guess.'

'Oh, fuck it.' Ted got up and pulled his wallet from the back of his jeans. 'Get me a fuckin' quarter.' He counted out two twenties and a tenner and handed them to Gaz. 'And for fuck's sake, don't let it slip around the wife.'

Gaz took the money and grinned. 'Don't worry, mate. The whole thing's invisible. Like doing business in another dimension.'

Ted shook his head. 'Whatever.'

Gaz went to the door. 'I've got to go and get it. Should be out for about ten minutes. All right?'

'Yeah.' Ted picked up his headphones and retrieved the joint from the ashtray. He settled the headphones back upon his head and re-lit the dead joint. He grimaced at the taste, inhaled hot smoke, then sat back in his chair and closed his eyes.

On the staircase between the flat and the pub, Gaz stopped to pull a tenner from his pocket and added it to Ted's fifty. He hated to rip Ted off like this, but he and the lads didn't have fifty quid between them right now, and Ted was rolling in it. He assuaged his conscience with the fact that he had done all the legwork in getting this gear. It was he who'd made the contact, he who'd taken the chances, and if this Adam geezer was a nark or something, it was he who'd get nicked. No, he'd earned the right to take liberties with Ted's money. And fuck it, it was just small change to Ted, regardless of how he might complain. Gaz stepped through the door and emerged behind the bar. He avoided eye contact with a few punters waiting to be served and quickly stepped out from behind the bar and walked over to where Adam sat nursing a glass of lemonade. He sat down. 'Okay.'

Adam raised his eyebrows. 'What is?'

Gaz looked about nonchalantly. 'I got the money.'

Adam made a small, mute, 'Oh,' with his mouth and nodded his understanding.

'Listen. We really appreciate what you've done for us, y'know? I was wondering if you fancied coming back to our place tonight for a bit of a smoke?'

Adam seemed momentarily taken aback. 'Well, if that's OK with you and your friends.'

Gaz nodded. ''Course it is, man. Don't worry about shit like that. You're one of us now, y'know?'

Adam smiled. 'Well, since you put it like that. Thank you, I'd be… very happy to.'

'Excellent.' Gaz smiled broadly and got up, 'Well, I gotta get back to work now, but we finish in a few hours. I dunno if you wanna stick around now or just come back later on, but afterwards it's all back to ours for a bit of a smoke and a bevvie or two. Alright?' He held out his hand to Adam.

Adam took it and felt the money rolled in Gaz's palm. He looked at him and smiled, shaking his hand. 'Yeah.' The money changed hands, and the hands then separated.

'Nice one.' Gaz winked and returned to the bar.

Adam looked down at the money in his hand. He smiled; it was all so delightfully arcane. The One enjoyed mystery. He seemed to revel in the covert and the underhand. He looked up to where He now cheerfully served a group of young girls at the bar. He was so seductive, so beguiling. Adam smiled. Oh, what they could teach each other.

Chapter 16

WAYNE SCREAMED AGAINST THE BALL GAG for what had to be the hundredth time in half an hour. He hated the sound; it was desperate, agonised and incomprehensible. He sounded like a strange animal that lies wounded and frantic in some long forgotten trap. He tried to laugh at the irony, but it came out as a wet, muffled sob. He sucked air noisily around the gag. His exhalations were nearly always nasal, snot ran from both nostrils, he could taste it as it seeped in around his spread lips. Where was she? What the fuck kind of whore was she? She wasn't even fucking here! Anger coursed through him afresh and he strained against the manacles that held his wrists and ankles tethered to the wall, but it was futile. He tried to relax, tried to forget the pain that made his eyes water. She'd think he'd been crying, perhaps he had been, he realised. And why not? Jesus, he had a right to cry! He whimpered against his gag and thought back to how she had snared him into this nightmare. He remembered how she'd let him in, all friendly and obliging after he'd put her on the spot about telling the freeholder about what she was doing.

'What are you wearing under the dressing gown?' Wayne had asked her.

'Oh,' Lucy said, coyly. 'Just a few work clothes.'

'Can I see?'

'Follow me.'

'Can I?' Wayne could feel his cock stiffening; just being inside her flat was sexually intoxicating. She closed the front door behind him.

'Maybe. Come this way.' She indicated her hallway. 'I have to take you to where you'll receive your punishment. You know you really have been very bad.'

'I know. Are you angry?'

'Oh, I'm very cross with you, Wayne.' Her voice lacked any trace of anger. She seemed kind of… amused. 'Very cross indeed.'

Wayne smiled uncertainly. 'I'm sorry.'

'I know. You're a sorry man alright. But I can cure you. Once you've taken your medicine, you'll be feeling a lot better – at least on the inside.' Lucy led him down the short corridor and they stopped outside a door. 'Open it.'

'Lucy, I-' Wayne began, but she cut him off.

'Don't call me Lucy!' she snapped at him. 'You will call me Mistress, and I will call you whatever I like. Is that understood?'

'I'm sorry,' he hesitated a second. 'Mistress.'

'Good,' she whispered. Wayne noticed a change had come over her. She wasn't remotely intimidated by the things he'd threatened her with earlier. He thought she might be a bit, sort of, obliging. But this was someone he'd never seen. 'Now open the door,' she said. He opened it. She pointed. 'Inside.' Wayne stepped inside the room. The room was lit by a naked red bulb in the centre of the ceiling. Three of the walls were painted mat black, one white. The white wall held a variety of hooks upon which hung a number of whips and other curious implements.

'Nice décor,' said Wayne.

'Shut up.' Lucy followed him inside. 'Get undressed.'

Wayne bent down and began to untie his trainers. He felt mildly foolish, but very excited. He wondered how much longer she'd go on with this bossy persona. When would she start pleasuring him? He cleared his throat. 'Mistress?'

'Did I say you could speak?'

'No, Mistress.'

'Then be silent. You speak only when you are spoken to. If you wish to address me, raise your hand.'

Wayne, having removed his trainers and socks, raised his hand nervously. 'What is it?'

'Will you be undressing?'

'What I do is not your concern, you turd. What I do is punish you, and how I punish you is for me to decide. How you take your punishment, however, is up to you; you can take it like a man or you can take it like a baby. I don't particularly give a shit. You will pay me now, while your trousers are still on.'

'How much?' Wayne asked, taking out his wallet.

'Seventy five pounds.'

Wayne looked up, shocked. 'Fuckin' hell!'

'You thought perhaps I was cheap?'

'No,' said Wayne, regaining his composure. 'I, I just didn't think you'd be quite that expensive.'

'If you can't afford my treatment, you may still leave.'

'No,' Wayne reached into his wallet and took out some notes. 'I can afford it.' He handed her the money.

She took it wordlessly, checking the sum before slipping it into the pocket of her dressing gown. 'Where do you get it?'

'Get what?' Wayne asked, pulling his T-shirt over his head.

'Your money. What do you do for a living?'

'I'm an invalid,' said Wayne casually.

She raised her eyebrows. 'Really? Anything I should know about before I begin?'

'No. I hurt my back at work awhile ago. Couple of years actually, lifting stuff, you know. I got big compensation since they never trained me properly in how to lift stuff.'

'Really?' Lucy sounded disinterested.

'Yeah. Now I claim disability.' Wayne began unfastening his trousers. 'I'll probably have to go back to work someday. But for the moment, I'm just kind of, you know, milking it.'

'I see.'

'Just so long as you don't, er, treat me too rough.' Wayne winked. 'I should be fine.' Lucy said nothing. Wayne pulled his trousers down and stepped out of them. His erection strained against the fabric of his shorts. She looked at it with mild contempt. Wayne looked down at his pants, embarrassed. He had hoped for at least feigned desire on her part. Part of him felt deflated, but thankfully, not the part that mattered. He pulled the shorts down and stood naked before her.

'Step over against that wall.'

Wayne stepped clear of his clothes and walked across the cool, black linoleum floor. For the first time he noticed the restraints that were fixed to the wall. Some hung approximately at shoulder height, the others were fixed at ankle level. There were two sets of four: one set consisted of leather buckled straps with some kind of padded lining, the other set looked like police issue handcuffs. He turned and looked questioningly at Lucy.

She nodded to the cuffs. 'Get your back up against the wall.'

Wayne smiled, 'But-'

'Who said you could speak?'

The smile vanished from Wayne's lips and he averted his eyes downwards. He raised his hand.

'Yes?'

'Do you...? I mean, do I...?'

'What do you think, Wayne?' Lucy raised her eyebrows. 'Get in between the restraints. Then bend forward.'

Wayne nervously did as he was told.

'Close the bracelets around your ankles.'

'But-'

'Do it!' she snapped. Wayne did it. 'Now stand up. Close the left bracelet around your wrist. Make sure it's tight. I'll check it. And if I find it's loose, you'll suffer.'

Wayne did as she instructed. 'Ow!' he cried. 'I think I did it too tight – can I loosen it a bit?'

'Silence!' she shouted. Wayne shrank against the wall. 'Put your free hand up there by the other bracelet.' He did so. She reached forward and took the cuff. Her gown fell slightly open and Wayne chanced a look within the darkened folds of the towelling. His thrill didn't last long. She snapped the other cuff closed and he shut his eyes, wincing in pain.

'Fuck,' he hissed.

'Tight enough for you?'

'Actually,' he squinted at her, 'they're like I said – a bit too tight. Can you loosen them a bit?'

'Perhaps later. For now I want you properly restrained.'

'I'm not going anywhere,' Wayne said.

'Oh, I know that, turd.' She leaned up close to him, so close that he could smell her perfume. 'You most definitely aren't going anywhere. Not until you've gotten everything you've paid for.'

'Which is?'

She smiled. A cruel smile that seemed to reflect a deep and genuine pleasure within her. 'Punishment.'

As she moved away from him, Wayne felt the towelling gown brush against the swollen glans of his penis. He bit his lower lip to withhold a gasp of pleasure. His mind raced, forgetting the pain from his wrists; what could she have in mind? What would his "punishment" be? He had to admit, he was enjoying this. It was like nothing he'd ever imagined, let alone experienced. Then he tensed, she was leaving. 'Mistress,' he called timidly.

She stopped and looked at him over her shoulder with what he felt was a mixture of amusement and contempt. It was an expression he recognised all of a sudden, one he had fallen in love with as a child: it was how Julie Newmar's Catwoman used to look at Batman when she had him tied up and heading for a circular saw.

'Are you leaving?'

She smiled. 'Yes, for a moment. But I'll be back.' She sauntered lazily from the room and closed the door.

Wayne bit his lower lip and looked from one manacled wrist to the other. He tugged against them, but they were securely fastened to solid metal brackets. 'Fuck.'

The door opened and she returned. Something wet and dripping swung casually between her fingers. Wayne recognised it as a ball gag. It looked like something you'd see on a horse; all black leather straps and buckles designed to enclose the wearer's head. He also noticed her dressing gown had fallen open at the chest. The tops of her breasts were clearly visible above the black lacy bra she wore. In his fantasies she'd always opted for something kinkier, PVC or maybe rubber. As she stood in front of him, he found he couldn't take his eyes off her chest. 'Nice bra.'

'Thank you.'

'Not rubber then?'

Lucy frowned. 'What?'

'Your bra. I, er. It's not rubber.'

'How observant of you. Do you like rubber then, Wayne?' She pronounced his name like it was a thing beneath contempt.

'No, no,' he stammered. 'That, that one's fine. It's very nice.'

'It's someone else's idea of heaven. It also happens to be mine; it's comfortable, unlike rubber.'

'I like it.'

'I don't care what you like, turdykins,' Lucy prodded him in the stomach. 'Open your mouth.'

Wayne squirmed against the wall. 'What?'

'Open your mouth!' she shouted. Wayne's mouth sprung open like a child's in front of a big spoonful of ice cream. She came up against him and pushed the ball into his mouth. He felt her firm breasts press against his flabby ones; the thrill was only lessened by the taste of washing-up water. As she tethered the gag in place, he tried to object. All that came out was a muffled noise. 'Shut up, you prick,' she snapped. She finished securing the gag and stepped back to look at him. 'Comfy?'

Wayne was still trying to cope with the taste of soapy water. He tried to tell her the ball needed rinsing. 'Unghhhh,' was what he actually communicated.

'Good.' She smiled. 'Now then, you're probably wondering when the fun is going to start, aren't you?'

He stopped wrestling his tongue about the ball and nodded.

'Well,' she reached both hands into the pockets of her dressing gown. 'Now seems as good a time as any.' She drew her hands from the pockets of her gown and held up the contents for him to see.

Wayne's eyes bulged with horror as she snapped the pair of bulldog clips rhythmically before him. He tried to scream his protest, wriggling frantically against his bonds as she reached forward and snapped the clips onto his ample nipples. The agony was overwhelming, Wayne felt as if she had plugged his tits into the electricity grid. He thrashed against the wall, straining against the handcuffs that bit into his flesh as he struggled. His screams were just suffocated noise, like a man buried alive.

Lucy smiled that Julie Newmar smile. 'There now, are we enjoying ourselves?'

Wayne screamed at her, a primal howl of utter rage. The air that should've been expelled through his mouth caused fresh snot to pour from his nose.

'Silence!' she shouted.

'Unghhhhh!' he shouted back.

Lucy stepped up, took the bulldog clips between her fingers and twisted them. Were it not for the gag, Wayne's scream would have been deafening. She let go and hissed into his face. 'I said silence!'

Wayne managed to get himself under control, gasping about the gag. His saliva bubbled around it, running down his chin and dripping onto his chest.

'Good boy. Now, I'm going to leave you alone in here for a while so you can think things over. I want you to think about what a little shit you've been. Not just to me, but to your lovely wife, or whoever she is, downstairs. Then, if you're good. I might let you go. Do you understand?'

Wayne nodded.

She smiled. 'Good. I'll see you later.' She turned and walked to the door in a sensual, provocative manner that Wayne knew was entirely deliberate. She wasn't just punishing him, she was playing with him. At the door she turned and gave him a little wave with her fingers.

He snorted something incomprehensible in reply as the door closed silently behind her.

Wayne's mind replayed all this again as he stared grimly at the white wall and its range of sexual curios. He found if he could immerse his attention elsewhere, then he could, at least in part, distract himself from the pain and humiliation of his immediate predicament. That for brief, fleeting periods he could transcend the agony that radiated outwards from his nipples, and the throbbing pain from his wrists that were, mercifully, almost numb due to poor circulation.

How long had she been gone? Twenty minutes? An hour? Time was something that he was trying to forget, but at the same time, it was something that he couldn't ignore. He was supposed to be preparing dinner for himself and Ellen tonight. The thought sent fresh panic and anger through him. He bellowed against the ball gag and strained against his bonds. He pounded his bare buttocks and shoulders against the wall behind him, thrashing like a fish out of water.

He had noticed, with a mixture of sadness and indignation, that soon after she left him in here, she had started typing in some other part of the flat. As he bucked and bellowed, he paused occasionally to listen to see if the sound had stopped. Every time he did so, he realised it hadn't. Whatever she was typing away at, it was obviously more important to her than he was; more enthralling than this, his terrible suffering.

'For God's sake, man', his mind screamed at him. 'Is this what you're paying for? Chained up and gagged! Tortured! While she sits there in some other room writing letters to someone? Love letters probably – but not to you, you dumb fuck! Not to – '

Suddenly his mind fell silent. The typing had stopped. Wayne's exertions had left him a little short of breath. It was hard for him to hear her distant movements as his ears were filled with the sound of his breath as it huffed and sucked around the gag. This uncertainty didn't last long. His messy breathing stopped altogether as the door opposite him swung open.

'What the fuck do you think you're doing?'

Wayne tried to tell her he demanded to be released. 'Uh-uh-uh-e-e-e.' Fresh snot flowed as he tried to pronounce the letter d.

'Shut up!' Lucy shouted. 'Who gave you permission to speak?'

Wayne made further insensible noises as he tried to tell her he had to go downstairs and get the dinner on.

'Silence!' she pointed to the white wall. 'Do you want a whipping, Wayne? Is that what you want?'

Wayne fell silent. He shook his head.

'I didn't think so.' She sauntered into the room. 'So then. What's got you all worked up all of a sudden? You were behaving yourself so well, I almost forgot about you.'

Wayne huffed.

Lucy smiled. 'Is that it? Afraid you'd been forgotten?'

Wayne nodded.

'Oh, I haven't forgotten you, Wayne. Much as I might like to. It wouldn't be...' she stepped up close him and look down pointedly at his erect penis, 'professional.'

Wayne's breath came in wet, snuffling gasps around the gag.

Her eyes met his. 'You sound like a piggy at the trough, Wayne. A hungry little pig with its face in the swill.'

Wayne stopped breathing.

'Oh, I'm sorry. I'm obviously upsetting you. Perhaps I should leave?' She turned and began to walk to the door.

Wayne wailed against the gag. She turned on him and shouted, 'Shut up, piggy! You think I don't mean it when I say I'll use the whip?'

Wayne whined plaintively. Snot bubbled in his nostrils.

'Or perhaps you'd like that? Is that what this is? Provocation? Too shy to ask for it out loud, so you push me to it with your babyish tantrums? Begging, simply begging to be flogged!'

Wayne shook his head emphatically. His body trembled with the force of his denial, causing the clips on his nipples to wobble and send fresh tremors of pain through him. He bit down on the gag and tried not to howl. His erection nodded lazily, as if contradicting him. Bizarrely, neither the pain, nor the shame and rage he felt in his heart, had done anything to cool his ardour.

'Very well, then. I'll be merciful, for now. But be warned. Keep up these tantrums and I'll be back. And next time, I promise you some real misery. Understand?'

Wayne and his erection nodded in unison.

'Good.' Lucy left the room and kicked the door shut behind her.

Wayne released a breath around the gag. Drool dripped onto his chest. What the fuck was he going to tell Ellen? His quick, illicit shag with his neighbour was turning into an afternoon from which he'd return black and blue – in all the wrong places. Try saying you slipped on a bar of soap and bruised both your nipples. He gasped noisily, sucking in cold saliva.

Then of course, there was the question of the dinner; what was he going to do about that? He looked down at his cock, which protruded beyond the small dome of his stomach. Why didn't it go down? Why was it so excited while the rest of him was in such turmoil? Aren't we on the same team? Wayne closed his eyes and struggled to vanquish whatever thrill his libido was getting from all of this by thinking of woodwork. But without success. Every time he became even remotely aware of the pain that assailed him from his tender bits, his penis seemed to swell, as though inflated by the suffering. Seminal fluid slowly emerged from its eye and fell in a slow viscous teardrop to the linoleum. Wayne blinked as his view of the world began to grow watery. He bit down on the gag and tried not to sob too loudly.

Lucy added a splash of milk to her coffee and gave it a quick stir before returning to the front room. She walked past Wayne's dungeon without so much as a glance at the door. She settled down in an armchair and picked up the remote control of the TV. She'd done her bit behind the keyboard for today. The fact that she'd accomplished little was irrelevant. It was the effort that mattered. She sipped her coffee and considered Leanne and Rick's strange relationship. Was the full on shagging a good idea, Mills and Boonwise? She flicked through the channels; the flickering, changing images were like a thought process in themselves. Maybe Mills and Boon were just the wrong target publisher for the book anyway, she thought. Maybe someone else? *Penthouse*? *Playboy*? Surely she'd written too much for a magazine. 'Fuck it'. Carry on regardless. Worry about a publisher later, when the damn thing's done.

Her mind, firm in its literary resolve, now turned to the wretch in her spare room. She unconsciously pulled the front of her dressing gown closed. What was she going to do about Wayne? Her channel surfing halted when Jerry Springer's face filled the screen. She watched for a moment as the participants solved their problems in that unique and highly entertaining fashion. It was a pity she couldn't stick Wayne on Springer and let the audience deal with him. The caption beneath him would read: "Wants to fuck neighbour." Oh he's fucking me alright, she thought. Giving me a headfuck and a half. She took her cigarettes from the coffee table and lit one. How would she go about releasing him? What if he got violent? What if he stormed downstairs and phoned the freeholder? He wouldn't do that, she reasoned. I'd tell his partner and that'd be his relationship down the toilet. She realised how handy a camera would be right now – if only she had one. Then again, what if he doesn't really care about his relationship? I mean, he's cheating on her isn't he?

She shifted and felt the notes in her pocket. She drew them out and looked at them. She could throw them in his face and tell him to fuck off, but there was no guarantee that he would. And besides, she could use the money. It was, after all, a transaction that was in the latter stages of completion. She drew on the cigarette and stared into the exhaled smoke, as if the answer might form itself in the thin blue cloud. Maybe it did. A smile slowly spread across her face. She sipped her coffee and wondered where she'd left the cat o'nine tails. She really had to get into the habit of tidying up after herself.

Wayne had been silently praying for salvation when the door swung open and Lucy stood in the doorway. He blinked. She was holding something in her hand. Wayne recognised it, cold dread flowing into the base of his spine as he did so. A cat o'nine tails. Oh, shit. His mind began to race in panic. As it did so, his penis stirred to new heights of attention. Lucy took a step into the room. Wayne tensed. Oh Jesus, I haven't been making a fuss. I've been quiet. He tried to tell her, wetly, 'Ie-e-ie-uh.'

'What did you say?'

Wayne looked down, chastened.

'That's right, piggy,' she walked slowly into the room. 'Hang your head before me. If you weren't chained there I'd have you on your knees begging for forgiveness. Would you like that?'

Wayne didn't move.

'Or do you still feel some of the old spirit?'

Wayne shook his head.

Lucy looked down between his legs. 'You seem to be in two minds.' She gathered the tails against the handle of the cat and pressed it gently but firmly to Wayne's cheek. His skin turned white and bloodless beneath the pressure. 'Which is it, Wayne? Which of you is telling me the truth?'

Wayne made a noise equivalent to, 'I am.' She seemed to understand. It occurred to Wayne that over the years, she had probably grown to understand and interpret the language of the gag.

'You are?' she looked down at his penis. 'He seems awfully keen to disagree with you.' Wayne frowned, his eyes pained. 'Ah.' Lucy smiled. 'As I suspected. Still a bit of the old salt left in you, eh?' She let the tails fall from her hand and brush against his face. He whimpered. She drew the cat slowly down his neck. 'You want this, don't you, Wayne? You want the sting of the tails against your bare, trembling flesh.'

Wayne, who was again making the sounds of a pig at the trough, shook his head in the negative. This caused ripples of agitation to run through his frame and his erection bobbed up and down, contradicting him as always. She drew the whip down his chest, pressing it mercilessly around the clamped right nipple. Wayne screwed his eyes closed against the pain, biting the gag and trying to not scream.

'I'm sorry, Wayne? What was that? I'm getting mixed messages. You want the cat? Yes?'

Wayne whined, "no" to the best of his ability.

Lucy laughed. 'No?' The cat continued southward, its tails tickling his stomach. 'You want me to stop then, piggy? You want me to go away again?'

Wayne felt the first brush of the tails against his erection. He made a small, keening sound in his throat.

Lucy smiled and allowed the tails to tickle the base of his penis. 'What was that, Wayne? Come on, speak up.'

'Uhhhhhhhhhhh!' Wayne howled, shaking his head.

She chuckled as she drew the tails slowly along the length his penis, just allowing the slightest touch against his skin. 'Oh, you like it do you, Wayne? You enjoy it, you snivelling little shit.'

Wayne felt the tails tickle the head of his penis, he shuddered uncontrollably and nodded his assent. She brushed the tails slowly back and forth along the length of his erection. Wayne's eyes rolled back in his head. She continued repeating the slow rhythm. Wayne snuffled about the gag. He had been averting his eyes from her, almost afraid to look for fear of punishment. Now he chanced a glance at his tormentor. She was looking down to where she teased him with the cat, and he felt a fresh wave of fear and desire flow through him.

She looked up and caught his eye. He looked quickly away. 'That's right, pig. Know your place. You're right to fear to look at me.' She drew the tails over his cock, base to tip, base to tip. 'But then, since that's a lesson you seem to have learned. I give you permission. You may look at your Mistress.'

Wayne looked up at her coyly.

'Not at my face, you shit.' Lucy pulled open the front of her dressing gown. 'Look at my tits!'

Trembling, he did as he was told. His eyes bulged with fear and desire.

'Now look down at my panties, you pig! Do you still want to get inside them?'

Wayne did as she instructed. He was afraid to respond to her question for fear of giving the wrong answer. He was breathing so hard he thought he was going to have a heart attack. The tails were moving faster and faster about him.

'Do you still want me, Wayne?'

Desperately, Wayne wailed his equivalent of, "yes". He repeated it, over and over, closing his eyes as he felt his spine begin to melt.

Lucy recognised the sign. She took a few steps back from him and released the coiled whip to the floor. She took a fraction of a second to measure the distance as she drew the tails of the cat back across the linoleum. 'Well guess what, piggy?'

Wayne's eyes snapped open.

'You can't have me!' The whip flashed out, its many tendrils flailing across the bulldog clips on Wayne's nipples.

Wayne threw himself back against the wall, screaming against the gag as the twin explosions of pain sent a single shockwave down what remained of his quivering spine. His orgasm, which had been slowly simmering since the moment he stepped into the room, suddenly erupted. He felt as if someone had jabbed his prostate gland with a cattle prod. He felt himself disintegrate; felt his molecules disperse and scatter, dancing in the air like sparks rising into the night sky from a bonfire. He swirled up into the void, away from the world and all that crawled upon it, up, up, up… and then he was thickening again, re-integrating; sucked back into reality, into wholeness, into trembling, solid Wayne.

Lucy watched his ejaculation from a safe distance. It flew across the room and splattered onto the linoleum. She enjoyed a momentary sense of professional satisfaction before setting the cat in its proper place on the white wall. 'Don't bother me again, Wayne. If you come anywhere near this place again, I'll tell your wife or whoever she is downstairs all about what just took place. You can tell the freeholder if you want to, but the same applies.' She came over and carefully removed the bulldog clips from his nipples. Wayne moaned with almost orgasmic relief and sagged back against the wall. She reached into the pocket of her dressing gown and took out a small key. She held it before his eyes. 'I'm going to unlock you now. I don't want any trouble from you, do you understand?'

Wayne nodded dumbly. She knew the look well. As she had planned, he hadn't anything left in him; he couldn't kick up a fuss even if he wanted to. She reached out and unlocked his left wrist. His arm dropped to his side as if he'd been sleeping on it, a dead weight attached to his shoulder. The same thing happened when she unlocked his right wrist.

She produced a second key and held it out to him. 'You can do your own feet. And take out the gag yourself.'

Wayne took the key and slid down the wall to his ankles.

'We had an agreement, Wayne. A transaction. It's completed on both sides. You got what you paid for, even if it wasn't what you expected.'

Wayne removed the cuffs from his ankles and fell forward onto the floor. He reached up and began fumbling with the gag straps behind his head. Lucy turned away and left the room. When she returned a moment later, Wayne was lying on his side, free of the gag and massaging his jaw. She dropped a damp cloth onto his face.

'Don't forget to clean up your mess.'

Wayne took the cloth from his face. She nodded at his semen. He sighed and began mopping it up. When he was finished he found he couldn't turn to look at her. He stayed on all fours, staring at the cloth. The moment didn't last long.

'You can keep that as a souvenir. Now get dressed and get out.'

Three minutes later he emerged from the dungeon to see her waiting by the front door. She was watching him with open contempt. He looked at his feet and walked down to where she now opened the door. At the door he looked up at her. He cleared his throat. 'Thanks,' he mumbled. 'I, I won't trouble you again.'

'Just fuck off, Wayne.'

He stepped outside, his eyes once again downcast. His mind fought desperately for something to say, something to diffuse and lighten the atmosphere. Then the door slammed at his back, the force of it causing him to stagger forwards onto the landing.

'Bye then,' he whispered.

Feeling slightly disorientated, he walked cautiously to the stairs. He took hold of the banister, suddenly feeling great need of its support. Slowly, he lowered himself to a sitting position on the top stair. Shame, remorse and despair; a trinity of misery swelled inside him and forced a sob from his lips. He gasped, cramping all the muscles of his face against a sudden, almost overwhelming need to cry. Tears forced their way from his eyes and he wiped at them angrily. What had happened to him? This… encounter hadn't been what he'd come upstairs for. He thumped his fist against the wall. Why didn't he just leave when she first asked him to? His nipples were burning like two hot coals inside his shirt. Then he remembered the dinner, as if he didn't have enough to be worrying about.

He allowed recipe ideas to occupy his thoughts as he began to slowly massage the blood back into his aching wrists. The need for tears passed and the practical considerations of the aftermath began to assert themselves. He had things to do, a life to be getting on with. He had to put this incident behind him and pull himself together. He stood up, took a deep breath and stepped forward. As he slowly descended the stairs to his flat, he reflected that his nipples were going to need some considerable working on with Ellen's make-up. Quite how effectively he was going to hide these wounds of shame he had no idea. Perhaps there was enough make-up to conceal the visible blemishes, but all the Max Factor in the world couldn't conceal the strange and fruity bruises that were blooming on his conscience.

Chapter 17

IT WAS AFTER MIDNIGHT as Adam walked with The One and his disciples back towards their house. The One was talking about women. He had many insights into the matter that had never occurred to Adam, and he listened intently.

'You leave ordinary life at the airport,' said Gaz. 'As soon as you're on board the plane, there are robot women waiting on you. If you want sex there and then – they oblige – they have to, it's in their programme. In fact,' he added, 'there'd very likely be wild orgies on the plane.'

'Nice one, man,' said Glen.

'Yeah. No getting-to-know-you, just sex. Filthy, dirty, anything-goes sex.'

'I think I'd prefer it one-to-one in the toilet,' said Jimmy. 'It's more traditional.'

'If that's the way you want it, man, that's the way you have it. Anything goes on the journey to the Island of the Robot Women.'

'Sounds like a film,' said Glen. In a cheesy American accent, he announced, 'In Technicolor, starring Doug McClure, "Journey to the Island of the Robot Women".'

In similar tones, Gaz added, 'Also starring, Mary Millington.'

'Isn't she dead?'

'Isn't Doug McClure?'

'Who cares?' said Jimmy. 'It's not like it's a real film or anything.'

'Ahhh, but we could make it real. We've got a cast of robot women, don't forget.'

'So who'll get the Doug McClure role?' said Glen.

'Me, naturally,' said Gaz.

'What about Mary Millington?' asked Jimmy.

'We have a robot Mary Millington.'

'Niiice,' said Jimmy. 'I could fuck an Elizabeth Hurley robot.'

'Oh yeah,' Gaz agreed.

'And I'd definitely have Samantha Fox – when she was young.' Glen rubbed his crotch. 'The eighties model. Classic stuff, like a Model T.'

'Model T and A, man.' Gaz moulded an hourglass female figure in the air before him. 'T and A.'

The three young men found this hilarious. Adam, not wishing to appear humourless, chuckled along with them.

'Who'd you be shagging then, Gaz?' asked Jimmy.

'I already said didn't I? I'm having the Mary Millingtonbot.'

'Who is Mary Millington?' asked Glen.

'She was a soft porn star in the seventies. Maybe you're too young to remember, but her films were always knocking about in video shops when video first took off. They were like Confessions movies, but better.'

'I've never seen a Confessions movie. They all look pretty shit.'

'Yeah well,' Jimmy put a hand on Glen's shoulder. 'That's because our generation has grown up with proper porno movies. But older generations, they had to put up with that kind of cheesy stuff. Like my brother's generation: I remember when I was about thirteen or so, and my brother used to rent all those old Confessions movies to watch with his mates. The next day he'd go to work and I used to wank myself blind over them before he took 'em back in the evening.'

Glen made a face like he'd just stepped in something. 'Ohhh, nasty.'

'Oh, I dunno. I enjoyed myself. I remember you used to get a lot of TV birds in 'em. I remember seein' that woman from the Oxo ads in one.'

'No way, man,' Glen's horror deepened.

'Oh yeah,' Gaz agreed. 'And Liz Fraser.'

'Who?'

'She was your classic bird on sixties TV. In fact, she can be on the Island of the Robot Women too. I could be in a young Liz Fraser and Mary Millington sandwich.'

'Alriiight, man,' said Jimmy. 'A seventies soft porn-tastic love knot.'

They all laughed, and again, Adam chuckled along sociably. As they reached their house, Gaz turned to Adam. 'What about you, Adam? Who'd you be shagging on the Island of the Robot Women?'

Adam felt embarrassed. The idea of an island populated by sexually servile robot females wasn't something he'd ever contemplated before. His mind plunged blindly into the well of his adolescent memories searching for the ghost of a fantasy. He smiled, uncertain. It was important to respond, and quickly. 'Does she talk like the real thing?'

Gaz frowned. 'Eh?'

'The robot likeness of the woman I have sex with; does she sound like her real life counterpart?'

'Fuck, yeah.' Gaz fished for his keys. 'They sound like 'em, look like 'em and fuck like 'em. It would be just like reality in every way, except you don't get any bullshit afterwards. You can have them programmed to do exactly what you want, exactly what you like.'

Adam nodded, understanding. He paused a moment to consider further, then a name rose to the surface of his memory. 'Raquel Welch. I always felt she was someone I would have liked to get to know better.'

'Shag you mean?'

'I confess, that would've been nice.'

'Yeeeah.' Jimmy ground his hips salaciously and the others joined in.

Adam was pleased to have struck such a note of approval. He moved his hips in the same manner. This went down well; they all said, "Yeeeah". He made a mental note to do it again sometime.

'Alright man.' Gaz laughed as he opened the front door and stepped inside.

Adam felt happy too. He followed Glen and Jimmy inside. As he entered he noticed the scorched surface of the skirting board near the front door. He bent to touch it. 'Fire?'

'Yeah.' Jimmy nodded. 'Some nutter poured petrol through the door and it caught on fire. We had to go to hospital and shit. The nut left a note on the door warning us to be quiet.'

Adam recalled Peter telling him his side of the story. Without looking up, he smiled.

'That's terrible. Has there been any repeat of the incident?'

'You mean has there been any more petrol through the door? No. Not yet anyway. I reckon the guy's realised he was playing with fire, if you know what I mean. That is, if we caught him, we'd kick his fuckin' head in.'

Adam nodded. 'I'm sure that's the case. He realised he was playing with fire. Good pun.'

'Yeah.' Jimmy nodded and grinned. 'Wasn't bad was it?'

They went inside and closed the door. They went down the hall and into the lounge. Adam felt strange being in this room. He had watched it from his window through the telescope for days now. He felt he knew every inch of it, at least those inches that he could see. He suddenly realised the importance of not disclosing such knowledge: it wouldn't do to know where the bathroom was, for example.

'Hey,' said Glen. 'Let's show Adam the fox.'

'What do you mean, show him?' Gaz sat down and put his feet up on the coffee table. 'We haven't even seen it ourselves yet.'

'I mean, later. We'll have like, a fox watch.'

Gaz turned to Adam. 'We've got this fox keeps coming into our garden and marking its territory.'

'Oh? How?'

'He pisses on our house,' Jimmy sat down next to Gaz. 'Bit of a nuisance to be honest. It's starting to stink a bit.'

'Yeah,' Gaz agreed. 'We have to wash that patch down sometime. It doesn't go too well with the warm weather does it?'

Adam rubbed his chin. He thought of the man who lived in the ground floor flat of his building. He'd observed the fellow making occasional nocturnal visits to the rear fence with a toy gun. Was there a connection? 'This piss? Where is it?'

'Outside the French window.' Glen was searching through the CD collection. 'Have a look if you like, but shut the window after you, it stinks.'

'Who's gonna skin up?' Jimmy asked. 'I don't mind kicking things off.'

'Go for it, man.' Gaz handed him the new lump of dope.

Adam crossed to the French window, turned the key in the lock and slid it open. He stepped out into the night, closing the window behind him. The pungent smell of urine filled his nostrils. It was concentrated in an area just beside the window. He hunkered down and sniffed. He grimaced. There was no doubt about it; this wasn't animal. It was human. He looked to the rear fence where the man from downstairs came with his gun. He saw the dim light shining through the knothole. It was the same spot that the ground floor guy seemed so fond of. He walked through the long grass and weeds to the knothole. He bent forward to peer through. As he did so he noticed the smell of urine was here too. He frowned, straightening up and looking back to the patio. Then the penny dropped. The man from downstairs was evidently using some toy water cannon to pump piss into this garden. But why? The answer presented itself immediately; the man suffered from the same condition as Peter Reynolds: insomnia as a result of The One's late night music.

Adam smiled and shook his head. He returned to the French window. Music suddenly began on the other side of the glass. The sound poured out around him as he opened the window and stepped inside. He chuckled and turned back to the fence. 'Wakey-wakey.' He closed the window and rejoined the group.

'What do you think, Adam?' said Gaz.

'It certainly smells bad.'

'We should put some bread and milk out for him,' said Jimmy. 'Lure him in, like.'

'Yeah,' said Glen. 'We'd better turn the music off too. They're shy, foxes. Don't like loud stuff.'

The idea struck Gaz as a sensible one. He got up from the sofa. 'Alright geezers.' He crossed over to the hi-fi and switched off the music. 'Let's go for it. Glen, turn out the lights.'

Glen got up excitedly and ran over to the light switch.

Jimmy put the joint in the ashtray. 'I'll go and get the bread and milk.'

Gaz returned to the sofa and offered the ashtray to Adam. 'Smoke?'

Adam sat down in an armchair and accepted the ashtray. 'Thanks.' He didn't take drugs as a rule, but he felt that the circumstances dictated a certain companionability. Also, the smoke may help him better relate to the mood of his new friends, rather like American Indians passing around the pipe and sharing visions. He drew in the smoke. He held it in his lungs as he had done in his youth, then exhaled leisurely. He passed it to Glen who came and sat beside him on the couch. The room was dark and the tip of the joint glowed red as he passed it.

'Nice one,' said Glen.

Jimmy returned with a saucer of bread and milk. The moonlight shone in through the French window and Jimmy went over and opened it. He stepped outside and returned a few seconds later empty handed. 'There,' he said, closing the window. 'Dinner is served.'

Adam was enjoying the buzz. His head felt pleasurably light. 'You won't need bread and milk to attract this fox.'

'Eh?'

'He responds to a different bait.'

'What?' Gaz looked confused.

'Put the music back on and open the window.'

Glen laughed. 'You're kidding?'

Adam shook his head, a dopey smile on his lips. 'Nope.' There was an awkward silence as the three young men looked at him with bewildered expressions. 'That's been the case so far, hasn't it?' said Adam. 'You change the setting and the fox may become suspicious and stay away.'

'Huh-huh-huh,' Glen laughed, stoned. 'Yeeeah, man.'

'Yeeeeah,' Gaz nodded with dawning comprehension. ''Course he will. Fuck. Well spotted, man. Quick, lads, everything as it was. Jim, get that saucer back inside, Glen, get the lights back on.' Gaz got to his feet and trotted over to the CD player. 'Jamiroquai? He seems to like Jamiroquai.'

'Yeah, nice one.'

'Leave the lights off, Glen,' said Adam lazily.

Glen stopped and looked from Adam to Gaz.

Gaz shrugged his agreement. 'Whatever. Adam seems to dig foxes better than we do.'

Glen returned to the sofa and sat down next to Gaz. Jimmy came back inside and put the saucer by the inside of the window and sat down on an armchair. Gaz passed the joint back to Adam, who accepted it with a smile.

'Fuckin A, man,' said Jimmy. 'A fox that likes Jamiroquai.'

'Yeeeeah,' said Gaz and Glen, almost in unison.

Adam smiled dopily and said, 'Wicked'. He was pleased to note it went down well.

Wayne had been too late to prepare the dinner as planned. Instead Mr and soon-to-be Mrs Dolan dined on a couple of frozen pizzas. Wayne had also nipped out to the off-licence to get a bottle of reasonably good red wine. The overall effect had been successful. Ellen hadn't made any noises of dissatisfaction with the meal, and now, following an enjoyable evening's televisual entertainment, she had gone to bed. Wayne had found the evening a little less enjoyable than Ellen since his nipples were still extremely sore. He'd realised soon after his ordeal that the pain wasn't going to be a fleeting thing. Every time his body moved against the fabric of his shirt his nipples screamed at him. He found comfort by covering them with two large, square plasters. While this arrangement was comfortable, it was by no means perfect. He still had to explain the plasters to Ellen. Subsequently, he'd concocted a desire to watch the late night snooker as a means of getting her into bed and off to sleep before he came to bed.

'Tape it,' said Ellen.

'It's not the same.'

'Since when do you even watch snooker, let alone distinguish between whether or not it's the same taped?'

'I'm cultivating an interest in sport,' Wayne shrugged. 'The guys in the pub watch snooker all the time. It's a common topic of discussion. If I tape it, there's no guarantee that I'll get to watch it before the outcome gets discussed down the pub.'

'Well God forbid that should happen. I can't imagine the nightmare – the sheer hell – of not having seen the snooker. Such a crippling social disadvantage.'

'Look,' Wayne addressed himself to the coffee table as if it were a naughty child. 'I'm going to watch the snooker tonight. I won't be up all night and I'm not going to be hurting anybody. I just want to do something that millions of other people do in their houses all the time. Is that so weird?'

'It's not snooker watching that's weird. It's you watching the snooker. You hate sport.'

'I want to like it.'

'Why?'

'I want to belong.'

'You do belong,' Ellen rolled her eyes to the ceiling. 'Who among your mates is going to disown you if you don't watch the snooker?'

Wayne put his face in his hands. 'Why can't you just let me watch the snooker, Ellen?'

'Because I want to cuddle up to you. I can't sleep properly if you're not there.'

'You slept alright before we met, didn't you?'

'That was a long time ago. I've gotten used to you being there now. Anyway, we always go to bed at the same time.'

'Well, I'm sorry, hon,' said Wayne sympathetically. 'But I really do want to watch the snooker. Just this once. Please?'

Ellen looked dejected. 'Okay'. She got up and left the room.

Wayne sat and listened to her switch on the bathroom light, a moment later she was brushing her teeth. He relaxed a little. He looked out of the lounge door across to the bedroom as he heard her approaching.

Ellen stopped outside the bedroom door and looked over to where Wayne sat on the sofa, watching her. ''Night.'

'Night, hon.' He waved as she went into the bedroom and closed the door. He sighed and shook his head. He didn't like having to go through this snooker pretence. He sat back and used the remote to lower the volume. The next few hours were going to be hell. He hated snooker.

Now, the snooker raged in all its infinite dullness before him. Men slowly inched about a big table, leaning over occasionally to knock balls about. Wayne yawned and looked at his watch. He'd seen enough ball knocking to be able to lie about it tomorrow. He picked up the remote control and turned off the TV. He got up and made his way to the bathroom. Once he'd urinated and brushed his teeth, he wandered back into the lounge to undress. There was no point in undressing in the bedroom, the whole point of the exercise was to allow Ellen to get off to sleep before him. His stumbling about in the dark with his jeans around his ankles wasn't exactly a bucket of cold water in the face for the sleeper, but it wasn't far off. Once he'd shed his clothes, he inspected himself in the big mirror that hung above the fireplace. Had they not been square, the two pink plasters on his nipples would've been like crop circles in the middle of the hair on his chest.

'Crop squares,' he said as he ran his fingers over the tender patches. His wrists were okay. Once the indentation in the flesh had disappeared he was left with a couple of mild pink rings that were barely visible beneath the hairs of his arms. Wayne looked at his reflection for a long time; he stared into his eyes as if trying to fathom the workings of the mind that lurked behind them. All he found there was Lucy. He sighed dejectedly and went to bed.

Having pulled on a T-shirt from the top drawer of the dresser, Wayne pulled back the duvet and climbed gently in beside Ellen. The springs creaked and groaned as he transferred his weight onto them. He cursed silently, wishing himself thinner. Thinner and unbruised. He'd be spending the night on his back, that was for sure. Just as he had lowered himself to a recumbent position, Ellen stirred beside him. He froze.

'Wayne?' her voice was drugged with sleep.

'Shhh,' Wayne whispered. 'Go back to sleep.'

'I haven't been able to sleep. Not properly.' She cuddled up against him, wrapping an arm across his chest. Wayne bit back a scream as fresh agony exploded in his nipples. A small noise escaped from between his clenched teeth, not dissimilar to the sounds of the constipated as they strain against the immovable. Gently, he reached up and moved her arm down to his stomach.

Ellen suddenly sat up. 'Toilet,' she mumbled. She got up and left the room.

Wayne's mind raced. How could he avoid a further affectionate pounding? He hit upon it in a flash. Feign sleep. He rolled away from Ellen's side of the bed, smarting slightly as the flesh of his chest sagged against itself. He was just about reaching some kind of compromise with comfort when he heard Ellen return. In the dark, he shut his eyes and began to snore lightly. Ellen climbed in beside him and cuddled up to his back. She put her arm across his side and reached around his front. His elbow blocked her.

'Stop pretending to be asleep. You can't fall asleep that quick.'

Wayne pretended to rouse, he groaned dozily in protest. 'Wha-? What are you saying?'

'I said stop pretending to be asleep.'

'I was asleep. Until you came in and woke me up.'

'Oh, you can talk,' Ellen prodded him gently in the belly. 'It's not like you woke me up or anything.'

'You said you weren't asleep.'

'Not properly.'

'Well I was.'

'No you weren't,' Ellen reached down to cup the front of his boxers. 'If you were you'd be poking out here.'

'I would not.' Wayne moved her hand away, as if disgusted.

'Oh yes you woo-ould,' sang Ellen, reaching again for his genitals.

'Ellen!' Wayne brushed at her hand. 'Leave off. I'm tired.'

'Oh? Got a big day tomorrow have we?'

'No, I'm just tired.'

'How tired?'

'Very tired.'

Ellen began to move down the bed, her head going beneath the duvet.

'Very tired?'

'Yes,' Wayne's voice was losing conviction. 'Very tired.' She gently pulled at his hip and he allowed himself to be rolled onto his back. She began to pull his shorts down. Wayne bit his lower lip. Shit! It had been ages since anything like this had happened. He raised his bottom, helping her as she drew the shorts down his legs. But something was wrong. He felt a growing unease in the place where he should have felt another kind of growing. The realisation of an eerie stillness in his loins caused terror to prickle over his skin like a wave of static electricity. His stomach turned over. Oh, Jesus, his mind raced. Maybe she won't notice.

'Oh,' said Ellen. 'You are tired.'

Wayne clenched his teeth and grimaced. 'I, I told you.'

'Well, I'll just have to wake you up then.'

Wayne felt her tongue began to play around his listless cock. He closed his eyes and focused his whole being upon the sensation. Nothing happened. He felt her lift it and take it into her mouth. Oh, God please! he screamed his silent prayer. He could feel himself flopping about like a chipolata in a washing machine. In his whole life, never had he presented himself to a young lady's affections in anything less than furiously rigid condition. Desperately, he pictured Lucy as her dressing gown fell open before him. Nothing happened. He envisaged Pamela Anderson standing over him naked and lasciviously biting into a bacon sandwich, the melting butter dripping into his open mouth. Nothing happened. 'See El? I really am tired,' he said, trying to keep the pain from his voice. He felt her take his cock from her mouth and begin to manipulate it with her hand.

'Just relax, baby,' her voice was muffled beneath the duvet. 'Leave everything to Ellen. We'll get you up and standing to attention in no time.'

Wayne felt tears of shame and frustration begin to prick at the edges of his eyes. 'No, really...'

'Shhhh,' she cut him off. 'Just be still and enjoy it.'

Wayne felt a tear roll first from one eye, then the other. He pictured Lucy and Pamela Anderson in a lesbian clinch; he added himself as the object of their mutual lust. Still nothing stirred.

Then, as if by magic, salvation came. Music began to thud into the night from the house over the back. Wayne quickly wiped his eyes and groaned with theatrical annoyance, 'Ohhhh, Jesus. Not again. How can I relax with this racket going on?'

Ellen threw the duvet off her head. She looked up to him, his flaccid penis held between her finger and thumb. 'Forget it, Wayne, for Heaven's sake.'

'I can't forget it, El. Listen to it! It's louder than ever.'

Ellen listened, she nodded. 'It is loud alright.'

Wayne began to disentangle himself from her. 'I'll deal with it. A few rounds from the piss cannon should take care of those bastards.' He got out of bed and put his slippers on.

*

'Watch the hole in the fence,' said Adam.

'What hole?' Gaz squinted into the dark.

Adam pointed. 'See the small knothole there? There's a certain amount of light from the other garden that shines through it and makes it visible.'

They all looked. Jimmy saw it first. 'Oh yeah. I see it – about half-way down, not too far from the right edge.'

'That's it.'

'Oh yeah.' Gaz sounded unimpressed. 'What about it? What's it got to do with our fox?'

'Everything,' said Adam. 'You want to catch the fox? Go and stand very quietly by the hole in the fence. Very quietly, mind you. Don't even breathe.'

Gaz got up and handed the joint to Jimmy. 'Silent running, baby,' he grinned and tiptoed to the French window.

'Silent running.' Glen got up and followed Gaz.

'No,' Adam reached out a hand. 'Only one outside. The fox has to see things much as they normally are or he'll suspect a trap.'

'We don't want to trap it,' said Glen. 'We just want to see it.'

'Same thing in fox terms. Stay here. Only one to the fence.'

Gaz nodded. 'You guys wait here. I'll go to the fence. How much longer, Adam?'

'Should be any minute now. You'd better be quick. We don't want him to see you.'

Gaz stepped outside. He strode through the garden's overgrown lawn, conscious of the rustling of the grass as he passed through it. Once at the fence, he turned to the house and gave the "OK" sign to the others. He had to imagine their response as they were invisible inside the darkened room. He squatted down by the knothole and peered through it. Beyond was a messy garden. No foxes, just everyday garden shit. He looked back to the house, shrugged and settled by the hole to wait. Quite what he was waiting for he wasn't sure. Foxes and knotholes? Weird.

Wayne stepped outside. He went to a corner of the yard and moved aside an old canvas sheet. Underneath was a two-litre clear plastic container that had once held turpentine. It now held Wayne's urine; he'd been stockpiling it for occasions such as this when his bladder was light. He lifted the container and began to pour its contents into the Super Drencher. He shook his head as he reflected on what had just happened in the bedroom. What the fuck was going on down there? It had to have something to do with Lucy and what she'd done to him today. Had he lost his masculinity? Had she so humiliated him that he was now little more than a eunuch? The thought was both terrifying and plausible. What else could it be? It wasn't tiredness, and it certainly wasn't anything to do with these bastards over the back.

Suddenly cold urine began to overflow from the gun. Wayne grimaced in disgust and put the container to one side before screwing the cap back onto the Super Drencher.

He held it carefully, not wanting to get any piss on himself. He tried to get back into the spirit of things. Listening for a moment to the music that thumped into the night from beyond the fence. It worked. He gritted his teeth and set off stealthily down the now well-trodden path to the back fence. When he arrived, he hunkered down behind the knothole and peered into the other garden. There were no lights on in the house, but the window was open. Open! His mind reeled at the enormity of the bad neighbourliness. What were they doing in there? Maybe they were having sex with each other in the dark? He listened keenly for the sounds of orgiastic struggle. But there was just Jamiroquai. Wayne shook his head indignantly. Either they were so stoned they couldn't speak or they'd gone to bed and left the fucking music on. That wouldn't be a surprise. He took the Super Drencher and brought it up to the hole. He swivelled the nozzle to bear upon the area to the right of the window and pulled the trigger.

Gaz heard the sound of movement on the other side of the fence. But it didn't sound much like the stealthy patter of the four-footed nocturnal predator. More like the slow, heavy crunch of the two-footed suburban bloke. He smiled and pressed his ear closer to the wood. There was a pause, then the sound of something solid making contact with the fence. He was about to return his eye to the hole when a jet of liquid suddenly spurted through it. He fell back onto his behind, shocked, and watched as the liquid arced across the garden and rained down next to the French window. He looked to the darkened room where he knew his friends were watching all this and contorted his face with disgust. Then he stood up, placed a foot on the fence's cross beam, and pulled himself up.

Wayne didn't have time to register what was happening. One second he was firing righteous urine into the garden of evil. The next there was a scrabbling sound from the fence, and now he stood held fast by the hair.

'What the fuck do you think you're doing?' Demanded an angry voice from above. Wayne looked up and saw one of the blokes from over the back. He was leaning over the top of the fence and had his hand firmly buried in Wayne's short, but graspable locks.

'I...' Wayne stammered. 'I'm watering your garden.'

'I can fucking see that,' said Gaz. 'With piss!'

'I... ow!' Wayne winced. 'If you just behaved like civilised people, I...'

'What are you going on about? Civilised people?'

Wayne heard the sound of other voices approaching on the other side of the fence. He looked up as two other heads popped into view.

'Whoa, nice catch, man,' said Glen.

'Yeah,' Jimmy agreed. 'Fox in socks, or rather slippers.'

'You were saying something about civilised people, cunt?' Gaz pulled Wayne's hair harder.

'Owwww! I... I only wanted you to shut your window. I can't sleep with the music so loud. If you'd just shut the window. I- my wife – she's pregnant,' he lied, 'she could sleep.'

'Is that what this is about?' Gaz demanded. 'Noise?'

'Yes,' Wayne squealed as his hair took a fresh twisting.

''Ere!' Jimmy's face was suddenly serious. 'Are you the cunt who tried to burn our fucking house down?'

'What?'

'I bet he fuckin' is, Gaz,' said Glen. 'He's obviously fuckin' mental.'

'No!' Wayne protested. 'I don't know anything about burning your house down. I just peed in a water pistol. That's all.'

'Rifle,' corrected Jimmy. 'Get it right, man.'

'Sorry. Rifle.'

Gaz twisted Wayne's hair. 'Yeah, well you're hardly going to confess to attempted arson, are you?'

'I'm telling the truth!' Wayne begged. 'Honest. I don't know what you're talking about. Whatever it was, it wasn't me. Honest.'

A new voice came from somewhere on the other side of the fence, barely audible. 'He's telling the truth.'

Gaz looked down at the unseen man. 'Is he?'

Wayne strained to listen, but there was no reply. Perhaps there was a non-verbal response, because after a few moments, he was pulled to attention.

'Well why didn't you just knock at the fucking door like a civilised person instead of stinking our garden up with a load of fucking piss?' Gaz demanded.

'I... I didn't think you'd listen. You seemed to be...'

'What?'

'You seemed to be enjoying it too much.'

'Do you hear that, Jim?' said Gaz.

'Yeah. Fucking nutjob.' Jimmy cocked his head at Wayne. 'What a fucking nutjob you are, man. What's the story with the gun?'

'It, it's just a toy,' said Wayne.

'Give it here,' said Jimmy. Wayne looked up. Jimmy had his arm extended towards him. 'Gizzit.'

Gaz gave Wayne's hair an encouraging twist. 'Give it over.'

Wayne reached out with the water rifle.

Jimmy took it and sniffed cautiously around the tank. 'Fucking hell, man. It really is full of piss.' He turned to Gaz. 'I reckon he deserves a taste of his own medicine, don't you?'

Gaz smiled and looked at Wayne. 'Alright you fucking mental cunt, I'm going to let you go now. But if you run away, we'll be over this fence before you can say "knife", and we'll kick your fucking nutjob head in. Understand?'

'Yeah, yeah,' Wayne held up an appeasing hand. 'I understand.' Gaz released his hair. Wayne straightened up and stared into the dripping nozzle of the Super Drencher.

'You should've come 'round and asked us to turn it down, man,' said Jimmy.

'I didn't think you'd listen.'

'We're not unreasonable,' said Glen.

'Or uncivilised,' added Gaz. 'Why, when we go back inside, the first thing we'll do is shut the window and turn the sound down.'

'That's... That's good of you, thanks.'

'Mind you, it's not like we've got much of a choice. All that piss outside our window.'

'I'm sorry.'

'Oh, I bet you are,' said Jimmy. 'But not as sorry as you're going to be.'

'No, honestly. I really am very sorry.'

'Any last requests?'

Wayne looked up. His eyes pleaded for mercy. 'Please,' he begged. 'Please don't.'

'Sorry, man,' Jimmy smiled. 'Live by the sword...'

'Die by the sword,' said Gaz.

'Pleeease,' Wayne pleaded. The Super Drencher seemed to be aimed squarely between his eyes.

'Is that your request?' said Glen. 'Please?'

'Please... Don't do it.'

'Request denied,' said Jimmy.

'Fire,' said Gaz.

Wayne managed to shut his eyes before the blast of cold urine hammered into the centre of his forehead. He staggered back, holding up his hands in an attempt to deflect the powerful jet, in seconds his arms and upper body were soaked. He was afraid to cry out in case he got piss in his mouth. They were laughing at him. He could hear their voices over the relentless splattering of his own liquid waste.

Gaz reached out for the gun. 'Give us a go.'

The attack ceased a moment as the Super Drencher changed hands. Wayne gasped for breath and wiped his eyes in time to see Gaz aiming at his face. 'No, plea -' His words were cut off as Gaz opened fire, fanning the jet up and down Wayne's body, soaking him from head to toe. When his face wasn't being hit, Wayne screamed, 'Please, stop!' His appeals were lost to the neighbourhood at large beneath the sound of Jamiroquai. His firing squad heard him however, and Gaz obliged for a moment as he handed the gun to Glen, who then took his turn as executioner.

'Niiiice one.'

Wayne took one or two blind steps back, flailing hopelessly in the yellow stream before falling, defeated, to his knees. The grass was sodden beneath him. He drew his hands over his head and rolled himself into a ball, cocooning himself against the terrible onslaught.

Gaz patted Glen on the back. 'Alright, man. That's enough. You're just about out of ammo.'

'Alright, geezer.' Glen took his finger off the trigger and laughed at Wayne. 'Check him out, man.'

Wayne found himself unable to speak. He listened to them laughing, heard their various jibes and jokes, but he couldn't bring himself to respond. He sat, balled in a tight foetal position, and waited for them to go away. That was all he knew now. He just wanted them to go away and leave him alone.

'Come on, lads,' said Gaz eventually. 'Fun's over.'

Wayne heard the Super Drencher land in the wet grass close by, but he didn't move. He heard them get down off the fence and walk away back towards their house. They were laughing and saying things about him that he couldn't make out and didn't want to. A few moments later and he heard the French window close. Then he heard the music volume turned down to little more than a funky murmur.

'Victory.' Inside his protective ball, Wayne wondered for a moment who had spoken. The word was whispered, almost inaudible, but he had heard it clearly. It must've come from within his cocoon. So it must've come from him.

PART THREE

Chapter 18

THE LONG HAIR at the back of Mick's neck fluttered gently in the warm breeze as he strolled into the public gardens. He wasn't generally inclined to sing in public, but for some reason he had "The Street Where You Live" stuck in his head and it kept forcing its way out of his mouth in little bursts. He didn't know all the words, so he whistled more than he sang. He held his jacket draped behind his shoulder and his lunch swung at his side in a small M&S bag.

Just inside the gates, he stopped and looked across the gardens to the bench that he and Sally had shared yesterday. She wasn't there. He frowned. Was he early? He checked his watch. No, she should be here by now. He looked around, searching for her among the people on the other benches and squinting against the bright sunlight that drenched everything in gold. There was no sign of her. His sandwich bag sagged a little in his fingers. He checked again, hoping perhaps she had been obscured for an instant by someone who sat next to her, maybe someone with a broadsheet newspaper. But there was nothing like that. She just wasn't there.

'Mick!' a voice called from way off.

He looked around and noticed a small scattering of people sitting out on the lawns. A short distance away from the group Sally was waving at him. His face broke into a smile. He hoisted his lunch into the air and waved it back at her. Then he set out towards her, enjoying the springiness of the grass beneath his shoes. 'Hiya,' he said as he neared her.

'Hi.' Sally gestured to the grass beside her. 'I hope you don't mind sitting on the grass. There was nowhere available on the benches when I arrived, and I'm kind of comfortable now.'

'Not at all.' Mick spread his jacket out and dropped down onto it. 'I like the lawn, it's… grassy.'

'It is, isn't it? That's what I like about lawn – the grassiness.'

Mick smiled. 'So, how are you?'

'Fine. How are you?'

'Oh, I'm good.'

'No bike today?'

'No, no I left it at work. I only got it out yesterday because I needed to get down to where you worked and stuff – to buy the book I mean.'

'*Captain Corelli*? How are you finding it?'

'Oh, I like it, so far.'

'Where are you?'

'Not far, only about a chapter or so.'

'But you like it?'

'Oh, yeah. It's good. But I didn't get much time to read it last night; y'know, between making my tea, eating it, watching TV and generally trying to figure out this Peter business.'

'Still puzzling it over, eh?'

'Yeah.' Mick opened his sandwiches. He held one up. 'Bacon, lettuce and tomato. Breath friendly.'

She smiled. 'I had a boring old cheese and pickle.'

'Oh? You find cheese and pickle boring?'

'Well it's not exactly a night at Raymond Blanc's is it?'

Mick took a bite of his sandwich. 'Cheese and pickle isn't boring though, is it? It's kind of, zingy.'

'I suppose so. But you know what it's like these days; so many varieties of sandwich on the shelf to choose from. If you pick cheese and pickle, people think your boring.'

'I think cheese and pickle is exciting,' said Mick. 'I get excited even thinking about it.'

Sally laughed. 'Why didn't you get cheese and pickle yourself, then?'

'Too exciting,' said Mick. 'I need to unwind with my lunch, not get in a froth over it.'

'I see. So a BLT is a good sandwich to unwind with is it?'

'It is. But my main concern was, as I said, not stinking up my mouth.' He took another bite and savoured the taste. 'Mmmm, relaxing and non-malodorous. What a combination.'

Sally smiled. 'You sound like a commercial.'

'Yeah. I missed my vocation. I should be in advertising.'

'So what are you in?'

'You mean workwise?'

Sally nodded.

'I work in an office. "Data entry clerk" is what it says on the job description.'

'Do you like it?'

'No. It sucks. But, hey, it pays the rent.'

'It's kind of common these days, isn't it?' said Sally. 'People not liking their jobs.'

'I'd say it's always been kind of common. It's just jobs today feel, I dunno, pointless. Take my job; I don't come home in the evening feeling like, "Hey, I really did that, didn't I? I really made a difference." You know what I mean?'

Sally nodded. 'Is this why you're attracted to the role of part-time private detective?'

Mick paused in his eating and frowned. 'I never thought about it that way, but you may have something there.'

'How's the investigation going?'

'Oh, nowhere really. Nothing more than I've told you already. It's like a mystery wrapped in an enigma that someone locked in a box marked, "puzzle"'. Mick popped the last of his sandwich into his mouth. 'And then to top it off, they went and hid it somewhere.'

Sally smiled. 'I see.' She thought a moment. 'What made you call in on that house where we first met that time?'

Mick removed his second sandwich from the pack. 'The loud music. I could hear it from Peter's street. Peter had a big problem with neighbourhood noise nuisance. The guys in that house used to drive him crazy. Assuming of course, that it's the same house.'

'Oh, I'd say it's probably that place,' said Sally. 'Three guys?'

'Hmmm,' he nodded, his mouth full.

Sally nodded. 'I understand. Noisy neighbours; they're a growing problem these days.'

'Mmm.'

'I can understand what he must've been feeling. I've had similar problems. I think most people in flats do at some point or other. It comes with the territory.'

'But you don't let it rule your life, do you?'

'That depends. You don't necessarily have a choice. It's not up to you whether or not your neighbours are arseholes, is it?'

Mick shrugged. 'I suppose not. Where do you live? If that's not an inappropriate question.'

'No, that's okay. I live in Alexandra Road; a flat. I get problems occasionally from the people above and below.'

'Bad?'

'Sometimes. Sometimes not. Sometimes it's as quiet as the grave, other times they're both kicking off at the same time.'

Mick raised his eyebrows. 'Sound's nasty. Why don't you move?'

'Where to? In my experience it's a roll of the dice as far as flats and neighbours go. The estate agent doesn't take you around at night after the pubs and clubs have closed. What you see is what you get. But what you hear? That changes from hour to hour.'

'I guess so.'

'People should have to have licenses to buy stereo equipment these days. I mean, once upon a time these things were weird, crackly things that had, like, French horns sticking off them for speakers, you know? Like the HMV dog listens to?'

Mick nodded.

'Now they're like lethal weapons. You can drive people literally insane with these things. If you can't sleep, the next day, you're in bits. At least I know I am. Imagine what it must be like night after night – boom, boom, boom! It'd be hell.'

'Peter used to say that,' said Mick. 'Literally that. He'd say, "We are in hell," talking about how people are all stacked up in flats. All of them hasty conversions – none of them soundproofed.'

'I'd say he was right there. I hate it when someone comes in after a night of, 'avin it, and they want to 'ave it, a bit more. Of course it's ten times worse when they bring their mates back. Then there's no amount of thumping on the floor or ceiling that'll stop them. The worst thing is when they turn it down, then a few minutes later, someone turns it up again. I really hate that. Do you know what I mean?'

'Fortunately, no,' said Mick. 'It's not like that where I am.'

'Oh? Where are you?' She smiled, and added, 'if that's not an inappropriate question?'

'Seaton Street. I've got the bottom part of a house, a maisonette-type thing. I've just got the people upstairs, and they're quiet. Most of the time I don't even know they're there.'

'You're lucky. Seaton Street's a bit more on the expensive side. People 'round there are a bit more relaxed.'

'You mean older?'

'Older, and a bit better off, perhaps. Maybe not so many rentals?'

'I rent.'

'Expensive?'

'No, but then the rent hasn't gone up since about 1992.'

Sally raised her eyebrows. 'Really – you jammy git. Where did you get that?'

'I got it yonks ago. The landlady lives in South Africa. I've got a standing order for the rent. It goes in every month. That's about the only contact we have.'

'Shit, that's unreal. You are so lucky.'

Mick smiled. 'I know.'

'How many bedrooms?'

'Just the one, with a box room that could be rented out if my landlady was like that. Thankfully, she isn't.'

'You don't share it then?'

'Nope. Just me.'

Sally smiled and looked away over the gardens. 'It sounds like paradise.'

'Well, I don't know about that. But I like it.' Mick shifted his position, bringing himself a little closer to Sally. 'But enough about me, lets talk about you. What is it with you and those guys over the back of Peter's place?'

Sally laughed and picked a blade of grass. 'They're just a bunch of idiots. I know them by association rather than by choice.'

'Oh? How come?'

'I have this friend – well, more of an acquaintance really. But – ' Sally tossed the blade of grass aside irritably. 'Oh, I don't know. She's... ' she waved her hand vaguely.

'Someone you just, sort of... know.'

Sally smiled. 'Yeah, that's good. She's someone I know. Anyway, this person, she has a crush on one of those guys.'

'A crush?'

'I know, it's ridiculous isn't it? But that's the best way of describing it. To say she fancies him falls hopelessly short of describing the way she totally and utterly adores him.'

'Hmm. Go on.'

'Okay. So she has this big-time crush on him. Anyway, she's always on at me to go on like, double dates with her, although they're not dates because I wouldn't touch any of them with a bargepole.' She looked at him to check his understanding. He nodded. 'So they're always playing loud music and getting really stoned and stuff after they finish work. They work in a pub, by the way.'

'Which pub?'

'Shenanigan's?'

'That awful-looking green pub?'

Sally nodded. 'Irish theme place, garish; bicycles suspended from the ceiling type stuff.'

'I know the one.'

'Well they work there. The thing is, I don't think this guy – the one she has this adolescent craving for – I don't think he fancies her.' She hesitated a moment. 'I think he fancies me.'

Mick raised his eyebrows.

'I know that sounds vain, but it's true. He seems to, you know, undress me with his eyes?'

'Oh? I take it you don't return the, er, compliment, then?'

'God, no! He's appalling. The whole thing's horrible, especially since Kay – that's my friendly acquaintance sort of person – especially since Kay seems so blissfully unaware of it.'

'Sounds like a situation to be avoided.'

'Oh. I wish.'

'I don't get it,' said Mick. 'Why don't you just do that? Avoid it?'

Sally sighed and picked a few blades of grass. 'You don't understand, Mick. I don't have that many friends.'

'You don't? You're kidding?'

Sally smiled. 'Thank you. Sadly no. It's like, you make good friends when you're in your late teens and you kind of stick with them, don't you?'

Mick shrugged. 'I suppose.'

'Well how many of those friends do you still have now?'

'A few.'

'You still see them, socially?'

'Kind of.'

'They all got married, right?'

175

'Some.'

'Had children?'

Mick nodded. 'Yeah, not uncommon.'

'And so you see these friends maybe a few times in as many months?'

'Or less.'

'Me too,' said Sally. 'Old friends in happy couples. They tend to invite you over only if they're inviting other single people too. It's like they're superstitious about having just one single friend in the house.'

Mick smiled. 'I know what you mean.'

'Oh, you meet new people; occasionally they become good friends. But more often than not they just wind up as, you know, acquaintances?'

Mick nodded. He turned to look at the people over at the benches. Sally did the same. After a few moments, Mick said, 'I have an idea.'

'What's that then?'

'I could go with you to this Shenanigan's place and we could sort of, be together? Then this idiot guy would see us and think we were an item. Maybe he'd leave you alone?'

'You mean like a date?'

'Sort of.'

'Are you asking me out on a date, Mick?'

'Sort of.'

'To Shenanigan's?'

'If you want. I'd prefer somewhere else, but if it would help get rid of this guy...?'

Sally smiled. 'Shenanigan's is a toilet. Being a turd, he belongs there. I, on the other hand, do not. Where else did you have in mind?'

'I dunno. I hadn't thought about it until now.'

Sally drew a hand across her brow, sweeping her fringe to one side and tucking it behind her ear. 'Oh. I'm flattered.'

'I mean I hadn't thought of a place to go.' Mick felt his cheeks reddening. 'I had, sort of, wondered if you fancied going out for a drink sometime though.'

Sally smiled.

'Why?' Mick grinned coyly. 'Had you? Thought about it?'

'Of course not. I'm a girl.' Sally smiled and looked away.

Mick, suitably baffled, changed tack. 'When would be good for you?'

'Actually, I don't know.' She shifted her position to face him. 'For someone with no friends I'm a bit busy over the next few days. Do you want to meet for lunch tomorrow?'

'Er, let me think about that a moment.' Mick scratched his head theatrically. 'Yes.'

'Okay. And we'll arrange an evening date then.'

'Sure.' Mick realised he was smiling like an idiot. He looked down at his empty sandwich packet.

'That's fine, then.'

'Oh, absolutely,' Mick said, feeling suitably composed to look up again. 'Tomorrow lunchtime.'

For a moment, neither of them said anything. Mick picked a daisy and twirled it by its stem. He glanced over at Sally. She was watching the people on the benches, some of whom were getting up and leaving. She looked at her watch. 'I suppose we ought to be getting back to work.'

'Yeah,' said Mick, gathering his lunch litter. 'Back to the old grindstone.'

They got to their feet. 'I'll see you tomorrow then?' Sally said.

'Same bat time, same bat channel.'

Sally smiled. 'Does that mean here?'

'Here, yes. Definitely'.

'Okay.'

'Okay.'

She started to walk away. Then she turned over her shoulder. 'I'll see you then?'

Mick held up his hand in a wave. 'Seeya.'

She turned and walked away. He stood watching her go, hoping she'd turn back and wave or something, but she didn't. He smiled and sat back down, he didn't want to go back just yet; he'd say he got lost or something. A pigeon approached him, bobbing about just to his right-hand side. He tossed the bird a piece of crust that remained in the packet and smiled. 'I reckon they'd probably believe me too.'

Chapter 19

'WELL?' Ron Chigley wrung his hands together impatiently. 'See anything?'

'Naa.' Jack was peering through Gaz's letterbox. 'Nothin'. No sign of life.'

'Bollocks.' Ron scowled at the house as if it were in league with his troublesome tenants. 'Imagine trying to pull this sort of thing back in our day, eh? Imagine the look on the landlord's face.'

'Don't have to imagine it. I'm lookin' at it, Ron.'

'Eh? Do I look like a landlord would in our day?'

'I reckon.' Jack took out his tobacco and started rolling a cigarette.

'What? How do I look?'

'All red in the face. Cross-looking.'

'Well I am cross. Those lads owe me rent, Jack. I think I've a right to be cross, don't you?'

'Oh, yeah. No one's sayin' otherwise. All I'm sayin' is that you look like any landlord would at any time in history what's been messed about.'

'I am being messed about aren't I?'

'I reckon.'

Ron shook his head and looked at the concrete path. 'I'm a soft touch, Jack. That's my problem. Ask my wife, she'll tell you. A soft touch. She's always tellin' me, "Ron, you should be more like our Martin. Don't take anythin' off those buggers," she says. "Don't take any of their shit, Ron. You're too much of a soft touch." That's what she says.'

Jack nodded. 'I'd say she's right there. You're your own worst enemy.'

'Oh, I know, I know. But, I want to be fair with 'em. You know what I mean? There's plenty of landlords out there like our Martin. Partitioning rooms up and taking youngsters for all they've got. But I'm not like that, Jack. I think people deserve better. We'd expect better wouldn't we? Why not these lads? We're all brothers, Jack. All brothers.'

Jack lit his cigarette and nodded.

'He ain't heavy, he's my brother. You know? Like the song?'

Jack nodded.

Ron looked away toward the street. Then he turned back to Jack. 'Try it again, Jack. Keep pressin' it till it falls off the wall inside.'

Jack turned back to the front door and pressed the doorbell. Both he and Ron stared at the door, listening to the long, insistent buzzing within.

'I saw the Hollies, y'know,' said Ron.

Jack gave him a sideways look. 'Oh yeah?'

'Yeah. Me and Margaret.' Ron nodded. 'Long time ago now.'

'Would be.' Jack's finger was still on the doorbell.

'I think they still go out touring. At Christmas and the like.'

Jack nodded.

They listened to the buzzing inside for a while. Ron sighed. 'Enough to wake the dead, isn't it.'

'I reckon they're out, Ron.'

'That would explain it.'

'Probably in the pub, having a laugh.'

'You said that last time we were here. You got them wrong that time, didn't you?'

'Did I?' said Jack, knowingly.

Ron frowned, 'What do you mean?'

'How do you know they weren't in the pub before they eventually turned up?'

'They were in hospital.'

'Oh. My mistake.' Jack didn't sound convinced.

'What are you saying, Jack? Are you saying they weren't in hospital? Is that it?'

'No. They may well have been in the hospital, Ron. But what time did they get out, eh?'

'You're saying they went to the pub after they were discharged? Even though they had an appointment with me?'

'I know what I'd do if I got discharged from hospital.'

'What?'

'I'd go and have a pint. Wouldn't you?'

'No,' said Ron indignantly. 'I would not.'

Jack shrugged.

Ron was about to say what he would do when the front door opened and Gaz peered around the door. He was bleary-eyed and unshaven. It was too early in the morning to recognise Jack. 'Jesus, man. Get your bloody finger off the bell will...' Then he noticed Ron. 'Oh, Mr Chigley and, er?'

'Jack,' said Ron. 'You remember Jack? Fixes things? He's come to paint the new door. We had an appointment, remember?'

Gaz thought for a second. 'Oh, sh... Yeah. Yeah, I remember now. Sorry, Mr Chigley. We, we had a bit of a late night last night. Working late, you know, at the pub?'

'I know. Old Jack here thought you might still be there, didn't you, Jack?'

Jack re-lit his cigarette. 'I know I would be if I had nothin' to do but lie about.'

Gaz managed a smile. 'Ha, yeah. Given the chance, eh? But we work in it, mate. Big difference.'

'If you say so.' Jack puffed on his cigarette.

'Anyway, we've come to do repairs and collect this month's rent. So if you don't mind?' Ron stepped up to the door, waiting to be admitted.

'Oh, whoa, Mr Chigley,' Gaz held up his hands defensively. 'The place is in a bit of a mess. Give us a few minutes to get it tidied up, eh?'

Ron raised his eyebrows. 'I don't mind a bit of mess, son. I know how lads are, I used to be one once. It's nothing new to us, eh Jack?'

Jack made a noise that sounded vaguely affirmative.

'See? Now let us in, lad. C'mon.'

'Two minutes.' Gaz closed the door in Ron's face. From the other side of the door he called. 'I'm naked. Just two minutes.'

Ron looked at Jack, aghast.

Jack sniffed. 'Probably making a run for it out the back way.'

'You think so?'

'That's what I'd be doin'.' Jack took a puff at his cigarette, only to find it had gone out.

The naked Gaz ran into the lounge where Adam slept on the sofa. In spite of the persistent ringing of the bell, the big man had apparently slept undisturbed throughout. 'Wake up, man,' said Gaz, gathering up empty bottles from the coffee table. 'Landlord's here.'

Adam raised his head from a cushion. He spoke in a voice fogged with sleep. 'Landlord?'

'Yeah. Our fuckin' landlord. He's come for the rent and probably intends to have a good old look 'round into the bargain.'

Adam sat up blearily. He hadn't undergone a night of such toxic intake for some time. His head throbbed dully and his mouth tasted rancid. 'Any water?'

'What?' Gaz stopped as he tipped the contents of an overflowing ashtray into a carrier bag.

'Water. I'm thirsty.'

'Listen man, main thing is to look lively. Get the place lookin' pukka, like he expects it to be, y'know?'

'Pukka?'

'Nice,' Gaz explained. 'Nice and tidy, yeah?'

'Oh.' Adam got to his feet immediately and began to help Gaz in clearing the debris of the night before.

In a very short while, the place was presentable. They had gathered all the bottles and assorted trash into three carrier bags. Spraying air freshener, Gaz took the bags to the open French windows. Adam was already outside washing down Wayne's smelly handiwork with bleach and warm water. Gaz sniffed. 'How's it going?'

'Smells okay to me.'

'Cool. That'll do it for now. Go on inside and act natural.' Gaz ran around the side of the house and dumped the carrier bags in the dustbin. Returning to the lounge, he took another sniff. 'Smell okay?'

Adam sniffed. 'Smells okay.'

'Look alright?'

Adam looked around and nodded. 'Looks alright.'

'Right. Now he's a bit on the square side, so don't say anything weird or dodgy, alright? And don't say anything about smoking – he won't have smokers in the house.'

Adam nodded. 'Nothing dodgy, no smokers.'

'Okay.' Gaz dashed back into the hall. 'Just getting dressed!' he shouted at the door as he ran past it. He ran up the stairs. 'Lads!' He burst through the door of the room where Jimmy and Glen slept. 'Chigley's here! Get up and get with it.'

'Chigley?' Glen rubbed his face. 'What's he want?'

'Money, obviously,' said Gaz. 'Now get the fuck up and look presentable. Jim, have we got the rent cheque?'

'No, man.' Jimmy was having trouble opening his eyes. 'Not that I know of.'

'Glen?'

Glen shook his head. 'Uh-uh.'

Gaz thumped the door. 'Oh, fucking brilliant.' Cursing as he went, he ran into the other bedroom to get his trousers on.

In what eventually transpired to be five and half minutes, Gaz re-opened the front door, smiling and wearing the clothes he had crawled out of the night before. Behind him, Jimmy and Glen groped their way down the stairs sporting similar dress sense. 'Sorry about that Mr Chigley,' said Gaz. 'I was in the altogether, you know? Not a pretty sight first thing in the morning.'

Ron tutted. 'First thing in the morning? It's nearly half past one in the afternoon.' He stepped inside.

Gaz gave a short, affected laugh. 'Well you know, Mr Chigley, when you work nights, the afternoons and mornings tend to blur a bit.'

'I'm sure.' Ron looked around at the inside of the doorway. 'New door alright?'

'Lovely. Opens and shuts. Does exactly what it says on the tin.'

Ron looked at him. 'Eh?'

'Like the advert,' said Gaz. 'For creosote or whatever it is, "Does exactly what it says on the tin."'

'Oh, aye,' said Ron edgily. 'I don't think I've seen that one.'

'It's a good one,' said Glen. 'Bloke holds up a tin of creosote and says -'

'Yes,' said Ron. 'I think I get the picture.' He felt the finish of the door. 'Nice bit of wood that, eh, Jack?'

Jack looked the door up and down and nodded. 'Well hung too, if I do say so meself.'

Glen smirked and dug Jimmy in the ribs.

'We'll be painting this today, then, if that's okay with you lads. That and tarting up the frame and the skirting board.'

'No problem, Mr Chigley,' said Gaz. 'We're much obliged in fact.'

Ron nodded. 'Well, Jack. If you want to go and get your paint and stuff, I'll just see the lads about the rent.'

Jack gave a grunt of assent and went off down the path to his van. When he was gone, Ron turned back to Gaz and the others. 'So then, gents. About that rent?'

'Cup of tea, Mr Chigley?' said Gaz cheerfully. 'I'm sure you and Jack must be gasping. I know I am.'

'Well, I don't mind if I do. And I'm sure Jack'll have one. He's not known for turning down cups of tea is our Jack.'

'Lovely.' Gaz looked at Glen and Jimmy. 'Okay then lads. Teas all round then?'

'Yeah,' Jimmy agreed. 'Teas all round.'

'Nice one,' said Glen.

Gaz smiled and lead Ron into the lounge. Jimmy and Glen followed, scratching themselves as they went. As they entered the front room, Adam, who had been sitting on the couch, rose to meet them. Ron looked at him with mild concern.

'This is our friend Adam, Mr Chigley,' Gaz explained. 'He stayed over last night. Missed the last bus, y'know?'

Ron smiled warily at the big man in the crumpled "Choose Life" T-shirt. 'Pleased to meet you, Adam.'

'Pleased to meet you, Mr Chigley.' Adam extended his hand across the back of the sofa.

Ron shook it. He smiled, surprised that a man of such formidable appearance should have such an agreeable handshake. Ron found himself warming to him. 'Used to like Wham! did you, Adam?'

'Pardon?'

'Wham!' Ron pointed at the T-shirt. 'My daughter used to have one like it in the eighties. Wore it ragged, she did.'

Adam, recalling his conversation with The One as to the origins of the garment, smiled. 'I picked it up in Oxfam. I've no real knowledge of the group.'

'Funny bunch. That George Michael – he was in it.'

Adam nodded, none the wiser.

'You take sugar Mr Chigley?' Gaz asked brightly.

'Two, please, Gary.'

'Okay. Won't be a moment.' Gaz left for the kitchen. Behind Ron's back, he gestured to Jimmy and Glen to keep things convivial.

Jimmy nodded aside then turned his attention to Ron. 'Have a seat, Mr Chigley.'

'Thank you.' Ron sat down on the sofa beside Adam. 'Nice day.' He gestured in the direction of the open French window.

'Lovely innit?' Glen agreed. 'Been really nice lately.'

'It has, yes.'

They sat for a moment in an awkward silence, then Adam spoke. 'I used to quite like heavy metal.'

They all looked at him. Ron smiled. 'Sorry?'

'In the eighties. The music I was listening to? I used to quite like heavy metal.'

'Oh,' Ron nodded, understanding. 'Not Wham! then?'

'No. AC/DC, Motorhead, ZZ Top. Things like that.'

'I used to like all them too,' said Glen. 'I've got some here if you fancy listening to some sometime.'

'I'd like that. What've you got?'

Glen got up and went to the CD collection. Ron watched with ill-disguised concern as Glen rummaged among the little plastic boxes, emerging a moment later and holding one aloft. 'What about this?'

Adam smiled at the box. 'AC/DC. That's a great album.'

'I'll put it on.'

Jimmy frowned. His disapproving looks went unnoticed by Glen, who inserted the disc and started pushing buttons.

'Who are AC/DC?' Ron asked. 'I don't think my daughter...' He was cut off by guitars.

Glen beamed at Adam and hoisted an invisible guitar into action. Adam smiled and began nodding his head to the beat. Ron remained open-mouthed, as if waiting to finish his sentence. Jimmy sank his face into his hands and tried to suppress a smile.

Gaz returned carrying a tray laden with mugs of tea. He looked quickly around, taking in the situation at a glance. 'Tea!' All eyes went to Gaz as he set the tray down. He made a face at Glen and nodded curtly at the CD player. Glen quickly turned it off and they were able to hear each other again. 'Thanks, Glen. I'm sure Mr Chigley doesn't need that at this hour of the morning, do you, Mr Chigley?'

'Er, no. It isn't really my cup of tea, no.'

Gaz offered him a mug. 'No, but this is.'

'Thank you, Gary,' Ron smiled and accepted the mug. 'Now then, about the rent?'

'Yes, Mr Chigley,' Gaz sat down in a chair opposite Ron. 'We are a tad overdue on that aren't we. Times have been a bit on the hard side around here lately I'm afraid.'

'Times are hard all over. You have to learn to prioritise. As I'm sure you have done with the rent.'

Gaz smiled. 'Of course, of course we have. It's just...'

'You don't have it, do you?'

'No,' Gaz looked down at his tea. 'We've had a lot of unforeseen expenses this month.'

'Like?'

There was a pause, then Jimmy said, 'Clothes.'

'Clothes?' Ron looked incredulous. 'Visits to C&A come over rent in priority do they?'

'Our clothes were burnt, weren't they, Mr Chigley? You remember? The fire?'

'Not all of them.'

Gaz looked up. 'Well enough, collectively. We pool our resources, Mr Chigley. All for one and one for all. When we all need stuff at the same time, it gets pricey.'

Ron set his mug on the coffee table. 'I see. Well, I'm sorry, but I need that rent and I need it now. I can give you another day or two, but I simply must demand what is owed to me. If you fail to deliver, I'll have no choice but to evict you.'

'Whoa, now Mr Chigley. Surely we don't have to get that drastic?'

'You've had all month to raise this rent, Gary, even a few days on top as a result of the fire. But I can't go on indefinitely postponing collection. It's the same every month. When are you going to set up a standing order?'

'This month, Mr Chigley, honest we will,' Gaz looked at Glen and Jimmy. They returned various "yeahs," and "absolutelys".

Ron got up and looked at all of them sternly. 'You've got two days, lads. Then I'll have no choice but to serve you with the paperwork. Understand?'

'How much is the rent?' Adam asked quietly. 'If you don't mind my enquiring?'

Gaz considered for a moment, then shrugged. 'Eight hundred quid.'

'Which is very reasonable in this day and age, I think you'll agree,' Ron said to Adam.

'Oh, very reasonable,' Adam agreed. He looked to Gaz. 'I should be able to lend you the money.'

Gaz's eyes widened. 'Really?'

'If you've no other means.'

Gaz looked around at Jimmy and Glen. They both shook their heads in the negative. He looked back to Adam. 'Thanks man. I mean, if you're sure that's cool.'

'It's cool.'

Ron straightened his shirtsleeves and cleared his throat. 'Well. That's fine, then. I will, as I say, be back in two days. Please have the cheque – or preferably, under these late circumstances – the cash, ready for me by then.'

'Of course, Mr Chigley. As you've just seen. That won't be a problem.'

'Hmm,' Ron sounded unconvinced. 'Well, thanks for the tea.' He turned to Adam. 'Nice to have met you, Adam.'

Adam smiled warmly. 'Nice to have met you, Mr Chigley.'

'Right then. I'll be off. Jack'll obviously be here for a while doing the painting.'

'No problem, Mr Chigley,' Gaz got up to see him out.

'Please, Gary,' Ron held up a hand. 'I know the way.'

'Oh, right you are, then.' Gaz dropped back into his seat.

'Cheerio, lads.' Ron walked out into the hallway followed by the various farewells of his tenants.

Once Ron had left the room, Gaz nodded to Glen to put the music back on. Once it had resumed, Gaz went to the door and peered out into the hall. Ron was chatting with Jack outside the front door. Gaz returned to his seat and leaned forward over the coffee table to Adam. 'What are you going on about? Are you sure you can stump up eight hundred quid?'

'If you've no other means.'

'Shit,' Gaz slapped his thigh. 'Where'd you get that?'

'Savings,' said Adam, truthfully. He neglected to mention that they were Peter Reynolds' savings.

'Leave it with us for today. I reckon we could tap Ted for some assistance on this. But thanks, man. I really mean that.'

Adam smiled. 'No problem, man.'

Gaz sat back and jerked a thumb in Ron's general direction. 'That fucking guy. He's like a fucking nightmare every month. Coming 'round with his hand stuck out like a fucking beggar.'

'Beggar in a Rover,' said Jimmy.

'Yeah, man.' Glen scowled. 'Bastard.'

Adam raised his eyebrows. 'You don't like him?'

Gaz recoiled in exasperation. 'Like him? Fuck off, man. He's a cunt. A full-on nightmare. He's been robbin' us blind for ages with this place. I mean look at it.' He waved a hand around the room. 'Eight hundred quid? Leave it out.'

Adam looked at it. The place seemed very reasonable to him. But what did he know about such things? He nodded, confident that The One knew best.

'I wish the cunt was dead,' said Glen.

'Fuckin' A,' Gaz agreed.

'That bad, eh?' Adam stroked his chin.

'Shit yeah,' Glen laughed. 'It'd solve all our problems.'

'What would you do?' Gaz asked the group in general. 'Lead piping in the conservatory?'

'Revolver in the billiard room,' said Jimmy.

'No way man,' Glen shook his head decisively. 'It's gotta be the rope. In the library.'

'Car accident,' said Adam.

'Eh?' Gaz frowned.

'Best way. No questions asked.'

'Oh, yeah. But it's not exactly Cluedo, is it?'

Adam shrugged. They were silent a moment. Then he said, 'You think lead piping would be the best way then? Like Cluedo?'

Gaz laughed. 'Fuck, who cares, man. Car crash, lead piping, tubular bells – whatever. Just so long as I don't have to give the cunt any more money. Know what I mean?'

'Alriiight, man. Dead Chigley!' Glen flicked his fingers.

'Shhh,' Gaz waved a hand urgently. 'He's only just outside the front door. You tit.'

Glen made a penitent face and shrank back a little.

Jimmy grinned. 'Did anyone else ever have a wank over Miss Scarlet?'

Gaz laughed out loud and slapped the arm of his chair. 'Oh, no man! You're kidding?'

'No, seriously, did you?'

'No, man. No way.'

Jimmy shrugged. 'Nah. Neither did I.'

'Oh, yes you did!' Gaz pointed at him. 'While your family was trying to figure out whose name was in the old black envelope, you were having a hand shandy under the table over Miss Scarlet.'

'Well she was hot, man!' Jimmy protested.

Adam got up. 'I have to get going.'

Gaz looked up at him. 'Really?'

'Yeah. Things to do.'

'Places to be.'

'Yes.' Adam walked to the door. 'I'll see you in the pub later, perhaps?'

'Yeah, man.' Gaz waved.

'Nice one,' said Jimmy.

'Rock on, Adam.' Glen played a note on his air guitar.

Adam held up a hand and left. Out through the open front door, he could see Ron saying his goodbyes to Jack. He stepped outside and smiled. 'Hello again.'

'Oh, hello Adam.' Ron smiled. 'This is Jack. My handyman.'

'Hello Jack.'

Jack nodded.

'Right then, Jack,' said Ron. 'I'll see you later.' Jack made a sound of assent and Ron started down the path. Adam followed him. Ron turned. 'Nice bunch of kids really. You known 'em long?'

'Not long.'

'Oh, they're alright,' Ron chuckled. 'Better than a lot of youngsters these days.'

'They are.'

'I don't like having to be hard with them. But you have to be, you know? They don't mean to be a nuisance, but they just don't realise that I've got my bills and expenses just like everybody else. I mean, who do you think's paying for the fire damage?'

Adam nodded. 'I know. It's not easy.' As they stepped through the garden gate, he stopped. 'Actually, if you're going anywhere near town, I can give you that money now. I just need to pop into my bank.'

'Oh,' said Ron. 'Well, that's very good of you. As a matter of fact I am going that way. I could drive you in. Are you sure now's convenient?'

'Sure. And it would save me walking.'

Ron led the way to his red Rover. He took out his keys and opened the driver's side door. All the other doors unlocked in unison. 'Hop in there Adam. It's unlocked.' Ron smiled. 'Central locking you know?'

'Very nice, Mr Chigley.'

'Call me Ron.' They got in and buckled their seatbelts. 'Now you're sure this is no bother for you? I don't want to leave you short.'

'Oh no, Ron,' Adam smiled. 'It's no bother. No bother at all.'

Chapter 20

IT WAS 8.30 ON THURSDAY NIGHT as Sally approached The Moon and Stars pub. She hesitated before entering. The front doors were open and she looked inside with some uncertainty. It was one of those big, new-style pubs that seemed to have sprung up all over the country. The walls were lined with thin, yellow wood panelling covered with all manner of ads from the first part of the last century. It was a big, noisy barn-like affair. Sally had walked past it on various occasions but never before had she stepped over the threshold. The décor, size and lighting made it feel more like a cheap casino than a pub. She took a breath, as if knowing it would be the last clean air she'd get for the next few hours, and stepped inside. Once in, she looked around for Lucy.

There seemed to be a lot of groups of single men sitting around in booths, far more than you tended to find in the average pub. Many of these men were staring at her now quite openly, almost defiantly. As her eyes searched the room, none of them looked away if she accidentally caught their gaze; none were embarrassed to have been caught gawking. Instead they continued to stare, as if she might find this an attractive quality in a man. She moved deeper into the pub, hoping to convey an air of purpose. She was beginning to steel herself for the potential ordeal of sitting alone and waiting for Lucy to arrive, when she saw her. She was in a booth about half way down, waving at her like a relative in an airport. Sally smiled and waved back. As she walked towards Lucy's table, the cigarette smoke seemed to grow denser about her. An unpleasant premonition of what her hair and clothes would smell like tomorrow flashed through her mind.

Lucy stood up. 'Hi, Sal. Wow, you're looking great.'

'Hi Lucy. So are you.'

Lucy waved her into the booth. 'What are you drinking?'

'No,' Sally held up a hand. 'Let me get this one. What are you drinking?'

'Oh, no. First one's on me. What is it?'

'Oh, I don't know… vodka. Vodka and tonic.'

'Ice and lemon?'

'Sure.' Sally settled herself into the booth. 'Thanks.'

'Okay, one vodka and tonic coming up.' Lucy took her purse from her bag and headed for the bar.

Sally made herself comfortable, removing her jacket and laying it on the seat beside her. She noticed that Lucy was half way through a pint of lager and wondered if she'd been waiting long. She looked at her watch to check that she hadn't arrived late. She saw that she hadn't, and relaxed.

'Here you go,' Lucy said, returning to the booth. She put Sally's vodka and a little bottle of tonic on the table. She up-ended the half-pint of lager she had bought for herself into her other drink, creating a pint. Foam flowed over the side of the glass. 'Shit. Should've poured it gently. Oh, well.' She sat down opposite Sally and raised her dripping glass. 'Cheers.'

Sally raised her glass. 'Cheers.' They clinked glasses and drank.

'So.' Lucy wiped foam off her top lip. 'What've you been doing with yourself all these years?'

Sally shrugged. 'Not much, really. You know, getting by. You?'

'The same. Getting by.'

'What are you doing for a living nowadays? You know I'm working in a bookshop, but what are you up to?'

'Oh, I read horoscopes. Private consultations.'

'Really? Could you do mine?'

'Now?'

'Well, no, not now,' Sally said. 'But maybe some time in future, if you can fit me in?'

'Sure.'

'I'd pay you, of course.'

'No you won't,' Lucy waved the idea away. 'It'll be my treat. What's your sign?'

Sally smiled. 'You tell me.'

Lucy looked penetratingly into Sally's face. 'Okay, let me think.' She squinted and pinched the end of her chin. 'Pisces.'

Sally shook her head. 'Libra.'

'Doh!' Lucy slapped her forehead. 'Well, I was close. Especially as it's been a long time since I've seen you.'

'So what sign are you?'

'Sagittarius.' Lucy took a sip of her drink.

'Is that good?'

'It's all good, Sal. It's how it mixes with everything else that makes it interesting.'

'Does that sort of thing pay well?' Sally leaned forward, interested. 'If that's not being nosy.'

'No. I mean, no it's not being nosy. And no, sadly, it doesn't pay well either.'

'How do you get by?'

'Oh, I'm pretty resourceful. I'm hoping to get a novel published in the not too distant future.' Lucy's eyes lit up. 'Hey, maybe you can offer me a few tips on getting published. Being a bookseller as you are.'

'Oh, I just sell them. I don't know anything about the mechanics of getting published. But we have a lot of books that deal with the topic.'

'Really? Well, that'd be a big help. Cigarette?' She proffered the pack to Sally.

'No thanks,' Sally held up a hand.

'Very sensible,' Lucy took out a cigarette and lit it. 'I hate these things.'

'Why don't you quit?'

'Have you ever quit cigarettes?'

'No.'

'It's not easy. I've tried several times.' She held up the cigarette and smirked. 'Without much success.'

'Again, there're a lot of good books written on the subject. Certainly some come highly recommended.'

Lucy shrugged. 'I'll think about it. To be honest, I kind of need them right now. What with the book and stuff. They help me concentrate.'

'What sort of book is it?'

'A romance. I'm going for Mills and Boon.'

'Really? They're very particular about what they want, aren't they.'

'I dunno, I haven't spoken to them. They sent me some guidelines though, and to be honest, I'm having trouble sticking to them. In fact, I seem to be totally abandoning them.'

'What's happening?'

'People are fucking. None of that 'punishing kiss' stuff. My characters are really getting down to it. They try, but they just can't seem to stay clothed in each others' company for too long.'

Sally smiled. 'Maybe you should consider one of the adult book publishers.' She dropped into a sultry voice. 'Erotic fiction written by women, for women.'

'And bought exclusively by men, I'll bet.'

Sally nodded. 'In my experience.'

'Dirty mack brigade?'

'All sorts. The manger of Woolworth's is a regular buyer of erotic fiction written for women by women.'

'My God,' Lucy's mouth fell open in mock horror. 'Such a pillar of the community, a masturbator!'

Sally laughed. 'Thankfully not in the shop.'

'That'd be nice wouldn't it? Getting all the pages stuck together before he's even got it out of the front door.'

'Oh, that's gross.'

'Lovely to look at, lovely to hold. But if you cum all over it…'

'Consider it sold,' they said together, and laughed.

There was a pause. They both took sips of their drinks. Sally sucked on a cube of ice. 'So you've not gotten married then?'

'No.'

'Boyfriend?'

Lucy shook her head. 'You?'

Sally shrugged. 'Not exactly.'

'Oh?' Lucy sat up. 'Tell me more.'

Sally fingered her glass, bobbing the slice of lemon absently. 'There's nothing to tell really. He's just this bloke I've met recently.'

'Just good friends?'

'Not even that.'

'But you'd like to be?'

Sally shrugged.

'What is that? A yes?'

'I dunno. It's a bit too soon to know. But enough of me, what about you? Any big relationships since we last met? When was it, eight, ten years ago?'

'Or more. I think the last time we really spoke to each other was when we all used to hang out at the Coach and Horses.'

'That's about right. Back at the start of the nineties. I remember bands like Right Said Fred being on the jukebox.'

'That's right,' Lucy ground out her cigarette. 'And you were going out with Andrew Collier.'

Sally smiled and shook her head. 'Yeah, old Andy Collier. He was a bit of a twit really.'

'Was he?' Lucy sounded surprised. 'I remember we all thought he was quite a catch.'

'Not really. He was more in love with himself than with me.'

'Nothing unusual in that. I'd say men spend at least as much – if not more – time in front of the mirror than what we do.'

Sally laughed. 'Well he certainly did. So come on, stop being evasive. Any significant others?'

'Oh, a couple. Nothing special.'

'I guess there's plenty of time for that later, eh?'

Lucy smiled. 'I'm in no hurry.'

As if on cue, two men came up to the booth. They wore sportswear, yet neither looked particularly athletic. The one with the moustache spoke first. 'All right, ladies? All alone are we?'

Lucy looked him straight in the eye and smiled humourlessly. 'Yes thanks.'

The other man, who wore his hair in the bowl-cut style, spoke next. 'Mind if we join you?'

Lucy nodded. 'Yes. Actually we do.'

The two prospective admirers stalled. Moustache rallied. 'What, waiting for the boyfriends are we?'

'You might be,' Lucy said. 'We just don't want company.'

Moustache sneered. 'You a couple of dykes are you?'

'Oh, I'm sure you've already made your own mind up about that, haven't you?' Lucy lit a cigarette.

'Come on, Rich,' said Bowl-Cut. 'Lets go and find some real women.'

Moustache managed a final sneer before allowing himself to be led away. 'Sweet eaters.'

'Lovely regulars in this place,' Sally said. 'Do you come here often?'

Lucy shook her head. 'No. I've never been here before tonight. I just figured it was big and easy to find.'

'Do you like it?'

'No. It's an armpit.'

Sally picked up her drink. 'Shall we go somewhere else?'

'Where?'

Sally took a deep swallow of her drink and shrugged. 'Anywhere. As long as the blokes who drink there can keep their knuckles out of the sawdust.'

'Well that's definitely this place out.' Lucy drank the remains of her pint and set the glass down with finality. 'Shall we?'

Sally finished her drink with equal emphasis. 'Let's.'

They wound up in the Coach and Horses. Both were shocked at how the place had changed. All the carpets had been removed in favour of bare

190

floorboards. The walls were painted in bold colours and pictures of jazz musicians hung everywhere. Plush leather sofas had taken the place of most of the old seating. The other chairs and the wooden tables they clustered around looked like they'd been scavenged from abandoned French farmhouses.

The punters all seemed to be younger than them. They lounged around the sofas and the bar laughing loudly and radiating what Lucy called "obscene levels of confidence".

'In our day we were a bit more restrained,' Lucy said from the corner table they'd managed to secure shortly after they first arrived an hour or so ago. 'A bit less cocky.'

'Were we?' Sally replied. 'I imagine we were much the same. The fashions were different; the music on the jukebox, and obviously the décor. But I'll bet we were just like this.'

Lucy smiled. 'I'm just getting old and bitter. Ignore me.'

'I would. But it's my round. Same again?'

'No. I'll have a half now. I've kind of reached my limit.'

'Okay.' Sally went to the bar.

A few minutes later they sat over fresh drinks. Sally said, 'So, your limit? Are you feeling tipsy, then?'

'I'm feeling pissed.'

Sally grinned. 'Me too. To be honest, I don't get out that often.'

'Oh?'

'Maybe it's my age? Maybe I'm just not interested? I just don't seem to bother much, y'know?'

'I have to admit, I'm not the social butterfly I once was.' Lucy smiled wryly. 'Or moth, depending on your point of view.'

Sally laughed. 'Don't get me wrong, I'm not a complete spinster. I do get out occasionally. I have this friend, sort of.'

'That bloke you mentioned?'

'No.' Sally shook her head. 'A girl. She's okay. I mean, she's nice enough. It's just she's a bit...'

'What?'

'Young. She can't be much older than these people.'

'Is she like these people?' Lucy raised her eyebrows. 'If she is, I can see why you don't choose to go out so much.'

Sally smiled. 'A bit, I guess. But she's certainly not "obscenely confident", as you put it. Quite the opposite, if anything.'

'So why do you hang around with her if you don't really like her? I mean, that's the way it sounds to me – that you don't really like her that much.'

'Oh, I do like her.' Sally stirred the ice cubes in her drink. 'I dunno, I guess you could say that she's all I've got.'

Lucy laughed. 'Oh, I see. Is that why you called me up out of the blue? Desperation?'

'No, of course not. I was going through my diary and I just saw you there. And I thought, "Hey, Lucy Conner. I wonder if she's still about." To be honest, I thought you probably wouldn't be there. Like you'd moved on, same as everyone else. In fact, I'm surprised you're still in the same place.'

'I'm not,' Lucy lit a cigarette. 'I took the phone number, but that's all.'

'So where are you?'

'Charrington Street.'

'Really? Fancy that? You know that guy I was talking to you about earlier?'

'The just-good-friends one?'

'Yeah.'

'What about him?'

'Well,' Sally leaned forward, 'he's, kind of, investigating in Charrington Street at the moment.'

Lucy frowned. 'Investigating? Investigating what?'

'His disappearing colleague.'

'Sounds like a magic act. Roll up! Roll up! Witness the spectacle of the amazing disappearing colleague. What did he use, smoke and mirrors? A trapdoor?'

'Not quite. This guy just left. No message, no phone calls.'

'Sounds odd. But at the same time, I can understand it. I quite fancy just packing my bags and just going off somewhere.'

Sally was about to take a sip of her drink. She hesitated. 'Where would you go?'

'I don't know.' Lucy stubbed out her cigarette. 'Australia, New Zealand, the States? Any place where the natives speak English – I can't be arsed learning a new language.'

'Fair enough.'

'I saved up the money ages ago. I just can't seem to, you know, let go.'

'So what's keeping you here?'

'Habit? I dunno. My flat, maybe?' Lucy shrugged. 'I should really just fuck off and have done with it, but...'

'I understand. It's hard to sever connections. Especially when you've spent time building things up: relationships, property...'

'But that's just it,' Lucy said. 'I don't have any real connections or ties. I'm just, I dunno, lazy.'

Sally laughed. 'Maybe you're just happy. You don't feel the need to travel because you're content.'

'Oh, I'm not content. Not by a long shot.'

'What? Astrology business not exciting enough for you?'

Lucy smiled slyly and turned her lighter over between her fingers. 'You know I said I was resourceful earlier when we talking about making a living?'

'Yeah?'

Lucy looked her in the eyes. 'You don't seem the judgemental type, Sal. Can I tell you a secret?'

'Of course.'

Lucy leaned forward. 'You sure?'

'Yes. What is it?'

Lucy smiled. 'I'm a dominatrix.'

Sally sat back suddenly and put her hand to her mouth. 'You're kidding?'

Lucy shook her head.

'A dominatrix?' Sally whispered.

Lucy nodded. 'I punish men for a living. I provide what the film called, "personal services", remember?'

'Jesus. Do you like, have sex with these men?'

'God, no! I don't even get my hands dirty.'

Sally leaned forward so her face was close to Lucy's. 'So what do you do?'

'I told you, I punish them. I smack their sorry old arses with a cane; I make them kiss my patent leather boots while they're bound and gagged on the floor. There's one who even comes around to clean my house while I call him names. But sex? Oh, no.'

Sally giggled. 'Blimey. Does it pay well?'

'It pays a hell of a lot more than doing horoscopes, I can tell you.'

'Isn't it dangerous?'

Lucy shrugged. 'I'm very careful. I generally only accept recommended clients.'

Sally raised her eyebrows. 'Who recommends people for a spanking?'

Lucy smiled. 'Oh, I have my connections.'

'Maybe that's why you don't just pack up and travel. You're worried about the needs of your clients?'

'Shit, no. I can always refer them on to another caring mistress somewhere. I stay because I'm lazy. I wish there were more to it than that, but there isn't.'

'Except maybe the book you're writing?'

'Yeah,' Lucy extinguished her cigarette. 'There is that.'

'Well stone me,' Sally sat back. 'Who'd've thought it? Lucy Conner, Miss Whiplash. What are they like? Your customers?'

'Just sad men, mostly. They've all got their stories. You tend to feel sorry for them after a while, but you don't show them that. They prefer to be despised. At least my ones do, it's kind of a prerequisite of mine. I don't want to deal with anyone who's too sure of himself. You know what I mean?'

'I'd love to be a fly on the wall sometime.'

'You can come around and help sometime if you like,' Lucy said. 'There's one guy in his fifties who visits once a year, every May bank holiday. He insists on being spanked by two women. I usually get a friend of mine to come over and lend a hand. Maybe you could do the honours next year?'

Sally raised her eyebrows. 'Er, I'll have to get back to you on that one. I have a feeling I may be busy.'

'It's easy money, honey. I bet you'd take to it like a duck to water.' Lucy took a sip of her drink.

'Thanks. I'll bear that in mind.' Sally pictured the scene and shook her head. 'Jesus. Once a year for a two woman spanking? That is so weird.'

'What, the regularity or the two women thing?'

'Both. All of it.'

Lucy smiled. 'You don't know the half of it, sister.'

The barman suddenly rang the bell. 'Last orders at the bar, ladies and gentlemen!'

'You want another drink?' Lucy asked.

'No,' Sally held a hand over her glass.

'Do you fancy coming back to my place? I can show you some of my outfits and stuff?'

'I bet you say that to all the little old men.'

'Oh no.' Lucy said. 'Only the ones who look like they'd weep at the prospect.'

When they arrived at Lucy's house, Sally looked around. 'You know this is really close to where Mick is investigating his disappearing friend.'

'What's his friend's name?' Lucy fished in her bag for her keys.

'Peter, something.'

Lucy looked up. 'Peter Reynolds?'

'That's him! Do you know him?'

'No. But this is the building where he used to live.' Lucy cocked her head at the front door. 'There's this big, bald guy seems to have moved in to his old flat. I wasn't sure whether Reynolds had let the place out or sold it. Or maybe the bald guy was a mate of his, flat-sitting while Reynolds went on holiday or something.'

'Well Mick – that's the just-good-friends guy. He says he called around here for Peter Reynolds, and a voice – I presume the voice of your big bald guy – this voice says that Reynolds has gone abroad. Ran out on his rent or something like that.'

Lucy smiled. 'I think he may have called here too. Does he ride a Chopper?'

'Yeah, that's him.'

Lucy nodded. 'He called here, alright. So he's your friend eh?'

'Friend,' Sally emphasised.

'Uh-huh.' Lucy nodded knowingly and opened the front door. She turned on the timed light in the hallway. 'Well, as for Reynolds, I didn't know him. Kept himself very much to himself. Quiet, y'know? Not the sort who would get into a serious financial pickle.'

'That's the impression I get from Mick too,' Sally said as they walked up the stairs. 'Efficient. Regular.'

'Right down to the bowels.'

Sally laughed. 'Oh yeah, every morning. Eight o'clock on the dot.'

'You or him?'

'Me,' Sally said, and they both laughed.

Lucy opened the door to her flat and turned on the light. She noticed a small sealed envelope on the floor just inside the door. It was addressed simply, "Lucy". She bent and picked it up.

'Love letter?'

'Not quite. Not if it's from who I think it's from.' Lucy slit the envelope open with her fingernail and removed the folded piece of paper within. She read it to herself then shook her head. She handed the note to Sally. 'As I suspected.'

Sally took the note, it was hand written; a small cramped style that took a moment to interpret. She read it aloud.

'"Dear Lucy. I know you told me not to bother you again, but I have to speak to you. You see, I think something's gone wrong with me. I'm damaged somehow. Maybe it's psychological, maybe it's physical. All I know is, things haven't been working quite right since the other afternoon. I really need to see you, just one more time, and only to talk, I promise. Please, please allow me this and I promise I'll never bother you again. Your friend. Wayne."'

Sally noticed that "Wayne" was signed with a flourish. She looked at Lucy. 'Who's Wayne?'

'Guy who lives downstairs. He thought I was running some kind of knocking shop and popped up here looking for a shag.'

'What happened?'

'Let's just say he left feeling sore in all the wrong places.' Lucy said. 'Tea or coffee?'

'Tea please.'

'Here,' Lucy went into the front room and switched on the light. 'Have a seat.' She went to the stereo and turned it on. 'Do you like Englebert Humperdink?'

Sally sat down on the sofa. 'Englebert Humperdink?'

'Yeah,' Lucy opened a CD case and removed the disc. 'I just love Englebert Humperdink. My mum used to like him when I was a kid and I kind of grew up listening to him – yet rejecting him – you know? As you do. It was what your parents liked, so it sucked.'

Sally nodded. 'My mum liked the Seekers.'

'And do you find you like them now?'

'I don't know. I haven't bothered to find out.'

'Do,' Lucy said. 'Buy a "best of" album and listen to it. I bet you'll love it to death.'

'Is that what happened with you and Englebert?'

'Kind of.' Lucy tapped at the buttons on the front of the CD player, selecting a track. 'I found an album of his, one of my mum's old LPs, among my records. I put it on for a laugh. Fuck me, I had to sit down; it was such an emotional ummmph! You know? I just sat there and smiled and cried and laughed and stuff, just remembering my mum and my family when I was little. You know what I mean?'

Sally smiled. 'Yeah. Your mother's dead?'

Lucy nodded. 'Cancer. Smoking. Stupid isn't it? Me smoking and all that?'

'I'm sorry.'

'Thanks. Anyway, listen to this.' She pressed play. 'Do you take sugar?'

'No thanks.'

The opening bars of "Les Bicyclettes De Belsize" began to drift from the speakers as Lucy went to the door. 'I'll be back in a bit. Just listen to this. It's so good.'

Sally sat back and closed her eyes. The vodka tingled pleasantly around her system as she listened to the music. The image of herself and Lucy spanking a man's bottom rose again in her mind. She grimaced and opened her eyes. Then she giggled, bit her lip, and closed them again.

It was approximately an hour later when the door buzzer rang.

'That'll be your taxi.' Lucy put her cigarette in the ashtray and rose from her armchair. She went into the hall and picked up the entryphone. 'Hello?'

'Taxi for Sally,' the voice at the other end answered.

'Okay. She'll be down in a second.' She hung up and went back into the lounge.

Sally looked at her, casually expectant. 'Is it?'

Lucy nodded. 'Only ten minutes late. They must be quiet tonight.'

Sally got up. 'Well, it's been a lot of fun. We should do this again sometime.'

'We should.' Lucy kissed her lightly on the cheek. 'You'll need to give me a few day's notice though. I have an unusual schedule.'

Sally laughed. 'I will, don't worry.'

They went into the hall of Lucy's flat. Lucy opened the front door. 'Thanks for a nice evening. I was beginning to forget what a normal night out feels like.'

'Well, like we said,' Sally stepped out onto the darkened landing. 'We'll have to do it again sometime.'

'Sometime soon.' Lucy switched on the hall light.

'Thanks,' Sally said. 'I'll see you.' She turned and walked softly down the carpeted stairs.

'Seeya, Sal.' Lucy waited until Sally had disappeared from view, then she went back into her flat and closed the door.

As Sally walked down the stairs, she smiled. She really should call Lucy up again soon. It was so refreshing to go out with a woman she could actually talk to on the same level. To talk about something other than that idiot, Gaz and his friends.

Just as she reached the door, the timed light went out. Sally stopped. There was enough light coming in from the window above the door for her to see the Yale lock. She reached out to open it, but before she could, it opened for her. She stepped back as the door swung slowly open and the silhouette of a large man filled the doorway. As he removed his key from the lock, his smooth head shone in the glow from the streetlamps outside. She realised that this had to be the guy who now lived up in Mick's friend's flat. She stepped uncertainly to one side and he saw her in the shadows.

'Oh,' he said apologetically. 'Excuse me.' He stepped aside for her to pass.

Sally smiled. 'That's okay.' She avoided making eye contact as she stepped past him, noticing as she did so, the odd T-shirt he wore. Once outside, she looked back to thank him for holding the door, but it was already closing behind her. She raised her eyebrows. So that was him, eh? Interesting. Especially the "Choose Life" shirt. She got into the waiting cab and gave the driver her address. As she sat back, visions of Wham! suddenly filled her head, their long forgotten songs rising with incredible buoyancy.

She sat forward and spoke to the driver. 'Do you have a radio or something?'

'Yes, love.'

'Do me a favour,' she said. 'Turn it on.'

Chapter 21

KAY OPENED HER EYES and saw the face of Gaz sleeping beside her. She smiled and lay still, enjoying the moment, letting it sink in through the residual effect of last nights' various intoxicants that lay over her senses like a morning mist. She wanted to remember it later on when she was at work, drowning in boredom and drudgery. She felt an ache inside as she looked at him, his face all stubbly and slept on, his breathing slow and slightly hissy through his nose. She kissed him gently on the forehead. He stirred a little but didn't awaken. She smiled, and wondered what the time was.

Kay rolled over onto her other side and looked over Jimmy's sleeping face at the bedside clock. It read 8.20. Shit! 8.20! They'd done it again. They were supposed to set the alarm for 7.45. She cursed herself for leaving the task to them. Sure, maybe they forgot. Then again maybe they did it on purpose to avoid being woken up early. 'Shit!' She clambered unceremoniously over Gaz's body.

'Unnh, eh?' Gaz writhed into consciousness beneath her. 'Kay? What's going on?'

'I'm late. You didn't set the alarm again.'

'I did. Check it, man.'

Kate strode around to the other side of the bed. She pressed the button that revealed the pre-set alarm hour. It read 7.45.

'See?' Gaz propped himself up onto his elbow.

Kay held up the display for him to see more clearly. She pointed to a small red dot in the corner, beside which were the letters, "PM". 'PM, Gaz. Not AM, but PM. You got the wrong part of the sodding day.'

'Shhh, low. Not now,' Jimmy mumbled, turning over in bed so his face lay upon his arms.

Gaz ignored him. 'Will you be late?'

'Not if I hurry.' Kay crossed the room and snatched up a T-shirt that lay discarded on the floor. 'I've got my work things in my overnight bag. I can catch a later bus if I'm quick.'

Gaz sat up and rubbed his face. 'Aw, shit. What a wake up call.'

'Oh, well I'm sorry to trouble you.' Kay pulled on the shirt and stomped out in the direction of the bathroom.

Gaz blinked a few times and smiled. He swung his legs out of the bed and got to his feet. He stretched and yawned, then cheerfully scratched his groin with both hands. He looked back to where Jimmy persevered with sleep and chuckled. 'Nice one, man. You sleep on.'

'Urrr,' was Jimmy's only response.

Gaz trotted out onto the landing in pursuit of Kay. The other bedroom door was open and the sounds of Glen's snores drifted out onto the landing. Gaz looked in to see Glen's naked form sprawled upon his bed, the duvet kicked off and tangled around his knees. Gaz seemed to remember Glen still being in with them when he'd nodded off last night. He must've crawled back in here sometime in the early hours.

He heard the sounds of Kay in the bathroom. She was showering. Just as well, Gaz grinned to himself. She'd need to. He went downstairs, wondering if he'd find Adam on the couch. He went into the lounge and checked the sofa, but the big guy had gone. He'd said he would. Gaz realised he was glad. There was something about Adam, something... amiss. He knew Kay was deeply uncomfortable with the idea of Adam getting involved with them at bedtime. He wondered if Adam sensed that, whether that was why he never joined them?

He went into the kitchen and filled the kettle. He opened the fridge and poked about until he uncovered a bottle of milk. He sniffed it. It was okay. He shut the fridge and took a couple of slices of bread from the packet that lay spilled over the work surface. He deposited them in the toaster and switched it on.

As the kettle boiled, he looked out of the window. He took a deep breath and sighed. Things just weren't happening with this Sally campaign. She should've been conquered by now; twisting and turning between them at night, unsure of where to turn for her next pleasure. He shook his head. The stuck-up bitch. She'd fucking love it. If only he could get her to be there in the first place. He heard Kay coming down the stairs just as the toast popped up. He picked up a knife and the tub of margarine that lay next to the bread. 'Breakfast?' he asked cheerily as Kay entered the kitchen.

She looked at him, surprised and delighted. 'Thanks. I wasn't expecting this.'

'Hey.' Gaz shrugged. 'If I hadn't messed up the alarm, you wouldn't be in this situation. It's the least I can do.' He spread margarine on the toast then dug out a jar of marmalade from inside one of the cupboards. 'Marmalade?'

'Yeah, thanks.' Kay sat down at the kitchen table and ran a brush through her damp and tangled hair. She wore a towel around her body, tucked into itself just above her breasts. Gaz felt an urge to remove it and make her really late for work, but resisted.

'Tea or coffee?'

'Coffee.' Kay smiled at him. 'Black and strong.'

'Hungover?'

'Just a bit.' She pulled a face as the brush encountered a stubborn knot in her hair. 'I don't know how you manage.'

'I go back to bed and sleep it off.'

'I wish I could, you lucky sod. Give us a kiss.'

He walked over and kissed her. She smelt fresh and clean, the vague perfume of shower gel mingled intoxicatingly with the smell of her skin.

Kay noticed things between Gaz's legs beginning to stir and she pushed him gently away. 'Down boy. No time for that sort of thing.'

'Are you sure?' Gaz came back to her, pushing his face into the damp hair that fell about her neck. 'I can be very quick, you know.'

'I'm sure you can.' Kay giggled. 'Shame we haven't got the time for you to prove it. Where's my coffee?'

Gaz allowed himself to be pushed away again and smiled. 'Your loss, baby.' He turned and plucked two mugs from the clutter of crockery on the draining board and began preparing coffee for them. 'So, you busy today?'

'Busy every day. God knows how I'll cope with a sodding hangover.'

'How do you normally manage?'

'Coffee and chocolate.'

'Well, we haven't got any chocolate.' Gaz handed her a steaming mug. 'But here's that all-important first brew of the day.'

'Thank you,' Kay said, accepting the coffee.

'And here,' Gaz passed her a small plate with two pieces of toast and marmalade, 'here's breakfast.'

Kay felt that ache again as she took the plate. There wasn't anything particularly emotionally intoxicating about the toast, it was just him. Standing there, bare-arsed naked and handing it to her. 'Thanks, Gaz. That's really... It's really nice of you.'

'Toast, Kay,' Gaz bowed, 'is my speciality.'

'Thanks.' She bit into the toast.

'Good?'

'Mmmm,' she munched.

Gaz sat on the chair next to hers at the table. 'Will you be seeing Sally today?'

Kay stopped chewing and looked at him. 'Why?'

Gaz shrugged. 'She's your mate isn't she? I just wondered if you'd be seeing her.'

Kay put down her toast and took a sip of coffee. 'You want to shag her, don't you?'

Gaz laughed. 'I think she'd be fun, yeah. But I'm thinking more of Glen and Jimmy than myself. If we can get her into the swing of things, it'll leave you and me free to get it together on our own.'

'You're saying you don't want to screw Sally?'

'No,' said Gaz. 'If she's gonna be there, sticking it in my face, then yeah, I'd probably get it on with her. I mean, I'm a geezer. But it wouldn't mean anything, y'know? What I'm saying is, if we had Sally around, she and the lads could take the double room, and we'd take the single all to ourselves. Push the two beds together, like.'

Kay scrutinised him over her coffee. 'You mean that? You and me alone?'

'Yeah, babe. Sally's not my type. Too uptight. You know that surely? Swinging guy like me?'

Kay picked up her toast and took a bite. 'She is uptight. I think she might be a bloody lesbian, either that or an escaped nun.'

Gaz ran his hand up her thigh and under the towel. 'Not like you, eh, babe?'

She smiled. 'No thanks to you. You animal.'

'I don't ask you to do anything you aren't begging to do anyway.'

'That is so not true.' Kay brushed his hand away from her leg.

'Oh yes it is.' He tried to bring his hand back onto her thigh but she swatted it away.

'I wanted us alone from the start. That didn't happen did it?'

'Ahh, come on. You enjoy it.'

'Sometimes I do, sometimes I don't,' said Kay. 'But I'd prefer it if it were just the two of us.'

'So get Sally 'round.' Gaz slipped his arm around her shoulders. 'Give the lads something else to do.'

Kay let him hug her to him for a moment before she changed the subject. 'Where's Adam?'

'Gone.' Gaz reached out and took his coffee from the table.

'Thank God.'

'You don't like him?'

'I don't know. He's odd.'

'You don't fancy him, then?'

'Jesus Christ, no. I mean, it's not that he's ugly or anything – he isn't. But the thought of him touching me.' She shuddered. 'No thank you.'

'What is it you find odd about him?'

'Why?'

'I wonder if it's the same things I do.'

'You find him odd too?'

'Oh, yeah,' said Gaz. 'How could you not?'

'I don't know what it is. Sometimes when he looks at me, or anyone for that matter, it's so intense isn't it? Especially when he looks at you.'

'Yeah.' Gaz sipped his coffee. 'I've noticed that.'

'Is that all? Have you noticed anything else?'

'I dunno.' Gaz rubbed the stubble on his chin. 'Just stuff, you know. Like the business with that piss in the garden. He knew exactly what it was, and exactly where it was coming from. And he knew, or certainly seemed to know, that guy with the squirt rifle wasn't the one who put the petrol through the door.'

Kay nodded. 'I thought that was odd when you told me about it.'

'That, and the way he just seemed to kind of, know us before we met. You know?'

'Yeah,' Kay said thoughtfully. She smiled at him. 'You know what I think?'

'What?'

'I think he fancies you.'

'What?'

'I think he fancies you. I know because I feel kind of... jealous sometimes when he looks at you. I feel like saying, "Oi! Get your eyes off him. He's mine."'

Gaz shook his head. 'Naaaa. If he fancied me, he'd come and get it on with the rest of us, wouldn't he? He'd make a move on me while we were all at it.'

Kay shrugged. 'Maybe, maybe not. Not everyone who fancies you wants to go to such lengths in order to have it off with you. Except me, of course. I'm so fucking crazy about you I...' She let the sentence trail off.

Gaz put down his mug and gave her shoulder a gentle squeeze. 'You what?'

She looked at him. 'Nothing.'

'What?' Gaz touched her chin lightly and turned her face to his. 'You can tell me.'

She looked into his eyes. 'No I can't.' She got up. 'I have to get a move on. I'm late as it is.'

Gaz watched her as she tipped the remains of her toast into the bin. She went to the sink, and seeing it full of washing-up, began to rinse the plate with great determination under running water. He decided to stay quiet.

She found a space for the plate on the draining board. 'I have to go.' She turned and left the kitchen without looking at him.

'Your overnight bag's in the lounge behind the sofa,' he said. 'I saw it just before I came in here.'

'I know. Thanks,' she called from the lounge.

He sat a moment longer, then got to his feet and followed her. He stood in the doorway and watched her. She had discarded the towel and was pulling on her underwear.

'Stop it,' Kay said.

'Stop what?'

'Stop looking at me like that.'

'Like what?'

'You know.' She fastened her bra and bent down to her overnight bag for her tights.

'You mean stop admiring you?' Gaz asked. 'Don't you want me to fancy you?'

'You know I do. But sometimes you make me feel like, I dunno.'

'What?'

'Like meat,' she said, pulling on her blouse.

He raised his eyebrows. 'Oh. Well I'm sorry. I'll look elsewhere if it bothers you.' He turned and walked away down the hall.

'You know what I mean, Gaz. Sometimes I think all I am to you is a fuck. And a fuck you can share with your mates at that.' She hesitated. 'It's not, it's not a nice thought.' She swore under her breath, stepped into her skirt and pulled it to her waist.

Gaz returned to the doorway. 'You think that? You really think that?'

Kay shrugged, pulling on her blouse. 'Sometimes.'

'Come on, Kay. You know I fancy you.'

'Oh I know that. But that's all isn't it? It's not like you ever look at me like that Adam bloke looks at you.'

Gaz grimaced. 'Leave it out, Kay. That's too weird when you say that. It creeps me out.'

'It's true though, isn't it?' Kay persisted. She took her shoes from her bag and dropped them to the floor, stepping into them one after the other. 'He looks at you like he loves you. You're not just meat to him.'

Gaz came into the room, he reached out and caught her gently by the arm. She stopped and turned to look at him. He met her eyes levelly. 'Is that it Kay? You want me to love you?'

'Well.' She shrugged. 'It would be nice, wouldn't it? I mean, I don't want you to say anything you don't feel, but it would be nice if you could try and make me feel a bit, you know… special.' She looked away.

'Don't I do that already?'

'No, frankly.' She bent and started rustling pointlessly in her bag. 'Where are my other clothes?'

He smiled. 'All over the place. Mostly in the bedroom.'

She straightened up and went to move past him, but he stepped between her and the door. 'Hey,' he said, 'forget about them. They can wait. Leave them here and I'll put them in the wash.'

She refused to look at him. 'Let me go, Gaz, I'm late enough as it is.'

'Kiss me before you go,' he said. His hold upon her arm was light, she could break free if she wanted to, but she stayed still. He lowered his head to look beneath her hair and see her face. She lowered her head further. 'Hey,' he said, 'where's my kiss? You can't just go off to work without giving the old man a kiss goodbye.' She raised her face to his. Tears welled in her eyes. Gaz said nothing. Her eyes held as much challenge as they did sadness. He took her face gently in his hands and kissed her eyes, spilling her tears onto his lips and down her cheeks. He drew his lips slowly over her face, tracing the warm, salt taste of her tears to her mouth where she met his kiss with her own.

When the moment was over, he brushed her damp fringe from her eyes. 'Why don't you phone in sick?' he whispered. 'You can't go in looking like you've been crying, babe.'

'I have been crying,' she sniffed.

'You know what I mean.'

'I have to.'

'No you don't,' he said. 'I can do it for you, say you were sick in the night or something?'

She sniffed and shook her head.

'Please? We can spend the day together. Just the two of us.'

She looked up into his eyes. Fresh tears spilling over her eyelashes. 'Do you want that?'

He smiled. 'Of course I do, Kay.' He held her face in his hands and brushed her tears gently from her cheeks with his thumbs. 'You're my girl aren't you? My special girl?'

'Your only girl?'

'Yeah. My only girl.'

'I love you, Gaz,' she said, her lips tightening.

'I love you too, babe,' he whispered.

'Do you? Do you really?'

'Course I do, babe.' He smoothed her hair. 'I wouldn't say it if I didn't mean it.'

Kay buried her face in his bare chest and drew her arms slowly but tightly about his neck and shoulders. He returned her embrace, holding her to him as she began to cry softly against him. 'Shhhh,' he whispered, still smoothing her hair. 'Nothing to cry about, sweetheart. You're safe now. Safe with Gaz.' He felt her murmur something against his chest, but he couldn't hear it. He kissed her head. 'But you understand I'm different, don't you Kay?'

She nodded slowly.

'I want more out of life than other people do. Isn't that what attracted you to me in the first place? Sure, we could just pair off and go out in a normal boy and girl type way. But I'd go crazy, and sooner rather than later.'

'I know,' she whispered, her face still against his chest.

'You're the same Kay.' He stroked a finger against her neck. 'You want more than the others. They're dead, babe. Not like us. We're different here – we experience it all, don't we?'

She nodded, a slow and single movement of her head.

'You'll help me then?' he said softly. 'Get Sally involved? For our sake? For us?'

Kay didn't move. For a moment Gaz thought he'd pushed it too far. Then she nodded; again, just a slow, single movement of her head. But it was enough. A smile rose on Gaz's face. He caught sight of his reflection in the mirror. He mouthed a single word to his image, savouring the feel of it on his lips even though he couldn't hear it. "Yesssss!"

Chapter 22

'WELL FANCY SEEING YOU HERE.'

Sally turned to see Mick standing behind her in the bustling crowd at the Marks and Spencer sandwich counter. 'Oh, hi.'

'What's the difference between us and the pigeons?' said Mick. 'Here we all are, clamouring after bits of bread. I ask you, what's the difference?'

Sally smiled. 'We don't make weird groaning sounds in the middle of the night.'

'Speak for yourself.' Mick selected a packet of sandwiches. 'Anyway, do pigeons groan in the night?'

'Oh good heavens, yes. I used to live in a flat above a shop and there were pigeons nesting outside my window. Every night, just as you'd be getting off to sleep, they'd start this weird groaning sound.'

'What were they doing?'

'I don't know. Maybe they were snoring.' She browsed the sandwiches. 'What have you got?'

'Turkey and bacon club.'

'Hmm,' Sally considered a moment, then made a decision. 'I'm going for the BLT.' She took a packet from the display.

'I had it yesterday. Very nice. Everybody came over to my desk to enjoy my fresh breath afterwards.'

'What, did they say? "Mmmm. Pig"?'

'How did you know?'

Sally shrugged. 'I hear pig is the new mint.'

Mick laughed and feigned astonishment. 'That'd explain why everybody was trying to kiss me all day. It was like living in a seventies toothpaste ad.'

'Oh? I hope you resisted.'

'Of course. I only hope you're as strong willed this afternoon when you go back to work smelling of swine.'

'Since Leonard's my only colleague, I think I'll be safe. Unless of course the great smell of bacon brings out a hitherto unseen side of him.'

Mick raised two crossed fingers. 'Here's hoping, eh?'

Sally smirked. 'Shall we pay?'

'Yeah. I think we're attracting attention standing here rambling on about pigs.'

They paid and left. They walked together through the town to the public gardens. 'So what do you think was really going on with those pigeons?' Mick said. 'Perhaps it was like, a mating thing.'

'Who knows? All I know is it just used to go on all night like some weird, tormented pump.'

'What does a tormented pump sound like?'

'Like, uuur-uuur-uuur,' Sally did her best rendition of a pigeon's nocturne. 'They'd get louder if you didn't stop them.

'It sounds more and more like a mating thing. Maybe they got louder as they got more passionate?'

'I don't think so,' said Sally. 'When it got to the point that I couldn't take it any more I'd open the window and they'd fly off. I never caught them inflagrante delicto.'

'Eh?'

'On the job.'

'Oh.' Mick nodded. 'Maybe they heard you coming and quickly packed it in, then acted all innocent.'

'Yes.' Comprehension dawned on Sally's features. 'That explains why they were standing around whistling nonchalantly with their hands in their pockets when I arrived.'

'Ahh, you see? There you are. The problem is solved.'

'How can I ever thank you?'

'You can select a spot for lunch.' Mick looked around the gardens. 'We seem to be spoilt for choice today.'

Sally pointed to the benches. 'There's a bench if you want one?'

He pointed to an area of lawn near a flowerbed. 'Or there's a lawn with a view.'

Sally shrugged. 'I don't mind. You choose.'

They looked from one option to the other. Mick shrugged. 'Lawn?'

'Lawn's fine with me,' Sally agreed. They headed toward the designated spot. As they got there and spread their things out, Sally suddenly looked up. 'Oh, guess what?'

'What?'

'I know someone who lives in the same building as your friend Peter. Or rather, the building where Peter used to live.'

Mick stopped trying to open his sandwiches. 'Really?'

Sally nodded. 'Really.'

'Who?'

'A friend of mine. She lives in the flat below.'

'Shit. What did she tell you?'

'Not much. Only that Peter didn't seem the unreliable type.'

'She got that right,' Mick finally opened his sandwiches and took one out.

'She also said the fellow who lives there now is a big bald guy. He'd be the one you spoke to on the intercom.'

'Yeah,' Mick said through a mouthful of turkey and bacon. 'Anything else?'

Sally bit into her apple. 'Mm-hm.'

'What?'

'I saw him.'

Mick leaned forward. 'You saw the bald guy?'

Sally nodded. 'Yeah. In the hall as I was leaving.'

'What did he look like?'

'Well, he was bald.'

Mick smiled. 'Yeah, and?'

'I didn't see really. It was pretty dark. But I think he's a Wham! fan.'

Mick frowned. 'Oh? What gave you that impression?'

'Do you remember those "Choose Life" shirts they used to wear?'

Mick made a face. 'Yeah, big things?'

She nodded. 'Yeah, but not on this guy. He was wearing one, and it was a pretty good fit.'

Mick chewed thoughtfully for a moment. 'Hmmm. Anything else?'

'No, not about him. But obviously lots of other stuff.'

'Like what?'

'Oh, you know, just things. She's an old friend of mine. I haven't seen her in years. At least not socially.'

'Until last night?'

'Yeah. Her name's Lucy. You'd like her.'

Mick considered. 'Big and bald you say?'

'Well no, she's about my height with lots of curly red hair.'

Mick smiled. 'You know who I mean.'

'Oh him, yeah. Big and bald.'

'I saw him too the other day.'

Sally stopped eating. 'Did you? You never told me.'

Mick shrugged. 'I didn't know who he was. I was watching the house and I saw this big bald-headed dude come out. I thought about following him for a bit, but to be honest, I couldn't be arsed.'

'Why?'

'I was pissed off and hungry.'

'Fair enough.'

They were silent for a moment, then Mick said, 'I wonder who the landlord is?'

Sally smiled at the memory of Lucy's collection of bondage implements. 'I got the impression from Lucy's place that she didn't have a landlord, so it'd be no good asking her.'

'Oh? What gave you that impression?'

'Oh, certain decorative ideas.'

'Like?'

'I can't say, I'm sworn to secrecy.'

'I see,' Mick said. 'But you reckon a landlord would object?'

'I think so, but you never know.'

'Hmmm. Well, let's change the subject.'

'I think that's a good idea.'

'Okay. Are you still on for a drink?'

Sally took another bite from the sandwich and nodded. 'Uh-huh.'

'So, when shall we go? And where?'

'How about tonight?'

'I thought you said you were busy over the next few days?'

'A woman's prerogative, isn't it? To change her mind?'

'I suppose so.'

'This time yesterday I had plans. Today, I don't.'

'Hmmm, you're a fickle breed.'

'Don't bring the breed into this,' Sally said. 'It's me who's fickle.'

'Really?'

She smiled. 'Only when it suits me.'

'I see.'

'Anyway,' Sally said, 'you're practically a stranger. I hardly know you. A girl has every right to exercise a certain... reserve.'

'Oh, absolutely,' Mick agreed. 'I quite understand. Though would you say that now, perhaps, that certain reserve is a little less... reserved.'

Sally gave him an appraising look, shrugged slightly, and then nodded.

Mick smiled. 'That's good, then.'

'I think so.'

'So, where do you want to go?'

'I can think of a lot of places I don't want to go. Have you ever been to the Moon and Stars?'

'That big place? No.'

'It's awful. We went there last night, Lucy and I. These horrible men tried to chat us up.'

'Lucky you.' Mick said. 'So where is a good place? Shenanigans?'

'Please!' Sally grimaced. 'That's the last place I want to go. Do you know The Coach and Horses?'

'Yeah.'

'Do you like it?'

'It's alright. A bit pretentious.'

'It is, but maybe that's what keeps the arseholes away.'

'Okay, shall we say the Coach and Horses then? Say about 8.30?'

'Okay, it's a date.'

They ate in silence for a moment, looking about at the other people in the park. Then Mick said, 'Could I ask you for your phone number? You know, in case I get stuck down a mineshaft or something and can't make it?'

'Sure, I'll give you my mobile. Do you have a pen?'

Mick fumbled in his jacket and came out with a pen and a used envelope. 'Fire away.' Sally gave him the number and he scribbled it down. 'Brilliant. Do you want mine?'

'Sure. You never know, I might get stuck down a mineshaft myself. Can you write it on that piece of paper?'

Mick wrote the number down and tore it off.

She looked at it. 'This is your home number?'

'Yeah.'

'You don't have a mobile?'

'No. Don't need one.'

Sally put the piece of paper in the pocket of her cardigan. 'Neither do I really. I just, you know, got one.'

Mick smiled. 'That's cool.'

Sally raised an eyebrow. 'Is it? Not particularly good for you are they?'

'That's what they reckon.'

'When you think of it, I suppose I should be grateful for a quiet social life,' Sally said. 'Can you imagine the brain-frying hell of popularity? All those microwaves frazzling your head twenty-four hours a day?'

'Damn.' Mick thumped the grass. 'Now I've come along and taken your number. It's the beginning of the end for your brain, sister.'

'Mmm.' Sally stroked her chin. 'Maybe I should give you my home number.'

Mick smiled. 'That would be nice.'

They sat and discussed various trivialities for the remainder of the lunch break before it was time to return to work.

'Oh, well,' Mick got reluctantly to his feet. 'At least it's Friday. The weekend lies ahead.'

'Not if you work in a shop. Though fortunately Leonard and I rotate our weekends. And this one's mine.'

'So you're off tomorrow? Are you doing anything special?'

'Not working. For me, that's special enough.'

Mick brushed down his jacket before putting it on. 'Well, I'll see you tonight, then? The Coach and Horses at 8.30?'

'Yep. Don't be late. I don't want to be sitting in there on my own like some sad old wallflower.'

'I can't imagine you'd be sitting alone for long, Sal. What were you saying about those guys last night trying to pick you up?'

'All the more reason for you not to be late, mister.'

He smiled. 'I won't be.'

They stood for a moment in silence. 'Well,' Sally said, 'I guess I'd better get going.'

'Yeah, me too.'

'Right, then.' She turned and began to walk away from him. After a few paces she looked back over her shoulder. 'See you at 8.30.'

Mick raised his hand. 'On the dot.'

Sally smiled and turned back in the direction she was walking. She considered glancing casually around again, just to see if he was still watching her go, but decided against it. She'd look like a teenager. Just leave, she told herself. Cool and casual. Her plan didn't work, when she got to the entrance of the gardens, almost without thinking, she turned back. Mick was walking towards one of the side exits. She felt a momentary disappointment. She realised she'd wanted him to be standing there, waving after her like she was riding out of some black and white movie on a smoky old train. Then Mick turned in her direction. She hesitated, then waved. He waved back. She smiled and headed back to the shop. Drat, she thought. There goes my feminine mystique.

She remained in a bright and cheerful mood all the way back to the shop. She was just about to enter when a hand fell lightly upon her shoulder. For one insane and strangely hopeful moment, she thought maybe Mick had chased after her with a bunch of flowers or something, just acting on impulse, as it were. She turned to see Kay.

'Hi, Sally. Are you busy? I really need to talk to you.'

'Kay? Hi, er, no, no I'm not busy. My lunch is over, but you can come in and talk to me. What is it?'

'It's about Gaz. Can we talk inside?'

Who else? thought Sally. 'Sure,' she said. 'Sure, come in.'

Mick was just getting out of the shower when the phone rang. It was six-thirty and the bathroom's acoustics were doing wonders for his version of "The Street Where You Live". He stopped mid-verse and listened to confirm the distant sound was the phone. 'Shit,' he muttered. He ran from the bathroom into the hallway, leaving a trail of wet footprints behind him. He snatched up the phone. 'Hello?'

'Mick?'

'Yeah?'

'It's Sally.'

Mick brightened. 'Hiya, what's up?'

'I'm sorry, but it looks like I'm stuck down that mineshaft after all. A friend needs some moral support tonight and I've been more or less press-ganged into lending it.'

Mick's smile waned. 'Oh.'

'Are you mad at me?'

'No. No of course not. These things happen.'

'She's got man trouble. You remember I told you about that girl and the blokes at Shenanigan's?'

'Yeah.'

'It's her. She wants me to add some extra femininity to the testosterone-heavy environment.'

'Oh. That, er, doesn't exactly sound like a great night out.'

'I know, but what can I do? She was wearing these sunglasses all the time, I think she'd been crying. She certainly sounded on the verge of tears when I spoke to her.'

'Why doesn't she just forget about it?'

'Have you ever been madly in love with the wrong person?'

'No, I can't say that I have.'

'I have. It's a nightmare that you don't want to end. There's always this persistent hope that things will get better. That things will somehow eventually change and go the way you want them to.'

'And they never do.'

'No, not in my experience. But Kay's got to learn that for herself. I kind of know what she's going through, and I know how much she needs a friend right now. I'm really sorry it messes things up for us tonight, but I can't refuse her Mick. Do you know what I mean?'

'Yeah, of course' Mick said. 'Maybe we can do something another night.'

'Tomorrow?'

Mick smiled. 'Sure, that'd be great.'

'What time?'

'Whenever.'

'How about midday? We can make a day of it.'

'Okay, where?'

'I could call for you. Seaton Street, right? What number?'

'Twelve A.'

'Okay, so midday then?'

Mick plucked at the telephone flex. 'I'm looking forward to it already.'

'Me too. And sorry again, Mick. Thanks for being so understanding.'

'Forget it. I'll see you tomorrow.'

'Okay, bye.'

'Bye.' Mick put the phone back on the cradle and sighed. 'Shit.' He looked at the puddle of water at his feet and dragged a line through it with his toe. 'Shit, bollocks and shit again.' He padded back through the hall to the bathroom where he picked up the towel and went back to drying himself. What now then? he thought. I could phone Dave and Clare, see if they're going out for a drink? Or I could get a video and a pizza or something, maybe a few beers? He gave his hair a vigorous towelling. Then another option occurred to him. Or I could stake out Peter's place. Maybe catch a glimpse of the bald guy?

He stopped, suddenly paralysed in the grip of a brilliant idea. Or I could call for him. Say I'm a Jehovah's Witness or something? Or canvassing opinions on local parking issues – getting a petition together? He grinned. 'Now that's what I call genius.'

Chapter 23

RICK RETURNED TO THE BEDROOM carrying a tray laden with sumptuous breakfast pleasures the like of which Leanne had never seen. He set the tray down upon her lap and sat next to her on the edge of the bed.

Leanne was almost speechless with delight. She managed to blurt out a sentence, pointing as she did so at a plate on the tray. 'What, what's this, Rick, darling?'

'Eggs Benedict,' said Rick. 'I made it myself.'

'Really?' said Leanne, impressed that such a complex yellow mess of egg, ham and muffin could be prepared in so short a space of time. But then she realised she had no idea how long Rick had been up before her. When she awoke and stretched out her arm to touch him, his side of the bed had been cold and empty. He could have been up for hours, she realised. She smiled, lovingly, and pointed to the next delicacy. 'And these?'

'Pancakes in maple syrup,' he said with an arrogant grin. 'Just like they have in the North.'

'Oh, Rick,' said Leanne. 'Will it always be this way? You bringing me breakfast – and such a wonderful breakfast it is too. Will you always bring me breakfast when we're married?'

Rick slid from the bed onto one knee at the side of the bed and grasped one of her delicate, flower-like hands in both his large, manly ones. 'Of course, Leanne. Every moment will be like love's first sight; every day like today, and every night like the night of our honeymoon – or,' he said with a rakish grin, 'if you prefer – every night will be like last night.'

She reddened and looked down at her glass of passion fruit juice, though she didn't know it was passion fruit juice yet. 'Oh, Rick, you're such a fine thing. How could I ever have been so... so blind to your charms? The Zodiac is such a complex and weird thing. I sometimes feel I'd be better off just judging people by who they are rather than what signs they were born under.'

'You must do whatever you feel is best, my love. But in all honesty, I tend to agree. The Zodiac kept us apart for so long. That, and the fact that I was kind of beastly on occasion.'

Leanne leaned forward with a gushing earnestness that spilled some of her hot, rich Brazilian coffee. 'Oh no, Rick, it was I who was beastly to you;

you were only responding like a wounded deer that has been stung by a stone, fired by a foolish and errant child from the catapult of ignorance.'

Now it was Rick's turn to redden. He said, 'Well, if you think so...'

'Oh I do, Rick, darling. I do.'

He looked at her, sitting there, propped up by her pillows, her long blonde hair spilling over her full, milk-white breasts. He reached out a tentative finger and dipped it into the hollandaise sauce that covered the eggs on her plate, then raised the finger to her lips. She extended her tongue and licked it off. 'Mmmmm,' she murmured, closing her eyes with delight. 'Lovely.'

He repeated the action, this time smearing her ruby-red lips with the creamy sauce as fast as her greedy pink tongue could lick it away. She giggled happily. Rick then picked up one of the hollandaise-heavy poached eggs and placed it against the swell of one of her breasts. She gasped, her eyes still closed. 'Oh, it's hot, darling.'

'Not as hot as me,' he said, and then pressed the egg flat against her, the yolk spurting out between his fingers like a thick, yellow ejaculation. Leanne opened her eyes and looked at the egg and hollandaise that Rick now massaged into her breasts using both hands.

'Oh, Rick,' she gasped.

'Oh, Leanne,' he sighed, then plunged his face onto her breasts and began lapping furiously at the savoury treat.

'Oh, Rick!' Leanne said, tears of joy filling her eyes. 'Eat it! Eat my Eggs Benedict!'

Rick, his face messy with egg, looked up and said

There was a knock at the door. Lucy looked up from the monitor and listened. It sounded again, louder than before. She saved her work, pushed her seat back from the table and got up. She went to the door, slid the safety chain on, then opened it wide enough to see who was outside. It was as she expected. She didn't register any emotion. 'Hello, Wayne.'

'I can't explain it,' Wayne said a short while later as he sat in her lounge nursing a mug of coffee with both hands. 'I just don't work right anymore.'

Lucy took a sip of her coffee. 'I'm sorry to hear that. Why don't you go and see a doctor?'

'I can't do that,' Wayne said with more than a hint of desperation. 'Ellen and I share the same doctor. He knows us both. How can I tell him I went to see a, a...?'

'Whore?'

Wayne balked. 'I didn't say that.'

'You wanted to.'

'No I didn't.'

'Forget about it. You were saying you couldn't see your doctor...'

'No. Well, how can I say what happened? What led me into this mess?'

Lucy shrugged. 'So go and see a different doctor.'

'No,' Wayne wrung his hands around his coffee mug. 'I need to see you. Just one more time. I need to know if what took place between us has, has changed me.'

Lucy looked wary. 'What do you mean?'

'I mean, what if I still – you know – get hard with you? At least I'll know if I'm damaged or just, just a bit... you know, a bit kinky.'

'You're not damaged, Wayne. Don't be stupid. It's the latter – you're a pervert. Now go downstairs and get Ellen to spank you. You'll be standing to attention in no time.'

Wayne looked at her intently. 'Why don't you spank me?'

'Oh, no,' Lucy shook her head wearily. 'Don't start that again, Wayne. I told you, it was a one off. And I meant it.'

'I could still tell the freeholder what you're doing up here.'

'And I could still tell your wife.'

'Fiancée,' Wayne corrected.

'Whatever,' Lucy said. 'I could still tell Ellen about your pestering me for sexual gratification.'

'I don't care.' Wayne held his nose defiantly in the air.

'Really? Well I don't care if you tell the freeholder about my business concerns. I've been meaning to move on from this life for awhile now and it would be the perfect spur to get me moving.'

'I don't believe you.'

'Try me.'

'I will,' Wayne said. 'Don't make me prove it.'

'I think you've overstayed your welcome, Wayne,' Lucy said coolly.

He put down the coffee mug and stood up. 'I won't go until you punish me.'

'You will go, or I'll call the police.'

'Ha! That's a laugh. Do you expect me to believe that?'

'I have friends on the force, Wayne. All girls in my line do. Don't you know that?' It was a bluff, but then acting was part of her job. Her performance was flawless.

Wayne pursed his lips into a thin white line. 'Call them then. But I won't leave voluntarily.'

'What did you say?' Lucy's voice dropped into sub-zero temperatures.

Wayne took an unconscious step backward. 'I, I said I won't go voluntarily.'

Lucy uncurled from her chair. 'Oh?' She moved slowly across the room and squared up to him. She stood some four or so inches smaller than Wayne, but height and stature, she had long since learned, aren't quite the same thing. 'You'll do what you're told, little man, do you understand?'

'I, I won't.' Wayne's voice trembled slightly. 'I won't go until you punish me. I've been bad. I'm being bad, Mistress.'

Lucy smiled. 'That's better, pig. At least you recognise who's in charge in here.'

Wayne smiled nervously. 'More than that, Mistress. I've recognised something else.'

'What's that?'

Wayne thrust his jogging pants down and his erection juddered free like a recently vacated diving board. 'I'm cured.'

'Put that away, pig!'

'I won't.' Wayne reached into his jacket pocket and took out his wallet. He drew out a handful of cash and held it out to her. 'Please, Mistress. Please. I've been so very bad.'

Lucy looked at the cash, then looked at Wayne. A cruel smile tugged at the corners of her mouth. She turned on her heel and went to her desk. Opening the second drawer she took out a length of telephone extension flex she'd been meaning to install. She turned and threw it at him. He caught it in his free hand. She walked over to him and took the cash.

'You'll need both hands.'

'Wh- what do you want me to do?'

'Take the wire and bind it around the base of your cock and balls. Do it tight, and leave a good length for me to pull on.'

Wayne did as he was told, wrapping one end of the flex around the base of his genitals and then slipping the knot tight. He gasped as the wire bit and his penis and testicles were bunched painfully together. He swallowed, and with uncertain fingers, held out the other end of the flex to Lucy.

She walked over and took it. 'Get down, piggy.'

'What?'

'Get down on your hands and knees, pig! Don't try my patience, you little fuck or you'll be really sorry. Understand?'

Wayne quickly got down on his hands and knees. 'Yes, Mistress. Sorry, Mistress.'

'Good slave. Good piggy.' She tugged on the flex and Wayne gave a small cry of pain. 'Does it hurt, piggy?'

'Yes Mistress.'

'Do you want me to stop?'

Wayne closed his eyes. 'No, mistress.'

Lucy smiled. 'Very good, then. Come with me.' She began to walk, taking up the slack in the flex as she did so. Wayne shuffled after her. Every now and then she gave a little tug to keep him alert. 'Come on, piggy.' She led him into the hall and past the front door. 'You're a dirty little pig, aren't you? A filthy little runt.'

'Yes, Mistress.'

Lucy turned and jerked on the flex. 'Then oughtn't you speak like a piggy? Come on...' She jerked again. 'Snort for me, pig.'

Wayne snorted.

Lucy smiled. 'Good pig. Keep it up.' She pushed open the bathroom door and stepped inside. A tug on the flex brought Wayne hurrying in after her. Lucy closed the toilet lid and sat down. The bathroom also doubled as the laundry. Against one wall stood a washing machine, tumble dryer and a wicker laundry basket. She placed her hand lightly upon the basket and smiled.

Wayne was again reminded of Julie Newmar; Catwoman with her hand on the lever that will drop Batman into the pit. He licked his lips.

'Hungry?' she asked.

Wayne's eyes darted nervously about. 'Er?'

'I said are you hungry, pig?'

Wayne snorted. It was a neutral snort, neither negative nor positive.

'Good.' Lucy's hand casually tipped over the laundry basket. It was full and densely packed. It hit the floor with a soft thump, the lid rolled away and a number of garments spilled out.

'Dinnertime, piggy. Find my knickers.'

Wayne gave a curious snort. He looked at the spilled laundry before him, then back to her.

'Piggies furrow for their dinner, don't they?'

Wayne nodded cautiously.

'So get your face in that basket and dig out my knickers.' She sent a quiver of tension down the length of the flex. 'There's several pairs in there.'

Wayne shuffled towards the overturned laundry basket. He could already see one pair of knickers, he leaned his face into the opening and took them in his teeth, drawing them out and dropping them on the floor.

Lucy smiled. 'Good pig. Now get the rest.' She got up and came around behind him, placing the flat sole of her tennis shoe on his naked bottom and pushing him so he fell face forward into the laundry. Wayne made a muffled sound of protest as his face disappeared into the basket. 'Go on, pig.' Lucy ground her foot against his buttocks. 'I can't hear you snorting in there. Snort for me, piggy.'

Wayne started snorting. The basket shifted and rolled as he foraged for her underwear. Every now and then, he'd emerge with a pair of pants between his teeth and drop them on a slowly accumulating pile.

Lucy looked dispassionately at his bottom protruding from the basket as he rummaged around inside. She kept her eye on the spot where the flex disappeared between his thighs, tugging on it occasionally just to keep herself amused. Wayne's pig noises were impressive; he was enjoying himself, literally burying himself in the part. 'Good pig.' She drew on the flex with a steady pressure. 'That's enough now, come out.'

Wayne emerged, red faced from the basket, a last pair of pants in his mouth. He looked at her for a second before dropping them onto the pile.

'Get up, piggy. Get up, step into the bathtub, and kneel down.'

Wayne nervously did as he was told.

Lucy picked up the small pile of knickers. 'Look what you've found, pig. Aren't you clever?'

Wayne gave a delighted snort in the affirmative.

'Do you want these?'

Wayne looked at the pants and snorted cautiously.

Lucy smiled and came towards him, wadding the knickers as she did so. 'Open wide, piggy.' Wayne opened his mouth and she pushed the ball of underwear in. He made a sound of protest, moving instinctively back from her. 'Be still!' she snapped at him. Wayne froze and let her fingers push the dirty laundry into his mouth until it was painfully full. Once she was satisfied, she stood back and admired her handiwork. 'Tasty?'

Wayne blinked, then nodded. He drew in a breath through the knickers and moved them around in his mouth.

'Good pig. See what a good Mistress I am to you? I feed you, don't I?'

Wayne nodded.

'Now you just stay there,' she said. 'Don't you move now.' She left the bathroom.

Wayne knelt in the tub, unsure of what to do next. He looked down at his cock and took a moment to enjoy its renewed rigidity. He touched it at the exact same moment that Lucy returned.

'Who said you could touch that?'

Wayne's hands fell to his sides like he'd been caught stealing. He looked at her with frightened eyes.

'Did I say you could masturbate? Is that what you were doing?'

Wayne shook his head.

Lucy sat down on the toilet lid and crossed her legs. She'd been to fetch a cigarette and now she smoked it casually while surveying her client. 'Touch it.'

Wayne pointed at his cock, unsure.

She nodded. 'Touch it.'

Wayne touched it.

'How does it feel to be hard again?'

'Uuuh.' Wayne nodded.

Lucy leisurely exhaled a stream of blue smoke towards him. 'Okay, pull yourself off. Entertain me.'

Wayne's hand fluttered uncertainly around his penis.

'Come on, slave! Masturbate for me.' She picked up the telephone flex and yanked it. Wayne squealed in pain. Obediently, he took himself in hand.

'Come on wanker. Show me how it's done.'

Tentatively, Wayne began to masturbate.

'Come on, piggy. Is that the best you can do? Spank that monkey!'

Wayne began to wank harder and faster, his breath coming in short, hissing gasps through the mouthful of underwear.

'Can you taste me?'

Wayne nodded, he shifted on his knees, his upper body rigid as he pumped his fist up and down.

She smiled. 'Is it nice?'

Wayne nodded, his empurpled face beginning to break a sweat.

She got up from the toilet, lifted the lid and dropped the cigarette inside it. It hissed as it hit the water. She closed the lid and walked slowly towards him. He followed her progress as she came alongside him. Her fingers brushed lightly over the fabric of his shirt. They snaked down over his chest and began playing with a button. Wayne continued to wank steadily as the button popped open. 'Don't you come,' she warned him. Another button fell open. Silently she slipped her hand inside his shirt.

Wayne's rhythm faltered. He hesitated as his attention shifted entirely to her hand.

'Did I tell you to stop?'

He shook his head and began pumping afresh. He closed his eyes as he felt her fingers moving gently through his chest hair, tracing the underside of his left breast. He could feel his heart pounding beneath her touch. A tingle of alarm ran through him as she touched the sore spot around his nipple. Then she squeezed. Wayne screamed through the pants.

'Mmmmm,' Lucy said. 'Painful?'

Wayne nodded, his gasping muffled.

'Keep wanking, pig.'

Wayne's nipple throbbed as he unsteadily resumed his rhythm.

She withdrew her hand from his shirt. He sighed through the gag in a long hiss. She smiled at his evident relief. 'Good pig.'

He looked up at her fearfully.

'Time for your reward.' She tore his shirt open. Buttons popped and flew from the fabric, scattering around his knees in the bath. Wayne's eyes widened in terror, his breathing coming in short, tremulous gasps through his gag. She smiled and stepped quickly into the bath behind him, reaching around the front of him and taking each nipple inbetween her fingers and thumbs. She could feel him shaking as she leaned in close to his ear. 'Come for me now, slave.'

Wayne's nipples exploded in agony as she squeezed them. His muffled scream filled his mind as his hand continued to pump away, faster and faster, with a will seemingly of its own.

'Come!' Lucy demanded. The pressure she exerted on his nipples was constant.

Wayne moaned, closing his eyes as pleasure and pain blurred into one, indistinct, overwhelming sensation. Somewhere deep within his balls, fluid began to churn.

Lucy felt his body tensing as his orgasm started to build. 'Come, pig!' she hissed in his ear. 'Let me see it. Show it to me.' She punctuated her demand with a savage twist.

Wayne screamed through the underwear as a bolt of semen shot from his penis and splashed along the side of the bath. His back arched, his upper body stayed tense and upright as though high voltage current was flowing through him. Lucy released him, the effect was like shutting off the current. Wayne sagged down onto the backs of his legs. His penis spilled residual semen onto his thigh as it rolled to rest.

Lucy stepped out of the bath. She gave him a friendly pat on the shoulder and said, 'Okay, now spit those knickers out and fuck off.'

Wayne pulled the wet panties from his mouth and rubbed his jaw. 'Thank you, Mistress.'

'That's it now, Wayne.' Lucy sat down on the toilet. 'There'll be no more of this. You know you're not impotent. There's nothing wrong with you, you're just sick. Talk to Ellen; tell her you want to try something different next time. But don't bother me again. Okay?'

Wayne nodded, wiping the cum from his thigh with her wadded knickers. As if realising a potential misdemeanour, he stopped and held them up. 'Do you mind?'

She shook her head. 'They've got to be washed anyway.'

'I, I won't bother you again.' Wayne got unsteadily to his feet. 'I'll take your advice. Thanks.'

'Yeah, well, get going. I've got other things to do today besides watching you degrade yourself.'

Nothing more was said after that. Lucy got up and went into the lounge for another cigarette. Wayne finished cleaning himself up and got dressed. A short while later she opened the front door for him. As he stepped out he turned back sheepishly. 'Never?'

'Never. I mean it, Wayne. If you so much as knock on my door again, I'll just push you aside, go downstairs, and tell Ellen. That's a promise.'

Wayne nodded and went sullenly down the stairs.

Lucy closed the door and slid the chain back into place. She turned and leaned against the door, drawing on her cigarette. Jesus Christ, do I need this? Do I really need this kind of crap in my life? Sad, sorry little men with their sorrier little hang-ups coming around here day after day?

'That fuck,' she thumped the door. 'That pathetic, annoying little fuck.'

She pushed herself away from the door and walked back into the lounge. She shook her head. 'He's no different to any of the others, not really. But he's,' she stopped and pointed at the floor, 'he's there.'

It was, she realised, his proximity to her that she was really uncomfortable with. When the others went, they were gone. But she had to live on top of this guy. Both him and his fiancée, Ellen. She'd seen Ellen in the hall a few times. She seemed nice enough. What had she done to deserve Wayne? Lucy gave a short, derisory laugh. What had either of them done to deserve Wayne?

She opened the top drawer of her desk. She rummaged a moment before taking out a building society book and opening it to inspect the figures. She nodded thoughtfully. 'Plenty.' She looked out of the window. Just rent this place out through an estate agent and leave the country. Travel. Get yourself a rucksack, fill it, and go.

She ground her cigarette out in the ashtray, she continued to stub and grind it for some time after it was extinguished. Then she looked back out of the window and smiled to herself. 'Yeah. Just go.'

Chapter 24

'SHE HAS A RARE QUALITY, MAN,' said Gaz. 'Not like most chicks. She's like…' he raised his hands and tried to shape his feelings in the air before him. 'She's like… got something else.'

They were sitting in Shenanigan's beer garden: Gaz, Glen, Jimmy, Adam and Ted, waiting for Kay and Sally to arrive. It was eight o'clock. Gaz was holding court, and the issue of the moment was Sally. 'Know what I mean?'

Adam nodded slowly. 'I think so. She is more than the rest?'

'Exactly.'

'But what about this Kay bird you're shagging?' said Ted. 'What's going on there?'

Gaz shrugged. 'Nothing much. She's a nice girl and all, but it's Sally we want, don't we lads?'

'Yeeeah, man.' Glen stood up from the bench and ground his hips back and forth.

'Come on, lads, I thought we wanted the pair of 'em?' Jimmy laughed. 'Get the old double-ender going, eh?'

A bawdy chorus of "yeahs" broke out around the table. Other drinkers in the garden glanced over. Ted looked furtively about to make sure Fiona wasn't somewhere among them.

'Double-ender?' Gaz shook his head, grinning. 'Don't say it, man, you'll have me running to the gents for a wank saying things like that.'

'No way, Gaz. You gotta save it for later, man,' Jimmy said. 'Don't waste it on the fantasy when the reality could be just a few hours away. Know what I mean?'

'Ohhh, fuckin' hell.' Glen started bucking his hips wildly. 'All over the reality, man. Spurting.'

Ted laughed and shook his head. 'I dunno, you lads.' He looked into his coke, swirling the liquid around. In the dark and fizzy depths he saw himself with them, naked and spurting furiously. He blinked and the image was gone. 'You're unbelievable.'

'Oh be-lieve it, Ted,' said Gaz. 'Be-lieve it.'

'Fuckin' A.' Glen sat down and took a slurp of his beer.

Adam had been smiling despite a sense of detachment. 'And you hope to see her tonight, then? This Sally? The special one?'

'If Kay's managed to talk her into it,' said Gaz. 'She phoned me earlier and she seemed to think she'd cracked it. So yeah, hopefully.'

Adam nodded thoughtfully.

'Whoa! Speak of the devil,' said Jimmy. 'Look who's here.'

Kay and Sally were coming out of the pub carrying drinks. Kay was smiling radiantly. She waved.

'Alriiiight,' Glen murmured. 'Party time.'

Kay came up to the table. 'Hiya.'

'Hey,' said Gaz, grinning. 'It's the girls. Hi, Sally.'

'Hi.'

'Alright girls.' Glen waved.

'Hey,' said Jimmy. 'How's it going?'

Ted ran his eyes up and down the new arrivals and sighed. 'I've got to be getting back, lads. Wife'll kill me if I spend much more time skiving off out here.' He got to his feet. 'I'll see you later.'

'See you later, mate.' Gaz held up a hand.

Ted took a last, quick glance at Kay's legs and withdrew into the gloomy interior of the pub.

Gaz noticed Sally was staring at Adam. 'So, how's it going, Sal?'

'Fine.' Sally diverted her attention to Gaz. 'I'm fine. You?'

'Oh yeah, cool, y'know.'

Sally smiled and glanced again over at Adam. He was wearing the same T-shirt he had been wearing the other night. She hadn't really been able to see his face then. Now she could see it clearly. He looked like he was in his early forties. A strange face, not unattractive, just kind of intense. He met her gaze steadily, but there was nothing challenging in his look. It was, if anything, appreciative. She looked away and saw another kind of appreciation in Gaz's eyes as he gestured for her to sit down beside him.

'Here, have a seat.'

Kay sat in the indicated spot. 'Thanks.' She set her glass down irritably.

Gaz put his arm around her. 'Hey babe.' He kissed her on the cheek.

Sally sat down in the space Ted had vacated next to Jimmy. She looked at the three lads and noticed without surprise that they were all deeply stoned. They were all nodding and smiling dopily.

Gaz gave Kay a squeeze and turned back to Sally. 'Sally, this is our mate, Adam.'

Adam bowed slightly. 'How do you do?'

'Very well, thank you.' Sally smiled. 'I was admiring your T-shirt a moment ago.'

'Wham!'

'I know. Where you a fan?'

'No. I can't say that I was.'

'Oh,' said Sally.

'I got it at Oxfam.'

'I see.' She nodded. 'I should think it's quite a collector's item,'

Adam smiled. 'I got some other ones too.'

Gaz laughed. 'I should hope so. When are you going to wear them?' He grinned aside at Jimmy and Glen.

Adam shrugged. 'I can wear one tomorrow.'

Gaz smiled and nodded approvingly. 'That'd be cool. Any other interesting designs?'

'I don't know. Some have things written on them.'

'Like what, Adam?' Glen asked.

Adam frowned thoughtfully. 'Not sure. I don't remember.'

'You don't remember your own wardrobe?' said Gaz.

Adam shrugged. 'It's just stuff.'

'Alriiight, man. Just stuff, I like it. That's the kind of attitude we should all have to our stuff, whatever it is – it's just stuff. Nothing special, nothing sacred – just stuff.' Gaz nodded, savouring the wisdom.

Glen and Jimmy nodded in unison. 'Yeah, man,' said Glen. 'Just stuff. Nice one.'

Adam smiled, happy to have been the prompt to The One's latest revelation.

'Though as far as T-shirts go, I doubt anything could top that. It's a thing of beauty.'

'You like this?' said Adam.

'Yeah, man. It's tasty. The only problem is, every time I see it, I get, "Wake Me Up Before You Go Go", stuck in me head.'

'Do you want it?'

Sally could tell from the earnest expression on Adam's face, that he not only meant it, he actually wanted Gaz to say yes.

Gaz laughed and shook his head. 'Nooooo mate, you keep it. Anyway, it looks like it'd be too big for me.'

Adam nodded and took a sip of his lemonade.

Sally found herself unable to take her eyes off the bald man. Certainly his appearance was unconventional, but offering to give the shirt off his back, that was downright weird. It reminded her of a gawky kid she'd known in primary school that used to try to buy the friendship of the popular kids with sweets. That was all well and good, but what was this guy's angle? He wasn't exactly primary school age, yet he definitely appeared to be trying to curry favour with Gaz. Her reverie was interrupted when the subject of her interest suddenly turned to her.

'Do you like it?'

'Me? Oh, what? The shirt?'

Adam nodded. He puffed out his chest so she could see the logo clearly.
'Yes. It's nice. It reminds me of my youth.'

Adam frowned. 'But you're not old.'

Sally smiled. 'Thank you. What I mean to say is that it reminds me of when I was younger.'

'Oh.'

'How old are you, Sally? If you don't mind me asking,' said Jimmy.

'I do.'

Jimmy looked sheepish. 'Sorry.'

'Oh, Okay. I'm twenty-eight. I wouldn't want you to think I had a hang up about it.'

Gaz noticed Adam was watching Sally with undisguised interest. He rolled his eyes. Oh, for fuck's sake, he thought. This is the last thing I need: old cue ball staring at her and weirding her out. He lit a cigarette. ''Ere Adam, any chance of your getting any more gear tonight?'

Adam turned to Gaz. 'Tonight?'

'If poss. We're getting low.'

'I can try.'

'Same amount again, yeah?'

'Same amount again. Okay,' said Adam.

There was an awkward silence. Gaz smoking and nodding slightly; Adam sipping lemonade, stone cold sober, also nodding slightly.

'Nice one,' said Glen.

'Yeah, nice one man,' Jimmy agreed.

'Should I go now?' asked Adam.

Gaz shrugged nonchalantly. 'Go whenever you like, man. Obviously the sooner we get the gear the better. But I don't want to put any pressure on you.'

Adam smiled. 'Thank you. I don't feel any pressure.'

'Cool.'

'But I'll go now,' Adam said, rising. 'The sooner the better.'

'Do you need the money up front?' asked Glen.

'Why? Do you have it?'

'Er,' Glen looked searchingly at Jimmy and Gaz. He received blank looks in reply. 'No,' he concluded.

'Then it's not necessary,' said Adam. 'You can pay me later.'

'Nice one, man.'

'I'll see you later, then.' Adam turned and walked away towards the pub.

The group said their various goodbyes, but Sally was silent, her attention arrested by Adam's trousers. They were slightly too small in the leg. His socks were plainly visible as he walked. When Adam disappeared into the pub, she said, 'Interesting fellow.'

'That's a polite way of saying it,' Gaz stubbed out his cigarette. 'He's a bit of a weird one is our Adam.'

'A real weird one,' said Glen, with a hint of Iggy Pop in his tone.

'You like his taste in clothes, then?' said Jimmy.

'He has a unique look, that's for sure.'

'He's always got that outfit on,' said Gaz. 'Right down to the Daffy Duck socks. I mean, jeans or something I can understand, but socks?' He cringed. 'I don't know if he washes 'em, or whether he's got a dozen pairs or what, but he truly loves those socks.'

Sally looked into the shadows of the pub, as if she might see Adam, staring back at her. 'I guess he just likes Daffy Duck.'

'That wouldn't surprise me,' Glen said.

'Why do you say that?'

'I dunno. He's a bit like a kid, isn't he.'

'Does he strike the rest of you that way?'

'He's a nutcase,' said Kay. 'He's like I told you, a weirdo.'

'So why do you hang out with him?'

'Hash,' said Gaz. 'He gets top gear at rock-bottom prices.'

'I see.' Sally thought again of the gawky kid in primary school.

'Why?' Kay smiled. 'Do you fancy him then, Sal?'

'Yeeeah,' said Gaz. 'I can just see you two at it – whooo!'

Sally smiled wanly. 'I don't think so somehow.'

'Oh? Maybe you're looking for something a bit closer to your own age?'

'Something a bit funkier?' Glen suggested.

'Something with hair?' said Jimmy.

Sally took a sip of her drink. 'Actually, I'm not looking for anyone.'

'Oh, come on, Sal,' said Gaz. 'Everybody's after a bit, aren't they – a bit of what does you good?'

'Not everybody.' She took another drink and wondered how this was benefiting Kay. Sally noticed that Kay was looking at her with the same, almost predatory interest as the others. She's one of them now, she thought. One of the lads. She wondered if Kay wanted to fuck her too; that was so transparently what the rest of them had on their minds. She looked away. The small qualm she'd had about not wanting to come in the first place was now becoming an overwhelming desire to leave. She turned to Kay. 'Do you need to use the toilet?'

Kay shrugged and got up.

'Why do chicks go to the bog in twos?' Gaz asked.

Sally smiled. 'To have a decent conversation?'

'Ow! You got me.'

'It's not like you present a small target,' Sally said over her shoulder as she and Kay walked towards the pub.

Jimmy and Glen both laughed. Jimmy pointed at Gaz, 'She's got you, man. She's got you on the ropes, baby.'

'Yeah,' said Gaz, slapping the table as if it were the canvas of a wrestling ring. 'And I submit, baby! I submit!'

Once inside the ladies toilet, Sally turned to Kay. 'Having a good time?'

'Sorry?'

'Are you having a good time? You know, a laugh?'

'Yes, thank you. Are you?'

'Not really, Kay. I certainly don't see what my being here is doing for you and Gaz.'

Kay realised Sally was ready to leave. She placed a hand on her shoulder. 'Sally, of course you don't see it. It's all a game isn't it – the mating game? They must call it that for a reason. We're out there in the middle of Gaz's weird mating game.'

'Correction. You're out there in the middle of Gaz's weird mind game. What I'm doing here is a mystery'.

'It's not a mind game, Sal. He's just very sexual. He expresses himself sexually.'

'Is that how you explain his overt interest in my private life?'

'He doesn't mean anything by it.' Kay shrugged. 'Why should he? He's got me.'

'Yes. He does, doesn't he.'

Kay hesitated for a moment, then smiled pleasantly. 'You're great, you know that? I know you don't like the guys much, and... Well, I want you to know that your just being here is really helping me.' She sighed, exasperated. 'Imagine what it's like just me on my own with them? Just the one girl and those three animals. God.'

'Hmmm.' Sally relaxed a little. 'So why don't those other two find themselves a couple of babes, or chicks, or whatever? Actually, you don't need to answer that. Obviously there aren't too many girls around who want the job.'

Kay smiled, but she didn't feel like smiling. She felt like asking Sally just who the fuck she thought she was? Miss fucking picky. As if Glen or Jimmy would want to go out with a boring bitch like you! They just want to fuck you, sweetie. Fuck you and dump you. This thought brought a smile to her face. She said, 'I know. It's difficult. But just having another girl around, even on a platonic level like in your case, makes it easier for me. Gives me and Gaz just a little more space, y'know?'

Sally, who most definitely did not know, walked to one of the sinks and turned on the cold tap. 'That's as may be, Kay. But I honestly don't think I can do this second girl thing anymore. I've met that guy, remember?' She washed her hands absently beneath the running water.

'Well that's okay,' said Kay, speaking to Sally's reflection in the mirror. 'You can bring him along. Sort of a double date?'

Sally smiled thinly. 'Somehow I don't think they'd get along. Mick's not one for "expressing himself sexually", as you put it.' She shook the excess water from her hands and turned off the tap.

Kay managed a small smile. 'I see. Oh, well. You're here now, that's the main thing. And I really appreciate it, honest.'

Sally put her hands under the drier. 'Yeah. Don't mention it.'

'Okay.' Kay felt confident that Sally's presence was secured for at least the remainder of the pub visit. However, she reflected, getting her back to the house might prove more difficult. Then an idea occurred to her. She smiled pleasantly. 'Do you want another drink?'

'No thanks. I'm fine for now.'

'Oh, go on,' said Kay. 'Vodka and tonic, yeah?'

'No, really. I'm fine. Anyway, it's my round.'

'Oh no. You're here for me. Buying you a couple of drinks is the least I can do.'

Sally smiled. 'Don't be silly.'

'I'm not being silly,' Kay persisted. 'Please? It'll make me feel better about dragging you down here.'

Sally sighed. 'Okay, but this is the last one.'

'Well done, Sal.' Kay pushed open the door to the pub and went through. She held it open for Sally to follow.

'Thanks. Do you need a hand? I don't really fancy going back to that table without you.'

'I can understand that. Like a lamb among the wolves, eh? Now you can imagine how I feel sometimes.'

Sally managed a vague smile, 'Yeah,' she said, uncomfortable with the image. 'I can imagine.'

Making cannabis compulsory, all night sex raves for the leaders of warring nations, and replacing morning prayers in mixed schools with masturbation. By the time they left the pub at 9.30, Sally was starting to see the funny side of Gaz's solutions to world problems. Kay and the lads had all managed to persuade Sally into accepting at least one drink from each of them. She had become more relaxed as the evening wore on, so much so that they had managed to talk her into coming back for coffee.

As they entered the house, Sally admired the newly painted door and frame. 'It's much better than the old one. Funny how so often from the ashes of disaster, something better comes into being.'

'Whoa,' said Gaz. 'Cosmic, baby.'

Sally smiled. 'It's true though isn't it? Your door is an irrefutable example.'

Kay grimaced in the shadows.

'Irrefutable.' Gaz laughed. 'Our irrefutable door.'

'Fuckin A, man.' Glen agreed. 'Our irrefutable door rules.'

'In the kingdom of the doors, the newly painted, irrefutable door is king,' said Sally.

'Nice one.' Gaz resisted the urge to put his arm around her shoulder. 'You know you should come drinking with us more often, Sal. I don't want to assume too much, but I think you've had a pretty good time. Am I right?'

Sally smiled and looked away from his expectant face. 'I suppose so. You guys can be quite funny sometimes – even if it's always for the wrong reasons.'

'Half a laugh is better than none.'

'I can't argue with that.'

Gaz grinned. 'So, was it tea, coffee or vodka for you Sal?'

'Coffee, please.'

'How do you like it?'

'Black, no sugar.'

Gaz turned to the rest of the group as they spread out on the various chairs around the living room. 'What about you guys?'

'We got any Red?' asked Glen.

Gaz nodded. 'Red for you Glen. Jim?'

'Red for me, man.'

Gaz turned to Kay. She sat on the floor in front of the fireplace. 'Kay?'

'Gin,' she said flatly.

'Anything in it?'

'I don't care. Ice, tonic, your cock, whatever.'

Gaz nodded, making a mental note to pay her some attention when he got back. He didn't want her getting up and leaving in a huff. Not tonight. If she went, he knew Sally was straight behind her. 'A gin and tonic for you, then.' He turned in the direction of the kitchen.

'Don't forget to stick your cock in it, mate,' Glen called after Gaz. 'She definitely said she wanted your cock in it.'

'Yeeeah.' Gaz laughed. 'Play some funky music, white boy.' He wandered into the kitchen and put the kettle on. From the fridge he extracted three bottles of Red. He took a glass from the draining board and grabbed the bottle of gin from under the sink. He didn't give Kay too much gin; she'd had enough already. He dropped a couple of ice cubes into the glass and filled it up with tonic water.

From the lounge, he heard the first beats of Fatback's "Yum Yum Gimme Some". He smiled salaciously and began to move his hips, humping to the rhythm. 'Nice one. Get 'em in the mood.'

The kettle was boiled. He spooned some coffee into a mug and filled it two-thirds full. Then he returned to the cupboard under the sink. 'There she is.' He reached in and drew out a bottle. The label, slightly faded from careful washing, identified the contents as Smirnoff vodka. That was only there in the unlikely event that he might've got stopped going through customs. Gaz unscrewed the top and sniffed the clear liquid.

'Woo!' He winced. 'Nitro glycerine.'

It was poteen, genuine Irish moonshine, given to him by his Uncle Frank the last time Gaz had been over to visit. Apparently it had been brewed in an illegal still. Neither Gaz nor his uncle had any idea of the alcohol percentage.

Though as Gaz tipped a generous measure into Sally's coffee, he recalled from his own experience of the poteen that it was more than adequate.

He lifted the mug and sniffed. 'Smells like coffee to me.'

He put the three Reds, the spiked mug of coffee and the glass of gin onto a tray. He was just about to set off for the lounge when he realised he'd forgotten something. He unzipped his fly, took out his penis, and dunked it into Kay's drink.

'Oooo!' he gasped. 'That's chilly, man.' He swirled it around for a moment before tapping it onto the rim of the glass and putting it back into his trousers. 'Just like the lady ordered.' He smiled, picked up the tray and went to rejoin the group.

It was shortly before ten when Mick rode down Charrington Street. He steered with one hand, in his other he carried a clipboard bearing the petition form he'd knocked up on his PC earlier in the evening. In the top few boxes he'd scribbled various names in various handwriting styles to give the illusion of authenticity. He looked up at the top flat of number thirteen as he cycled past it. It was dark. Maybe the guy was out. It was a Friday night after all. He spun the Chopper in a slow arc, bringing himself alongside the kerb and facing back in the direction he'd just come from. He dismounted and pulled the bike up onto the pavement. He wheeled it over to number thirteen and kicked down the stand. He walked up to the door, paused a moment to compose himself, then pushed the buzzer of the top floor flat. A few moments passed without a reply. He pushed it again. Still no response.

'Shit. The fucker's out. All this – ' he gestured with the clipboard. 'A fucking waste of time.' He looked up at the dark windows above and sighed. Then, shaking his head, he turned back to his bike. 'The perfect end to the perfect evening.' He kicked up the stand and threw his leg over the saddle.

As he reversed back onto the road he weighed the options that remained open to him. He could head back home, there was still time to get a video. Alternatively he could go down the pub and get a few pints in before closing time. Then again, he looked up and down Charrington Street, I could stick around here and stake this place out for a bit. Maybe the guy'll come back soon. He looked at his watch and frowned. If he was in a pub, he was likely to be ages yet. But then maybe he wasn't in a pub. Maybe he'd just gone up the road to buy a pint of milk? He tugged pensively on his lower lip. Bollocks, I'll give him ten minutes. Seems a shame to come all the way over here to just bugger off again. He free-wheeled a hundred yards or so down the street and pulled in behind a parked car. He looked again at the darkened windows of number thirteen's top flat.

'So this is a detective's life,' he muttered. 'I hope it fucking pays well.'

*

From his seat on the floor beside Kay, where he was gently massaging the back of her neck, Gaz watched as Sally took her first sip of coffee. No reaction: she continued to listen to Jimmy rhubarbing on about when he went to America. Beautiful. Good old Uncle Frank. Nobody does it better. He turned back to Kay. 'How are you feeling, babe?'

Kay's eyes were closed, a smile of deep contentment played upon her lips. 'Better now that you're here.'

'How'd you like the drink?' he grinned.

Kay opened her eyes. She saw his expression and smiled. 'You didn't?'

He nodded. 'Better than an olive, innit?'

She took a sip from the glass. 'Mmmm, much better.'

'And that's not all. Coz this a double-pronged delight see? Now the drink tastes like my cock, but later, my cock'll taste like gin. Nice one, eh?'

Kay giggled. 'Nice one...' she took a drink and withheld an ice cube in her mouth. 'Man.'

Gaz nodded. 'Alriiight.'

'Gaz?' Glen's voice was constricted as he held down a lungful of smoke. He held a joint out to Gaz.

'Cheers, man.' He drew on the joint and then brightened suddenly. 'Hey. Let's get the bong.'

'Oh, no,' said Sally. 'Not that thing.'

'Aw, come on, Sal,' Gaz prodded her foot. 'Don't start whinging. You don't have to smoke anything if you don't want to. We're your hosts, not your camp commandants.'

Glen chuckled, then said in a dopey German accent, 'You vill smoke da bong, Englander.'

Gaz got unsteadily to his feet and sauntered over to the sideboard. A moment later, he returned holding the bong. 'Right then,' he passed the joint to Kay. 'It's bong time.'

'Water?' said Jimmy.

Gaz looked up. 'Water?'

'In the bong?'

Gaz swilled the bong. 'There's some in there, man.'

Sally grimaced slightly. 'I bet it tastes lovely.'

Gaz smiled. 'Point taken.' Then an idea occurred to him. His smile widened mischievously. 'I'll, er, I'll go put somethin cool and fresh in it.'

'Nice one, man,' said Glen.

Gaz left the room, the bong clutched to him like a precious thing. Everyone watched him go. Then Jimmy said, 'Cool and fresh. Like a mountain spring.'

'Yeah,' said Glen. 'Like toothpaste.'

'No, man. Not like toothpaste. That's too thick.'

Glen smiled, drunk and stoned. 'Toothpaste's cool and fresh.'

'Yeah,' said Jimmy. 'But it's thick. That's why it's called paste. You don't smoke through paste. You smoke through water.'

'Maybe if we put toothpaste in the water it'd be cooler and fresher. Minty.'

Jimmy looked to Sally appealingly. 'You see what I have to put up with?'

Sally smiled politely. After Masturbation Assembly and some of the other things she'd heard these guys discuss lately, toothpaste in the bong sounded almost intelligent. 'Why not? Maybe it'd be like smoking menthol cigarettes.'

'Ahhh!' Glen pointed at Jimmy, vindicated. 'See? Not so stupid after all, eh?'

'Yeah, yeah,' Jimmy slapped at his finger. 'But who smokes menthol cigarettes?'

'Old ladies.' Gaz returned with the bong. 'Old ladies and kids, why? Who's got menthols?'

'No one. Glen wants to put toothpaste in the bongwater.'

Gaz made a face of unbridled disgust. 'What? No fuckin' way, man. That's like... insane.' He sat on the floor by the coffee table. Glen, Jimmy and Sally sat on the couch opposite him.

'Sally said it'd taste like menthols, didn't you Sal?' Glen looked to Sally for support.

Sally shrugged. 'What do I know?'

Gaz, who had just filled the bong's water well with poteen, now contemplated adding a generous squeeze of Colgate. He grimaced and shook his head. 'Sorry, but, it'd ruin the bong forever.'

Glen, suddenly faced with the sanctity of the bong, quickly relented. 'Oh. I wasn't serious, man. Just a laugh, y'know?'

'Yeah,' Gaz said. 'It'd have to be, wouldn't it?'

'Yeah. Just a laugh. I mean, toothpaste in the bong,' Glen shook his head, laughing. 'Crazy talk.'

Jimmy pointed to the small lump of cling-filmed hash hiding among the general debris that was scattered over the coffee table. 'There's the gear, Gaz.'

Gaz found it, unwrapped it and held it up. 'Mmm. Good job we sent old Adam on a mission. We're getting low.' He picked up a lighter and warmed the lump in the flame.

'Tell me more about Adam,' said Sally.

Gaz noticed a slight drunken slur to her words now; not noticeable unless you were listening for it, but then he was listening for it. He smiled. 'What do you want to know?' He broke off a heated piece of hash and placed it into the firebowl of the bong.

'I dunno. He seems unusual. Tell me something unusual about him.'

'He won't stop wearing that T-shirt.' Kay put her arms around Gaz's neck. 'It's starting to smell. That's unusual.'

'He likes it,' said Gaz.

'He thinks you like it.'

'He does not,' said Gaz dismissively.

'Oh?' Kay moved around so she sat beside him. 'What was that shit earlier then when he asked you if you wanted it?'

'He's just being friendly.' Gaz put the bong to his lips and sparked the lighter into flame.

'Oh, come on, man,' said Jimmy. 'It is a bit weird, you have to admit.'

Gaz shrugged and drew on the bong. The poteen bubbled like a witch's cauldron as smoke was drawn through it and up into Gaz's lungs. He pulled his face away with an expression of surprise and placed his hand over the top of the pipe. He mouthed the words, "fuck me" silently as he held the smoke down and passed the bong to Sally.

'No thanks,' said Sally. 'Remember, Commandant?'

Gaz let the smoke out in a long stream. 'I know, but you have to try this, it's unreal.'

'What is it, man?' said Glen.

'I put a secret ingredient in. That's all I'm saying.' Again, he silently urged Sally to take the bong.

'No thanks. Give it to Jimmy.'

'Please?' Gaz persisted. 'Just to be sociable?'

Kay looked at Sally with an imploring expression. Sally hesitated. It was enough to get Jimmy and Glen going. 'Come on, Sal,' said Jimmy placing a hand upon her shoulder. 'Just to be sociable eh?'

'Go on, Sal,' said Kay. 'It's only a giggle.'

Gaz still held the bong out to her. 'It's an experience. You'll have plenty of time to take life seriously when you're old and grey.'

She sighed and reached out for the bong and the lighter. 'Oh for heaven's sake'.

A chorus of whoops and general applause broke out around the room as Sally put the bong to her lips and touched the lighter's flame to the lump of hash. The smoke coursed through the poteen and up into her lungs. Was there a difference? She wasn't familiar enough with the practice of bong smoking to appreciate any subtle changes or secret ingredients. It felt much the same as it had on the previous occasion: like sucking on an exhaust pipe. She took her mouth from the bong and handed it to Jimmy, again to much applause from around the room.

'What do you think?' Gaz asked.

Sally gave a thumbs up. She was surprised at the improvement in her ability to handle a lungful of smoke since the previous occasion. Obviously she was becoming a hardened pothead. She exhaled the smoke, and quite without warning, found herself giggling. 'What can I say? It's disgusting, but...' she shrugged. 'It's okay. It's better than last time.'

Gaz felt a rush of pleasure that owed more to a sense of impending sexual conquest than anything he'd just inhaled. 'Alriiiiight.'

Jimmy passed the bong to Glen and exhaled smoke theatrically. 'Fucking hell, man. What's the secret ingredient?'

'It's a secret, innit! I can't tell you what it is or it wouldn't be a secret.'

Jimmy, now deeply stoned, nodded, his heavily lidded eyes smiling dully as he did so. 'Nice secret, Gaz.'

Sally suddenly felt very out of it. She reached down for her coffee mug. As she lifted it she noticed how light it was, she looked into it; it was empty. She held up the mug. 'Can I have something to drink?'

'Sure.' Gaz started to rise. 'What do you want?'

'No,' said Sally. ''S-okay, I'll get it. I only wannaglass o'water.' She used the arm of the sofa to help her to her feet. When she was upright, she touched her brow. 'Oh, my.' She smiled and shook her head. 'I'm goingtotheloo.'

Gaz chuckled. 'Okay, Sal. You know where it is?'

'I know where it is.' Sally waved a hand behind her as she left the room.

'She's pretty gone, man,' said Jimmy once Sally was down the hall.

'I know it.' Gaz grinned. 'I put poteen in her coffee, and in the bong.'

'Shit!' said Glen. 'That explains it. That's the secret ingredient? That Irish stuff? Fuck-a-doodle-doo!'

'Shhhh,' said Gaz. 'She'll be back soon. I think we should start setting the mood.'

'How?'

'Play it by ear. But don't touch her before I give the nod. I know the signs, okay?'

'I know the signs, too,' said Jimmy querulously.

'And me,' said Glen.

'I know, I know. What I mean is, I don't want to have to blame either one of you two if this gets fucked up, know what I mean?'

'Oh,' said Jimmy. 'That's alright, then.' He looked at the now dead bong. 'Let's go back on the spliffs, eh? Too much of this beast and we'll all be too zonked to party.'

'Go for it, man.' Gaz turned to Kay. 'Feeling horny, baby?'

Kay smiled and put her hand between his legs, 'I'm always horny when I'm around you.' Gaz leaned over to her and kissed her sensuously on the mouth. She offered no resistance as he gently leaned toward her, easing her down onto her back.

When Sally walked back in to the lounge, it was to see Gaz and Kay entwined on the carpet. She stopped and watched them for a second, suddenly unsure of how to behave. She looked around. Jimmy was rolling a joint and Glen was watching Gaz and Kay with undisguised enjoyment. Sally sat down heavily and took a sip of the water she'd just poured herself. Well at least Kay and Gaz are together, she thought. She looked at Jimmy and pointed at the couple on the floor. 'They make a lovely couple.'

Jimmy looked up and grinned. 'Yeah. They're pretty hot.'

Sally nodded, stoned, drunk and feeling awkward. 'You come here often?'

'Uh?'

Sally noticed how all the muscles in Jimmy's face had slackened. She waved a hand. 'Nothing.' She sat back and looked at the couple writhing together on the carpet. This was weird, she thought. I mean, I know he's an exhibitionist, but this is still weird. She shifted in her seat. She sensed a definite change in the atmosphere of the room, it wasn't just Gaz and Kay, things were different. Or were they? Am I just picking things up differently because I'm stoned? She felt a sudden wave of panic. Am I paranoid? she thought. Are they behaving normally and it's me that's got it all wrong? Am I freaking out?

She closed her eyes for a second, trying to adjust her perception, but it just made her dizzy. She opened them again and looked with fresh consideration at Gaz and Kay. No, she decided. It's not me; this is weird. She sipped her water. Shit, I wish I wasn't so zonked. I'd just get up and go, just stand up and say, "Well, I'm leaving now". As it is, I get dizzy when I stand up. The last thing I want to do is throw up in front of them. I'd never hear the end of it. She sipped her water again. I'll just sit here and wait for Kay and then we'll go together.

On the floor, Gaz had his hand inside Kay's blouse and was openly fondling her breasts. Kay was massaging the bulge in his jeans with equal enthusiasm. Sally just sat and watched them. The peripheral world seemed to fade out as her whole attention became absorbed by the couple on the floor. What would happen next? she wondered incredulously. How far was this going to go?

Gaz and Kay separated for a moment with mutual understanding. Sally watched dumbly as Kay helped Gaz lift her blouse up over her head. Then, smiling dreamily, Kay unfastened her bra. Gaz stooped his head to kiss her breasts. Sally continued to watch with mounting disbelief as Kay reached down a hand and slowly unbuttoned Gaz's fly and released his erection.

'Yeeeah,' came a voice to Sally's left. She turned to see Jimmy and Glen, sitting as she was, watching the strange show in front of the fireplace. However there was no disbelief in their eyes: they were enjoying it, excited, perhaps even expectant.

'Do you guys do this kind of thing a lot?'

Jimmy turned to her and smiled. 'It's a beautiful thing, man.' He offered her the joint.

She shook her head. 'No thanks.' Then she watched as Glen got off the couch and crawled over to start kissing and fondling Kay's other breast. Kay moaned, her eyes closing as the two men suckled her like kittens. This is too much, thought Sally. I don't believe I'm seeing this.

Kay's rhythmic grip on Gaz's penis was causing him to groan with almost theatrical delight. She opened her eyes and looked straight at Sally. She smiled and bit her lower lip lasciviously.

Sally looked away. There had been something in Kay's eyes; a mixture of invitation and challenge that had sent a cold shot of sobriety into her fogged perception. She looked at Jimmy. He was stroking the bulge in his jeans and grinning like a lunatic. Sally said, 'Aren't you going to join them?'

Jimmy turned his mad grin to her. 'Aren't you?'

Sally laughed. 'No. Oh no. You go ahead, I'm gonnaphone a cab or somethin'.'

At this Gaz disengaged his face from Kay's chest. 'You're not going, Sal?'

'Er, I think I am,' said Sally, as if Gaz had just made the understatement of the century.

'Oh, come on,' said Gaz, leaning forward so Kay had to release his cock. 'You can't go now. Things are just getting interesting.'

'They might be for you. But for me, things are getting jus' a bit unpleasant.'

'Look,' a hint of panic entered Gaz's voice. He reached behind an armchair to his right and drew a big plastic picnic box to his side. 'Wait.' He took off the lid and rummaged inside a moment, then came out holding a large dildo. 'You don't have to join in if you don't want to. You can just... enjoy yourself alone.'

Sally stared speechlessly at the dildo. She saw with deepening horror that it was unwashed. A number of black pubic hairs clung to its lustreless pink surface as if they had died trying to embed themselves in it. 'I don't believe what I'm seeing.'

'Or, maybe if guys aren't your thing...' He rummaged again in the box. This time he drew out what Sally initially thought was a huge, pink frankfurter. Then she saw the penis heads at either end. 'You and Kay can groove on this number.'

Sally got to her feet too fast. The room spun and she fell back down onto the sofa. She put her hands over her face. 'Phone me a cab.'

Gaz crawled over the carpet, pushing the coffee table aside and bringing his face down to her feet. 'You don't want a cab, Sally. You want to stay here and make love.' He kissed her feet. 'Have you ever made it in a group before?'

'No,' said Sally, her face still behind her hands.

'You've never felt the affections of more than one man at a time. Never experienced the multiple pleasures of – ' Sally kicked out with the foot he was kissing and caught him full in the face. 'Ow!' Gaz's cry was one of shock rather than pain. He looked stunned, touching his face lightly as if making sure it was still there.

'Get out of my way, you creepy fuck.' Sally got unsteadily to her feet using the arm of the sofa for support. 'I'm leaving.'

Kay came to Gaz's side and put her arm about him. 'Are you alright, Gaz? What did she do to you?'

'She?' said Sally. 'Is that who I am now? She? What's going on here Kay? What are you doing there with your tits out calling me she all of a sudden?'

'Oh shut up, you frigid bitch!' Kay snapped. She glared at Sally as she stroked Gaz's hair, protectively clutching his head to her bosom. 'Why can't you just loosen up and get your tits out? You might actually enjoy yourself for once.'

Sally looked at her a moment, too shocked to say anything, too stunned to move.

'Now, hang on there, Kay,' said Gaz.

It was enough to break the spell. Sally turned and walked out of the room. She suddenly felt very sober. She was down the hall and at the front door by the time Gaz came running out after her, struggling to get his still erect penis back into his jeans. 'Wait, Sal, wait a minute'. She ignored him, and after a moment's fiddling with the new catch on the front door, she opened it and strode down the garden path. She felt a tear fall onto her cheek and wiped her eyes angrily as she stepped out onto the street.

'Sal!' shouted Gaz. 'Please?' He stumbled out of the house, stopping at the gate and leaning over, watching her go. 'I'm sorry, Sal!' She didn't look back. She turned the corner and was gone. 'Shit.'

Kay, her blouse back on in crumpled disarray, came down the garden path to stand at his side. 'She gone?'

'Yeah,' said Gaz quietly.

'Frigid bitch.' Kay put an arm around his waist and leaned against him for support. He turned his face to hers. For a moment, she felt there was a coldness in his eyes. She moved away slightly. Then the moment was past.

Gaz smiled and gently stroked Kay's hair. 'Oh well. At least we've still got you, eh?'

Kay smiled wanly as he put his arm around her and led her back to the house. Inside she could see Jimmy struggling to take his jeans and pants off over his shoes. 'Yeah,' she said in a small voice as he closed the front door behind them. 'At least you've still got me.'

Chapter 25

LIKE MANY A CLASSICAL GUMSHOE on stakeout duty, Mick had accumulated a small number of cigarette butts at his feet. Into this number he dropped what he absolutely considered to be the last one.

'Fuck this.' He ground out the cigarette with his shoe. 'Enough is enough.' He looked at his watch, it was 10.30. The guy's obviously out having a laugh somewhere, like any normal person would be on a Friday night. He rolled his lower lip between finger and thumb for a moment. Then looked at his watch. He calculated that if he were to leave now, he might still catch last orders at his local. 'If you get a move on.'

He shifted the Chopper's gear stick into first and pointed the bike toward the top of Charrington Street. He switched on his lamps, kicked up the stand and pushed off. Allowing for traffic and the time it would take to drop the Chopper off at home – there was no way he was leaving his wheels outside a pub on a Friday night – he reckoned he'd catch last orders with ease. Then he heard a shout behind him.

'Mick!' it was a female voice. Mick stopped and looked back. There was someone out in the road waving at him. She stood just out from the junction with Barrow Street. She wasn't standing near enough to a street lamp for him to be able to discern any features at this distance. He turned the bike around and let gravity roll him back down the hill. The wind stirred his hair, it fluttered over his collar as his speed increased.

'I knew it was you,' called the girl. 'You couldn't mistake that bike anywhere.'

Mick's features brightened as he recognised Sally. But as he drew nearer, his expression changed to one of concern; something was wrong. Her eyeliner was all smudged. That, and she looked kind of… unsteady.

'Sally? Sally, what's happened to you?' He pulled on the brakes, squeaking to a halt beside her.

'I'm drunk. No -' she held up a hand. '- I'm intoxicated. Multiple horrors.'

'I see,' said Mick cautiously. 'Are you okay? You look like you've been crying.'

'I have been crying. Not that I wanted to, but the bloody things jus' come don't they.'

Mick smiled. 'They do. But why? What's brought this on all of a sudden? I thought you were going out with your friend, Kay.'

'Ha! That bitch! I don't fucking believe how stupid, I've…' her voice began to tremble slightly. 'How stupid I've been.' She looked away and pressed a hand to her mouth.

Mick quickly dismounted, he lay the bike down in the road and put an arm around Sally's shoulders. 'Hey,' he said softly. 'Hey there. It's okay.' He gave her shoulder a squeeze. 'I'm sure you haven't been stupid. Not you, Sal.'

She looked at him, her tear-filled eyes sparkling in the streetlight. Without saying anything, she moved into his arms and buried her face in his jacket. 'I feel such a fool. I'm such a chump.'

Mick smiled and closed her in his arms, unconsciously breathing in the fragrance of her hair. 'A chump? Is that what you've been?'

'Yeah. I'vebeenabigchump.'

He stroked her back. 'What is it that you've done to be a big chump?'

She stepped back from him and sniffed, wiping her eyes now that she had once again regained her composure. 'Well, I went with Kay like I said on the phone earlier.'

'Uh-huh,' Mick said encouragingly.

'But, the whole thing, I think, the whole thing wasn't about Kay needing girlie support with those, those wankers who live over there.' She pointed back in the direction from which she'd just come. 'It was more like, I dunno, it was more like they, they all just wanted to shag me.'

'Shag you?'

She nodded. 'They started – Kay and Gaz – they started getting off with each other on the floor.'

'Uh-huh.'

'And then, then they started,' she gestured. 'Gettinundressed.'

Mick raised his eyebrows. 'Really?'

Sally nodded. 'Yeah. She got his… thing out.'

'You mean… She got his…?'

Sally abandoned decorum. 'She got his cock out and started wanking him off in front of me.'

'Oh,' said Mick quietly.

'And it wasn't jus' me. The other two – those two glove puppet pals of his – they were sitting there watching them like it was Match of the bloody Day.'

'I see.'

'No, not yet you don't. Because then, Glen got up and joined in.'

Mick raised his eyebrows. 'Wanking Gaz?'

'No.' Sally smiled at the thought. 'Doing things to Kay.'

'Oh, I think I… get the picture.'

'No. There's more. I say, I'm going to leave, right? And then, when I say this, Gaz gets all…' she mimicked him. '"Oh, no, don't go Sal," And then he gets this weird picnic box and pulls out these horrific dildos. And then he says I don't have to join in – I can just amuse myself, or something.'

'He said that?'

'He did.' Sally nodded emphatically. 'Then he, he crawls over and starts kissinmyfeet.'

'What did you do?'

'I kicked him in the face, and left.'

'Really?' Mick laughed.

'Yeah.' Sally sniffed. 'Right in the chops.'

'That's brilliant. Well done.'

'I know,' said Sally, laughing a little. 'I didn't hurt him or anything, but he didn't like it.'

'I bet he didn't. Shit, what a rotten night you've had.'

'I have. Totally.'

'But I wouldn't say you've been a big chump,' said Mick. 'You were just being a friend.'

'She called me a frigid bitch.' Sally glowered at the memory.

'She didn't!'

'She did. She said I should get my...' Sally faltered a moment as her brain quickly re-edited Kay's words. 'She said I should have joined in and not been such a frigid bitch.'

'Sounds to me like she's the bitch.'

'Isn't she! I'm not a frigid bitch just because I don't want to get involved in their sordid little gang-bang, am I?'

'Of course not.'

'I just have some self-respect.' She turned and pointed back into Barrow Street. 'Unlike you, Kay Oliver, you... tart.'

'Slag,' said Mick.

'Yeah, slag,' Sally amended. 'I didn't want to say it, but yeah.' She looked to where she imagined Kay to be right now. 'You slag!'

'Feeling any better?'

'Yes, thanks,' Sally brushed away a lock of hair from her wet cheek. 'Mick, I'm so sorry about blowing you out earlier over this... this bunch of shit.'

'That's okay.' Mick reached out a hand and stroked her shoulder. 'You didn't know what was going to happen, did you? You were just being a good friend to someone who, unfortunately, wasn't being a good friend to you.'

'I know. But it doesn't make me feelanybetter. I've been such a fool.'

'Not a chump anymore?' said Mick with a reassuring smile.

'No. Not a chump. Jus' afool.'

'Well that's okay, then, isn't it? Everybody's allowed to be a fool every now and then.'

Sally sniffed. 'Thanks.'

'There's nothing to thank me for.'

'There is. But there's no point arguing about it. I think you'll deny it, won't you.'

'I will.'

'Okay, so we'll leave it then.'

They stood a moment in silence, then Mick said, hesitatingly, 'Can I, can I give you a lift anywhere?'

'What? On that?' she pointed at the Chopper.

Mick bent and picked it up. 'Yeah. On this.' He patted the big, cushioned saddle. 'You can sit here.'

Sally laughed. 'You're kidding?'

'No,' Mick shook his head, smiling. 'I'll give you a backie.'

'Where will you sit?'

'I won't. I'll be pedalling, won't I.'

'But what...? What do I hang on to?'

'You can hang on to the bottom of the seat. Or, which is more traditional, you can hang on to me.'

'Mick, I dunno.' Sally put a steadying hand to her head. 'I'm not exactly with it.'

'That's okay, you're not the one driving.'

'But I still might fall off.'

Mick thought for a second, then gave a slight shrug. 'Okay. I just, thought it might be helpful.'

Despite her foggy mental condition, Sally perceived a note of regret in his tone. She suddenly got the impression that he really wanted to do this. She smiled. 'You're sure it'll be safe?'

Mick brightened. 'Oh, absolutely. You just hang on tight and I promise you'll arrive safe and sound.'

'Okay. But my house is too far. Why don't we go somewhere for last orders.'

Mick looked surprised. 'Er, I don't know Sal, aren't you a bit pissed already?'

Sally laughed. 'I don't want alcohol. Jesus! I mean a coffee. I want a black coffee to help me sober up a bit.'

'Who's going to serve you black coffee at last orders?'

'Roy and Tony. At the Black Pig. It's not far from here. We could get there on your bike in no time.'

Mick shifted his position slightly. 'Isn't that a gay pub?'

'Discreetly gay. Don't worry, I'll look after you.'

Mick looked at his watch. 'Y'know the Lion and Lobster's nearer.'

Sally laughed. 'What are you afraid of? Do you think everybody's gonna come runnin' over to pinch your arse or something?'

'Oh, I'm not afraid or nothing,' Mick shrugged. 'It's just the Lion's nearer, that's all.'

'Aw, c'mon. I like the Black Pig, it's different.'

'Yeah, so I've heard.'

'There's nothin' to be scared of, Mick. You're not scared are you?"

'No, but,' Mick sighed, exasperated. 'Look, I'm not some kind of homophobe Sal, I just haven't been in a gay pub before. The occasion just hasn't presented itself, if you know what I mean.'

'Well, I... suppose your not being gay probably had somethin' to do with that.'

'Gosh. After all these years of trying to figure that out – you come along and crack the nut in an instant. How can I ever thank you?'

Sally smiled. 'You can buy me a coffee. Come on. They'll be closing soon. You fancy a pint don't you?'

'Yeah, but, what about the bike?'

'Whataboutit?'

'I can't leave it outside a pub, someone'll nick it.'

'You can leave it around the back. Don't worry, I go there all the time with Leonard. In fact, he's probably there now.'

'Oh… okay, then.' Mick patted the saddle. 'So, you want a lift then do you?'

Sally smiled. 'I don't see how else we can possibly make it in time.'

Mick beamed and straddled the Chopper. He stepped forward over the crossbar and leaned the bike towards Sally. She came in close behind him and tentatively put one leg over the saddle.

'Oh, blimey,' she said, easing herself back onto the saddle. 'You know I've never done this?'

'What? Had a backie?'

'No,' Sally slapped his shoulder. 'I've had a backie before, obviously. I've just never had a backie on a Chopper. Deprived childhood eh?'

Mick looked back at her as he selected first gear. 'You know what else?'

'What?' Sally nervously took a hold of his back.

'I've never driven anyone either.'

'You're kidding?'

Mick stood on the right pedal and they began to move. 'Nope. You're my first passenger.' Standing up and pedalling slowly, he began to get an unsteady rhythm going. 'I just wish Malcolm Barnes was here to see it.'

'Who?'

'Oh, no one.' Mick smiled at the memory. 'I'll tell you later.'

The Black Pig was one of the town's less bustling watering holes that Friday night. Indeed, The Black Pig seldom bustled in the same manner as other establishments at all. It was more like a member's bar than a public house, and that was the way the landlords liked it. Mick and Sally spent a minute or two outside the pub as Sally corrected her ruined eye make-up. Once she was reasonably comfortable with the patch-up job she'd done, she pushed opened the doors and led Mick inside. Mick looked about, not sure what to expect; if anything, the ordinariness of the pub surprised him. Then he saw the mirrorball. It hung still and dark over the centre of the public bar. The area beneath it was clear of tables. 'A dancefloor?'

She turned and nodded. 'Pretty cool, eh?'

He raised his eyebrows and nodded approvingly.

Of the mostly male crowd, no one seemed much younger than forty. Several heads turned to look at them, but for the most part they were ignored. Those who did pay them any attention warmly acknowledged Sally. She returned the various greetings as they stepped up to the bar. The ride here had done a lot to sober her up, there was nothing like hanging on for dear life to focus the mind. She turned to Mick. 'What do you want to drink?'

Mick quickly surveyed the pumps and taps that glowed and glittered along the other side of the bar. 'I'll have a pint of Guinness, thanks.'

Sally turned and caught the eye of one of the bartenders, a man in his fifties with a shock of white hair.

Mick blinked as a vision of Tony Hart moved towards him through the stale bar smoke.

'Hi, Roy,' said Sally.

As Roy came over, Mick saw his mistake: the Hart similarity vanished when you looked below the hairline.

'Hello Sally. What can I get you?'

'Is there any chance of a coffee?'

Roy drew a sharp intake of breath. 'Well, not ordinarily. But since it's you I think we can stretch to it. How do you like it?'

'Black and strong.'

'Like your men?'

'Ho ho,' said Sally. 'Good one.'

Roy laughed and nodded to Mick. 'So I take it you two aren't together then?'

Sally turned to Mick and placed a hand on his shoulder. 'Roy, this is my friend Mick.'

'Only a friend, Sally? How sad.' Roy leaned toward Mick in a mock aside. 'You need to put a bit more work in on this one, Mick. It shouldn't take much though; she's a pushover. Ask anyone in here.'

Sally smiled sarcastically. 'Yeah, yeah. Well, the sooner you pour him a pint, the sooner I can get him drunk and start taking advantage of him.'

'Get in line, girl,' said Roy. He gave Mick a reassuring wink, then touched Sally on the hand. 'Just messing about. Aren't we love?'

'Oh, of course.'

'So a black coffee and a Guinness?' Roy confirmed. 'Is that right?'

'Please.'

Roy put a glass under the Guinness tap and drew off about two thirds of a glass. 'I'll just pop out to put the kettle on, Sally. Won't be a tick.' He exited through a door at the rear of the bar.

'No fancy coffee makers here then?' said Mick.

'No fancy anything. They keep things traditional here.'

'Unlike the music.'

Sally smiled. 'Roy and Tony make up their own tapes. I rather like them.'

'Who the hell is this? I expected seventies disco classics. Pardon my thinking in stereotypes.'

'Oh they play that stuff sometimes. But not tonight. This is...' Sally listened for a moment to the pop-orchestral sounds that swam around them.

'No… I've heard it here before, but I don't know who it is.' She put her hand out and the other barman, a chunky-looking man with a blond crew cut, came over. 'Hello, Sal, how are you, dear?'

'I'm fine Tony. This is my friend, Mick.'

Tony smiled at Mick. 'Hi, Mick.'

Mick smiled. 'Hi.'

'We were wondering who this is on the tape?'

'Bert Kaempfert. Lovely isn't it? There's a mixture on this tape: Bert Kaempfert and James Last. Roy prefers James Last, but I'm definitely a Kaempfert man.'

'It's nice.' Sally nodded. 'I think I'm with you on that.'

Roy came back. 'With him on what?'

'She says she's a Kaempfert woman,' Tony explained.

Roy raised his eyebrows and handed Sally her coffee. 'Well you only to need to look at the way she walks to see that.'

'Are you saying Bert Kaempfert effects the way you walk?' said Tony.

'It effects the way *you* walk, Tony. You ought to see yourself sometimes.' He went back to pouring Mick's pint and set it down on the bar. 'Waltzes, he does,' he confided to Sally and Mick. 'Swishes around the place like Ginger Rogers. Wouldn't be so bad if he were holding a mop at the same time. Two pounds fifty, please Sally.'

'How much is the coffee?' Sally asked.

Roy waved his hand dismissively. 'Don't be daft, girl.' He took the five pound note she offered and deposited it in the till.

'Well at least I can dance,' said Tony. 'Not like you with your two left feet – both size twelves at that.'

'I have not got size twelve feet,' said Roy handing Sally her change.

Tony seemed surprised. 'What? Don't tell me they've grown?'

'Not so big as I can't lift one to kick you up the arse.'

Sally turned to Mick aside. 'They're not normally this affectionate, I think it's for your benefit.'

Mick smiled. 'Are they an item?'

'Oh yeah,' said Sally. 'And quite an item at that.'

'Do you want to sit down?'

'Yeah. Let's see if Leonard's here.' She led him away from the bar and around a corner. There, sitting with a late-middle-aged woman with a small dog on her lap, was Leonard. He looked up and smiled as he saw Sally approaching. The woman with the dog, who had been talking, stopped and followed Leonard's gaze. She recognised Sally and dipped her head to address the dog. 'Look who's here, Chippy,' she said, pointing at Sally. 'Look who's here.' The dog stared happily in a different direction to the one indicated. Its small tail thumped against her lap and she rubbed its head.

'Hi, there Leonard,' said Sally. 'Hiya Jean.'

'Hello, Sally,' said Leonard.

'Say hello to Sally, Chippy,' Jean urged the dog.

Chippy noticed the new arrivals, wagged his tail and carried on staring happily into space.

'Chippy says hello.'

'Hi Chippy,' said Sally. 'Everyone, this is Mick. Mick, I think you caught everyone's names, didn't you?'

'I think so,' Mick nodded at Leonard and Jean in turn.

'I'm not Chippy. That's Chippy.' Leonard pointed to the dog with cool disdain.

'Right,' Mick followed Sally's lead and sat down at the table.

'What brings you here so late?' Leonard picked up his cigarettes.

'Well,' Sally sighed. 'I've had a bit of a colourful evening to say the least. Things were all but gone to hell when Mick here found me and brought me to the pub.'

'That's very decent of you, Mick.' Leonard offered Mick a cigarette. 'Gasper?'

Mick took one. 'Thanks.'

'Oh,' Sally said, surprised. 'Do you smoke, Mick?'

'I'm quitting.' Mick accepted a light from Leonard's slim, silver lighter.

'Leave him alone girl,' said Leonard. 'A chap's got to have some pleasures in life.'

'But cigarettes aren't a pleasure. If they were he wouldn't be quitting.'

'If he's on a date with you, Sally. He'll need all the support he can get. Let the man smoke.'

'I don't have to smoke if it bothers you,' Mick said to Sally. 'Like I say, I'm quitting. I've mastered the art of stopping so many times it's second nature to me now.'

'You should stick with your first nature,' said Leonard. 'The one that led you to the weed in the first place. There lies your true self.'

'Oh shut up, Leonard,' said Sally. She turned to Mick. 'No, you do what you want, Mick. I don't want to hector you into not being yourself.'

'Well said,' Leonard agreed.

'I'll just finish this one,' said Mick. 'Then I'll knock it on the head.'

'For good?' Jean asked.

'Yeah.' Mick looked at Sally. 'Why not?'

'Why? Would be a better question,' Leonard exhaled smoke luxuriously. 'The hazards of smoking are overwhelming. Think of it not as a habit, but as an adventure.'

'What about the unadventurous advantages of not smoking?' said Sally.

'What advantages? Clean fingers, more money in your pocket, less risk of fatal diseases? How mundane. How ghastly.'

Mick smiled. 'You think the idea of not getting a fatal disease is ghastly?'

'Hideous. The prospect of premature death is the reason I started smoking in the first place. The other benefits, the stained fingers, the penury; these are little treasures I've picked up along the way.'

'Oh stop talking rubbish, Leonard,' said Sally. 'You don't mean a word of it.'

'On the contrary. I mean every word.' Leonard finished his drink and set the glass down with a flourish. 'Tide's out, Jean. Your round.'

'Oh, is it?' said Jean. 'What are you drinking?'

'Gin and bitter lemon. Same as I was twenty minutes ago, same as I always do. You really must start paying attention, dear.'

'Oh, well, yes,' Jean put her hands under the dog's lap. 'Will you take Mr Chips, Leonard?'

'Don't be absurd, woman,' Leonard cringed. 'Why on Earth would I want that huge rodent sitting on me?'

'I'll take him,' Sally volunteered.

'Thank you Sally.' Jean handed the dog across the table. 'Would either of you two like a drink?'

They both declined with thanks and Jean left to go to the bar.

'Another date with Jean then, Leonard?' said Sally.

'We're not lovers, Sally. We're cellmates. Her and that hound there. Jean's the Dogwoman of Alcatraz.'

'No plans to marry then?'

'I'd rather marry Mr Chips. And that's saying something. Anyway, enough of my non-existence. Tell me about this colourful evening of yours.'

Sally recounted the evening's events again, this time in detail. Mick and Leonard listened intently until Jean returned and fussed about transferring Mr Chips from Sally's lap back to hers. Then Sally continued, ending with their cycle ride here.

'Well, well, well,' said Leonard. 'Not the sort of people you'd want to frolic with anyway by the sound of it. I imagine they're probably diseased.'

'How big was the dildo again?' Jean asked.

Sally held her hands about two feet apart. 'The big one was about this big; the one with two heads.'

'I believe they call them double-enders,' said Leonard. 'I trust you managed to secrete it about your person before you fled the scene?'

'Gosh, Leonard,' said Sally, assuming a regretful tone. 'If I'd known you wanted it, I would have. Sorry about that.'

Leonard smiled thinly. 'Thank you, but I already have a fine collection. Mother polishes them every Sunday morning, along with her horse brasses.'

Mick laughed as he was taking a drink. He managed to inhale some Guinness and Sally had to slap him on the back a few times until he raised a hand. 'S-alright,' he said. 'I just got this mental image of a little old lady polishing big rubber cocks. I'm okay now.'

'I'm glad it amuses you,' said Leonard. 'Personally I wish she'd just leave them alone. After all, they are mine.'

Mick looked incredulously at Leonard. 'You're kidding?'

'Of course he is,' said Sally. 'Aren't you Leonard?'

Leonard raised an eyebrow and lit a cigarette. 'I'm afraid it is a mild fib.' He smiled whimsically. 'A fantasy perhaps.'

'That sounds about right,' said Sally.

Mick looked around as Roy and Tony began pulling the pub's curtains. 'What's going on?' he asked no one in particular.

'Lock-in,' said Leonard. 'The only reason that sane people come here.'

'So why do you come here, Leonard?' said Sally. 'The music?'

'I come here to be insulted by the likes of you, Sally. It keeps my hide tough enough to cope with the book buying public.'

'I see.' Sally's knowing smile alluded to more than Leonard's riposte. It said, *yes, but I know the real reason you come here.*

Leonard returned her expression with a similar smile, a reply that said, *But you'll never know for sure, will you?*

Mick was oblivious to all this subterfuge; he was looking at the bar with all the excitement of a kid in a sweet shop. 'When do they start serving, Leonard?'

'I don't know. Why don't you try them now? I'm fairly parched.'

'Gin and bitter lemon?' Mick asked.

'See, Jean?' Leonard tapped her on the arm. 'He's only been here five minutes and already he knows my tipple.'

'He does seem a bright, chap, yes,' Jean nodded.

'What's that you're drinking, Jean?' Mick pointed to her empty glass. 'Baileys?'

'Yes. A Baileys. Thank you.'

'Sally?'

'Nothing for me, Mick, thanks.'

'Look here,' said Leonard. 'I know you were saying you were three sheets to the wind earlier on, but frankly you look fine to me now. Have a drink.'

'Oh no. I'm only just starting to get my head together. The last thing I need's a drink.'

'Oh, tosh. What is it? Vodka and tonic?' Leonard turned to Mick. 'Get her a vodka and tonic, Mick.'

Mick looked at Sally and raised his eyebrows.

Sally sighed, 'Oh, get me a coke. Thanks, Mick.'

Mick smiled and went to the bar.

The moment Mick's back was turned, Leonard lunged forward towards Sally. 'So who is he?'

'He's Mick. I met him... Well, I just met him.'

'He seems nice enough,' said Leonard, conspiratorially. 'What's going on with the neck blanket?' He reached behind his head and toyed with invisible hair.

Sally smiled. 'I think it's quite nice. It's quirky.'

'It's revolting,' said Leonard. 'He looks like he arrived with Jon Pertwee in the Tardis.'

Sally laughed. 'I think it's more eighties, isn't it?'

'No. That model comes straight out of the Bay City Rollers book. Very "Shang-a-Lang".'

Sally laughed. 'I'll tell him you said that.'

'Tell him what you like,' said Leonard nonchalantly. 'I couldn't care less.'

'But you like him?'

'I think he's very nice,' said Jean.

'Thank you, Jean,' said Sally.

'And Chippy likes him, too,' Jean stroked the small dog's head. 'Don't you Chippy?' Chippy's only response was to continue to pant on her lap like a small, furry engine.

'Well if the dog likes him, he's sorted,' said Leonard. 'Such a sterling judge of character; any friend of Mr Chips is a friend of mine.'

'In other words,' said Sally. 'You like him?'

'He's charming. It's about time you found yourself a man.'

'It's about time you found yourself a man,' said Sally. 'Or a woman.'

'Sex doesn't interest me, Sally. "Man delights not me," he quoted airily, "no, nor woman neither". Think of me as a eunuch.'

'Who's a eunuch?' said Mick, returning with drinks.

'I am,' said Leonard. 'I was getting playful with Mr Chips one afternoon and he got snappy with me. Terrible mess, but it gave him something exciting to bury in the garden. If only I could find the spot, I might find a surgeon somewhere who could restore me to my former glory.'

Mick sat down, smiling uncertainly.

'He's being an arse,' Sally explained as the lights in the bar grew dim.

Mick frowned. 'Something to do with the lock in?'

'You could say that,' said Leonard wearily.

Mick blinked, startled as suddenly the bar came alive with myriad swirling stars of light. He looked up to see the mirrorball on the ceiling had awoken. He gave a short, delighted laugh. 'What's going on?'

'"Autumn Leaves," Leonard groaned. 'Wait for it.'

From behind the bar, Roy led Tony out onto the dancefloor. Those who had been standing around dutifully moved aside. 'Come on, people,' Roy beckoned the audience to join them. 'Don't be shy. They're playing our tune.' He and Tony embraced and began to slowly move around the floor.

Mick gaped. 'Does this happen often?'

'Too often,' said Leonard. 'You'd think that they'd get bored, but oh, no. It'll go on now for hours.'

Mick noticed other couples joining in. He turned to Sally. 'Shall we?'

'What?'

'Shall we dance?'

'No way,' Sally said emphatically.

'Oh, go on, you miserable cow,' said Leonard. 'I can't remember the last time someone asked me to dance.'

'Would you like to dance, Leonard?' said Jean.

'Don't be absurd,' said Leonard. Seeing Sally's expression, he added, 'My corns are playing up. You go.' He ushered Sally and Mick towards the floor. 'Leave me; I'll only slow you down.'

Sally looked at Mick. 'I really don't know if I'm up to it.'

'You seem fine to me.'

'I'm still technically hammered.'

Mick held out his hand. 'Then why not make a fool of yourself? You've got the perfect excuse?'

She smiled, slightly embarrassed, then took his hand and allowed him to lead her onto the floor. Leonard clapped languidly as they did so. 'Bravo.'

Sally turned back to him and hissed, 'Leonard, shut up!' Leonard sat back and winked as they stepped to the periphery of the dancers.

'Can you do this properly?' asked Sally, stepping into his arms.

'No.'

'Neither can I.'

'Good. Then we've nothing to lose.'

'Mmm,' Sally said, doubtfully. She squeezed his hand and allowed him to lead off.

Mick held her close to him as they moved in slow, shuffling steps along with the other dancers. Their eyes met. Mick held her gaze. 'Not so difficult, eh?'

'Stop it,' Sally looked down. 'You're embarrassing me enough as it is.'

'Are you embarrassed?'

She paused a moment, then looked back at him, smiling coyly. 'No. Are you?'

'Not a bit.'

She turned her head in the direction they were moving. Roy and Tony were laughing and making passing remarks to other dancers as they drifted about the floor. Mick noticed them too. He said, 'So this is their tune, is it?'

Sally nodded. '"Autumn Leaves", I've been here before when this has happened. Leonard's right, the dancing'll go on for quite a while now.'

'So I guess this must be our tune as well,' said Mick. She looked at him quizzically. 'Since this is our first dance,' he explained.

'I suppose.' She became conscious that their faces were only inches apart. She looked away quickly and changed the subject. 'You like it here then?'

'Yeah. It's different.'

'It certainly is that,' Sally turned to him again. 'Where else could you dance the night away to Bert Comfort, or whoever he is?'

'With a beautiful girl in my arms,' added Mick.

Sally felt a heat rising in her cheeks. She looked down. 'Stop it Mick, you're making me blush.'

'Am I?' he said softly.

She looked up at him, feeling again the closeness of him. Mick held her eyes, then cautiously, he moved his face a little closer to hers. Sally hesitated, then she moved a little nearer to him. Their lips met in a kiss. It only lasted for the briefest time; they stopped dancing, their eyes closed, oblivious to all around them. Another couple accidentally bumped into them and they were awoken. Instantly they began to dance again.

'Blimey,' said Sally.

Mick laughed. 'Blimey.'

'I hope Leonard didn't see us.'

'Why?'

'I'll never hear the end of it.'

'I hope not.'

She looked back at him. He moved to kiss her and she responded. This time they continued to dance as they kissed, drifting slowly with the crowd, their bodies held close together. Then suddenly, Sally broke off, an alarmed look in her eyes. 'Oh shit.'

'What is it?'

Sally put her hand to her mouth. 'I think I'm going to be sick.'

Mick looked about for the toilets. 'Do you – ?' he began, but she moved quickly away from him through the crowd. Feeling naked on the floor without a partner, Mick walked anxiously back to the table and sat down.

'I saw you,' said Leonard. 'You old dog.' He gave Mick a friendly nudge. 'Where's she gone?'

'I think she's being sick.'

'Oh?' said Leonard. 'Do you always have this effect on women?'

'Here,' Jean held Mr Chips out to Mick. 'I'll go and check on her.'

Mick took the plump little dog – it looked like some kind of corgi – onto his lap, and Jean hurried off in the same direction in which Sally had disappeared.

'I'm sure she'll be fine,' said Leonard. 'Though it sounds like she's had rather a skinful. That and that horrible pipe business. If it'd been me I'd be in intensive care.'

Mick looked anxiously after Sally. 'I suppose so, I just wish I could go and help her out.'

'What, you? Venture into the Ladies in this place? That'd be a picture. Here,' Leonard proffered his cigarettes. 'Have a fag.'

Mick took one and accepted a light. 'Thanks.'

'It must be love.'

'What?'

'I'd say you've stirred the seat of her emotions: the stomach. All this nonsense about the heart aching and what not – it's tosh. It's the stomach that aches when we're in love, not the heart.' Leonard nodded towards the Ladies. 'Hence Sally's problem.'

'So why do they say it's the heart?'

Leonard shrugged. 'Can you imagine a poet going on about his belly aching every time he sees his own true love? Or a Valentine's Day card with a couple of entwined, glowing stomachs on the front? Not very romantic is it?'

'No, I don't suppose it is.' Mick looked back to the toilets. 'Do you suppose I ought to call a taxi?'

'Unless you plan on giving her a ride home on the back of your bicycle, I'd say that might be a good idea.'

Mick handed Mr Chips to a reluctant Leonard and got up to find a phone. When he returned he was pleased to see that Sally was back at the table. She was ashen and the hair of her fringe was damp with perspiration. Mick sat down beside her and placed his hand lightly upon hers. 'Are you feeling okay?'

She shook her head, no.

Mick looked at Jean.

'She's not very well, I'm afraid, Mick.'

'Did you get a cab?' asked Leonard.

Mick nodded. He tenderly swept a few damp hairs from Sally's face. 'I've phoned a cab, Sal. Do you feel okay with that?'

She nodded.

'Okay,' said Mick. 'Shouldn't be long now.'

'Thanks,' Sally's voice was barely audible above the music.

'Can I get you anything? Maybe a glass of water or something?'

She shook her head. 'No, thanks.'

'Good job you're off tomorrow, Sally,' said Leonard.

Sally smiled weakly and nodded. 'Yeah.'

Roy, having resumed his landlord role, called out from the bar. 'Taxi for Mick outside!'

Mick put his arm around Sally's back. 'Taxi's here. Ready Sal?' Sally got slowly to her feet and pushed her hair back from her face.

'How are you feeling?' asked Mick.

'Dead.'

'Do you think you'll be alright in the cab?'

She nodded.

'Okay.' Mick turned to Leonard and Jean. 'Nice to have met you both. Hopefully I'll see you again sometime.'

'Don't forget Mr Chips,' Jean gently agitated the little dog's body.

'Of course not. Bye Mr Chips.'

The dog moved his head a little at the mention of his name, then resumed its contemplation of only he knew what.

'Go!' said Leonard. 'I don't imagine Sally has the strength to endure Jean's torturous dog farewell rituals. I'll keep the hound occupied while you escape.'

Mick nodded and steered Sally in the direction of the exit. She raised a hand to the table as she went. 'Seeya.'

After they were gone, Leonard turned to Jean. 'Well, looks like it's just the three of us again. What are your first impressions of that Mick chappy then?'

'He seems quite nice. If I were twenty years younger, I'd consider myself to have done quite well if he were on my arm.'

'He's not a peregrine falcon, Jean. Spare me the pleasantries. Are you trying to say you'd shag him?'

Jean nodded. 'Yes. I'd shag him.'

'Mmm,' said Leonard.

'And Chippy would shag him too,' said Jean, talking directly to the dog. 'Wouldn't you Chippy?'

For the first time that evening, Mr Chips looked up at her, gave a little bark and lapped at her face.

'Charming,' said Leonard dryly. 'Quite charming.'

Chapter 26

GAZ WOKE UP IN DARKNESS to find Kay sleeping alone beside him. He looked about, but neither of the other guys was around. Then he remembered: Kay's mood after Sally had walked out hadn't exactly been amorous. To go from that to Jimmy and Glen stripping off for a party in the lounge – it wasn't quite the soothing balm she needed. They'd all sat around bitching about Sally for a bit longer, after deciding that another spin on the bong was a good idea after all, then he and she had come up to bed alone. The lads understood; chicks need to be mollified occasionally. Tonight, Kay had needed to feel special. He'd as good as promised her a night alone, and to rescind on the deal in the eleventh hour just because Sally was an old maid was unwise, not to mention unfair. Anyway, he'd gotten his leg over, that was the main thing.

He looked to where numbers glowed from the face of his alarm clock. It was half past two. He climbed out of bed and scratched himself before going to the bathroom for a piss. As he stepped out onto the landing he could hear music still playing downstairs. Snoring from the room to his left told him that Jimmy and Glen had long since come up to bed. They'd obviously gone to bed leaving the CD player on. It was working on random selection and would go on all night unless someone actually shut it down. He decided to go for a piss first, then take care of it.

As Gaz directed his pee stream at a couple of stubborn streaks of excrement that had been hanging around on the interior wall of the toilet for a few days, he heard what sounded like the doorbell chime. He frowned. Who the hell would be calling at this hour? Sally? Maybe she'd had a little re-think and realised what she was missing. Or perhaps the sight of him and Glen getting to work on Kay had done something for her after all? The doorbell rang again. He finished urinating, gave himself a shake, then hurried downstairs. He didn't bother putting anything on. If it was Sally, it'd save time just being naked. If it wasn't, he could just keep himself behind the door.

The doorbell rang again as he approached it. 'Yeah, yeah. Hang on.' He opened it just wide enough to see who was outside. It wasn't Sally. He blinked, surprised. 'Adam?'

'Hi.'

'What do you want, man? It's like, half two in the morning.'

'Is it? I don't know. I came as quick as I could.'

Gaz frowned. 'What do you mean?'

'The gear?' Adam fished in his trouser pocket. 'I got it. I was as quick as I could be. The sooner the better, remember?' He produced the cling-filmed lump and held it out to Gaz.

'Shit, man. Don't go waving that about outside.' Gaz stepped aside, opening the door as he did so. 'Come on in.'

Adam stepped into the house. 'Thank you. It's getting pretty cold outside.'

'How long have you been there?'

'I don't know. A while. I don't have a watch.'

Gaz managed a laugh. 'You're crazy, man. Standing out there in that T-shirt, no jacket or nothin'.' Then he slapped his forehead. 'Damn, there it is again, "Wake Me Up Before You Go-Go". You gotta stop wearing that shirt, geezer. It's driving me insane.'

'I will. I've got some others.'

'Good.' Gaz patted him on the back. 'Wear 'em, eh? That one could use a few days off.'

'I will.' Adam smiled, pleased at the approval.

'Come on. Come into the lounge and sit down. Do you want tea or anything?'

Adam followed Gaz into the lounge. 'No thanks. Maybe a glass of water?'

'Sure, no problem. By the way,' Gaz said as they entered the kitchen. 'I hope you don't mind me being naked. I just got out of bed, y'know?'

'No. I enjoy the sight of you naked. Nudity is a good thing. I should be naked more often myself. It's a good thing.'

Gaz, who was filling a glass with water as Adam spoke, suddenly realised the glass had overflowed and water was running all over his hand. What had he just said? He turned off the tap and turned to Adam with the glass. He tried to keep his expression as neutral as possible. 'Yes, yes it's a good thing.'

Adam took the glass. 'Thanks.' He drank it off and handed it back. 'Do you want the gear now?'

'Er? Hang on,' Gaz stepped towards the kitchen door. 'It's a bit chilly innit? I just wanna get some things on. Help yourself to more water.'

'Thanks.' Adam went to the tap and poured himself another glass of water. He wondered if he should've suggested that he undress too? Perhaps that would make The One feel more at ease, but now it seemed that clothes were in order. It was chilly after all. The nights are still cold. Not good naked weather. He heard the sound of The One returning.

Gaz came in wearing jogging pants and a singlet. 'Now then,' he rubbed his hands together. 'Let's get down to business. Lounge?'

'Okay.'

Gaz led the way into the lounge. The music had stopped for a moment as the CD player randomly selected the next track. A moment later, the Doors' "Moonlight Drive" began to drift from the speakers. Gaz sat down in an armchair and motioned Adam to the sofa. He noticed Adam looking into the picnic box. 'Love toys,' Gaz explained. 'Quite a selection, eh?' He reached in and pulled out the double-ender. 'We like to get a couple of chicks on either end of this one.' He laughed. 'You should fuckin' see it. Me and one of the other guys getting sucked-off by these chicks as they fuck each other on this?' He shook his head, smiling at the memories. 'Fuckin' wild, man.'

'It certainly looks... used.'

'Sorry?'

'Kind of, sticky?'

Gaz grinned and rolled the dildo under his nose like a cigar connoisseur. He sniffed meditatively. 'Mmmm, interesting bouquet. Could it be Kathy and Mel? Yes, yes I think so.' He laughed and tossed the dildo back in the box. 'Haven't seen either of those two for a couple of months now. Maybe we should call them up?' His eyes widened a little. 'Hmm, maybe we should at that.'

Adam shifted a little in his seat and looked down between his knees.

'What?' said Gaz. 'Does that make you uncomfortable?'

Adam shrugged. 'Not exactly. I just... I don't know if that kind of thing is really...'

'Really you?' Gaz suggested.

Adam nodded thoughtfully. 'Yeah. Really me.'

Gaz picked up a joint that had been laid prematurely to rest in the ashtray and lit up. 'Well, each to their own, man. If you ever change your mind you're, er, always welcome.'

'Thanks.'

'Mind you, Kathy and Mel aren't exactly good-looking. But who cares, eh?'

Adam smiled. 'I don't care about looks. They're only skin deep.'

Gaz nodded, exhaling a stream of smoke. 'That's what they say.'

'It's true, though.'

'Oh, yeah,' Gaz agreed emphatically. 'It's true alright.'

Adam shook his head and gave a little laugh. 'Hell, here I am telling you what's what. Ignore me. I'm sorry.'

'No, man, don't be daft. Everybody's got an opinion, man. No one's any more right than anybody else, that's what I say.'

Adam nodded. 'Wise words.'

'Thanks, man. Now, about that hash, what do we owe you?'

Adam took the lump of hash out of his trouser pocket and set it down on the coffee table. 'Same as before?'

Gaz, who had been holding down a lungful, coughed. 'Same as–? Are you sure? Is it the same gear?'

'Same gear, yes. Why? Didn't you like it?'

'Fuck no,' said Gaz. 'I mean fuck yes. We loved it. It was great. But are you sure you don't want more for it? I mean, the first time was like a special offer wasn't it?'

Adam shrugged. 'So's this – a special offer.'

Gaz smiled broadly and shook his head in a slow, incredulous manner. 'Jesus, Adam. What can I say? Thanks a lot, man.'

'It's my pleasure. It's always a pleasure to help you. To assist.'

Gaz drew on the joint and held the smoke in his lungs. There was something decidedly odd about some of the things Adam said, and despite what Kay thought, Gaz wasn't blind to the possibility that maybe the big man did fancy him. That bit earlier about liking the sight of him naked would be enough to put the wind up anybody. And now this stuff about it being a pleasure to please; it was creepy shit alright. But then look at that lump of hash on the table. Just fucking look at it! He let the smoke go in a long blue stream. 'Do you mind if I open it up?'

Adam shook his head. 'Do want you like with it.'

Gaz put the joint in the ashtray and picked up the big lump of resin. He unwrapped the cling film and sniffed it. 'Mmm-mm. Fuck-ing A, man.' He looked at Adam. 'I hope you don't mind, but I'll sell some of this shit on. It'll go a long way to paying off Ron.'

'You don't need to worry about Ron.'

Gaz, who had been sampling the texture of the dope, didn't quite catch what Adam said. 'Sorry?'

'Ron. Your landlord. You don't have to worry about him anymore.'

'Oh?' Gaz chuckled. 'Don't tell me you paid our rent for us as well, man?'

'I took care of him, like we said.'

Gaz's smile lingered uncertainly. 'Like what?'

'Like we said.' Adam took the joint from the ashtray. 'May I?'

Gaz nodded, his expression now one of disquiet.

Adam drew on the joint and winked. 'He's out of the picture. You don't need to worry about him anymore.'

Gaz put the dope down on the coffee table. 'Hang on a minute, man.' He put his hand to his head. 'Don't go fuckin' with my head, eh? Coz I've had a busy night, stimulation wise. What, what are you telling me, man?'

Adam exhaled smoke and shrugged. 'A car crash. Or that's what it looks like.'

Gaz stared silently at the big bald man on his couch as if seeing him for the first time. 'Are you… Are you telling me that Ron Chigley is… dead?'

'Don't be afraid. No one'll suspect anything. I was careful.'

'Careful?' Gaz felt slightly dizzy. 'You were careful?'

'Yes. I was careful.' Adam offered Gaz the joint. 'And don't worry for Ron. He didn't suffer.'

Gaz shrank back into his chair. 'Oh, Jesus. You... You murdered Ron?'

'I took care of him. You wanted it done; now it is. He isn't a problem any more.' Adam indicated the joint. 'You want this? Or shall I put it out?'

Gaz got unsteadily to his feet. 'I think, I think you'd better go now Adam.'

Adam smiled nervously. 'Is there something wrong? I told you I was careful. You've nothing to fear.'

'I, I know that.' Gaz spoke carefully, trying to keep the panic out of his voice. He smiled. 'I've just had a bit too much to smoke. I want to go to bed now, man, okay?'

Adam frowned. 'What is it? Did I do something wrong?'

'Wrong?' Gaz laughed nervously. 'Oh, no, you just killed my landlord. I should thank you. In fact,' he added, 'I do. I do thank you. Thanks.'

'You're welcome.'

'You're not winding me up are you, Adam? You're not fucking with my head, are you, man? Tell me if you're fucking with my head, man because I don't need that shit, you know? Tell me. Tell me, Adam.'

'You are The One.' Adam looked at Gaz steadily. 'Surely you know whether I speak the truth?'

'What? What are you talking about man?' Gaz thrust his hand out before him as if to deflect Adam's strange vibes. 'What do you mean? Please, please stop fucking with my head, okay? I... I really think you should go now.'

'You aren't, are you?' There was regret in Adam's voice as he spoke.

'Not what, man? Who... ? What are you talking about?'

Adam lowered his face into his hands.

Gaz listened for a moment as the other man breathed heavily through his fingers. 'What? What's the matter now?'

Adam drew his hands slowly down his face.

'What?' Gaz shook his head in slow denial. 'What are you crying for, man? Stop it.'

Adam got up. 'I'm sorry. There's been a misunderstanding.'

'Has there?' Gaz attempted a laugh. 'What? What's misunderstood? Me?'

'No. I've misunderstood. Not you.' Adam began to move towards Gaz around the coffee table. 'I fear you could never understand me.'

'Yeah. You got that right.' He took a step back and held up his hands as Adam drew near. 'That's close enough, man. Don't come any closer. I can do kung fu.' His hands assumed a classic defensive pose. Adam kept coming. 'I mean it man, it sounds like shit, but it's true.' Gaz bent his knees, poised to strike.

Adam kept coming.

Gaz spun around and lashed out with his foot. It would've caught Adam square in the chest – if Adam hadn't caught it. Gaz had a moment to gape in astonishment at his captured foot before Adam twisted it, sending him tumbling to the floor. 'Fuck!' Gaz's cry was lost beneath the swirling music that still played about them. His head struck the picnic hamper, knocking it over and scattering sex toys across the floor.

Gaz, his eyes closed, lay stunned among the latex oddities. A shadow fell over his eyelids and he opened them to see Adam looming above him, bending down with his hands wide open. 'No!' Gaz tried to strike at him but he had no room to manoeuvre, all he managed was to punch Adam in the side of the face. Adam flinched a little, then he drew his own fist back. Gaz bolted, but too late. Adam's fist caught him full in the face as he tried to rise, smashing his head back to the floor with terrible force. Gaz felt nothing, it all happened too fast; there was an explosion, then darkness.

Adam drew back and looked at the young man on the floor. He looked around at the sex toys, his eyes lighting upon one particular dildo that had a pair of solid-looking testes at the base. He took a few steps and bent to retrieve it. Behind him Gaz began to stir. Adam held the dildo up and examined it closely. Clutching the base in one hand, he prodded curiously at the head; it quivered. Gaz began to moan incoherently. Adam turned and went back to where he lay.

Gaz tried to move but his head was spinning. Tiny dots swam and exploded before the image of Adam bending towards him with a dildo. Gaz tried to move away, but Adam reached out and took him by the front of his singlet. Gaz managed to shake his head slightly. 'No. Lemme go.' The big man ignored him, taking a single step over Gaz's body so he stood with one foot either side of him.

'Please, Adam,' Gaz raised his hands weakly in front of his face. 'Please, lemme go –'

His appeal was cut off as Adam sat down heavily upon his chest, forcing the air from his lungs in a violent rush. Still stunned and now winded, Gaz was unable to offer any resistance as he felt his shoulders pinned beneath the other man's knees.

'Cuuunt,' Gaz wheezed. He tried to find the breath to spit into Adam's face but couldn't. Air hissed in shallow gasps through his clenched teeth. He writhed and kicked futilely beneath the other man's weight, thrashing his head from side to side.

What was he doing with that fucking dildo? Why did he just sit there, staring and holding it? Then a memory struck him. Kay saying Adam fancied him. Jesus, was she right? Was that it? Was Adam getting off on this? Was he going to… to fuck him with that thing? 'Fff-fuck off, man!' his voice was tight and constricted, but it seemed to have an effect.

Adam reached out his free hand and began squeezing the flesh around Gaz's mouth so his lips curled out from his teeth in a snarling pout. Gaz felt the powerful hand pressuring his jaw to open; he tried to wrench his face free of Adam's grip but it was too powerful. As Gaz's teeth were prized apart he saw the dildo moving in towards him. His terrified eyes darted from the dildo to Adam, trying to read some kind of intention in the other man's face; and then he knew. He tried to scream, but the rubbery head of the dildo was already pushing in-between his lips.

'Nn, No!' Gaz managed to blurt out before the dildo cut him off. His taste buds registered latex, dust and female as it slid over the surface of his tongue, filling his mouth. He tried to jerk his face aside but Adam's grip was like a vice. The dildo slid deeper, entering his oesophagus. Gaz choked, his eyes widening as Adam's full intention dawned on him. His throat spasmed as it tried to choke up the hideous intrusion. Adam pushed down and Gaz felt the solid rubbery testes press against his front teeth. He tried to scream but all that came out was a guttural choking noise. He could feel his teeth straining against their roots, then breaking individually. Blood flowed into his mouth as the latex phallus filled his throat entirely. Gaz's struggles intensified as overwhelming terror began to black out his sanity. He heaved frenziedly against the weight on top of him, his legs thrashing and kicking out wildly. One foot struck the racking that held the CD player, the shock causing the music to cut out. The CD spun for a second, then fell silent.

The only sound in Gaz's ears was the furious beating of his heart as it strained for oxygen. Blackness began to prickle at the periphery of the world, and his wild eyes fell upon the words on Adam's T-shirt. Black on white, bigger now than ever:

"CHOOSE LIFE"

He'd never understood the significance of the message; why would anyone choose anything else? Then the words became indistinct, lost behind waves of myriad colourful stars that began to close across his field of vision. It was trippy, Gaz thought. I'm tripping. A new sound seemed to come from out of the rushing of his blood, rising in volume over the pounding of his heart. Music: a happy song that belonged to a summer long ago when he was a boy. He remembered a man clapping and dancing, another playing guitar. It was Top of the Pops, and he was watching it with his sister on the sofa. "Wake Me Up Before You Go-Go". His sister sang along. She knew all the words. All of the words to all of the songs.

Adam sat beside the body with his head in his hands. For about a minute he was still. Only his back and shoulders moved, rising and falling as his breathing gradually steadied. Then slowly, he raised his eyes to look at the corpse. The dildo still jutted from the bloody hole that had once been Gaz's mouth. Adam sighed; he took the dildo by its base and carefully disgorged it. A horrible sucking noise accompanied its withdrawal, as though Gaz's body were reluctant to give it up. The body sighed as the phallus finally cleared its throat. Adam put a hand beneath the dildo to prevent blood from dripping onto the carpet. He got to his feet and walked quickly into the kitchen where he dropped it into the sink. Fortunately someone had washed up that day and there were only a few dirty items in the wash bowl. Adam rinsed the dildo clean and tipped the bloody water away. He then carefully filled the bowl to the same level as before, adding a little squeeze of washing-up liquid so that, come the morning, it would appear exactly as it had a few moments earlier.

He held the dildo up before him to examine it. There were a few small gouges into the rubber where Gaz's teeth had broken and scored it, but nothing serious; nothing the others here would ever notice as they put the thing to its proper use. He went back into the lounge and tidied the other sex toys away in their picnic hamper.

When all was as it had been, Adam opened the French windows and looked out into the night. All the houses were black and silent; the neighbourhood was finally asleep. And they could keep on sleeping, Adam reflected. Now the source of their insomnia was vanquished forever. He looked back to the body on the floor. What to do with this one? He looked out again at the dark houses beyond, up to the window of the room he had recently claimed as home. His eyes found the fire escape that snaked downward from the window, past the second floor, and down to the ground. He looked back again at the corpse.

'Time to go.'

Upstairs, Jimmy, Glen and Kay slept the dreamless, comatose sleep of the profoundly intoxicated. To all intents and purposes, they were dead to the world.

PART FOUR

Chapter 27

'THUNDERBIRDS ARE GO!' The bold announcement was distant, but distinct. The adrenaline-soaked music that followed it, though quiet, was evidently very nearby. *What the hell am I doing in the same environment as "Thunderbirds"?* she wondered. Her eyes opened. Someone had removed her ceiling and replaced it with a different one. No, she realised; this wasn't her room. She raised her head from the pillow and slowly took in the scenery, letting it filter in gradually as she moved her head in a slow arc. On the wall at the far end of the bed was a poster of a thing with a face like a crab, holding a bloody skull over its head. A single word ran along the poster's lower half in bold red letters: "PREDATOR". Sally's head flopped back onto the pillow.

'I've died and gone to hell.' Speaking awoke the unpleasant taste in her mouth and she grimaced. The events of the previous night began to flicker in her mind like a movie trailer. She saw Gaz, Glen and Kay in their fireside threesome; Kay calling her a frigid bitch, a big bald man in a Wham! T-shirt and trousers that rode too far up his ankles. She saw Mick's back as she held on to it so as not to fall off his bike – *Jesus, I rode on the back of that thing?* Then there was the pub, the music, dancing with, and then kissing Mick. That incident played itself through again. She smiled as she remembered how she had felt in his arms. Then she remembered the sudden nausea. The flight from the dancefloor, the ladies' toilet, Jean stroking her back as she heaved into the toilet bowl, and finally a taxi outside. The rest was gone. She closed her eyes and put her hands over her face. 'Shit.'

From what she assumed must be the next room came the muted sound of big rocket engines. *I must be at Mick's,* she reasoned. Then her eyes sprang open. *My God! Am I...?* She pulled up the duvet and looked at herself. She was fully clothed – minus her shoes, she noticed, wiggling her toes beneath the fabric of the duvet. She sighed and lowered her arms. An alarm clock informed her it was 11.20.

11.20! Shit, she was late. She sat up and the world swam violently. 'Ohhh,' she closed her eyes and pressed her hand to her forehead. After a few moments, the nausea subsided, though it didn't leave altogether, it clung to the edges of her consciousness like a bad smell. She lowered her feet to the ground where they bumped against a plastic bucket. She looked into it and saw with relief that it was empty. She got slowly to her feet and padded over to the door. She opened it a crack and looked into the room outside. It was a big lounge and dining room in one. Over on the other side of the room was an armchair with its back to her, it faced a television where a puppet was dangling on a string into a smoky pit. The puppet looked hot, but otherwise fairly sanguine.

'Mick?' she croaked.

Mick's head appeared around the side of the chair. He smiled. 'Hiya. How are you feeling?'

'Awful. Do you have anything for a hangover? I have to get in to work. Leonard'll be having kittens.'

'Aren't you forgetting something? You're not working today. You have a midday date with the most eligible bachelor in town.'

Sally sagged against the doorframe with relief. 'Of course I do. Thanks.'

'Oh, it's my pleasure. Can I get you a coffee or something?'

She nodded. 'Thanks. Coffee and a blood transfusion.'

'Will some Alka-Seltzer do?'

'Wonderful.'

Half an hour later they were sitting on Mick's sofa. Sally was on her second cup of strong, black coffee and the plight of the imperilled cast of "Thunderbirds" was forgotten, the TV having been switched off.

Sally had been hearing from Mick certain details she had forgotten about the night before. He was just getting to the bit where the mirrorball came on. 'And then what?' she asked, though she knew perfectly well. Her legs folded beneath her, she fiddled distractedly with her toes.

'We danced.'

She smiled. 'You were quite good, I seem to recall.'

'So were you.' Mick grinned. 'I seem to recall.'

'Then what?'

'Then we,' he hesitated a moment. 'We kissed, sort of.'

'Sort of?'

Mick shrugged. 'Well, no, actually there wasn't any "sort of". We kissed. Don't you remember?'

Sally nodded. 'I remember.'

'Oh. I, I thought for a moment there you might have forgotten.'

'Oh no. I remember it quite vividly.'

'A happy memory?'

Sally smiled. 'Very. Thank you.' She went back to perusing her toes.

'I was wondering,' Mick said cautiously. 'If it was an isolated incident?'

She looked back to him. 'What do you mean?'

'I mean, I was wondering if it was just...' he shrugged. 'Like, a one-off thing? You know?'

'Oh. I see.'

'Well, was it?' he asked quietly. 'A one-off thing?'

'Not if you don't want it to be. Do you?'

Mick shook his head. 'Oh, no. No, I'd like to see repeat incidents. Regular, frequent, repeat incidents. If that's okay with you?'

'That's okay with me.' Sally leaned towards him and kissed him gently on the mouth.

Mick smiled. 'Thanks.'

'You're welcome.'

'Can I have another one?'

Sally nodded. 'But you have to come and get it.'

Mick brought his arms up gently around her and kissed her, this time for longer than before.

'Thank you,' said Sally.

'Oh, it was my pleasure.'

She remained in his arms, settling against him. 'Sorry about being sick and stuff. It's all very embarrassing.'

'Don't be daft. It wasn't your fault. Anyway, we've all been there.'

Sally smiled. 'Though not always quite so publicly.'

'I'm sure no one really noticed.'

'Except Leonard and Jean.'

'And Mr Chips.'

'Especially Mr Chips,' said Sally. 'That dog's an awful gossip.' She looked up at Mick again. 'Thanks for looking after me.'

'It was my pleasure.'

'You're a gentleman. A dying breed if Gaz and his mates are anything to go by.'

'I'm sure they're in the minority. Most men don't behave like they do.'

Sally said nothing. She thought again of the incidents of the previous evening, how they had started. First Kay, then going to Shenanigans… She sat upright suddenly as a forgotten detail suddenly occurred to her. 'Oh, I didn't tell you did I? I saw that guy again – the bald guy who's living in Peter's flat?'

'Really? Where?'

'I met him. It turns out he's an acquaintance of Gaz. He gets them their dope.'

'He's a dealer?'

'Yeah. Apparently he gets them a very good deal on it.'

'Mmmm,' Mick murmured thoughtfully. 'The plot thickens. What was he like?'

'Weird. That T-shirt? The Wham! one? He was still proudly wearing that.'

'Really?'

'Yeah. It was getting pretty ripe, too. Not eye-wateringly bad, but a bit whiffy alright. Apparently he absolutely lives in it.'

Mick raised his eyebrows. 'Oh?'

'Yeah. Gaz commented on the shirt to Adam – that's his name – and he said to Gaz, "Do you want it?" Meaning the T-shirt. You see, the reason he'd been wearing it was because he thought Gaz liked it. Isn't that weird?'

'It's pretty weird, alright. So did Gaz take this stinky shirt then?'

Sally smiled. 'Of course not. He was pretty diplomatic about it, saying he didn't think it would fit him and stuff, but Jesus. I mean who'd want a Wham! T-shirt under the best of circumstances? Let alone a smelly old one right off this guy's back?'

Mick pouted slightly. 'I wouldn't mind a Wham! T-shirt. Mind you, it'd have to be clean.'

'Really? You're a Wham! fan?'

'Sure. Everybody likes Wham! It's just that not everybody realises it.'

'I don't like Wham!' Sally said with firm conviction. 'I never liked Wham!'

'Ahhh. That's the thing, you see. When we were young, Wham! Were a bit...' he grimaced. 'You know, naff. And that feeling has stayed with us as we've grown because we've never had any cause to rethink it. But if I was to start singing a Wham! song, I bet you'd join in.'

'I bet I wouldn't.'

'Not openly perhaps, but inside.'

Sally shook her head. 'Not me, mister.'

Mick started singing the chorus to "Club Tropicana".

Sally picked up a cushion and buried her face in it.

'Oi! Why are you hiding?'

'I'm embarrassed.' Sally lowered the cushion and peered over the top.

'You mean you're trying to stifle the urge to sing along.'

Sally laughed into the cushion. 'Oh yeah, that's it. I'm gagging myself.'

'I knew I was right. That Adam guy's not the only Wham! fan in town after all.'

Sally put the cushion aside. 'No, there's the two of you. Maybe you can go and see George Michael in concert together sometime.'

'Maybe we will.' Mick turned his nose up. 'Since you're so obviously in Wham! denial, I take it you won't be joining us?'

Sally grew serious. 'I wouldn't like to go anywhere with him. He's not quite right, you know?' She tapped the side of her head. 'He was staring at me in a weird way in that beer garden.'

'Was he?'

'Yeah.' She rubbed her upper arms as if a chill had passed through her. 'He gives me the creeps. Thank God I won't have to socialise with him again.'

'Maybe he fancies you. Perhaps that's why he was staring.'

'Oh, God, don't.'

Mick smiled. 'What? Not your type?'

'That's not the point. It could've been George Clooney sitting there, it wouldn't have made any difference.' She laughed. 'I can just see George Clooney sitting there in that T-shirt, funky trousers and Daffy Duck socks.'

Mick frowned.

Sally was surprised by his expression. 'What? Don't tell me you're jealous?'

'Daffy Duck socks?'

'Yeah. He was wearing these socks with Daffy Duck's face embroidered on 'em. Apparently he's been wearing those for a good few days as well. And like the trousers, they looked too small for him, you know? Short and tight?'

Mick said nothing. He seemed suddenly far away in thought.

'Mick?'

'I'm just thinking.'

'About Daffy Duck?'

Mick nodded slowly. 'Daffy Duck and Peter.'

'What about them?'

'Peter was into Daffy Duck. I mean, in a sort of blatant way, you know? Like he had this Daffy Duck tie he used to wear? And sometimes,' he pointed thoughtfully to his breast. 'He'd wear this little Daffy lapel pin.'

'You didn't notice if he wore Daffy Duck socks?'

'No, I didn't get down on an ankle level with old Pete that often. But it would follow, wouldn't it? That he'd have Daffy socks as well?'

Sally nodded. 'It would. You think that maybe, there's a connection?'

Mick looked at her. 'Big guy moves into Peter's flat, Peter having,' he made quotation marks in the air with his fingers. "Gone away". Then this guy, Adam, starts walking about in clothes slightly too small for him. Part of his outfit is a pair of socks – precisely the kind of socks that Peter would buy.' He raised his eyebrows. 'What do you think?'

'I don't know,' Sally said thoughtfully. 'You think this guy's wearing Peter's stuff?'

Mick shrugged. 'Could be. It makes a certain sense, doesn't it?'

Sally nodded slowly. 'So, where's Peter?'

'Last time I saw him he was driving off in the back of a bus with a guy he was genuinely frightened of.'

'The tramp?'

Mick nodded. 'The big tramp.'

'You said he was hairy-looking.'

Mick shrugged. 'Maybe he went to the barbers.'

'You don't think he's got Peter up there in his flat? Sort of... hostage?'

'I dunno. Maybe sort of... dead.'

Sally's hand went to her mouth. 'Oh God, you don't think he murdered Peter?'

'I honestly don't know what to think. But it's not impossible is it? I mean, like you said, he's weird. Creepy.'

'But homicidal? How could a man like that just be walking around in society?'

Mick shrugged. 'It happens. Every now and then, someone who should be receiving serious professional help winds up doing something that gets them in the papers, you know what I mean?'

Sally nodded, almost reluctantly. 'And you, you think this guy's one of those people?'

Mick shrugged. 'Could be. Could be he's living at Peter's house, walking around in Peter's clothes. Shit, maybe he even thinks he is Peter.'

'Do you think we should go to the police?'

'With what? Some story. My friend's moved abroad and there's a man in his flat wearing the same socks as he used to. I believe this man is a homicidal maniac. Please go and arrest him?' Mick raised his eyebrows. 'I think we'd get some pretty queer looks, Sal.'

'Well what else can we do?'

'I don't know. Watch him. Stake him out – seriously though, not in the half-arsed way I've been doing it. Watch him; follow him. See what he does, who he sees.'

'That's pretty ambitious isn't it? What're you going to do? Take the month off work just so you can hang around outside his house waiting for him to come out? And even if you did, just how long do you think it'll take him to spot you? A bloke sitting outside on a Raleigh Chopper day in, day out? Come on, Mick you might as well let off a smoke flare.'

'I dunno. I'm making this up as I go along. Feel free to bung in a more sensible suggestion anytime.'

'We need evidence.'

'Yes, evidence would be good. But where are we going to get evidence from?'

'Peter's flat.'

'And how do you propose we get into Peter's flat?'

'Those buildings all have fire escapes, don't they?'

Mick shrugged. 'I don't know.'

'I think they do.'

'Alright, assuming they do, so what?'

'So my friend lives in the flat below, remember?'

Mick said nothing for a moment as the fact sank in. 'You're proposing we go up the fire escape into Peter's flat and then look about for evidence?'

Sally nodded.

'It's kind of Scooby Doo, isn't it?'

'Do you have a better idea?'

Mick thought a moment, then shook his head, no.

'Following him could take months. And there's never going to be any guarantee of finding anything. I don't imagine he goes and puts flowers on Peter's grave every Sunday. Assuming of course, that he has murdered him'

'No,' said Mick, gazing thoughtfully out of the window. 'I don't imagine he does.' Then he turned to Sally. 'When should we do this?'

Sally shrugged. 'We have a date, don't we?'

Mick's eyes widened. 'You mean today?'

Sally shrugged. 'Do you have any other plans?'

'I, I need to go back to the Black Pig and get my bike. I phoned them up this morning and they said I can go 'round anytime today.'

'So you go and get your bike back. Then what?'

Mick shrugged. 'I guess a trip to the zoo's out of the question?'

Sally smiled. 'Do you still have that petition thing you made up?'

Mick nodded.

'How do you feel about canvassing a few opinions down Charrington Street?'

Mick sighed. 'Do you mind if I postpone giving up cigarettes until tomorrow?'

Sally smiled. 'Attaboy.'

Mick smiled back, nervously.

Chapter 28

ELLEN WOKE UP AT ABOUT ELEVEN O'CLOCK. She always slept in on weekends, catching up on the sleep she lost out on during the week when she had to get up at the ungodly hour of 6.30 every day in order to get into work for nine. As usual, Wayne's side of the bed was cold and empty when she awoke. She got up, put on her dressing gown and fluffy rabbit slippers, and went into the lounge.

Wayne was looking out of the window, dancing on the spot to whatever was filling his head through the stereo headphones he wore. He was still only in his boxers and T-shirt. Ellen smiled, and rolled her eyes. She tapped him on the shoulder. Wayne started, turning around with a hand to his heart. He pulled the headphones off. 'Fuck, you gave me a shock.'

Ellen smiled. 'Serves you right, you shouldn't be shaking your fat arse at the neighbours at this hour of the morning. You should be making me breakfast in bed.'

'Well, I thought you wanted to sleep.'

'I did. Now I'm awake.' Ellen patted his bottom. 'I don't suppose you fancy making breakfast?'

Wayne gave a smile of regret. 'I've eaten, babe.' He rubbed his stomach. 'No room for any more.'

'I mean do you fancy making me breakfast?'

Wayne frowned. 'I was having a dance. Notice how I unselfishly used the headphones.' He held them up as if in evidence.

'I'm touched,' said Ellen. 'Does this mean I'm making my own breakfast?'

'Well I did make dinner last night. And the night before that.'

Ellen shrugged. 'Okay, it was worth a try.' She turned around and padded off in the direction of the kitchen. Just as she was about to leave the room, Wayne called after her.

'Hey, El? If you're up, do you mind if I listen to this without the headphones?'

Ellen waved a hand without turning. 'Go ahead, but not too loud, we don't want to annoy the neighbours, do we?'

'Thanks, babe,' said Wayne. Then as an afterthought, he added, 'Oh, El? Are you going to be making tea?'

Ellen stopped in the doorway with her back to him. 'Yes.'

'Couldn't make me one, could you?'

Ellen stood still a moment, then continued into the hall without speaking.

Wayne looked after her for a second, shrugged and removed the headphone jack from the stereo. The sound of OMD's, "Electricity" filled the lounge and Wayne resumed his rhythmic writhings.

Presently, Ellen returned with a mug of tea which she set down on the table. She straightened. Wayne was smiling at her. She stuck her fingers up at him, then turned to go.

'El!' said Wayne, hurt. 'Wait!' He switched off the CD and jogged after her, catching her by the shoulders. 'Are you cross with me?'

'I only get two mornings off a week, Wayne. It would be nice if you'd – I don't know – consider making them a little special.'

'I do consider.'

'And the result of these considerations is – ?' Ellen looked at him expectantly. He was silent. 'Is you can't be arsed.'

'Well, like I said, I thought you wanted to sleep in.'

'But when you knew I was up, when I actually asked you if you'd make me breakfast, still, you declined. So I think I'm right in saying you can't be arsed.'

Wayne hung his head. 'I'm sorry. I was listening to my music and I just... got absorbed.'

'Sure.' Ellen turned to leave.

'I'll do it now. I've finished rocking.'

'Don't bother, Wayne,' said Ellen as she walked away. 'I've as good as done it myself. I just heard the toast pop.'

'I'll butter it.'

Ellen made no reply.

Wayne pulled a sour face in her general direction then sat down in an armchair and aimed the remote at the TV. He began flicking through the channels. As the pictures flashed in front of him, he found his thoughts turning to Lucy. She was no longer afraid of his threat to inform the freeholder of her business antics, nor was she making any bones about coming down and telling Ellen if he bothered her again. He swore silently under his breath. He muted the TV and looked up at the ceiling. It was silent. Maybe she was out? Perhaps she was sleeping? He unconsciously raised his hands to his nipples and pressed them gently, biting his lower lip and closing his eyes as blood began to flow quickly into his penis.

'Stop it,' he gritted his teeth and set his hands firmly on the arms of the chair. Stop torturing yourself. What's the point? You've told her you won't bother her anymore. She's told you not to bother her anymore, and you agreed.

Just like you did the first time, another voice in his head pointed out. You said you wouldn't bother her again last time, and then you did, and what happened?

'She told me to get lost,' Wayne said aloud.

Until you did... what?

Until I threatened her with the freeholder?

No. Think.

A smile spread slowly over his face. Until I offered her money.

That's it, boy.

'Money,' he whispered. Lucy likes money. Maybe even more than she dislikes me. He smiled a cruel smile and peered sideways to where he could see the bedroom door. 'Ellen?' 'What?'

'Listen. I've had a thought. Why don't I go out and do some shopping? Save you the bother? I'll buy you a newspaper and the new *Radio Times*. What do you say?'

There was silence for a moment, then Ellen called, guardedly, 'That's very nice of you.'

Wayne got up and strolled into the bedroom, he leaned against the doorframe and smiled at her. 'It's the least I can do. After being such a selfish dickhead, and all.'

Ellen sat propped up by pillows in bed. She was eating a piece of toast. She lowered it to the plate on her lap and smiled at him. 'Oh Wayne. Don't feel you have to do that for me.'

'Oh, I do though, El. Like you said, it's your day off. You work hard all week while I sit around here on my arse. It's only right that you should get a chance to relax when you can.'

'That's very sweet of you, darling.' She popped the last of the toast into her mouth. 'Thanks. And you're not a dickhead.'

Wayne beamed. 'If you say so. So, I'll just get dressed. Then I'll be off.'

'Thanks.' Ellen took a sip from her tea.

'Forget it.' Wayne assumed an American accent and said, 'Don't thank me ma'am, I'm just doing my job.' He saluted, then ran off to the bathroom.

Ellen smiled with an air of weariness and went back to her magazine.

Exactly forty-nine minutes later, Wayne, a carrier bag of shopping in his hand, knocked on Lucy's door. A few moments later, it opened, though only as far as the safety chain would permit. Lucy's face through the gap was a picture of contempt. 'Well, what a surprise. The prodigal shithead returns.'

Wayne was silent, the sight of her in her dressing gown having momentarily arrested the speech centre of his brain. He simply held up the money that he'd withdrawn from the cashpoint ten minutes ago.

Lucy looked at the money, then at Wayne. 'Is this supposed to speak to me in some way? Am I looking at some kind of password?'

'Punish me.'

'Fuck off.' She went to close the door. His foot stopped her.

'Please, Mistress. I can pay.'

She looked at him hatefully. 'I neither need, nor want, your money.'

'But I need you. I need your discipline. I can't function properly without it. I'm changed Lucy. I'm not the same man anymore.'

'You seem like the same fucking bastard to me. Now do like I told you: get your girlfriend to smack your arse and stop bothering me. I have a life you know.'

'You are my life. Please, let me in.'

'Get your foot out of my door.'

'Punish me.'

'I told you I'd tell your fiancée if you came back here, Wayne, and I meant it.'

'I don't care,' said Wayne. 'Our love is dead. She can't make me hard like you can. She can't fulfil me like you can. Our life together is a sham. Tell her anything you like, I don't care.'

Lucy glowered at him. 'Wayne, I'm ordering you to go away.'

Wayne hung his head. 'And I must disobey that order, mistress. See how bad I am?' He held up the money.

'You utter, utter shit,' she hissed.

Wayne nodded plaintively, his head still lowered. 'He waggled the wad in his hand.'

Lucy looked at him, then at the money. She looked down at his foot in the doorway, and back to him. She hesitated for a moment, thinking. Then, reaching a decision, she sighed. 'Move your foot and I'll let you in. But I promise you, pig – you're going to be very fucking sorry.'

'I hope so.' Wayne looked up and smiled. 'I really do.'

Lucy unslipped the chain and opened the door.

Fifteen minutes later, Wayne was on his knees in Lucy's lounge. He was naked and his hands were cuffed behind his back. She had fixed a dog's collar tightly around his neck and tethered it, via a short leash, to a solid fitting screwed to the wall just above her skirting board. Wayne was wondering if there was going to be a dog's bowl involved in his punishment, and if there was, what was going to be in it?

He shifted uncomfortably. He was ungagged, but found it difficult to turn around without falling forward or chaffing his knees on the carpet. His conversation with Lucy took place mostly with him facing the wall. 'What, what are you going to do to me?' Wayne simpered.

Lucy was in the bedroom getting dressed. She wore jeans and a T-shirt and was pulling on a light sweater. 'Punish you.'

'I've been very bad.'

'I know.' Lucy re-entered the room. 'Don't try to turn, pig! Face the wall.'

Wayne did as he was told. He bit his lip as he heard the sound of a cane swishing through the air. 'Is that,' he said, nervously. 'Is that, a cane?'

'It is. And you're going to get what you deserve. What you came here for: six of the best.'

'Oh no,' said Wayne, a tremor in his voice. 'Oh no, please not that.'

'Silence! I'll decide what you will and you won't get.'

Wayne heard her pacing around behind him, the cane slashing through the air intermittently. 'I want you to think about this, pig. I'm going to leave you here alone for a while and I want you to think. To contemplate what a bad pig you've been. Do you understand me?'

'Oh, not the lonely treatment again. Shi –' Wayne's protest was cut off by the cane striking his backside. 'Shit!'

'What did you say?'

'I said shit!'

'Did you dare to question me?'

Wayne gritted his teeth. 'Sorry mistress. I just, I just didn't want to be alone.'

'Do you want me to gag you? Because that's what happens to whingers. We have to silence their whinging with the gag.'

'No. No mistress,' Wayne begged. 'I'll be quiet. Just don't be too long. I'm uncomfortable.'

Lucy smiled. 'Good.'

Wayne lowered his head.

'That's it. Good pig.' Lucy went out into the hall and shut the door. She opened her front door and went downstairs. When she got to the door of Wayne's flat she took a deep breath and knocked.

A few moments later, Ellen opened the door, a puzzled expression on her face. 'Yes?'

'It's Ellen, isn't it?'

Ellen smiled. 'Yes.'

'Can I speak to you for a moment? It's about Wayne.'

How long Wayne actually had to think about his misdemeanours was difficult for him to accurately determine, since his watch was on the sofa along with the rest of his clothes. Not that he could read it at the moment even if it were on his wrist. An hour? He speculated. Two?

'Fuck!' His arms and wrists ached harmoniously, and his back was beginning to join in. A chorus of pain – none of it inflicted by that bastard whore in person. Where did she go? I heard the front door go, then that was it. Has she gone to the shops? Jesus – has she gone on fucking holiday?

The ache in his back suddenly flared up into a full-on pain. It centred around the spot where he had injured himself at work. A wave of panic went through him. My back! Oh Christ, not my back. Please God, not my back. He tried to straighten up, but the collar and leash forbade him. Desperately, he fell onto his side. Oh shit, that was better. He stretched his legs out. Oh, God, yes. Then he had a thought: what if she came back and found him this way? Not squatting in shame, contemplating his folly? Would she give him a really hard time? If spanking were involved, and he kind of hoped it was, would she be merciless? He fretted for a moment before deciding to lie down anyway. 'When I hear the door, I'll just get back into position'.

As if on cue, he heard the front door open in the hallway. 'Shit!' he hissed. He rolled over, chafing his knees as he scrabbled about trying to right himself. He made it just as the door to the lounge opened. 'Mistress?' he whimpered. 'Where have you been? I've been so worried about you?'

There was no reply.

'Mistress?'

He heard the sound of a cane slicing the air behind him.

'Oh, mistress. Oh, please. I've been so bad.'

'Yes,' said Ellen. 'You have been haven't you?'

Wayne froze. When the cane whacked against his buttocks, his scream was as much of fear as of pain. 'Ellen!' he cried. 'Ellen, oh God, I'm sorry!' The cane slashed down again, striking the same spot. The pain was incredible.

'You bastard!' Ellen remained behind him, her voice was thick with emotion. She struck him again.

Wayne clenched his teeth and tried to bite back his scream. When he was able to catch his breath he stammered, 'Please! Darling, I can explain!'

'How can you, Wayne? How can you explain the man I see before me?'

Wayne screwed up his face as he felt tears pricking at his eyes. 'Please,' he cried. 'I'm...'

Ellen struck him again. 'Yes?' she shouted. 'What are you?'

'I...' Wayne's head reeled, he felt sick. When the truth came out of him, it did so as though his body were expelling a toxic substance. Even he didn't recognise it. 'I'm... I'm bored.'

'Bored!' Ellen nearly screamed in disbelief. She slashed the cane against his buttocks again. 'You're bored! That's what this is all about?'

'I can't help myself. I just,' he gasped, choking back a sob. 'I just sit around thinking about it all day, and it drives me insane.'

'Well why don't you go back to fucking work then?' Ellen shouted.

In the doorway, Lucy watched the proceedings with a mixture of pity and despair. What a piece of work is man? What a piece indeed.

'Because I'm getting paid time off!' Wayne bellowed.

'And it's driving you insane, you fucking arsehole!' shouted Ellen. 'Look at you! Just take a look at yourself Wayne! Is this a sane man I see before me? Well is it?'

As best as he could manage, Wayne looked at himself. He looked at his cramped and aching naked body; he felt his hands manacled behind his back;

his knees, carpet burned and trembling beneath him; the pull of the dog collar around his neck; and the eyes of the woman he loved upon him. The full horror of his demise suddenly overwhelmed him. He closed his eyes, all his remaining energy draining from him as slowly, he lowered himself onto his side and rolled his knees to his chest. A sob escaped him and he turned his face to the carpet, his body finally abandoning any attempt to suppress his tears.

Ellen, whose own eyes had done their fair share of crying, turned back to look at Lucy. She didn't have to say anything. Lucy nodded and gave her small reassuring smile, then stepped back into the hall closing the door behind her.

Once outside, Lucy gave a sigh of relief. Thank fuck that's over – at least as far as I'm concerned. Now I can just leave them to sort it out alone.

She was just getting to the kitchen when the front door buzzer sounded. She turned and looked at the door. Who could this be? She checked her watch, she wasn't expecting anyone. She went back and picked up the entryphone. 'Hello?'

'Lucy?' said the tiny voice at the other end. 'It's Sally.'

'Sally?'

'Yeah. Listen, can I ask a favour of you?'

Lucy looked to the closed door beyond which Wayne and Ellen were getting to know each other better. 'Wait there,' she said. 'I'll come down.' She hung up the phone and opened the door.

Chapter 29

THE FIRST THING LUCY SAW when she opened the door was the mullethead on the kid's bike. She recognised him, or rather his bike, from when he came around the other day looking for the old tenant in flat 3. She grinned. 'Sally, don't tell me, this must be Sam Spade, right?'

Sally smiled. 'Lucy, this is Mick. Mick, this is Lucy.'

'Hi.' Lucy nodded at the Chopper. 'Nice bike.'

'Thanks.'

'We need to ask a favour of you,' said Sally.

'Oh? What's that?'

Sally looked anxiously at Mick, then back to Lucy. 'Can we borrow your fire escape?'

Lucy smiled. 'As long as you remember to bring it back.'

Sally nodded, embarrassed at her mistake. 'I mean, can you allow us access to your fire escape?'

Lucy looked doubtful. 'Er....Why?'

'We, erm…' Sally looked at Mick.

'We need to check out the upstairs flat.'

'The guy we were talking about the other night?' Sally explained. 'The bald guy?'

'What about him?' Lucy frowned.

'We suspect he may be involved in something…' Sally sought the right word. 'Untoward.'

'Untoward?'

'We think he may have killed someone,' Mick stated flatly. 'We need to check a couple of things out while he's not around.'

Lucy looked at him, then at Sally. 'Oh. Is that all?' She gave a short laugh. 'Why didn't you just say so in the first place? That sounds perfectly reasonable. Not in the least insane.'

'I know it sounds nutty,' said Sally. 'But there's good reason to suspect that it's true. That's all I can say really. We just need to eliminate him from our enquiries, as the police would say.'

'By breaking into his flat?'

'No,' said Mick. 'We don't intend to break in. We just want to take a look through the window. Check it out without checking in, as it were.'

Lucy looked at Sally. 'This is kind of irregular, Sally. You know what I mean?'

'I know it is. But I'm begging you, please, just trust us. It is important, even if it sounds… irregular.'

Lucy leaned against the doorframe. 'How do you know he's out?'

'Mick's just rung his bell. Pretending to be gathering signatures for a local petition about parking spaces.' Sally shook her head. 'There was no reply.'

'I rang about five times, too. He's either out or deaf.'

'And he's not deaf,' said Sally. 'I met him yesterday.'

'Did you?' said Lucy. 'What's he like?'

'It's a long story, Luce. I'll tell you next time we go out for a drink. We can look back on this and laugh.'

'As long as we're not laughing on either side of the Perspex during prison visiting hours,' said Lucy.

'Honestly, Lucy,' said Mick. 'We're not going to do anything hooky.'

'Okay.' Lucy shook her head in disbelief and opened the door wide. 'But if he's up there listening to headphones or something, I never saw you before in my life. You came over the fence or something. Got it?'

'Absolutely,' said Mick. He indicated his bike. 'Could I bring this into the hall?'

'Sure.'

'Thanks.' Mick dismounted and wheeled the bike into the hallway behind Sally. Lucy closed the door behind him and then walked to the front of the group. 'You'll have to be careful when you go through my flat. There's a kind of sensitive situation going on.'

Sally touched Lucy on the arm, suddenly aware of potential indelicacies. 'This isn't a, er, a bad time for you is it, Lucy?'

'No, nothing like that. At least...' Lucy considered a moment. Then she smiled. 'No, nothing like that, not anymore.'

'You're sure?'

'I'm sure.' Lucy gave Sally's hand a reassuring squeeze. 'Come on.' She turned and led the way upstairs. They entered Lucy's flat, following her as she led them down the hallway and into her kitchen. She pointed to the window. 'Fire escape's just outside there.'

Mick went over to the window and looked out into the garden beyond. 'Are all these flats laid out the same way?'

'What do you mean?' Lucy asked.

Mick indicated the ceiling. 'Is the room above this a kitchen as well?'

Lucy shrugged. 'I've no idea.'

Mick looked through the window at the fire escape. It was of a spiral metal design, rusty, but solid looking. 'Okay if I open the window?' Lucy nodded. It was a large sash window; Mick released the catch and drew the lower half of the window up. A warm breeze lightly lifted the net curtain.

Lucy looked at Mick and Sally in turn. 'You're really going up there?'

Mick looked at Sally questioningly.

Sally shrugged. 'It's the only way to be sure.'

Lucy shook her head. 'And you seemed so sane the other night, Sally. This guy's obviously a bad influence on you.'

Mick raised his eyebrows.

'Oh yeah,' said Sally. 'He's mad, bad and dangerous to, er, accept bicycle rides from.'

Mick smiled. He noticed a butter knife on the kitchen work surface and picked it up. 'Mind if I borrow this?'

Lucy frowned. 'Why?'

'In case my mate's bound and gagged to a chair. I'll need to get the window open to rescue him.'

'I see. That's a possibility is it?'

'You never know.'

Lucy turned to Sally. 'He wants to take a knife upstairs in case his mate's bound and gagged to a chair. You heard that too, right?'

Sally shrugged. 'You never know.'

Lucy nodded. 'I see. Well, that's fine then.' She turned to Mick, 'Okay, SAS boy, take the knife.'

Mick slipped it into the back pocket of his jeans. He looked at Sally, 'Who's going out first?'

'You are.'

'Why me? It's your plan.'

'He's your friend.'

Mick sighed and put one knee up on the sill and climbed out of the window. Once he was out on the fire escape, he took a few tentative but firm steps to check the sturdiness of the structure. When he was satisfied that it was sound, he leaned back in through the window. 'It's okay. You coming?'

Sally looked at Lucy. She gave her a brief smile, then followed Mick out onto the fire escape. She came up face to face with him and quickly kissed him on the lips.

'What was that for?'

'I don't know. Good luck?'

'Oh.' Mick kissed her back. 'I don't want to be the only lucky person around here, do I?'

Sally prodded him affectionately in the ribs. 'Thanks. Now get going, Mister.'

Mick began to carefully ascend the stairs. Sally followed; their footsteps rang out dully on the metal as they climbed. 'If anyone is in there,' Mick said over his shoulder, 'we're not exactly doing a good job of sneaking up on them.'

'I know. We sound like the Bells of St Clement's.'

As he came within sight of the top floor window, Mick held out his hand for her to stop. He looked back at her and whispered. 'The window's open.'

Sally's eyes widened. 'What do you want to do?'

Mick shrugged. 'I dunno. Take a look I suppose?'

Sally nodded.

'Did you bring the Milk Tray?'

Sally frowned, confused.

'All because the psycho loves Milk Tray?'

Sally rolled her eyes and waved him on.

Mick crouched down and took the last remaining steps to the top window. Slowly, he raised his head to peer inside. An unmade bed stood opposite the window. Around the walls were photographs of young men. Mick's eyes widened. Maybe there was an element to all this he hadn't previously considered. There didn't seem to be anyone around, so tentatively he stood up and leaned his head inside. An expensive camera, still fixed to a tripod lay on the floor; next to it lay a telescope, also fixed to a tripod. Mick turned back to where Sally crouched on the stairs behind him. 'Check this out, Sal. Things have just taken a turn for the weirder.'

'What is it?'

'Take a look.' Mick moved aside so she could join him.

Sally peered into the room. Mick saw her expression change from curiosity to astonishment. 'Bloody hell.' She looked back at him. 'Those pictures on the walls? They're of Gaz and his mates.'

Mick raised his eyebrows. 'Jesus. You think he fancies them? Like in a peeping Tom kind of way?'

'I don't know. But I think we should go in and check it out some more. We may not get the chance again.'

Mick nodded. 'After you?'

'Oh no.' Sally took a deferential step back. 'After you.'

Mick pushed the lower sash window higher up in the frame and clambered into the flat. He stepped over the camera tripod and into the middle of the room. Despite the open window, it smelled mildly unpleasant. Mick noticed various dirty plates and cups lying down on the floor beside the bed. Clothes were piled on a chair in the corner. Mick could see a number of tags dangling from them and he bent to look at one. They were from Oxfam. There were also a number of garments on the floor by the open wardrobe.

Behind him, Sally stepped into the room. 'Mmm,' she murmured. 'Chic.'

Mick went over to the wardrobe and looked inside. Peter's work clothes and a few other shirts hung crookedly from hangers. Mick riffled through the clothes. He came to a tie rack. After a moment's fumbling, he withdrew a particular tie. He showed it to Sally.

Sally looked at the motif. 'Daffy Duck?'

'The one and only.' Mick put the tie to one side and looked down at the clothes that spilled out from the bottom of the wardrobe. He hunkered down and began to rummage. 'These're all Pete's. They–'

'They what?'

'Take a look at this.'

She looked to where he was holding some shirts aside. There was something red in the bottom of the wardrobe that she couldn't quite make out. 'What is it?'

Mick pulled the clothes out altogether, revealing the petrol can.

Sally's hand went to her mouth to cover her surprise. 'Jesus. Could he have been the one who poured petrol through Gaz's door?'

'Eh?' Mick frowned.

'Is it empty?'

Mick pulled the can free and shook it. He nodded.

Sally went to the nearest picture-strewn wall and pointed to a picture of Gaz, by far the most photographed subject. 'That's Gaz. Someone put petrol through his letterbox and he managed to set it on fire.'

Mick dropped the can into the clothes. 'When?'

'Last week.'

'Was Peter still around?'

Sally calculated. 'Yeah. Yeah this was a few days before we met.'

'Oh Jimminy,' Mick whispered.

'You think Peter could have done it?'

'I dunno. He was certainly pissed off with them, but... Who knows?' Mick looked at the photographs around the room. 'But I'll tell you one thing, Sal, I don't think our bald friend is the photographer here. Look at this one.' He pointed to a black and white picture of Gaz and Jimmy in their back yard. 'They're wearing big coats and winter hats. It's cold. This was taken a while ago.'

Sally shook her head slowly. 'Did Peter ever seem...' she thought a second. 'Did he ever seem kind of, crazy?'

Mick shrugged. 'No more than anybody else.' He pointed at the photographs. 'But these guys, they used to really do his head in. Maybe more than I suspected.'

Sally looked at the petrol can. 'Enough to make him want to do… that?'

'I dunno. I guess it's possible.'

'So it was Peter, then. Peter poured the petrol.'

Mick raised his eyebrows. 'Try saying that when you're pissed.'

Sally smiled, despite her anxiety. 'Should we look further?'

Mick nodded. 'Might as well.' He opened the bedroom door a crack and peeped into the next room. Over in the far corner it looked like a small dark room had been set up. Pictures hung from a small indoor clothesline over a couple of shallow trays. Mick opened the door and went inside. He walked into the middle of the room and looked about. Plates and cutlery lay all around the lounge and adjoining kitchenette. Mick went over into the kitchen area. He noticed the rubbish bag was overflowing. It stank too. He looked at Sally who was taking it all in from where she stood in the doorway. 'Quite the bachelor pad, isn't it?'

'Yeah, but where's the bachelor?' Sally stepped into the room and noticed the closed door in the opposite corner. She went over and opened it.

Mick noticed a pair of sunglasses on a shelf. He picked them up and inspected them, turning the lenses to face him. As he did so the memory of the tramp standing outside McDonald's rushed into his mind, his eyes inscrutable behind the impenetrable black shades he wore. Mick dropped the sunglasses as if they were suddenly white hot. He was just about to call out to Sally when he heard her cry of alarm. He turned in time to see her walk quickly from the room and shut the door behind her.

'We have to get out of here, Mick. We have to call the police.' Her face was ashen.

'What?' Mick came over to her. 'What's in there?'

'Not now. We have to get out of here.' She took his hand and walked away from the door.

'Wait.' Mick resisted her pull. 'What is it? I should know.'

'I'll tell you when we're back in Lucy's place. Please, come on.'

Not letting go of her hand, Mick turned and opened the door. 'It won't take a second.'

'Mick!' Sally let go of his hand as he went inside.

'I'll just be a – '

Sally brought her hands to her face. 'It's Gaz.'

After a few moments, Mick appeared unsteadily at the door.

Sally reached out and took his arm. She tried not to look back into the room, but it was impossible not to notice the blood that screamed from the white-tiled walls. 'Let's go.'

Mick pointed at the body in the bath. 'He's been butchered.'

'I know, come on.' Sally pulled at him and he started forwards. 'We have to get out of here before Adam comes home.' No sooner had she spoken than they both froze. She looked at Mick; his expression was a reflection of her own. He had heard it too. Beyond the front door came the sound of footsteps. They were heavy, and getting closer.

Chapter 30

ADAM ENTERED THE TOP FLAT and kicked the door shut behind him. Immediately he began unbuttoning the old raincoat he wore. It was the first time he'd worn it since he moved in here. He hadn't intended to wear it again, but he'd been in a hurry. As it fell open he looked down at the bloodstained clothes beneath it. He tutted and shook his head. 'Should've put the damn coat on before I started cutting him up.'

He opened his carrier bag and reached inside. He withdrew a large roll of heavy-duty garden refuse sacks and tossed them onto the sofa. Then he pulled out a large hacksaw. Discarding the bag, he ran a finger over the hacksaw's teeth. 'This should sort out those damn tough bits.'

From the bedroom came a dull metallic clang. Adam looked up, and heard the sound again. He moved quickly to the bedroom and flung open the door. The room was empty. Then he heard the sound again. It was coming from beyond the open window. The fire escape – someone was on the fire escape. In a few strides he was at the window, he thrust his head outside. Footsteps below, voices. He climbed out onto the fire escape and looked over the rail. He saw a woman's hand, and then she was looking up at him. Adam found himself looking into the terrified eyes of the girl from the pub. The one that Gaz, the last sign, had considered special. A feeling, Adam now realised, that he shared. 'Of course,' he whispered.

Sally looked up to see Adam staring down at her. 'Shit!' she screamed, the sound of her own fear started her running again. She went headfirst through Lucy's open window, diving onto the linoleum and rolling to a halt by the fridge. She looked up to see Mick entering in similar style. Sally got to her feet and ran to the window, pulling it closed and twisting the latch closed.

'He's coming,' said Mick. 'I could hear him.'

'I know.' Sally grabbed him and ran towards the door as Adam's shadow filled the kitchen window. 'He's here.'

Mick stumbled after her as the window exploded behind him. He glanced back to see Adam's elbow withdrawing to strike again. 'Oh fuck.' He slammed the kitchen door behind him and ran after Sally down the hall.

Lucy came out of the room at the far end. 'Hey, if isn't Jonathan and Jennifer Hart. Was that my window I -'

'Lucy, call the police!' Sally shouted. 'Get out of sight and call the police!'

Lucy stood aside as Sally and Mick charged past her. As Sally opened the front door, Mick looked back at her. 'It's us he's after, but get out of sight. Hide.' He disappeared after Sally through the front door.

Lucy stood dumbstruck. The sound of more breaking glass from the kitchen seemed to shake her into motion. She didn't think, she just ran, finally catching the sense of fear that Sally and Mick had left in their wake. She burst into the room where Wayne, now clothed, sat talking quietly with Ellen. Lucy threw her back to the door and held her breath. On the other side of the door she heard the sound of fast, heavy footsteps. She closed her eyes as the sound drew nearer, she could feel the floor resonating with the man's weight. For one terrible instant she was certain that he was going to ignore the open front door and keep coming, crashing through this door, knocking her across the room and... and then the footsteps where receding again. Mick had been right. It was them he was after. She ran to the telephone and grabbed the receiver.

Wayne looked nervous. 'What's going on?'

'I don't know,' said Lucy, stabbing out 999 on the dialpad. 'But apparently it's a serious fucking emergency.'

The bike. Mick saw it as they came down the stairs; it leaned where he had left it in the hallway. 'Should we – ?' He began, stopping alongside it.

'Don't be bloody stupid,' Sally pulled him towards the front door. 'We wouldn't stand a chance.'

As they passed the Chopper Mick reached back and knocked it over. It clattered onto its side, blocking the passageway as Adam rounded the top of the stairs.

'Which way?' Sally looked up and down the street.

'This way.' Mick took her hand and started uphill towards the main street. 'It's busier, maybe he'll give up with so many people around.'

Sally ran after him. 'Oh? I don't know – I get the feeling that shyness is the least of his problems.'

Adam came upon the bike in the hall. He bent to pick it up. As he did so, a thought occurred to him. He pushed the bike out backwards through the still open front door. Once on the street he looked right and left. He saw them running up towards the junction with the main road. He threw one leg over the bike and sat down as if trying it for size. He smiled, and stood up on the pedals.

Mick glanced back as they got to the junction. 'Oh, fucking hell.'

Sally stopped, panting for breath, and looked back.

'He's got my bike.'

Sally saw Adam toiling up the centre of Charrington Street on the Chopper. 'Come on,' she pulled Mick's hand. 'Keep going, we can lose him.'

They ran onto the Eastern Road, the bustling shopping street that ran across the top of Charrington. Saturday afternoon shoppers milled around with vague directional purpose. Sally and Mick ran through them, occasionally bumping against one and receiving indignant looks. 'There!' shouted Mick, pointing ahead. 'The bus.' Sally nodded and they ran down to where a double-decker bus was just getting ready to pull out into traffic. Mick ran up alongside the doors and hammered on the glass doors. 'Hey! Please! Let us on, mate.'

The driver opened the doors. 'Oi! Who do you think you are banging on my doors?'

Mick and Sally clambered aboard. 'Sorry,' Mick gasped. 'Anywhere. Take us anywhere.'

'That's no good, mate,' the driver shook his head. 'I need a proper destination.'

'What's your last stop?' Sally asked, desperately.

'Hollingdean.'

'Take us there,' said Mick.

The driver punched out the tickets. 'Two pounds.'

'Mick!' Sally was staring down the aisle of the bus and out of the rear window. Mick followed her gaze. The bald guy must've seen them getting on. He was pedalling straight towards the bus.

Mick turned to the driver. 'Just go, man!' he shouted. 'Move it!'

'I don't have to take this.' The driver pointed at the doors. 'Get off my bus.'

Mick clenched his fists in desperation, thinking furiously as Adam closed the gap between them. Then the light of an idea spread over his face. In a single movement, he grabbed Sally and pulled her in front of him. He grabbed the butter knife from out of his back pocket and brought it up against her throat. 'Get rolling, mister. Or I'll carve her!'

The driver's mouth fell open.

Sally, understanding Mick's ploy immediately played along. 'Please,' she begged. 'Please, do as he says.'

Still speechless, the driver closed the doors and put his foot on the accelerator. The bus growled into motion, moving away from the kerb and out into traffic.

Mick nodded. 'That's it, mate. You're doing great.' He looked down the length of the bus, past the frightened faces of the passengers and out of the back window. He smiled to see Adam was losing ground. He looked again to the anxious faces of the passengers. 'Don't anybody get any ideas now. I don't want any of that have-a-go-hero shit. Anybody tries anything and the girl gets it, okay?' There was some nodding of heads, but the majority of the passengers just looked on in stunned silence. Mick was just about to relax a little when, suddenly, he noticed the bus slowing down and pulling in to the side of the road. 'What?' he looked at the driver. 'What're you doing?'

The driver indicated the queue of people who waited at the bus stop ahead of them. 'Passengers. I'm picking them up.'

'What? Don't be daft!' Mick brought the butter knife up close to Sally's throat again. 'You don't stop until I say stop, understand?'

Sally cried out. 'Oh God!'

'Alright, alright. Take it easy.' The driver swerved the bus away from the kerb, speeding up again.

'Good man.' Mick looked out at the queue of abandoned passengers. As the bus sped past them they made a range of angry gestures.

'I'll tell you son,' said the driver, keeping his eyes on the road. 'I don't know what this is all about, but you've got to see no good's gonna come of it.'

'Yeah, yeah. Thanks for the advice. Now just drive the bus. And don't stop unless I say so.' He looked out of the rear window. There were several other cars between Adam and the bus now. Mick relaxed a little.

'I'm scared, Mickey,' said Sally, evidently beefing up her role a little. 'Why can't you just let me go?'

'Shut up, Sally. I warned you what'd happen if you carried on seeing Tony. Now it's payback time.'

The driver looked at them anxiously. The passengers, who resembled a spellbound theatre audience, just sat and stared.

'Is he still coming, Mickey?'

Mick looked through the back window. 'Yeah. But we're losing him.'

The bell rang. The driver looked sideways at Mick.

'Keep driving.' Unsteady footsteps descended the stairs and a man emerged. Mick met his eyes steadily. 'Sorry mate. We're not stopping.'

The man saw the knife. 'Wh- What's going on?'

'You're going to get a little bit more mileage for your money,' said Mick. 'Take a seat.'

'But that's my stop we just passed. I want to get off.'

Mick tightened his grip on the butter knife. 'Nobody's going anywhere until I say so, okay?'

'Sit down, please sir,' said driver. 'I'm afraid we're in a hostage situation. Don't worry. I'll be dropping everyone where they want just as soon as it's all over.'

'But this is outrageous. I've never – '

'Shut up and sit down!' Mick shouted, 'Or her blood's on your hands. Get me?'

The man raised his hands in front of him. 'Okay, okay,' he pointed vaguely at the seats. 'I'm going to take a seat over here.' He moved away from the stairs and sat down on one of the front seats beside an old woman.

'Good boy.' Mick's eyes were suddenly drawn back to the stairs by the sound of more people descending. 'Oh, for fuck's sake.'

He watched as a teenage girl, laughing and talking to a friend behind her came into view. When the girl reached the bottom step she looked up, straight into Sally's eyes. She froze. 'Oh my God.'

'What is it?' Her friend asked.

'Oh my God.'

'It's okay,' Mick assured her steadily. 'No need for alarm. Just be cool and nobody'll get hurt.'

The second teenage girl ducked her head into view. 'Oh my God.'

'It's okay.' Sally smiled. 'He won't hurt me if everybody stays calm and does as they're told.'

The bell rang.

'Oh for crying out loud.' Mick's head slumped onto Sally's shoulder. She shrugged it back to attention. 'Listen,' he said to the girls. 'You two go upstairs and tell everyone up there to stop ringing that damn bell. Nobody's getting off till I say so. Okay?' Then he noticed the bus slowing down. 'What the fuck?' he turned to the driver. 'Did you hear me, driver? I just said – '

The driver pointed ahead to where the traffic became a slow moving knot. They were approaching the shopping centre. Buses limped after one another, slowly inching in and out of stops, bringing the traffic to a virtual standstill.

'Shit.' Mick gritted his teeth. He looked out of the rear window of the bus. Another bus filled the view. 'Shit!'

The bus slowed to a crawl.

Sally steered Mick around so she could look out of the front window. 'Ohhh -'

'"Shit" seems to be the popular word of choice miss,' said the driver.

Adam smiled as he gradually overtook the cars that idled between him and the bus. He could see the double-decker ensnared with all the others in what he had once correctly identified as a bus trap. Soon he would be upon them. They knew about the body in the bath, that much was obvious. Perhaps they had shared their knowledge with others as they fled through the flat below his? He sighed. He couldn't know, neither was he concerned; it was too late for that. Time was running out now. All signs had led to her. She could no more escape her destiny than he could his own. He sat back and closed in on the knot of buses. He could smell the exhaust already.

Mick punched the windscreen. 'Can't we turn out of this?'

The driver held up his hands. 'Where?'

Mick looked about desperately. 'Why?' He shook his head, exasperated. 'Why did they stick so many bus stops in such a tiny area? It's mental.'

'Lots of routes lead in here,' said the driver. 'People drop off here from miles around.'

'Well it's stupid. They should spread them out a bit.'

The driver shrugged. 'Town was never designed to cope with this much traffic.'

'They should bring back the trams!' shouted an elderly woman among the passengers.

Mick looked back to see other elderly heads nodding in consent. He whispered in Sally's ear. 'What do you think?'

Sally frowned. 'I think she has a point.'

Mick gritted his teeth. 'Yeah, forget about the trams. I mean what do you think we should do next?'

'Oh. I think we should get off. Quickly.'

'I think she's right,' said the driver.

Mick smirked. 'Yeah, okay mate, thanks for your opinion. Just open the doors willya? We're getting off.'

'Where? Here? In the middle of the road?'

'Yeah. In the middle of the road. Now get those doors open quick and all these people can get a nice ride back to wherever it is they're going.'

Shaking his head, the driver threw the lever that opened the bus doors and they rolled back with a hiss.

With the butter knife still to Sally's throat, Mick stepped cautiously to the doors and looked out. His grip on the knife suddenly went slack and it fell from his fingers. 'Oh fuck!'

Adam was cycling in easily, coming alongside the back of the bus. Unimpeded by traffic, he was upon them.

Mick released Sally and pushed her towards the stairs that led up to the top deck. 'Go!' He shouted. 'He's here!' Sally saw Adam's head as it glided past the windows towards the front doors.

The two teenage girls, who still stood rooted to the spot on the stairs now stood aside as Mick and Sally clambered past them. The first girl, relieved that the mad knifeman was no longer between her and the exit, looked to the open doors of the bus. A big bald man in a dirty raincoat was getting on board. Her friend must've seen the bloodstained clothes beneath at the same time she did. They screamed in unison.

Adam ignored the screaming girls and stood calmly beside the driver. His eyes searched the lower deck for Sally but she wasn't there. He turned to the girls. 'They go upstairs?'

The first girl blinked, then screamed again. Her friend joined in.

Adam grew tired of waiting for a sensible reply. 'Excuse me.' He reached out and gently but firmly moved the first girl aside.

'That must be Tony,' said one of two old women that sat among the foremost of the passengers. The woman beside her nodded excitedly.

'Now where?' Sally looked about the upper deck desperately.

'The back.' Mick pointed to the rear window. 'The escape hatch.'

There were only a few passengers on the upper deck. One of them, a big man in a black puffer jacket saw the panic in their eyes. 'What's going on?'

'Nutter on the bus.' Mick gave the guy a worried look as he and Sally ran to the back of the bus. He saw there were instructions on the window telling passengers what to do in an emergency.

'Here,' Sally pointed at a central red handle at the bottom of the pane. 'It says turn it.'

'So let's turn it.' Mick grabbed the handle and twisted it in the direction indicated. There was a click as the window unlocked. 'Okay, let's push it as wide as it'll go.' They pushed against the glass and the window, hinged at the top, yawned open.

The man in the puffer jacket got to his feet and went to see what was going on with the screaming girls in the stairwell.

Mick and Sally had pushed the window open to its fullest extent. Sally looked out and down at the street. 'Now what do we do? Fly?'

'No.' Mick pointed at the single-decker bus that idled behind them. 'We jump over onto that.'

Sally looked at the other bus. Its roof was roughly level with the floor beneath their feet. What concerned her was the gap between them. It had to be about four feet. She looked doubtful.

Mick gave her a squeeze and kissed her hair. 'It's just a short hop. We'll easily do it.'

Sally looked back into the aisle. Somewhere, girls were screaming. She felt like joining them. She looked at Mick. 'Okay, let's go.'

Mick was already taking hold of the bottom edge of the window. He sat on the window frame and lifted out first one foot, then the other.

Behind them the man in the puffer jacket had gone to the rescue of the two teenage girls. The scene that greeted him on the stairs was confusing. A big, bald man seemed to be hassling the teenagers; they were screaming hysterically. 'Oi!' he bellowed.

Adam looked up at the man for a moment, then continued in his efforts at manoeuvring past the struggling girls.

'What's your game?' Puffer Jacket demanded.

'No game,' Adam finally extricated himself from the girls and began moving up to where Puffer Jacket blocked his path. He ignored the man's bulk and looked beyond him to where Sally was climbing out to join Mick on the window's edge. Adam watched as Mick launched himself from the window, jumping out and landing on the roof of the single-decker outside. Sally hesitated for a second, then she too jumped.

Adam began to push past Puffer Jacket. 'Excuse me.'

'Don't you push me, you cunt,' Puffer Jacket snarled. He grabbed Adam by the coat and yanked him back. Without hesitation, Adam punched him full in the face and he went sprawling backwards into the aisle. He was out cold before he hit the floor.

*

Mick looked around. He started to walk tentatively towards the edge of the bus. The road seemed an awfully long way down. 'Shit!'

Sally came up alongside him. 'What? Too far?'

'I dunno, I guess we'll – ' Mick's voice trailed off as he saw Adam appear in the rear window of the double-decker. 'I guess we'll have to.'

Sally followed his gaze. 'Oh, fuck.'

Suddenly Mick was pulling at her hand. There was a renewed conviction in his voice. 'C'mon, I've just seen another way off this thing.'

Sally looked in the direction Mick was pulling her. Another double-decker had moved up and now idled behind them. The single-decker was sandwiched between two double-deckers. Some kids in the top front seats of the new bus were pointing at them excitedly. Sally couldn't quite see what Mick had in mind. 'What? Where are we going?'

'We're going to catch that bus.'

Sally resisted his pull. 'What do you mean?'

Mick looked back over his shoulder to see Adam climbing out after them. 'We've got to get onto that bus.'

'That's insane.'

'Maybe,' Mick nodded back to the first bus. 'But if we stay here, we're definitely fucked.'

Sally felt the impact of Adam's landing resonate through the roof beneath her. She turned around. He was in a kneeling position, the jump hadn't been so easy for him, but he had made it. He looked up at her, and smiled.

'C'mon!' Mick tugged at her hand.

Sally looked from where Adam was now slowly getting to his feet back to Mick. 'I – '

From below, a voice shouted up at them. 'Oi! You up there!'

Sally glanced down over the edge of the bus. The driver had got out and was looking angrily up at them. 'Get the fuck off of my bus!'

'Gladly!' Mick shouted. He looked at Sally, 'It's wide enough for two Sal.'

Sally looked at the new double-decker. The entire population of the top deck was gawking at them through the front window. She turned to look behind her. Adam took a step towards them.

She was running before she had time to think of the consequences.

Their bodies hit the front windows of the new double-decker in unison, hands slamming onto the roof and finding purchase along the riveted seal that held the front of the bus to the body. There were gasps and screams from within. Sally found herself eye to eye with a mesmerised teenage youth. The youth managed a smile. Sally closed her eyes and concentrated on pulling herself up. Beside her, Mick was already getting one knee up onto the roof. She gasped. 'I can't get the right angle.'

Mick rolled up onto the roof and spun around on to lie on his stomach.

'Here,' he offered his open hands. 'Take my hands.'

'Don't be an idiot,' Sally managed to shout. 'You're not exactly anchored!' Her feet scrambled at the front of the bus for a moment before they found the lower edge of the window. She boosted herself up and managed to roll up alongside Mick. 'Jesus Christ.'

Mick smiled at her. 'Nice going.'

'Wait!' the voice came from the top of the single-decker behind them. Mick and Sally looked to where Adam was now walking towards them along the roof. 'Wait for me.'

Mick made a face of utter incomprehension. 'This guy is truly insane. Like we're going to wait for him to catch up?'

Sally pushed herself instinctively back and away from the edge of the bus, getting to her feet and trying not to look down. 'Go away!' she shouted. 'Just... Fuck off!'

'No,' Adam reached out placatingly, revealing the bloodstains on his shirt and trousers. 'You don't understand.'

'Get off of my fucking bus!' The bus driver, his face the colour of beetroot, continued to shout from below. A large crowd had gathered around him and was staring up at the drama on top of the buses.

Mick got to his feet and stepped away from the front of the bus feeling slightly giddy. He shouted at Adam. 'I understand there's a butchered corpse in your bathtub, mate! I think that pretty well covers the whole understanding thing!'

'He wasn't The One.' Adam replied. 'He was a mistake. You,' he pointed at Sally, 'you're The One.'

Sally took a step backward.

'Oi!' A new voice from below bellowed. 'What the fuck do you think you're doing up there?'

Sally looked over the edge to see another driver, no doubt from the new double-decker, standing beside his colleague. 'Get the fuck off there.'

'Call the police!' Sally shouted.

'Oh, I've called the bloody police, darlin',' shouted the first driver. 'Don't you worry about that.'

Sally reached out and took Mick by the hand. 'Let's get into the middle of the roof. I don't feel safe here.'

'Me neither.' Mick squeezed her hand and they both moved a few steps back. 'You hear that?' he shouted to Adam. 'The coppers are coming. You might as well give yourself up!'

Sally took a step closer to Mick. Adam was staring straight at her. The look in his eyes was intense. Mad, her mind corrected. Then he was running. Sally and Mick stepped back as the big man launched himself from the end of the single-decker and slammed against the front of the bus they were standing on. 'Oh Jesus, Mick!' Sally cried. 'Doesn't this guy pay attention?'

Mick ran to the front of the bus. 'Get off! Get off or... I'll stamp on your fingers!'

Adam's feet found purchase on the lower rim of the window. He eased himself forward.

'Get off!' Mick shouted, backing away. 'Or I'll bloody well kick you off!'

Adam's knee came up onto the roof of the bus.

'Get off!' Sally screamed.

Adam's arm moved forward. He began to ease himself up.

'I fuckin' mean it, man!' Mick ran forward and stamped his foot a few inches from Adam's fingers.

Adam instinctively recoiled, slipping back and catching hold of the front of the bus. Beneath them there was a collective gasp from the crowd. Adam spoke through gritted teeth. 'You don't understand...' His hand again grabbed the riveted seal and secured his position. 'I can't... '

Before Mick could react, Adam's other hand shot out and grabbed him around the ankle. Adam pulled hard. Mick had barely a second to register what was happening before he was falling backwards. His back slammed down onto the roof of the bus and he felt the air leave his lungs in a rush. For a moment, the world swam; Sally cried his name, then he felt the grip tighten around his ankle. He looked down to see Adam using him as a means to climb up onto the bus. Instinctively Mick's other foot kicked out, but he was still stunned, his aim was off. Adam caught his foot with his other hand and pinned it down beneath his weight. 'Oh shhhhhhit,' Mick wheezed.

Sally watched as Adam pinned Mick's ankles down and began to heave himself onto the roof. Adam looked over the length of Mick's body and smiled at her. 'Don't be afraid,' he said through gritted teeth. 'I'm here to help you.'

Sally couldn't quite connect Adam's words with his actions. She watched numbly as the bald man brought his knee up onto the roof of the bus, then reached forward, grabbing Mick's jeans. 'Mick!'

Mick was still stunned. He felt his grip on the edge of the bus slip as Adam pulled at his leg. He strengthened his grip, then suddenly he felt the other's weight shift, he was no longer being pulled. Instead, Adam was now pressing down upon him; he was on the roof and keeping him pinned as he moved upwards over his body.

Then Sally was there, she had taken off her shoes and was using one of them to strike at Adam. 'Get... off... him!' Adam raised a hand to deflect the blow and caught the shoe in the same movement. Sally staggered back as he threw it away.

Mick's reeling mind seized the advantage, forming the image of a course of action before it could formulate the words to describe it. He tried to imagine exactly how he might do it; it was something he'd only ever seen done on TV. The thought scared him – it was violent and could easily backfire, but as he felt the pressure of Adam's weight upon him, pinning his legs beneath him as he moved, he knew he had no other options open to him. He raised his head cautiously. Adam was looking over him, saying something to Sally – he obviously felt Mick posed little problem. Mick held his breath and tensed his stomach muscles, waiting for the precise moment, calculating height and distance. Adam reached out and grabbed Mick by the belt.

Now! Mick's mind shouted. Do it! Mick lunged forward from the waist, the big man's weight on his legs acted as an anchor allowing him maximum thrust as he sprang up like a rake that someone had unwarily stepped upon. The top of his forehead struck Adam squarely between the eyes. To Mick, the sound of impact was like an explosion in a padded cell. He immediately felt the grip on his belt slacken. Mick opened his eyes in time to see Adam fall sideways, rolling as his body slumped onto the slight curvature of the roof before falling away over the side of the bus.

There were screams from below, and Mick realised that Adam had fallen into the crowd. He rolled over onto his stomach and looked over the edge of the bus. Adam's body lay on the road close to the side of the bus. Blood was already spreading out around his head. In the shadow of the bus, the blood looked black. Mick felt a hand fall lightly upon his shoulder.

'Are you okay?' Sally's voice trembled slightly.

Mick turned. She stood over him. He put his hand over hers. 'Yeah. You?'

She nodded and got carefully down beside him. She pushed his hair away from his forehead and kissed it gently, her arms going about his neck. 'Your poor head, it must really hurt.'

'No, surprisingly.'

'I didn't realise you were such a hard nut.'

Mick laughed, more from relief than humour. 'Oh yeah, I'm a fucking nutter, me.'

Sally's eyes darted about his face, taking in all the little details; perhaps seeing them for the first time. A little bloom of pink was rising on his forehead, but otherwise he was intact. She kissed him. 'You were so brave.'

'So were you, Sal – much more than I was. You went for him with your shoe.'

Sally laughed nervously. 'It was all I had to hit him with. I saw him climbing up onto you and I just... Well, I had to do something.'

Mick smoothed her hair back with his hand. 'Thanks.'

'Thank you. You stopped him.'

'No.' Mick shook his head. 'We stopped him, you and me.'

Sally smiled and moved away to look over the edge of the bus. Her expression changed as she saw the body that lay still in the middle of the crowd below. 'Christ. Do you think he's dead?'

'I fucking hope so.'

Sally watched the commotion for a few moments, then turned back to Mick. 'What was he talking about? Saying he wanted to help us?'

'Help you,' Mick corrected. 'I got the distinct impression he didn't really give a shit about me.'

'Okay, so help me. What did he mean?'

Mick shrugged. 'Fucked if I know. Maybe he wanted to help that guy in Peter's bathtub as well.'

'Oh God, don't say that.' The memory of Gaz's butchered body arose in Sally's mind.

'I'm sorry.' Mick touched her shoulder. 'I didn't mean to be...'

'No,' Sally stopped him. 'You weren't. It's just... It's all just so horrible.' Her last words faltered slightly. Mick put an arm around her shoulders and she moved close to him.

'We're okay, Sal.' Mick stroked her back gently. 'We're safe now.'

'He said I was "The One", didn't he. He said that Gaz was... a mistake?'

'He did. But he was crazy. And now he's dead.'

Sally nodded slowly, her head moving against the fabric of Mick's shirt. Somewhere in the distance came the sound of sirens. 'Just like in the movies.'

'What?'

'The sirens,' said Sally. 'Just like in the movies. The police always arrive too late.'

Mick smiled. 'Oh yeah. That's right, they do.' He gave her a hug. Then a thought occurred to him. Somewhere in this clamour, his bike was lying unlocked and unattended. For a moment, panic seized him. Then, just as quickly, it seemed to melt away. It would be okay. Everything was going to be okay now.

He moved his face gently against her hair, awakening the fragrance. Was it apple? Something from the Body Shop perhaps?

'What shampoo do you use?'

'I don't know. Something I found in your bathroom. Why?'

Mick smiled. 'Oh yeah. Of course.' He looked up as the sirens grew louder. 'It smells different on you. Nicer.'

'Thanks.'

Mick couldn't hear her voice over the wail of the sirens. 'Sorry?'

Sally looked up at him and smiled. 'I said, "thanks".'

Mick returned the smile and kissed her on the forehead. 'You're welcome.'

'What?'

'I said, "you're welcome".'

'Oh,' Sally moved to her previous position, drawing his arm tightly around her shoulder. 'Okay.'

Mick moved his face against her hair again and let the strange, appley fragrance fill his senses once more. The sound of the sirens and the pulsing blues and reds of the police lights bounced back at them from buildings all around. They seemed to be coming from everywhere and nowhere at the same time.

Just like on TV, thought Mick. Just like in the movies.